Praise for Charles Shee
Prayer at Ruma

Bleak and disturbing... dead-on-target ...This first novel is a work of pure psychological conflict.

Gone are the game-like "smart" bomb videos, computerized reconstructions of death, and bloodless explosion photos from thousands of feet in the air.

They are replaced with the gritty, sometimes depressing, sometimes exhilarating, dangerous daily existence of a man who finds that gore and killing in the short term don't really bother him as much as he thought – but in the long run drive him crazy with guilt, remorse, and self-directed anger.
- Pulitzer Prize winning journalist John Hanchette, Reno Gazette-Journal, Gannett Newspapers

Prayer At Rumayla: A Novel Of The Gulf War is as timely as tomorrow's newspaper headlines. Written by Gulf War veteran and novelist Charles Sheehan-Miles, this is the story of a returning Gulf War veteran in the early 1990s who comes home to apathy, estrangement, and loss on behalf of his family, lover and friends. Brutally honest, direct, and meaningful, *Prayer At Rumayla* is a compelling novel of coming to terms not only with dangers and traumas of the battlefront, but with its aftermath upon the lives of the surviving combatants.
- Midwest Book Review, April 2002

Charles Sheehan-Miles was an on-the-ground at-the-front grunt during the Gulf War. His honest and unsparing account of that war is one that no American reporters could provide, and the American public could not learn about—because no reporters were allowed at the front. His memoir is a much-needed corrective about a much-misunderstood war.
- Seymour M. Hersh, Winner of the Pulitzer Prize, The George Polk Award, the National Book Critics Circle Award and the Los Angeles Times Book Award

Charles Sheehan-Miles's *Prayer at Rumayla* is a fast-paced, in-the-trenches Gulf War novel that provides vivid word pictures of the little-known tank war, as well as the war's aftereffects on main character Chet Brown. Sheehan-Miles was a loader on an M1A1 tank during the Gulf War and has been a leader in the Gulf War veterans movement.
- VVA Veteran Magazine

Profoundly moving, raw, exceptionally well executed vision....an expertly written psychological thriller...*Prayer at Rumayla* is easily one of the most impressive books reviewed in this blog. The writing is spectacular....
- The PODler Book Review

...Exposes the dirty underbelly of war...This book is a must for anyone interested in the Gulf War as it really happened... Cover-to-cover, the author places the reader right with Chet. In his tank and in his thoughts, we are offered an up close look at the psyche of a warrior in America's TV war. This book is highly recommended and should be on the shelf of every military history fan.
- Desert-Storm.com

Sharp and concise... takes on the simple poesy of a modern day Hemingway... *Prayer at Rumayla* showed that no war is a victory.
- Prince George's Sentinel

Sheehan-Miles has the ability to turn raw emotion into a riveting story...
- Amy Coffin, The Book Haven

"This book is only partly fiction ... *Prayer at Rumayla* captures the insanity and the humanity of the Gulf War...highly recommended."
- Patrick G. Eddington, Former CIA Intelligence Analyst; Author: Gassed in the Gulf

Killing is the toughest thing we ask of soldiers in combat. To bear the fury of smoke and fire, to stand your ground in the fight, is much easier than pulling the trigger. *Prayer at Rumayla* is a dark journey through the mind of a soldier who tries to come to terms with his acts of war. A timeless tale placed against the backdrop of the Persian Gulf War, it is a story of courage, betrayal, and anguish. Charles Sheehan-Miles draws from his own experiences in combat to create a story that delves into the ugliest side of war changing forever those who have been there. This is a must-read for those who have gone to war or have imagined that they want to. Prayer at Rumayla firmly establishes that indeed war is hell."
- Lieutenant Colonel David Pierson, Author, Tuskers: An Armor Battalion in the Gulf War

Republic

ALSO BY CHARLES SHEEHAN-MILES

Prayer at Rumayla A Novel of the Gulf War

Saving the World on $30 a Day
(forthcoming from Cincinnatus Press)

Republic

A Novel

Charles Sheehan-Miles

Cincinnatus Press
Cary, North Carolina

IF YOU ENJOYED THIS BOOK, PLEASE SHARE IT WITH A FRIEND, WRITE A REVIEW ONLINE, OR SEND FEEDBACK TO THE AUTHOR!

WWW.SHEEHANMILES.COM

Copyright © 2007 Charles Sheehan-Miles

All rights reserved. No part of this book may be reproduced in any form or by any electronic or mechanical means, including information storage and retrieval systems, without permission in writing from the publisher, except by a reviewer, who may quote brief passages in a review.

Any resemblance to real people, living or dead, is unintentional, with the exception of certain named historical characters.

ISBN-13: 978-0-9794114-2-7
ISBN-10: 0-9794114-2-4

Printed in the United States of America
Cincinnatus Press
www.cincinnatuspress.com

Dedication

In Memory of

Private Fred Harrison Miles
2nd Battalion, 131st Field Artillery
"The Lost Battalion"

Captured by the Japanese on Java March 2, 1942.
Prisoner of war until August 1945.

I wish I had had the opportunity to know you.

Author's Note and Acknowledgements

On April 19, 1995, a bomb made of improvised materials was detonated in front of the Alfred P. Murrah Federal Building by a young Gulf War veteran named Timothy McVeigh. The bombing, one of the first major terrorist incidents on American soil, killed 168 people, including nineteen children and three pregnant women. The youngest victim was only three months old.

For years after the bombing I was obsessed with the question: how could a man who had honorably served his country in wartime become a terrorist? What sequence of events led McVeigh and his co-conspirators to conclude that the only solution was to launch a murderous attack killing hundreds of people?

From there the question naturally arose: what circumstances in our modern era could bring about a massive domestic terror campaign, or an actual civil war? This novel arises from those questions.

Much of the original manuscript was complete by the time the September 11, 2001 attacks occurred. The response of the federal government provided much of the fodder for a rewrite, especially the creation of the massive federal bureaucracy known as the Department of Homeland Security. The passage of the Patriot Act, the rumors of an even stricter one which included provisions to strip Americans of their citizenship, domestic spying scandals, accusations of rigged voting machines and moves by Congress to consider the repeal of *Posse Comitatus* have all provided ideas and fears which fed this book.

Please note, however, that while I make reference to many of these developments in the book, this is indeed a fictional world. In some cases I've strayed significantly from current practice and law for dramatic purposes. I make no apology for this. In other cases—particularly the use of torture for terror suspects—I haven't touched on here, simply because it didn't make sense in the context of the story.

So, while this is a fictional world, perhaps ten years in our future, it is also the world we might one day live in. In a civil war, all sides believe they are in the right. The real danger we face, as individuals and as a nation, is that we all become so convinced that our own point of view is the correct one that we become unable to listen to anyone else's. It is not an accident that much of rhetoric I read in blogs, from both the left and right, mirrors in tone and in some content the speeches, newspapers, and pamphlets of the early 1860's, prior to beginning of the Civil War that killed more than one million Americans.

Now we talk about red and blue, fascists and traitors, but the words mean the same thing—*those people*. Those other people, who we don't understand, and who we believe don't have the best interest of our country in mind.

This is a novel of people fighting a war against each other, all the while believing that they are the ones fighting for our liberty and our country.

If you enjoy this book, please take the time to post a review online or to tell a friend about it. Word of mouth—from one reader to another—is what makes books successful or not. Please also feel free to drop by my website, make comments, and sign up to find out when the next book, tentatively titled *P@TRIOT*, will be out (currently planned for Summer 2008).

A book like this requires a lot of help from a lot of people. In particular, I'd like to thank my tireless editor, Shakirah Dawud, who helped me reshape this into a much better novel than it otherwise could have been. Also Paul Sullivan, Donna Price, Helen DeRamus, Richard Miles and Rhonda Miles for reading early drafts and sending me valuable feedback. Any oversights and mistakes present in the current volume are my fault, not theirs.

Finally, thank you to Veronica, Khalil and Amirah for putting up with me being distracted for long hours while I thought about the story, and the many hours you sacrificed so I could work on it.

Thank you,

Charles Sheehan-Miles
May 7, 2007
Cary, North Carolina

Email: Charles@sheehanmiles.com
Web: www.sheehanmiles.com

Prologue
April 14

Martha Murphy walked her son to his teacher and kissed him goodbye. Kenny shook away, in a hurry to get into the classroom so he could play with the computer before the day officially started. One step away from her he stumbled, arms and legs splayed out. A keening wail rose from the boy.

"Oh, honey."

Lifting her son, she examined him. His hands were scraped red, and he inhaled great shuddering gasps that expanded his cheeks. His green t-shirt and blue jeans were a little scuffed, but nothing serious. Even so, his blue eyes started to water, and the lower lip puffed out, the preliminaries of an explosion.

"There, there," she said. "No permanent harm done. Do you still have all your fingers and toes?"

He nodded. His eyes, wide and wet with tears, focused on his mother.

"Are there any big gobs of blood? Any serious injuries? You've still got all your head, right?" She gently tapped on the side of his head as she spoke the last words.

This time, he giggled as he responded with a shake of his head.

"All right then, you better get inside if you're going to have time to play with the computer. I'll see you tonight, chickpea."

Kenny didn't hesitate. If he arrived at school early enough, his teacher let him play on the computer until the other kids arrived. This time he didn't trip.

Mrs. Hayes, his teacher, put her hand up in the doorway, and said, "Martha, I wonder if you could find the time for a bit of a talk this week. We've got some concerns about little Kenny."

"Of course. Is something wrong?"

"Naw, nothing like that. But, well…we've been a mite concerned about his development. Not saying anything's wrong, but it's always best to check these things out early. We can talk in detail. How about tomorrow, at three?"

"I'll be there. Should I bring Ken?"

"Lord, no. It's nothing serious, Martha."

Martha nodded, then headed away. *Worried about his development.* There was nothing wrong with Kenny, he was doing just fine. She would meet with them, and find out what the worry was. Probably because he was a boy, and he acted like a boy, and these days that in itself was sometimes treated as a behavior problem.

Back at the pickup, she squeezed herself into the driver's seat, and then took a couple of deep breaths. Winded from walking thirty feet. Well, this was her third pregnancy, and certainly the last. Only three months to go. She was so stiff, and really too old to be having another baby. Kenny had come and slept in her and Ken's bed again, too, sometime after midnight, which had meant a whole night of tossing and turning.

Martha and her husband Ken had debated at length about whether to go ahead with the pregnancy. Their daughter Valerie, born when Martha was just eighteen years old, was twenty-two now, starting her first job as a congressional aide to Congressman Al Clark. Valerie was a stern young woman, ambitious and aggressive. Martha was simultaneously proud of her daughter's accomplishments, and—at least sometimes—secretly ashamed to think Valerie was cold. But facts were facts. She had certainly never let anything as silly as a boy get in the way of her career, but that was the way you were supposed to be these days.

Valerie had been an only child. Then Kenny came along like a shock to the system, and suddenly a newly adult woman an infant brother. Valerie took it easier than either of her parents, who had long ago forgotten the sleepless nights and stress attendant with being a new parent. Now they were doing it again.

Ken, stoic as always, struggled over the pregnancy, then announced that he would support whatever decision she wanted to make. She knew he wanted the baby, desperately. It cost him a lot to hold himself back and let Martha explore her emotions about having another baby in her forties. But in the end, there wasn't really any question about what she would do. Now, the questions all centered on the baby's health. The doctors were able to tell a lot, and she had been having the full range of tests since early in the pregnancy. She told herself that if anything serious were wrong, they would know by now.

All the same, sometimes she was frightened.

Her phone rang as she cranked the engine. With a glance at the phone—it was Valerie—she put the headset behind her ear and clicked the talk button.

"Hi, Valerie!" she said, backing out of her parking space.

"Hi, Mom. I just wanted to let you know I *will* be able to make it next weekend; I got Friday off. What do you think Kenny will want for a present?"

Martha looked both ways at the traffic on Route 340. Traffic was picking up, and over the years, this had become a dangerous intersection. The heaviest fog had lifted, but patches still limited visibility and gave the morning a grey, forlorn cast. A fat raindrop streaked the windshield. One more stop to make, at Haggett's Mart a couple miles down, then she could head into town.

"I think your best bet are some Ranger Heroes, he's been playing with those a lot. You can ask about them at the toy store. Just a small one, not one of the big sets—

we're having some of his classmates over for the party, so I expect there will be too many presents as it is."

"Thanks, Mom. How are you?"

"Well, I'm as big as a house. It's getting to where I have to ask Mr. Chapman next door for help whenever I need to do any lifting at the shop. And he's moving along in age himself—I expect one of these days I'll have him keeled over on the floor."

Valerie laughed. "You've always charmed the guys, Mom. How's the store?"

"Good, good! About three weeks ago they had some shindig in Harpers Ferry for some diplomat, a Russian I think, and they came into the shop and bought every flower I had! They cleaned us out."

"That's wonderful!"

As she was talking, Martha came to the turnoff for the small convenience store.

"Valerie, I've got to get going. Can we talk tonight?" she said as she made a left into the parking lot.

"Okay. I love you."

Martha clicked the "Talk" button and heard silence. She took off the earpiece and slowly climbed out of the truck.

Haggett's Mart could only charitably be called a shack, an old, clapboard building that had been whitewashed sometime in the last couple of decades. A single cracked but clean window was crowded with tin cans and a broken neon sign. The parking lot, once paved, had degenerated to mostly gravel and broken pavement, and the gas pumps in front had not operated in decades. The store still did thriving business, however. The chain gas station across town, though clean, well lit, and with lower prices, wasn't a place to find gossip, and it wasn't locally owned.

As she walked toward the door she glanced at the headlines on the newspapers out front. All of them were variations on the same theme: "DHS Raids Compound in Maine," or "Two Agents Killed in Gun Raid." The *Post* was dominated by a photo of a wounded DHS agent in full battle gear, a hint of blood on his black uniform.

The news had been all over since yesterday: a team of agents from the Department of Homeland Security had raided a compound in rural Maine. A gun battle ensued, killing two agents and seven of the suspected terrorists. The other suspects were in custody now.

Martha opened the door and waved to the cantankerous old man with thinning white hair and a face full of deep creases and wrinkles sitting behind the cluttered counter. Walter Haggett was pushing ninety, but looked seventy. He still ran his own store, and knew just about everyone in Highview. Walter was usually good for an interesting story or two about goings-on in town, which accounted for the popularity of his store. Certainly the décor didn't.

"Good morning, Martha. How's the flower business?" he asked.

"Just fine, Walter. How is the convenience business?"

"Well, if I get any older, it won't be very convenient for me." He laughed out loud. The joke wasn't all that funny, but he said it the same way nearly every day.

"There's fresh decaf made, Martha. But there's a price."

"What's that?"

"You talk to that husband of yours, ask him to find me a place in his battalion."

Walter was a Vietnam veteran, and liked to kid Ken about the computerized monstrosities his National Guard battalion was equipped with.

Martha smiled at the old man. "I'll talk to him, Walter, but I'm pretty sure you're past the enlistment age."

Haggett pursed his lips. "I'm pretty sure I was past the enlistment age forty years ago, young lady. Rules are for Yankees and lawyers. You talk to the Colonel."

She laughed and nodded, and said, "I will, but you have to promise to let me bring some flowers from the shop when we get some new shipments. Liven the place up a bit."

"*Flowers!* What do I need flowers for? Be useless as teats on a boar hog."

She laughed and walked through the cramped aisle to the back of the store; poured herself some decaf, looking longingly at the regular coffee. As she fixed her cup, she patted her stomach. Only three months to go, she thought.

The bell at the front door rang as she stirred the sugar and cream in her coffee, and someone muttered something up at the counter. She turned and walked back to the front, then stopped and gasped when she saw the man with the gun.

The unfamiliar man—boy, really—was rail thin, in ill fitting, tattered clothes, with dirty shoulder-length hair. His face was gaunt, with eyes that stared out from darkened sockets. His right hand, holding a pistol, shook.

"Come on, old man, just give me the money," the man said. As he spoke, his whole body shuddered. *Drug addict,* Martha thought, *Or he's really sick.*

Walter grimaced. "All right, don't get your panties in a wad," he said, working the register. His eyes darted to Martha, then to something below the register.

With a smooth, quick motion, he reached beneath it and lifted a shotgun to his shoulder.

He wasn't quick enough. The young man fired twice, the explosions rocking the tiny store. Walter fell backward in a shower of blood.

Martha shrieked, her hand rising to her mouth, and the man jumped and fired again, the muzzle blast bright in her face. She fell backward as if a truck had hit her; her head hit the floor with a loud crack. Dazed, she lay there as the man stepped over her, reaching behind the counter. Then he ran for the front door and out into the fog, leaving behind the sound of the bell ringing over the door.

Her vision was dark, pinpointed, as if she was looking out from a dark puddle of water. Slowly, she rested her hand on her stomach and felt a mass of blood and torn flesh. As the blood flowed from between her fingers, she began to feel the pain.

"Oh my God, my baby."

The phone. Despite the pain, she struggled for her purse as bright red blood washed across the dirty linoleum floor. Where was the damn phone? The purse fell open, pens and her checkbook spilling out onto the floor. There was her pistol, which Ken insisted she carry. Lot of good it did now that she really needed one.

No phone. *Must have left it in the car.* She fell back in exhaustion, waves of pain wracking her body, a fog clouding her mind.

What about Kenny? Who was going to pick him up from school?

Martha stared up at the ceiling, thinking of her little boy, and his father whom she'd loved for more than twenty years. She started to drift away into the darkness. A vision of dancing with him at their junior prom a lifetime ago came unbidden to her mind's eye. He'd worn a white tuxedo, and had given her a matching orchid. Now when she thought of him dressed up, it was always in his dress blues, with the yellow piping of an Armor officer.

Ken—what will you do when I'm gone? Oh, I love you.

Book One
Three Years Later

Chapter One
May 24

Kenny Murphy, Jr. waved goodbye and turned to go into the school building. The faint lines at the corners of Ken Murphy's eyes crinkled just a little as he watched the little blonde boy walk away. He'd changed so much that Martha wouldn't have recognized him if she'd still been alive. A very serious boy, he had problems they'd never imagined when he was just three, problems Murphy felt ill-equipped to deal with by himself, even three years after she'd died.

He got back on 340 moments later, hands tapping impatiently on the steering wheel as the slow moving traffic crept up the four-lane highway. At least he had an automatic shift now; the clutch in his old truck hadn't agreed with the prosthetic he'd worn since Iraq. His eyes glanced off the wedding ring on his left hand, then back to the congested road. Brake lights flashed in the heavy fog. Murphy hated foggy mornings.

When he'd first moved to Highview with Martha back at the turn of the century, the town had less than five hundred residents. There were at least four times as many now, and the rest of the county had grown even more, with thousands who commuted all the way to Baltimore and Washington, DC. Traffic got worse all the time; what had once been a five-minute drive to work had turned into twenty.

He grimaced as he pulled into the plant. A new fence had been under construction for some weeks. Security, said the executives. Hadn't been any need for a fence in the last twenty years, and he didn't see the need for one now. Waste of money.

He parked the pickup in his reserved spot near the entrance to the building. A small hybrid pulled in next to him, in the spot reserved for the employee of the month. Karen Greenfield. A little older than his daughter, Greenfield was a rising star at the plant, and one hell of a leader. He knew her well from the National Guard. She was a company commander in his battalion, confident and assertive. Attractive young lady, too; every junior officer in the battalion, plus most of the men at the plant, had tried at least once to get her to go out on a date. They rarely tried more than once—when provoked, her eyes could blister enough to crack your skin. Like Murphy, Karen wore stout jeans and a casual shirt.

"Morning, Colonel."

"Morning, Karen. You can call me Ken when we're not on drill."

She smiled. "If I did, I'd be the only person around here who did. Any word on what's going on in Vienna?"

He shook his head. The day before, his boss, plant manager and vice president of production, had been called to northern Virginia for a meeting of the executives that was supposed to be secret. Nothing stayed secret around here. The rumors said they were considering layoffs.

"No, nothing. I wouldn't worry too much. We're one of the most profitable units in the company. They'd be fools to mess with a good thing."

Karen smiled as they walked toward the entrance of the plant. "There's no shortage of fools in the world, Colonel."

"I suppose you're right. Nothing to be done for it now, though. We've got to get those bugs worked out of the new run. Best to think about that instead of rumors."

They entered the building and she headed off to her office, while he went to his. Despite the confident front, Murphy was worried. The fence was just part of it: spending thousands of dollars on security for a building that had never suffered a break-in? It was a very visible reminder that the company was changing, and quickly, since it had been bought by Nelson Barclay's Vienna Holdings.

Barclay had a nasty reputation in the high-tech industry. An incredibly wealthy man, he'd built his company by gobbling up smaller competitors, and avoided regulators by keeping plenty of campaign dollars flowing into the right pockets. He was a good friend of President Price, which didn't do him any good in Murphy's eyes. Murphy had voted for Price's opponent, a struggling underdog who'd been trounced in the election.

Murphy walked past his assistant's desk and into his small office. Like most of the rest of the plant's workers, she wouldn't be in for another hour. Murphy's habit, for more than a decade, had been to get to the office at least an hour or two earlier than the rest of the shift. Without interruptions, he was usually able to get more done then than he did during the rest of the day.

Every detail of the office was organized. His desk, usually clear of everything but the framed photograph of Martha, was currently stacked with the reports that had been rushed through yesterday for the executive meeting. Like the fence, the reports, describing the efficiency of the plant and its workers, made him uneasy. They showed a solid profit, but Murphy wondered if it was enough to satisfy Barclay.

They'd know soon enough.

The next morning was apparently soon enough.

The new twenty-foot high chain link fence surrounded the plant, topped with razor wire. Raw earth was exposed where the posts had been buried. New security cameras mounted on the high fence posts pointed at the roadway and the gate. The gate was locked tight with a chain and padlock, and unfamiliar security guards stood outside the door of the plant, well inside the grounds behind the gate. A brightly painted sign hung on the fence.

EFFECTIVE IMMEDIATELY, THE SATURN MICROSYSTEMS HARPERS FERRY PLANT IS CLOSED.
PERSONAL ITEMS AND SEVERANCE PAY WILL BE MAILED TO ALL EMPLOYEES ON COMPLETION OF INVENTORY.

Murphy climbed out of the car where he had parked it off the side of the long drive leading to the gate, his lips curled into a frown. Karen Greenfield stood next to her rusted pickup across the drive, slapping at the buzzing insects swarming around them. She looked at him, the query in her eyes clear enough that she didn't have to say a word.

He wiped sweat from his forehead and stared at the sign and the fence in disbelief. He was Director of Operations at the plant, the number-two man, and he'd gotten no word. Why the hell had they done this?

More cars drove up the tree-lined drive to the plant and parked on the gravel next to the drive, and a small crowd formed at the gate. He'd known all these men and women for two decades. He'd worked with them and seen them around town. Now they all wore the same puzzled look. No anger had surfaced yet, but that would come. In singles and pairs, they approached him for guidance and information. He had nothing to give them.

David Firkus stepped out of the passenger side of an electric van and walked toward Murphy and Karen. David's expression carried a noticeable lack of focus that made him seem younger than his thirty-five years, with the mannerisms and speech patterns of a ten year old. Mildly retarded, David had worked at the plant for several years. As always, he smiled when he saw Karen; he'd had a crush on her for a long time. She returned a reassuring smile. David was one of the few men in Highview who hadn't found himself wanting to crawl away in response to a cutting glance from her.

Murphy surveyed the growing crowd as Karen tried to explain to David what had happened. David started to look confused and upset as she spoke quickly in a low contralto. He didn't understand.

Murphy didn't either.

By seven, the crowd had swelled to hundreds of men and women, including some from other shifts: the word had spread. They talked in low murmurs, bunched in small groups.

Murphy's eyes darted upward when he heard a helicopter.

A ripple of voices surged through the crowd as a helicopter with the "blue blob" of the Saturn Microsystems logo on its sides appeared over the trees. It landed in the parking lot where their cars should have been, and two men jumped to the ground and approached the gate. Murphy's boss, in a suit and tie, carried a megaphone. He must have come from corporate headquarters: no one wore a suit at the plant. The other man wore the West Virginia State Police uniform. Murphy heard the indignation of the men and women behind him. Why did he bring a state patrolman with him? Was he afraid of them?

The crowd fell silent as the two men approached the other side of the fence, but the tension remained—a tension Murphy didn't like at all. Take away people's livelihood all of a sudden, and there was no telling how they would react. Murphy's boss's eyes met Murphy's, then looked away. No answers there.

The plant manager raised the megaphone to his lips.

"Folks, I can't even begin to tell you how sorry I am. You know that for the past couple of days I've been in Vienna for a meeting with Mr. Barclay. There isn't any way to break this easily, so I'm just going to lay it out. All three of Saturn's US-based plants closed this morning. Everyone is laid off, effective immediately."

An angry roar rose from the crowd.

"Hold on a minute," he yelled into the megaphone. "Let me have my say, please. This will hit me just as hard as all of you. There's nothing we can do. The board decided this months ago, and a new plant in Jakarta opened today. Now listen to me. The company is making a…a generous offer…of new positions for some of you. If you accept the offer you'll have the same seniority you have now. The company will even pay your relocation expenses, and there is a good English school near the new plant."

Someone in the crowd shouted, "Where the hell is Jakarta? We're Americans!"

Another yell, "How much is the pay cut? What will they pay us there?"

"Is this how you saved your job, you bastard? You sold us out to some other country?"

The plant manager frowned, and then spoke again, his voice shaking, barely audible even with the megaphone. "I didn't save my job—I can't move to Indonesia. I'm staying on to supervise shipping out all the equipment, then they're letting me go, too."

"Liar!"

"Folks, listen to me. You have to keep your cool on this. Next week, checks will go out to everyone for six weeks' severance pay, plus extra depending on how long you worked for the company. Also, for some of you there will be an enclosed job offer at the new plant, with the new salary, doing the same job you have today. The company will pick up moving expenses. This is a generous offer. All the details on the move will be in the information packet. Now please. Go home. Go back to your families and try to figure out what is the best move for you, all right? I'm sorry, I wish I had better news, I really do. Good-bye."

He shook his head and walked away, the state trooper following.

Someone pitched a glass bottle, the sun glinting off the glass as it spun end over end before shattering against the fence and showering the two men with broken glass. The trooper spun around and fumbled for his pistol, and someone in the crowd shouted.

Murphy backed away from the fence. Half a dozen men stood on the hoods of two trucks, shouting at the plant manager's back.

Murphy said in a tone he expected to be obeyed, "Captain Greenfield." He motioned to Karen and they grabbed David by the arms. Murphy hadn't been in an angry crowd like this since Iraq, and didn't want to be in one now. This could get ugly real quick, and David didn't need to be in the middle of it.

"Come on, Dave, let's get away from the gate," Karen said. She smiled at him, attempting to keep him calm even as the crowd grew more raucous. They pulled him away from the gate, toward the woods beside the road.

David said, "What's going on, I don't understand!"

Another bottle bounced against the fence, then shattered against the pavement. One of the workers started to climb the chain links.

"Sir, you're going to have to get down," shouted the state trooper. He unhitched the strap over his pistol.

Murphy pushed against the surge of the crowd, trying to move David and Karen out of it as screams rang out.

Behind him, Murphy heard a gunshot as the trooper fired into the air. Murphy's ears rang, and David screamed, then started to cry.

The crowd fell back from the fence, as if from the crack of a whip. The gunshot seemed to drain the angry energy from the crowd, or at least frighten them enough to back off.

Karen said, "It's all right, Dave," and hugged him.

"Go on," the trooper yelled. "Get out of here."

People started to move back to their cars. Much more quickly than the area had filled this morning, it began to empty. Murphy and Karen helped David back to his carpool as with a funereal air, the former employees headed back to their homes. Murphy looked back at the fence. The trooper still stood behind it, Murphy's boss not far behind him.

That was all the good-bye he got, after nineteen years with the company.

He looked at Karen, and she back at him, both of them helpless to do anything about the situation. Without another word, they got back in their cars and drove away.

※

Sally's Diner in Highview was as busy as Murphy had ever seen it. The usual lunch crowd was there of course, but the place was packed with an extra twenty people or so: folks like him, who would have normally been down at the plant. The old building, with its rundown interior and flaking paint, was a favorite meeting spot in Highview. On the corner of Main and Tipple streets, it was a small standalone building, a wood frame with peeling white clapboards.

Murphy had a seat at the scuffed counter, a cup of coffee set before him and an unread *Washington Post* next to it. The coffee had been sitting, getting cold. He absently rubbed the joint between his knee and the prosthetic left leg he'd worn for more than a decade. He needed to get some new liners; it had been irritating him lately.

Walter Haggett's teenage great-grandson Frank frantically washed dishes behind the counter, slinging the trays of dishes and glasses around with a crash. Frank was sixteen, and should have been in school; he'd dropped out earlier in the school year. It was hard for Murphy to see the gangly, greasy-haired teenager with acne and rings in his ears and nose: he'd been a confused young kid at Haggett's funeral three years earlier. Walter had been laid to rest during a closed-coffin service the day after Martha's.

"Hey, Colonel Murphy, look at the tube—isn't that your daughter?"

Murphy looked up at the aging television, tuned to CNN. Someone turned it up. Congressman Al Clark stood in the chamber of the House of Representatives. Directly behind him was Murphy's daughter Valerie, Clark's assistant. At the bottom of the screen the words "Welfare Reform Bill" flashed.

Clark spoke, a lopsided grin on his face. "The wisdom—no, the celestial guidance—behind this proposal is almost too stellar for me to see clearly. Applaud, I tell you. Applaud! Now, I have only one suggestion, one little morsel—an amendment to offer to Mr. Skaggs's wise proposal. Let us send a mission to the moon to carve up the cheese and give it to our senior citizens. Let us send it back in huge rockets to land in the ocean, not only providing for our dear sainted grandmothers, but at the same time revitalizing the shipping and dairy industries."

The diners in the restaurant broke into laughter as the screen switched to Representative Mark Skaggs from Kentucky, his face flushed. It appeared the other representatives onscreen were also gripped with hysterical laughter.

"My suggestion will have just as much opportunity to help our country as the one proposed by the gentleman from Kentucky," Clark said. "Gentlemen, Ladies: this proposal will likely bring revolution down on our heads. Our people are bleeding, fellow members of the House. *Bleeding.* Yet there he is, the gentleman from Kentucky who wants to take away their last bandages so the wealthy can use them as fancy headdresses."

Voices rose in the diner again, as if by common consent, and someone turned the volume back down on the television as the screen shifted back to the anchors. The goings-on in Washington had little to do with them, anyway. If it hadn't been for the brief view of Valerie Murphy, the news would have attracted little interest.

Murphy's waitress poured him a cup of coffee and said, "That Clark, he sure is a card, isn't he? How's Valerie doing working for him?"

"She loves the job, got promoted again last year; she's running his whole office now," Murphy said.

"Well, isn't that something. I remember when she was nothing more than a toddler, thought she owned everything."

"Well, some things never change," he said, grinning.

She laughed and walked away, and Murphy returned to the newspaper. Depressing stuff. Unemployment. War in the Middle East. Someone had poisoned the reservoir in Milwaukee.

Murphy looked away from the paper for a moment and his eyes landed on a couple he knew, holding hands over the table as they talked. He jerked his eyes away and returned to the bad news in the paper. Of course it was always bad news—at least what they chose to print. All the same, lately things just seemed to be getting worse.

"This seat taken?"

Murphy looked up at the words. Karen stood to his left, still in the jeans and flannel shirt she'd worn to the plant earlier in the morning.

"Sit down," he said.

She did, apparently unaware of the appreciative glances from the men across the room. Karen didn't socialize in town very often.

"What are you planning to do, Colonel?"

"Well, first I'm going to ask you to stop calling me that when we're not on drill status."

She smiled. "Seriously."

Murphy shrugged. "Don't know. I'll get a job somewhere. Kenny can't go without health insurance. But I'll be damned if I know what to do. I've been making chips at that plant for twenty years."

She nodded, her expression serious. "Yeah. I'm at a loss. It's for sure there's no other decent jobs around here."

Murphy tossed back the rest of his cold coffee, then waved to the waitress for a refill. "Maybe you should think about applying for active duty status."

She grunted. "Maybe. But they'd probably make me switch branches, be a nurse or finance officer or something."

She was probably right. President Price's predecessor had signed an executive order integrating women who applied into the combat arms, and Karen had received her Armor commission as a result. Then Price had rescinded the order; consequently, only a small number of women were grandfathered into Infantry and Armor.

"You're probably right," he said, "But they'd be fools to do it. Don't repeat this, but as far as I'm concerned, you're the most capable company commander I have."

"Why thank you, Colonel. I don't have any illusions though."

"Maybe I could talk to my brother. He might be able to swing something."

She raised her eyebrows.

"Tommy's taking command of a brigade down at Fort Campbell."

"Infantry?"

"That's right. West Point." He grinned. "I never thought my little brother would outrank me."

"Do you believe them about the severance pay?"

"I imagine so. If only to avoid lawsuits, they'll be scrupulously fair. But six weeks pay won't go very far. Not for most of these folks."

"Yes. Definitely not for me. I'm still paying off my damn student loans."

"You went to Bowling Green, right?"

"That's right. And this all has a familiar feeling. I grew up in Kentucky coal country. When they finally closed the mine for good, it seemed like the town was going to dry up and blow away. A lot of folks never recovered."

"Yeah," he replied. "I never thought I'd be facing a layoff at this age. Happened to me once, a lifetime ago it seems. I got laid off from the GM plant in Atlanta twenty-five years ago."

"What'd you do?"

He laughed. "Joined the Army. All I had was a high school diploma, Martha, and a new baby to feed."

He looked around the crowded diner, and said, "This sure is going to hit Highview hard. Eight hundred families…I guess more than half the town worked at that plant."

He didn't finish the thought aloud. Desperate people tended to do desperate things.

Chapter Two
May 26

Valerie Murphy hung up the phone and finished typing her notes. Another call from Highview. This was the fifth one this morning, plus the long talk with her father last night. Folks back home were starting to panic. A tall, well-dressed woman with a sharp mind, she knew that other staffers in the office—some of whom she'd been promoted over—privately called her a bitch, or worse. She didn't care. Her job was to take care of the Congressman, and that meant keeping the office running efficiently.

She pulled the file together, printed her notes from the latest call, and dialed Al Clark.

"You ready, Boss?"

"Come on in. Bring Ambrose."

Two minutes later she and Ambrose Hall, the Congressman's legal counsel, sat across from Clark in his spacious office. Clark briefly switched on his campaign smile; then switched it off, moved to a stuffed leather chair, and put his feet on the coffee table. He wore what could easily be called the Washington uniform: dark suit, solid blue shirt and tie. He didn't often pay attention to his appearance, and had been wearing the same ratty shoes he'd worn when he'd first been elected. One of these days she was going to make them disappear.

Ambrose sat next to her, carefully adjusting his well-tailored suit. Ambrose was a thin, well-dressed African American man who sported a rather unusual handlebar mustache. He was also gay—an open secret no one cared about on the Hill, but one that wouldn't go over that well back home.

"So what's the story?" Clark asked, struggling out of his coat. The office was oppressively hot: like much of everything else, funds for maintaining the aging House office buildings had been cut. Valerie's only concession to the heat was a lighter suit.

"We're short on details," she said. "Yesterday morning, Saturn Microsystems announced it was closing all three of its US-based plants—Highview, West Virginia; Roswell, Georgia and Phoenix, Arizona. They're moving their entire operation offshore to Indonesia. All told, about three thousand people were laid off, including nearly a thousand in the district."

Clark frowned. "Sons of bitches. Saturn was bought out by Nelson Barclay recently, wasn't it?"

"That's right. The company is profitable, but margins have been falling lately. It was the last chip manufacturer in the United States."

"Jesus Christ," Clark said, drawling the words out slowly.

Ambrose creased his eyebrows with a falsely stern look, then launched into his standard lecture. "Boss, you're not supposed to say that. Your constituents will take a dim view."

Clark laughed. "If there's ever a time to swear, it's now. I'd think we'd be able to get the folks on national security interested. Aside from the unemployment issue, it's for damn sure a weakness for our country to lose its only ability to make high-tech gear. Are they at least giving a decent severance to the employees who were let go?"

Valerie shook her head. "Six weeks, plus extra for seniority. My understanding is that final checks were delivered express mail to folks this morning. We've had a lot of calls—this was the biggest employer in the district. What happens to those folks?"

Ambrose, the attorney, said, "Most of them will be eligible for unemployment, but we've got another worry. The Skaggs bill, if it passes, will eliminate most federal benefits. There won't be much for those people to fall back on."

"Same story all over the country," Clark replied. "I can't figure out why the goddamn bill is so popular."

"Boss..." Valerie said.

"Right, I guess Congressmen aren't supposed to say goddamn, either."

"It's true, sir," Hall said. "It's bad enough you have a gay black man working for you."

"Right," Clark said, shaking his head. "Get me some options, folks. I don't know how much we can do, but we can't let this one slide."

Valerie and Ambrose nodded, and then stood. As she walked toward the door, Clark said, "Valerie, doesn't your father work for Saturn?"

Valerie looked back. "He did until yesterday, sir."

Clark met her eyes and nodded. "Find me some options, please. Let's see what we can do to help those folks out."

Back at her desk in the largest cube in the back of the office, Valerie lost herself in her work. A series of calls to the much reduced labor department produced no result but frustration. On top of that, a series of visitors were coming this afternoon. Representatives of the United Mine Workers and lobbyists for several different trade associations would keep her occupied most of the remainder of the day.

The phone rang, and she picked it up and answered, "Valerie Murphy," without taking her eyes off the report she was reading.

"Hi, it's David! Can I persuade you to drop everything and come up to New York this weekend?"

David. A year, even six months before, her heart would have jumped at the invitation. Now it seemed more like an invasion.

"I don't know, David. I may have to work through the weekend. We're pretty busy right now."

"I've got something that will change your mind," he said, his voice teasing. "Tickets to *Jumping Through Fire.*"

She smiled. *Jumping Through Fire* was the new stage play by Steve Chapman, one of her favorite playwrights. And David hated going to the theater.

"David, that's sweet… I just don't know if I can get away."

A sigh on the line told her he was defeated. "When you start turning down plays, I start thinking you're having doubts about us."

Valerie bit her lip. He was right. She had doubts, plenty of them. On the other hand, she'd be a royal bitch to turn him down. It had been nearly two months since she'd been to New York. He must have spent a fortune on those tickets—the show had been sold out six months in advance.

"All right. I'll come up on the train Saturday morning."

"Great. Call me on the way, I'll meet you at Penn Station. You know I love you."

"I know," she said.

A loud crash outside rattled the windows. She looked up up in annoyance, then back at the desk.

"David, let's talk this weekend. You know me too well. I *am* having doubts."

There was a sharp inhalation at the other end of the line. "I know. It's been pretty clear for a while."

"It's not you," she said. "I just don't know if I'm ready to settle into something permanent right now."

Several of the interns were crowded at the window nearest her, strangely hushed. A faint line appeared over Valerie's forehead. Why weren't they working?

"If it's not me, what is it?"

Another loud thump rattled the windows, and one of the interns squealed. Valerie frowned.

"David, I don't know if this is the right time to have this discussion. Let's talk in person this weekend."

"Well Christ, Valerie, if this isn't the time to talk about it, why did you bring it up?"

"I don't know. You're right."

Ambrose appeared at the door of the office and waved at her urgently.

"David, I've got to go. Something's happening."

"What?"

"I have to go right now. I'll see you Saturday."

"I love you," he said.

She hung up the phone without replying. A dozen steps took her to Ambrose. "What is it?"

He pointed at the television playing in the reception area. The words at the bottom of the screen told her all she needed to know:

"Explosions at the Pentagon."

⌘

"I'm sorry, sir. According to this, you've been provided severance pay for nearly four months. You'll just have to come back and apply in October."

Murphy swallowed his frustration. It was galling to be in this position, begging help from a government beauracrat. But he had a six year old to take care of, and didn't have the luxury of pride. He leaned forward, resting his arms on the neat, precise desk, behind which sat a woman whose smile didn't illuminate her eyes.

"I get that. The issue is, the severance pay doesn't extend to health insurance. I have a very sick son at home, and it is critical he stays covered. And I can't get him covered until you certify that I'm unemployed and seeking work."

The woman behind the desk tilted her head as if to say, *so what?* Murphy was unnaturally irritated by her heavy makeup.

"There's nothing I can really do about that, sir. You're not unemployed until the severance pay runs out."

Murphy closed his eyes and took a deep breath, fighting for patience. He looked up and said, "Without treatment, my son might be dead by then."

"Sir, I'm very sorry, but there is nothing I can do. You might consider contacting someone in the state health department, but we cannot list you as unemployed until October 1, at the end of your severance period."

Better to not say anything. Nothing at all. Murphy stood, unintentionally scattering papers onto the floor, and walked away.

Outside, it was grey and wet, rain coming down in a flood, despite the fact that it was nearly June. Half a dozen cold, rainy springs in a row. So much for global warming.

It could be a lot worse, he thought. He owned the old house outright; though it had been a real struggle, they'd kept with a fifteen-year mortgage and even paid it off two years early. When the deed came, delivered certified mail, they framed it, then drove to Washington to catch a play at the Kennedy Center and celebrate. Murphy wasn't much of a drinker, and neither was Martha, but that night they'd gotten drunk on happiness. She'd grown rounded at the edges as they'd grown older, but that night she was radiant. It was likely as not that Kenny Jr. had been conceived in the Hotel Harrington around the corner from FBI headquarters.

In addition to the house, he still owned Martha's shop in the center of the town. It had been a hideous indulgence to close and lock the doors, keep paying taxes on it, fending off all offers of a quick sale for the prime retail spot. Just never seemed right to sell off all that was left of her life's work. Now he'd have to. That alone ought to cover Kenny's insurance premiums for a few months, maybe a year. Long enough to find a new job, anyway.

Too bad about that bill from the IRS; he'd just written them a check for twenty thousand dollars. Just about cleaned out his savings.

"You look like you're doing a bit of woolgathering there, Colonel."

Startled by the bass voice, Murphy looked up, embarrassed to be found just standing outside the door of the unemployment office. It was Joe and Mandy Blankenship. Mandy had worked at the plant, in Karen Greenfield's department. Joe was a coalminer, which meant that he was more often unemployed than not.

"I confess. You can tell you're getting old when you think of ten years ago like it was this morning."

Mandy smiled, but the smile wasn't genuine. "Somehow seeing you here makes it all real, Ken."

"It's real enough," he replied. "How are you two? Kids okay?"

"Oh, Joe's an old hand at this, what with the coal mines," Mandy said. "We'll be all right, I suppose, long as we can keep up on the mortgage. I didn't get much in the way of severance pay, though. Hadn't been around long enough."

"Oh, that's too bad."

"By the way," Mandy said, "Have you heard any of that talk from Tim Wagner about forming a union?"

Murphy shook his head. "No. Tell you the truth, I can't see how a union would make much difference at this stage."

"I thought I heard he's trying to put together a deal for the workers to buy the plant."

Murphy grunted. That would be a hell of coup. "I'll definitely check into it, that could make a big difference," he said.

They said their goodbyes, and Murphy made his way out into the rain as the couple entered the unemployment office. In the car, he turned on the radio and heard the news: there had been a bombing in Arlington, Virginia, outside the Pentagon. Without a second thought, he dialed Valerie's number in Washington.

Chapter Three
May 26

Captain Mike Morris pulled the car to a stop in front of the house, where boxes from the move were stacked on the front walk. He had turned off the radio as soon as he got in the car; he didn't want to hear another word about the Arlington bombing. He suspected he'd soon know more about it than he could ever hope to. Rumor at battalion was they were going to be deployed as security near the Pentagon.

He turned off the car and listened to the engine tick, watching the house. Worn paint, dry-rotted siding. A line of paving stones led to the front door, some of them uneven, with weeds poking through the cracks. Inside, the carpet was a hideous orange. It was going to take a lot of work to make this place feel like home.

Enough stalling. Alicia was going to go bananas if they did get deployment orders; he'd been dreading coming home all afternoon. There'd be a round of recriminations, and she'd be off to her parents in Kentucky or Washington or wherever the hell they were right now. Another lecture about how Morris should be *stable*, more like her own father. He didn't need that.

Morris got out of the car and walked toward the house. The front door opened and his six-year-old daughter ran out, blonde mane flying behind her.

"Daddy!"

"Hi, kid. How you doing?"

Savannah jumped up for a hug. He carried her lightweight thirty-five pounds inside.

"Michael," Alicia called from the living room. "It's your company on the phone."

Morris groaned. This had to be it—right outside Washington, DC, who else would deploy for something like this? And why else would they be calling at dinnertime?

"Coming."

Lowering Savannah to the floor, he said, "Savannah, can you do your daddy a great big favor?"

"Yeah."

"You mean *yes*," he said, handing her his uniform cap. "Can you take this upstairs for me and put it on the hatrack?"

"Yeah," she said.

Morris sighed. Some battles you just couldn't win.

"Thank you, honey."

She ran upstairs as Morris walked into the living room. Alicia stood, legs spread shoulder-width apart, one hand on her hip, the other holding the phone toward him. She wore an old pair of jeans and a t-shirt smeared with paint and dust. She'd spent the day unpacking and painting, and looked very tired. She frowned, her blue eyes cold.

He took the phone from his wife. She met his eyes, but the look was not warm. Then again, was it ever any more?

"Captain Morris speaking."

"Captain, this is Sergeant Diamond at the company. We've received an alert message from battalion. I think this one's for real, sir; Sergeant Meyer up at battalion said we're going somewhere. Something about that bombing today."

"Roger, I'll be back in fifteen minutes. Check with Top about getting me some field gear issued; I don't have any equipment."

As he spoke, Alicia's frown grew more severe, twin lines forming on her forehead between her eyes. Her back was straight, her arms crossed under her breasts. Five years ago he would have found her posture fetching.

"Yes, sir."

Morris put the phone down and sighed.

"What's going on, Mike?"

"We're being alerted. I don't know anything more, yet."

"It never stops, does it? I mean, you just got home from a year in Korea, and now we've moved halfway to the end of the earth. Will you be home tonight, or am I going to see you on the news getting on a plane to somewhere?"

"I don't know, Alicia."

"I didn't sign up to be a single parent, you know."

Knowing she was right, Morris couldn't help biting back. "I guess you should have thought of that before you married an infantry officer."

He turned away so he didn't have to see her face harden; then marched upstairs to grab his always-packed alert bag. Her shout caught him by surprise.

"No, I should have thought of that before letting a drunk college boy get me pregnant!"

He reached the top step and told himself to calm down, take a deep breath, and relax. She had every right to be upset. Sometimes the alerts between the field deployments—not to mention the real deployments—turned everyone's lives upside down. For the last several years they'd lived like carnies, traveling where the job took them, punctuated by Mike's long absences, including one that lasted over a year. Morris knew that in her position, he'd be pissed too.

That didn't make dealing with her any easier. It was like walking through a minefield—he just never knew what was going to infuriate her. When he was out of town, she took Savannah back home to Kentucky, where her father, Congressman Mark Skaggs, constantly harped on how she'd screwed up her life. Just the thing Savannah needed to hear from her pig of a grandfather.

He started collecting his things, and then he heard Alicia's voice from downstairs. But it was the way her voice shook that caught his attention.

"Mike, you better get down here and see this."

He grabbed his bag and the cap Savannah had just brought upstairs, and headed downstairs. Alicia stood in front of the television, right arm clasped across her chest, left hand covering her mouth. The scene of devastation on the television was dramatic: burning buildings, chaos, smoke rising into the sky.

It took a moment for Morris to realize that this scene wasn't from a bad movie. It was just down the road in Arlington, Virginia.

"I better get back to the company," he said.

She glanced over at him, and in a small voice said, "I'm sorry."

"Me too," he whispered. But he left without kissing her goodbye.

♻

An hour later, the company commanders and battalion staff gathered in the briefing room in the battalion headquarters, a small, windowless cube with a long conference table stretching down the middle. All of the officers but Morris wore field gear, battle dress uniforms with pistol belts, gas masks and helmets strewn on the conference table. Morris, the odd man out, had no field gear as of yet, though his first sergeant had probably procured it for him by now.

Why the hell did this have to happen on his first day in charge of a new company? That morning he had released half his company on pass so he could spend time with the other half. As a result, he had several stragglers who hadn't gotten word of the alert. His new battalion commander, Lieutenant Colonel Barksdale, was pissed. Not a good way to start his new command.

The battalion intelligence officer, Lieutenant Elaine Gurewich, a strikingly attractive woman in her early twenties, stood at the head of the table and spoke. Morris had met the Army Intelligence officer only briefly when he'd been assigned to the battalion. Now she commanded everyone's attention as she pointed out locations on a map of Arlington, Virginia.

"An hour after the initial bombing, additional car bombs went off at three locations surrounding the initial bombing. These were devastating; the area was packed with rescue personnel when the bombs went off," Gurewich said. "They were timed to inflict as much damage as possible to rescue and security personnel. There are likely to be additional devices."

She turned and faced the group.

"It's clear the bombings were the coordinated actions of a terrorist group. No one has come forward and claimed responsibility at this time, and the news has indicated no leads. I've heard some scuttlebutt from Brigade headquarters—I don't know how reliable—that they suspect Middle Eastern origin, maybe Al-Qaeda. There's some evidence these were suicide bombers. DHS is pursuing the investigation."

Someone whistled low in the back of the room. Morris sighed. *Suicide bombers inside the United States.* It was bound to happen sometime.

Colonel Barksdale asked, "Has there been any looting?"

"Some. There's a large homeless and poverty level population in Arlington, and one of the shopping centers was heavily damaged. However, our last report has it that there are hundreds of civilians throughout the area, some of them wounded and trapped under rubble. It's going to be a bear. The Virginia and DC National Guard are already on station conducting rescue operations, so our mission will be security."

Barksdale stood. "All right then. Everyone have your maps? I want the battalion to roll out in thirty minutes. Major Granville, Lieutenant Gurewich: you go with the Scout Platoon for the quartering party. See if you can set up a liaison with the National Guard, and whoever else is down there. I want all our units on station no later than midnight. Understood? Good. Dismissed."

The officers filed out of the room and hurried back to their units.

༄

Private Jim Turville sat in the dark back of a two-and-a-half-ton truck, cramped and uncomfortable, with twenty other soldiers jammed in behind him. His nostrils filled with the smell of diesel and sweat; closing his eyes didn't shut out the overwhelming sounds and smells.

"All right, all right, get on the truck, no more screwing around. We're moving out in ten minutes," shouted Sergeant O'Donnell as the last of her platoon boarded the truck.

Turville looked up when he heard the new company commander's voice outside the truck. "Sergeant O'Donnell," called Captain Morris. "Did your wayward private ever show up?"

"Yes sir, about ten minutes ago. He's already on the truck."

"It looks like we're going to be sitting for a few more minutes, why don't you send him over."

"Roger, sir."

Hearing the exchange outside the truck, Turville frowned. *Oh, man.* He hadn't thought they took the travel limit stuff so seriously once you were out of basic training. What a way to make a first impression on his new commander. *Idiot.* This one mistake could screw his chances for promotion down the line.

"Private Turdville," called Corporal Meigs, his fire team leader. "Yo, get your butt off the truck."

Turville shot Meigs a vicious look and stood up, his heavy combat gear weighing him down. The nickname—*Turdville*—had been with him since elementary school, but it hadn't been a big deal until Turville's drill sergeant at Fort Benning thought of it, believing he was the baddest, most original dude to walk the earth. Making Turville's life miserable had been his major preoccupation for three months. That wasn't so bad; after all, being miserable was what basic training was all about. But to finish basic and end up in this candy-assed company with a 19-year-old corporal as his first line supervisor and a woman for a platoon sergeant—it was too much. There couldn't be more than a dozen women serving as platoon sergeants in the entire infantry, and it was Turville's luck he'd gotten one of them.

Turville climbed over the tailgate of the deuce-and-a-half and stood at parade rest. "Private Turville, reporting as ordered, ma'am."

O'Donnell, a foot shorter than him, her brown hair bunched up under her helmet, looked up at him with a frown. "Do I look like an officer to you, Private?"

"No, Sergeant."

"Then don't call me ma'am, you know better than that. What were you thinking going outside the mileage limit, Private Turville? We've got a new company commander, and you went and messed it up with him on the very first day."

"Sergeant, that was not my intention—"

"I don't care what your intention was, Private."

Turville shifted on his feet. "Yes, Sergeant."

"Now. These are the facts. Our brand new company commander gave everyone two days off, with the stipulation that you call in twice a day and that you stay within fifty miles of post, because we are detailed for rapid deployment should such a deployment become necessary. You, with your boneheaded reasoning, decided to blow that off. You, a brand new private in the Army, decided that your judgment was better than that of the senior officer of this company. Even more offensive, you decided your judgment was more important than mine. Do I have it pretty much straight?"

"Well, Sergeant, I—"

"That's what I thought. You have been summoned to speak with the Commander himself. You will conduct yourself in a military manner when in his presence, though I personally doubt you will ever make much of a soldier. When he asks you what you were thinking, you will respond by saying 'No excuse, sir.' You will then accept whatever punishment he deems suitable. You had better hope he doesn't leave that punishment up to me. Do I make myself absolutely crystal clear?"

"Yes, Sergeant."

"Good. Let's go see the Commander then, and you better pray that he is merciful and just."

"Yes, Sergeant."

※

Turville could smell and hear it long before they arrived. Crammed in the back of the truck at the end of a long drive, he couldn't see much, but the sounds and smells were more than enough. A roar rose from the still burning buildings, and acrid black smoke filled the truck, burning his eyes and throat. He saw flashing blue and red lights in the darkness, heard sirens and the sound of a single gunshot.

The truck jerked to a stop. Turville peered out between the canvas panels, then gasped and jerked his head back, blinking. On her back in the street, in a pool of light cast by one of the other trucks, lay a beautiful redhaired young girl around sixteen, her athletic body in a flowered and bloodstained sundress. She had no legs, and the ground all around her was soaked in a pool of blood.

"Off the truck! Off the truck!" The first sergeant waved his arms at them, directing the company to line up near the truck.

Turville didn't move until someone clapped him on the shoulder: Corporal Meigs, his lanky, African American fire team leader. "Move it, Turdville."

He jerked, and then climbed out of the bed of the truck, unable to take his eyes off the dead girl. He was followed by the rest of the platoon, someone muttering, "Holy shit, look at that," behind him.

"Second platoon, over here," shouted Sergeant O'Donnell, a wisp of hair falling out from under her helmet. The platoon gathered around her, no more than a hundred yards from the burning Crystal City Mall, just across the highway from the Pentagon. "Fall in."

Turville obeyed the order, standing in his rank to the left of Meigs. O'Donnell stood in front of the platoon, face set in grim lines.

"Listen up," she said. Turville had a hard time looking away from the body. "If you need to puke, go ahead, that's fine. No one will think any worse of you. But here's the deal: this won't be the only body you are will see in the next few days. Don't let it interfere with your job. Understand?"

No one responded. Most of the men looked anywhere but at the body, or, for that matter, at Sergeant O'Donnell.

"They've got about a thousand rescue workers out here helping clear the wreckage and find people. Our job is simple: along with the rest of the battalion, we provide perimeter security for the area. The LT will brief us shortly on our positions, so just stay here and stay calm. Got it?"

No one replied.

"Rest," she ordered. The members of the platoon sat down on the sidewalk. Most of them lit cigarettes. One of the older sergeants took out a deck of cards and started a game of solitaire on the sidewalk.

Meigs muttered under his breath. Turville couldn't catch the words. Their squad leader did, however. He shoved Meigs's shoulder and said, "Shut up. She's a hell of a good platoon sergeant, a damn site better than you, worm."

"Roger, Sarge," Meigs replied. He ducked his head and looked away.

Turville looked up at the sky. It was a clear night, but the smoke and lights obscured most of his view of the stars. *All right, damn it.* This is what he'd enlisted for, to help protect his country. Here was his chance. *Don't think about it. Just don't think about it.* But his thoughts kept returning to the girl.

Meigs lay on his back, his rucksack a makeshift pillow. "Don't let it get to you, Turville. This is normal—rush all over the place in a big hurry, then sit around waiting. Good chance to take a nap."

"You can nap with… that?" Turville said, indicating the girl's body thirty feet away.

"One thing you gotta learn: take every chance you get to sleep. You won't get many."

Turville tried to close his eyes. It was pointless. He lit a cigarette and looked around, then shifted position, uncomfortable sitting on the ground.

He sat up.

"Hey, Sarge," he said to the squad leader. "Can we at least cover the body with a tarp or something? Show her some respect?"

The squad leader, a bulky blonde man with striking blue eyes, replied in a biting tone. "Good idea, Turville. Why don't you use your shelter half?"

Turville didn't understand what their problem was; seemed like the non-commissioned officers in his squad had taken a disliking to him without even giving him a chance. "You'll cover me with the supply sergeant?"

"Yeah, Turville, I will."

Turville removed his shelter half from where it was tied underneath his rucksack. The shelter half was a large piece of green canvas. When joined with a partner's shelter half, it would make a functional tent. Turville untied it, not thinking about what he was about to do, then walked toward the body, watching his step.

Jesus. She was exquisite: red hair splayed about, green eyes wide open, the dress gathered around her breasts; she looked like somebody's prom date. It was creepy, looking at someone so beautiful lying there dead. Her skin was ivory pale.

Turville grimaced. *Idiot. Of course her skin is pale.* Her blood was run out all over the street, soaking the ground so that it looked black. He wanted to cry, looking at her. Could have been his sister, or one of the girls he'd wished he'd dated in high school. With a snap, he spread the shelter half as far as it would stretch, and then laid it over the girl.

It settled on top of her, obscuring the contours of her body. Turville stared at it, then turned to walk back to his squad.

Meigs muttered something to one of the other NCOs, then laughed out loud. Turville felt his face burn and didn't meet their eyes. He sat back down and pretended to sleep. Meigs was right about that: in the Army you had to learn to sleep anywhere.

Ten minutes later, Sergeant O'Donnell and the lieutenant returned. O'Donnell looked at the body and nodded in approval.

"Fall in," ordered O'Donnell.

The men and women in the platoon jumped to their feet.

The lieutenant didn't speak, his eyes going from soldier to soldier in the platoon. He was still new—someone told Turville he'd just finished college and this was his first assignment. Looked like it, the way he was rocking on his heels, his hands clenching and unclenching.

"Okay, here's the deal," he said, his voice high pitched, "We're to provide perimeter security for the search and rescue operations. What that means is, we don't let civilians into the area. Any we find, we get them to medical personnel and law enforcement regardless of whether they think they need help. The entire area between the Pentagon and the mall is closed to civilians. The triage tent is two blocks over there, next to the mall. I've got tourist maps of the area here for the squad leaders; you can use them to orient yourselves. Our positions are marked."

He pointed with his right hand.

"Now, there has been some looting. The word is caution. Each man will be issued a loaded magazine, but you are not—I repeat *not*—to lock and load your weapons without approval. Everyone understand? I will hold the squad leaders responsible for enforcing this.

"Next: this wasn't just a single bomb. About an hour after the initial bomb, a couple more went off, killing a bunch of paramedics and firefighters. It looks like this was a well-planned terrorist attack."

Turville's stomach twisted and he looked away. *Had to be the Arabs again.* They didn't have any respect for life. He still remembered the day the Pentagon and World Trade Center were hit—he'd been in first grade then, and everything was crazy. Somehow they'd got it in their heads that their parents were picking them up because a plane was going to hit the school, too. One kid didn't come back for almost three weeks: his mother, an accountant who consulted for the Department of Defense, had been injured in the Pentagon.

"We suspect there are more bombs scattered about the area," the lieutenant went on. "You will exercise extreme caution when approaching vehicles, or anything you see lying in the area. Our platoon will be a screening force along Army-Navy drive between Route 1, over here, and South Lynn St, over there."

The lieutenant gestured to the map as he pointed out the locations. "I want one squad to maintain position at the top of the exit ramp from 395 to the mall. The rule is simple: police, rescue, fire, and military vehicles may pass. No one else. If someone tries to force their way past, call for help and use the minimum force necessary to stop them. That includes the press—especially the press. They are not to be allowed in this area. Sergeant O'Donnell or myself will be the contacts if anyone needs to be taken into custody. Any questions?"

The men stood in silence.

"Everyone on the truck. We'll go the circuit and drop off each squad," said Sergeant O'Donnell.

With the others, Turville climbed back on the truck. It moved toward Army-Navy Boulevard, depositing each group of soldiers at their posts.

Turville's squad got off the truck at the corner of Army-Navy, about two hundred yards from the still burning mall. Macy's was at this end, the huge store windows smashed from the concussion, smoke still pouring out of the building. Two fire trucks stood to the side of the building, near an olive drab Army tent. The triage tent, the lieutenant had said.

In front of them, across the street, was the sweeping ramp from Interstate 395.

The squad leader spoke to the fire teams. "Leo, Gomez, I want you to set up a position about a hundred yards over there, right up against the second office building. Sergeant Nguyen, you set your team up to block the on-ramp there and the approach from Army-Navy over there. Meigs, Turville, you guys walk the position, up to Fern Street and back. We'll work out a shift schedule shortly."

Meigs and Turville dropped their rucksacks near the Sergeant and began walking their post. It was going to be a long night.

☙

Three hours after the explosion near the Pentagon, Murphy still hadn't reached Valerie, though he'd called her office and her cell phone repeatedly. He was sure she was okay; she worked in the Rayburn House Office Building, miles away from the Pentagon. All the same, he was on the verge of panic.

He drove back into the Highview town square, scanning for a parking space. The spaces in the square were all filled. Very unusual; folks must still be crowded into Sally's Diner, watching the news coverage of the bombing. He circled the square.

"Daddy, stop, I want to get some ice-cream," Kenny said, kicking the back of Murphy's seat and pointing out the window at the ice cream shop.

"Not right now; we're in a hurry."

"Daddy hates me," Kenny said the words in a sing-song, whining voice like fingernails scraping across a blackboard.

Murphy glanced back at his son in the rearview-mirror. It was so frustrating: they would have one or two good weeks, and then Kenny would slide back, with mood swings and tantrums, behaving like a two or three year old rather than a six year old. Murphy reminded himself that the boy had no idea that something terrible had happened. And he wasn't responsible for his steadily worsening neurological condition.

What the hell was Murphy going to do without health insurance? And why couldn't he reach Valerie? He spoke, an edge in his voice.

"No time for that now. I need to get you to Samira's so I can get to my meeting. All right? No more complaining. We'll do something fun tomorrow; it looks like I won't be going to the office anytime soon, so I'll pick you up straight from school."

The town square included a well-manicured green area in the center, surrounded by shops. He parked the car in front of the Al-Khoury Lebanese Grocery.

"Okay, kiddo," he said, stepping out of the car. He walked around to the other side and opened the rear passenger door. Kenny climbed out. Murphy was lucky this time: it hadn't turned into a full-fledged tantrum. He didn't have time for that right now.

Murphy took a deep breath when they walked in. He loved the fragrance of the spices. Ahmed, the owner, waved to him from the counter as he came in the door.

"Ken, Ken, I heard about the plant. Is everything okay? Can I get you anything?"

"No thanks, Ahmed. I'm all right, just dropping Kenny off with Samira."

"Go on up."

Murphy and his son headed down the narrow, crowded aisle to the stairs. Ahmed's family lived in the small apartment upstairs. Samira, Ahmed's twenty-year old daughter, was a student at Jefferson County Community College and had been babysitting Kenny off and on for the last three years. He paused and tilted his head, listening as he heard Ahmed's radio. More bad news from Washington.

He jerked as the door burst in with a crash.

"Everybody freeze! Don't move! Don't move!"

At the shouts, Kenny screamed. Murphy pulled the boy close to him and backed against the wall, all thoughts gone but escape for his son.

"I said don't move!" shouted a man, dressed in all black, wearing a flak vest and helmet. He pointed a folding stock rifle straight at Murphy's head. Murphy looked back at the rifle, the barrel gaping. Near panic struck, his heart thumping wildly as he held his son close. The boy shook; Murphy gathered him close. His eyes narrowed when he noticed the letters embroidered above the man's pocket: DHS. Department of Homeland Security.

Several other men, all dressed the same as the first, had shoved Ahmed against the wall. Two more men pounded up the stairs. Murphy listened to their pounding footsteps, then screams upstairs as they entered the upper floor. What was this?

He took a breath, then spoke, enunciating each word to keep his voice from quivering. "Mister, I don't know who you are, but you are scaring my son."

"Shut up!"

One of the men at the counter, short and balding with pale blue eyes framed by thick glasses, looked up at the shout, frowning, and said, "Bobby, chill out. Just keep an eye on the guy; he's not what we're here for."

The man guarding Murphy glanced back over his shoulder, then back at Murphy. He didn't say anything further.

Two of the men bent Ahmed over the counter and cuffed his hands behind his back. Two more came down the stairs, leading the entire family, including Ahmed's wife Maryam and their three children. The middle child, Hayder, was seventeen, a senior at Jefferson County High School. The agents pushed him to the counter next to his father; then pushed the women and girls to the back.

"Look," said the balding man at the counter. "You gentlemen cooperate and we'll have you home right quick. We just want to ask you some questions."

"Excuse me, sir," Murphy said. "Are you in charge of these people?"

The man looked up at him.

"You need to mind your own business, sir."

Murphy felt his eyebrows begin to twitch. "Now look. You men came in here brandishing guns at my six-year-old son without identifying yourselves. I say this is my business. I want to talk to you, right this minute."

Kenny grabbed Murphy's waist tighter.

The man walked across the aisle toward Murphy.

"Sir, I suggest again that you mind your own business."

"What's your name? Who are you?"

The man pulled a small folder out and held it up in Murphy's face. "I'm Agent Justin Hagarty with the Department of Homeland Security. I'm with the Harpers Ferry extension office. We're here to investigate a terrorist attack that took place today, and you, sir, are dangerously close to obstruction of justice. These men may have knowledge of the attack. They'll be detained briefly, questioned, and released—assuming everything is in order."

"Do you have a warrant? Where are you taking them?"

"I don't need a warrant to detain and question men suspected of involvement with terrorism."

Murphy took a breath and replied, "According to the United States Constitution you do."

Hagarty shook his head and spoke in a calm, cool tone. "Mister, you can debate that in the courts. My job is to protect people, not hold a debate. We all have to give up some freedoms in order to be safe, so let me be clear: if you give us any more trouble, we will hold you on charges of obstruction of justice, and maybe as a material witness while we look into your connection with these suspected terrorists. You don't want that to happen."

Murphy recoiled. "Are you threatening me?"

"What do you think is going to happen with that boy if you're in jail? A widower like you? I think they call it child abandonment when a single parent goes to jail."

Murphy felt his face heat, and he clenched his fists.

Hagarty looked down at the shaking boy, then met Murphy's eyes. "You know, a boy in his condition—he wouldn't do well in foster care."

"Let's go," he called to the other men, and they led Ahmed and Hayder toward the door.

As Hagarty reached the door, Murphy called out, "Hagarty!"

When the agent turned around and looked back, Murphy went on. "How do you know my son's condition? And that I'm a widower?"

Hagarty looked back and smiled.

"That's my job, Colonel Murphy. To keep an eye on things."

He left, and the bell chimed as the door closed behind him.

Chapter Four
May 27

"Kenny, it's time to go," Murphy called. He'd had his coffee and his shower, but the horror of a nightmare the night before still clung to him, though he could no longer recall the specifics. Dreams featuring Martha—sometimes real freak-show dreams—were sometimes a staple in his life. The last couple years, they'd come even more frequently than the sometimes bizarre dreams he still occasionally had about Iraq.

Kenny didn't answer his call. Murphy stood, balancing on a cane, and walked to Kenny's room. The boy had crawled under the sturdy oak bed Murphy had built for Valerie twenty-five years ago. He leaned over just far enough to see Kenny's face.

"Come on, kiddo. It's time to get going to school."

Kenny shook his head. "Why do I have to go? I want to stay home!"

The squeal in Kenny's voice was like fingernails scraping across a chalkboard. Again.

"We've been through this a hundred times, Kenny. Come on."

"No. I'm not coming out."

"*Kenny.* We've both got things to do, and I have to get you to school. I'm counting to three. One. Two. Three."

"No! Not coming out!"

Damn it. Murphy reached under the bed and grabbed the boy's arm. He pulled, hard, and Kenny slid out from under the bed.

"Ow!" he shouted, "You hurt me!"

"Kenny, come on."

"Mean Daddy. I'm not doing anything with you!" Kenny tried to twist away. Murphy tightened his grip on his wrist and dragged him into the living room.

"Kenny is this for you, or is it for me?"

"You just want to hurt me."

Murphy stopped. *Breathe. Calm down.*

"Kenny, I do not want to hurt you."

Kenny screwed up his face. "Daddy's fault!" he shouted.

Murphy looked his son in the eye, bending so there were about three inches between them. "You're right. It's my fault. I want to hurt you. I practice every night, thinking up new ways to torture you."

Kenny backpedaled. "No you don't. That's silly."

He finally settled down for breakfast while Murphy began making his lunch.

Kenny had been diagnosed with cerebral adrenoleukodystrophy, ALD, about eighteen months after Martha died. The disease caused fatty-acid chains to build up in his nervous system, triggering an immune response that was slowly destroying his nerve tissue. It had been getting progressively worse, and the only treatment—administering oil composed of saturated fats—only helped if it was introduced before the onset of symptoms. It was too late for Kenny. As the long chains of fatty acids built up in his nervous system and adrenal glands, he slowly deteriorated, had more and more seizures, and one day they would kill him.

A daily exercise regimen, combined with vitamins and drugs to control seizures, acted together to hold back the deterioration and hopefully prolong his life. Maybe one day there would even be a real treatment, or a cure. A good number of studies were underway, but Murphy knew of none that were making any real progress.

No work for Murphy today, but he got dressed and prepared regardless. His closet was still organized the way Martha had set it up years before, his casual and work clothes within easy reach, the dress uniforms and suits high to the left. The spare leg, socks and gel padding occupied a box below the suits. Her side of the closet stood empty, even after three years; he had given the clothes to the Amvets Thrift Shop in Harpers Ferry, but he couldn't bring himself to hang anything there.

Murphy carefully changed the sock and padding on the stump of his left leg, then dressed in a coal grey suit, a gift from Martha on their twentieth anniversary. After he dropped Kenny off at school he would drive to Charleston—a three-hour trip since they built the new 340 Extension—to see Major General Harris Peak. Samira would pick Kenny up from school. They still had heard nothing about the whereabouts of Ahmed and Hayder, though Valerie had promised him the night before that Congressman Clark would look into it.

It had been well into the evening before he'd finally reached her. He was well aware that only on the rarest occasions did she have business across the river at the Pentagon, all the same, for hours he'd dialed her office and cell phone numbers trying to get through, in a half-panicked daze. He'd never really gotten over the loss of his wife, and he knew it. To lose one of his children—that would be unbearable.

With any luck, General Peak would be able to get the battalion activated to help deal with the emergency in Arlington, Virginia. If nothing else, activation would help some of the guys with immediate income needs while they tried to figure out what to do. *And ladies,* he thought. Even after five years, he couldn't get his mind around the idea of having women in tank companies. Of course, he still only had to deal with one.

It'd be easier if Karen Greenfield were ugly. Then at least half his officers wouldn't be chasing after her. But she wasn't, and rumor had it every captain and lieutenant in the battalion had hit on her at least once since she'd joined the unit. It was the same at the Saturn Plant. Had been the same, anyway. So far as he knew, she'd never dated anyone local. He knew the scuttlebutt—the managers at Saturn said she was a lesbian. Sounded like a case of sour grapes to Murphy. Dressed, he went back downstairs.

Kenny was sitting at the oak kitchen table. An angry red handprint on his wrist marked the spot where Murphy had yanked on his arm to pull him out from under the bed. Murphy swallowed, hard. He had never done anything like that when Valerie was a kid. He'd never done that before Martha died. A wave of shame and sadness washed over him, and for just a moment, he wished he could just sit down and quit.

He sighed and looked at his son again, eating his breakfast and reading a book about Mars exploration. Time for Kenny to go to school, and for Murphy to go, hat in hand, begging. There would be time to sit when Kenny was taken care of.

⌘

At an outside table overlooking the sluggish Kanawha River, swollen with mud from last week's rain, Major General Harris Peak, Commander of West Virginia's National Guard, sat across from Murphy. The sky was clear and blue, wispy clouds high above, and a light breeze carried the smell of blooming flowers to them from the landscaped garden next to the river. They were eating at one of the several outdoor restaurants overlooking the plaza in downtown Charleston.

"Look, Ken, I understand what you're saying. I just don't think there's much we can do. The Army's already decided what units to activate. They don't need tank battalions for this. It's all rescue and security work. The only Army force deployed right now is an infantry battalion out of Fort Meade, and the DC National Guard." A slight breeze from the river ruffled Peak's steel-grey hair.

Murphy leaned forward as he spoke, his hands flat on the table.

"General, this could make all the difference in the world to the people in Highview—the folks in my battalion. Almost every last one of them lost their jobs, sir. They've got no means of support. You understand what this will do to our retention, our combat readiness? I won't have fifty percent of those folks in eight weeks; everyone will be leaving town to find jobs."

"I know, Ken, but the Guard isn't a jobs program. Besides, where do you think they're going to go? Where the hell are they going to find jobs? It's no better in Charleston. It's no better anywhere, from what I can see. The whole damn economy is tanking. Look, I promise you if anything comes up anywhere in the world that looks like it will require activating Guard units, I'll get your name up there. But more than that I can't do."

"Thank you, sir."

It was as much as he could expect, he supposed. Not enough. He took a sip of his coffee and sat back, eyes scanning the river.

"All right, enough of this," said the General, his eyes glancing at the wedding ring on Murphy's left hand. "How is your family? Isn't your daughter working up on the Hill now?"

"She is, sir. She's working for Al Clark now. It took a while, but I finally got a hold of her last night. All the phone lines into DC were tied up all day yesterday. They're going pretty crazy with the bombing."

"I imagine. Al Clark—he's a democrat? Well, I can't hold that against her; that is great, just great. Look, we'll talk again in a couple weeks, all right?"

"Yes, sir," Murphy said.

Peak wiped his face with his napkin and placed it on his plate, then stood. "Well, I've got a one o'clock meeting. Keep me informed, Murphy. I want to know right away if people from your unit do start to leave town."

Peak marched off.

Murphy frowned. He'd known General Peak twenty years, and had hoped he would be more helpful. Not this time.

Murphy settled with the waitress, then went back to his car. What was he going to do? It had been twenty years since he'd conducted a job search.

The drive back to Highview was slow, and Murphy found himself thinking in circles, frustrated, and especially afraid for his son.

Two hours into the drive, the phone rang, interrupting his thoughts

"Mr. Murphy, this is Sarah Hughes at Highview Country Day School." Sarah was the administrator at his son's school.

"Hi, ma'am. What can I do for you?"

"Mr. Murphy, Kenny seems to be having trouble—I think you need to get here as soon as you can." Her voice shook.

"What's the problem, Ms. Hughes?" Murphy asked, unable to suppress the alarm in his tone.

"Well, he was holding his arm and wrist and screaming. It was—terrifying. I think they were muscle spasms. He's in the nurse's office right now, lying down, but he seems to be in a lot of pain."

Murphy interrupted. "Ms. Hughes, I am on my way, but it will take me an hour to get back, and that's if I speed all the way. I need you to call an ambulance and get him to the hospital right now. Right this instant. The nurse has her instructions already; she's to give him his autoinjector right away, ma'am, you understand? Right now. Then call 911 and get him to the hospital. I'll meet him there. This could be very serious, even life threatening."

Murphy disconnected the phone and accelerated.

※

An hour later, Murphy slammed the door of his car and raced for the emergency room, long familiar with the way there. The first time had been for Martha.

"Excuse me, Miss. My name is Ken Murphy. My son was brought here from school."

The woman at the desk looked up at him. Her eyes were bloodshot, with dark circles under them.

"Hold on just a moment, Mr. Murphy; one of the nurses will be right with you."

Five minutes later he stood next to his son. Kenny was wearing an oxygen mask, but at least there was no respirator this time. His eyes were closed. Attached wires and electrodes led to computers that monitored his heart rate, blood pressure, and breathing.

Murphy sat down in the chair next to the bed and touched his son's hand. He was grateful they hadn't had to use the respirator this time. Last time, Kenny had awakened with the tubes down his throat and panicked until Murphy could calm him down.

"We've given him an anesthetic to help him sleep," said the doctor, a young man with already thinning black hair. "In the short term, there's not much we can do."

"Understand," Murphy said. "At least he's comfortable now."

The doctor looked a bit hopeless. Murphy was familiar with the routine.

"Colonel Murphy."

Murphy looked up. One of the nurses.

"Can you come to the desk for a moment, sir. We've got a small problem."

"Sure." He followed her out to the desk.

"Sir, I don't know how to approach you with this—we got a call from the front office. They indicated your insurance coverage has been cancelled as of yesterday and that they will refuse to pay any claims."

Murphy felt a sharp pain in his stomach. "That can't be right. I've been laid off, but my insurance is still good, at least through the end of the month. I'll call them."

"Don't worry about your son, sir. We'll treat him, of course, no matter what. But the front office is going to insist you pay, if the insurance won't."

"Can I use your phone?"

Thirty minutes later, Murphy was red-faced and frustrated. The number on his insurance card led to a computer system that seemed to go around in circles. None of the choices led to a human being, but he received the same answer from the computer, over and over again: his coverage had been cancelled.

One of the nurses approached. "Mr. Murphy?"

"Yes?"

"Your son is awake sir, if you want to come see him."

Murphy hung up and hurried to the room. He'd deal with the insurance later. Kenny lay in the bed, his face pale.

"Daddy!"

He smiled as he looked at his father and his eyes crossed, the left eye turning inward. Murphy swallowed his anxiety. The crossed eyes were new, and a very bad sign. The disease was progressing. He sat next to his son and smiled, trying to hide his distress.

"Hey, little man. You doing ok?"

"Yes. I'm feeling better now. When I was at school my arm hurt really bad."

It was the same arm Murphy had grabbed that morning. "I know. Does it still hurt now?"

"Just a little. Am I going to have to stay in the hospital long this time?"

"I don't think so."

"When we leave here, can we go to the toy store?"

Murphy smiled. "Sure. Maybe we can pick out a new train for your set. Would you like that?"

"Yeah, Daddy."

They sat for a few minutes, and then Kenny said, "Daddy, will you read me a book?"

Murphy wiped his eyes, then answered his son. "Sure, little guy. Whatever you want."

Chapter Five
May 27

Valerie Murphy arrived at work early the day after the attack and found the office in chaos. The phones were ringing off the hook, and already there were four people waiting in the reception area, without appointments, hoping to see the Congressman. She quickly sorted out the office, allocating emergency jobs to the staff to quickly deal with the onslaught of constituent calls, then prepared for a brief meeting with Ambrose.

Al Clark was in meetings this morning, so they used his office, away from the rest of the staff. The walls of his office were covered in plaques, mementos from campaigns, photographs from the district. Opposite his desk, at the other end of the long office, a leather couch faced matching chairs over a glass coffee table overflowing with files and documents.

First on the agenda was the bombings. The Department of Homeland Security had come down unusually strong across the country: according to some reports, they were picking up immigrants off the street and arresting them with virtually no due process. Given that one of the main targets was a DHS office, she wasn't terribly surprised.

From there, they moved on to the Skaggs bill.

"What we need to do is make sure the hearings are a complete circus," Valerie said. "Get hardworking Americans who will be devastated by this bill as witnesses. Get half a dozen to sit in front of the committee and speak, maybe appear in media interviews. We need a public groundswell against the bill if there's to be any chance at all to kill it."

"You know Senator Parkinson endorsed the bill this morning?" Ambrose said. He twirled the tip of his mustache between his fingers.

"No, I didn't. That means most of the democrats will follow suit."

"They will if they want to preserve their political careers."

"It just means we'll have to work harder, that's all. We can win this."

Ambrose grinned. "You know something, Valerie, that's what I like about you. It doesn't matter who we have against us, you are always confident."

"I usually win, don't I?"

"True," he conceded. "But when I look at the support this thing is generating, I feel the same thing I felt living in Morgantown when I realized I was gay—like there was a very bad dude just around the corner ready to kick my ass into the next county."

She took a sip of tea, then set the cup back down on the table, away from the pile of papers. "I know what you mean. It did work out for you in the end, though."

"Of course it did, honey, after I fled West Virginia." After he said the words, a tremendous smile appeared on his face.

"Well, for God's sake, we've got to make people see it. The people in our district will be killed by this, with all the job losses in the last couple years. Even the high technology folks aren't immune; Christ, my father got laid off along with everyone at his plant. He worked for his company for twenty years. His wife is dead, and he's raising a son with a terminal illness that costs hundreds of thousands of dollars a year to treat, and what will he do if this bill goes through? Don't they understand what this will do to people?"

Ambrose leaned forward. "You're right. Valerie, you need to tell that story. Better yet, your father needs to. Isn't he a general or something in the National Guard, too? And a war hero?"

"He's not one to talk about anything in public," she said, her voice subdued.

"Look, don't hit me, Valerie, but he could be the story. Christ almighty, we couldn't pick a better poster child if we made him up. You get your father on the cover of Time, and maybe you can win this one."

She felt her cheeks grow hot. Ambrose seemed to sense the approaching explosion and leaned away.

"Now don't get mad at me; you have to see it." He ticked off fingers on his right hand. "Look, everyone likes and respects your father, I've seen it. One, he's a hardworking American. Two, he's a veteran of a war."

"Two, actually."

"Even better. Third, he's a widower, and his wife was killed by the very type of random crime people are so afraid of."

She sat up straight, now truly outraged. "Damn it, Ambrose. That's going too far. There's no way I will ask him to talk about that in public. It'll kill him."

"Do you want to win this, Valerie? Stop trying to take care of your father for a change and look around. He might just be able to do it. Number four, after all that, he paid his daughter's way through college. Number five, his beloved son is very ill and now that he is out of work the only help he'll get will be from the government. The only thing that could make it better is if he were a disabled vet."

"You cynical bastard," she said, laughing in half admiration. "You didn't know, did you? He hides it so goddamn well. He lost his left leg below the knee in Iraq."

"I rest my case," Ambrose said. He leaned back, a smile on his face.

She sighed and closed her eyes, annoyed that Ambrose looked so pleased with himself.

"All right, I'll talk to him. But I'm telling you now, he won't have anything to do with this trash."

"All you can do is ask."

⌇

That Sunday, Valerie slipped away from the office and drove north on Interstate 270, then west on US 340 until she passed Harpers Ferry and reached home in Highview.

The newscasters on the radio went on incessantly. The Department of Homeland Security had announced they had a suspect in the Arlington bombing, a radical militia group called the Shenandoah Sons of Liberty, operating out of the West Virginia mountains. Agents were at a standoff with the terrorists at a remote compound near Baughman Settlement. At least they weren't rounding up Arabs all over the country anymore.

She changed radio stations without any luck: all the news stations were talking about the same thing. She had heard a little about them before; Baughman Settlement wasn't close to her home, situated in the mountains near Front Royal, but because of the most recent redistricting, Baughman had ended up in Clark's district. It was a strange group. Situated just a few miles out of town in the backwoods, they weren't connected to the outside world: no running water, electricity or telephone lines. It seemed odd to her that they were involved in terrorism—they seemed almost fanatically apolitical, and terrorism was by nature a political act.

Experts were being interviewed, as well as obscure professors and former military analysts, most of whom probably knew nothing. The current speaker on the radio was hysterically calling for a national database to track everyone, so people could be profiled based on their movements, their purchases, their religious affiliations. Valerie grimaced. Didn't they know the Defense Department had had that set up for ten years now?

She switched off the radio.

She reached home after an uneventful drive, and was immediately thrown off balance. Normally, when she arrived, Kenny barreled out into the driveway to hug her, soon followed by her father. Not this time: when she arrived, Murphy came to the door without his young son and waved. She felt a sigh of relief when she walked in the door, embraced her father, and saw Kenny listlessly reading a book on the couch.

Now that Kenny was home from the hospital, she spent the morning playing games with him while her father cooked. She tried to hide her distress. Kenny's left eye didn't track with the right, and seemed to wander aimlessly, and his hands shook like an old man's. He hadn't been so bad when she'd last seen him, only two months before. It was hard to believe how much he had detiorated in the two months since she'd been home.

Every once in a while she looked up at her father, in the kitchen, and wondered how he would survive losing his son so soon after Mom died. Since her mother had died, he seemed more and more like an old oak tree, strong on the outside, but hollow, ready to break. He'd lost a lot of weight, though he'd been fit and muscular all his life. Now his clothes hung too loose. Then there were the spells—they'd talk, and something would make him think of Mom, and he would stop talking and just stare out into space, remembering, not aware that his face had gone slack, and at moments like that she thought he was nearer to death than life, or wished he was.

Valerie knew it was morbid, but visiting her childhood home sometimes felt like visiting a mausoleum. Her father was so burdened, with sadness, with worry about Kenny. Sometimes after a visit, she would cry all the way home, though she didn't know whether it was her mother she cried for or her heartbroken father.

After lunch, Kenny went around the side of the house to play in his sandbox. Murphy brought out a pitcher of iced tea and poured glasses for both of them. They sat in rockers overlooking the side yard, and he eased his left leg off with a sigh, setting it on the ground next to the chair. He rubbed both hands in the stump, massaging it.

"He's much better now," Murphy said. "Yesterday it was all he could do to sit in his room and read books; he just didn't feel well enough to go out. Thanks for coming. I think seeing you made a big difference."

"Thanks, Dad. I just wish I could be here more often." As she said the words, she felt guilty. Visits to her father were so emotionally charged that it was almost impossible for her to visit more often, whatever the circumstances of her job.

He reached for her hand. His hand was large, calloused and scarred, around her small, delicate hand. All the same, his ring hung too loose. "I understand. You've got a very demanding job, and an important one. Tell me, how's it going with you and David? You haven't mentioned him much."

"I thought you didn't like him."

"Well, I don't. But he's yours. I suppose I have to try."

She looked down and shrugged. "I don't know how things are going, Dad. Did you know—with Mom—when did you know? I mean, that you wanted to be with her?"

"Well, it was a little different for us, I guess. We met in grammar school; I was about twelve when we dated at first."

"So you knew—you really knew what you wanted when you got married."

"Hell, I don't know. We got married right out of high school. My father said I was dumb as a post, and wouldn't ever amount to nothing if I got married at eighteen. But I didn't want to be with anyone else, and neither did she, and we loved each other, and it just made sense."

Valerie shrugged. "I don't know if I feel that way about David. He's pretty mad right now—I was supposed to meet him in New York yesterday, and had to cancel. I don't miss him anymore."

"Well, you need to do what's right for you. I won't tell you what to do; you wouldn't listen to me anyhow. Follow your heart. You may end up with regrets, but at least they'll be worth it."

"Do you have any regrets, Dad?"

He glanced over at her and smiled, a stark smile. Looking in his eyes was like stepping up to the edge of a cliff.

"Only that you and Kenny are still so young I can't go with her, wherever she went. I miss her so much… I'd follow your mother anywhere."

Oh, Dad. Don't say that, we still need you so much. She changed the subject.

"How is Kenny, really? Has he been any better?"

Murphy shook his head. "No. He's slowly getting worse. Sometimes I'm afraid he'll wake up one day and not recognize me. He gets these attacks; this was the third one, excruciating pain in his wrists and hands. Nobody can tell me what's wrong, it doesn't fit the normal profile for ALD. He gets these mood swings—makes him seem more like a two year old than six. And you know how many doctors and specialists I've talked to, all over the country. Last time they had to put him on a respirator to keep him alive."

She shook her head. "I didn't know that."

"You were at work then, and it—it just didn't make sense to call you until I knew…" His eyes watered and he paused. "It didn't make sense to call until I knew if he was going to make it."

He shook his head. "I don't know what I'm going to do, to tell you the truth. I got the mess with the insurance straightened out, but it's so expensive I'm only going to be able to pay it for about three months. After that I guess… We can probably get him on disability, I talked to the social security office about it. That may cover the insurance. He won't be eligible for Medicaid for another year—my income was too high. The sad part is I just wrote a check to the IRS for almost twenty thousand dollars."

"What!"

"Yeah, that was my tax bill this year. I sold some stock last year to pay off some debts—student loans and the like—I got whacked on capital gains. I really could have used the money now."

"You know about the Skaggs bill, don't you?" she said.

"Yeah, isn't he trying to cut welfare rolls, shift the money to social security?"

"Well, yes, but they are also cutting social security disability and veterans disability," she answered.

"You're kidding. Would Kenny be covered?"

"I don't think so, Dad. He'll probably lose any government assistance, unless the state has something."

"People are so overtaxed here by the feds, the state government has to hold the line. There's not much in the way of services. I'm sure you deal with it every day, in your job."

She nodded.

"You can't let that bill pass, if there's anything you can do, hon."

"That's part of what I wanted to talk with you about, Dad. I think—I think you can help."

☙

The noise of the crickets and cicadas drowned out the creak of Murphy's rocking chair as he sat on his front porch, staring out at the falling darkness. Murphy rocked; the sound was soothing, a reminder of so many nights before on this porch, listening to the same sound. Through the trees, he saw headlights as a car passed on the highway.

Two weeks had passed since he'd been laid off. Two weeks since the bombing, and the day his son went back to the hospital. Not much had changed. School would be out in another week, and normally Murphy would be worried about day care for the summer, but that didn't look to be a problem this year. In two weeks, he'd sent a hundred resumes, made fifty cold calls, and received no response.

He was starting to think there just weren't any jobs out there for him. He wasn't just looking at a job change. After nineteen years with the same company, he faced a complete career change. It wasn't like there were any chip manufacturers left in the United States. And he'd be damned if he'd move to Indonesia, after serving his country 26 years.

So the question was, what could he do?

He closed his eyes. If only Martha were here.

That thought brought a fresh bout of pain. They'd known each other since third grade, dated in junior high and high school. Voted "Most Popular Couple" by their senior class. Murphy lost his job with GM in '90 when she was six months pregnant with Valerie. She stood by him while he searched for work, with almost no luck. For a while he found work with a big landscaping company—cutting grass, that sort of thing. After she had Valerie, she kissed him goodbye and saw him off at the airport when he enlisted in the Army.

They lived together in Germany, at Fort Knox, Kentucky. He'd been deployed to the Gulf War and later the Balkans. Whenever he left her behind, she wrote almost every day. After the Army, when the position came up at Saturn's new chip manufacturing plant in West Virginia, she'd picked up and moved there with him.

In October 2004—by that time he was an officer—his National Guard unit mobilized and went to Iraq, where he'd seen more of his share of death and pain than anyone deserved. He'd been gone over a year that time, a year he almost never talked about, but that sometimes haunted him, especially when he looked at his son and remembered the children who'd died in Iraq. The year had ended with a roadside bomb that destroyed his humvee, killing his driver and shredding Murphy's left leg below the knee. Martha had nursed him back to health when he got home, helped him work himself back into shape, then stood by him when he fought the Army National Guard to get back on duty. Except for short periods training in the Guard, he'd never again left her.

They had made their lives here, in this ramshackle old farmhouse built of grey stone, with a tin roof and a wraparound porch. The dirt driveway led a half-mile out to US 340. They had experimented with various crops in the fields closest to the house—tomatoes and cabbage—but neither of them were meant to be farmers.

Over the last two decades he and Martha had redone the house's interior, making a wide open, bright space. She loved music and art and had decorated the house accordingly, with unknown artists from rural West Virginia. Murphy had once believed that if she died, he couldn't live a day longer. But she died early, and left responsibilities behind, and he had to meet those responsibilities.

That day in February three years ago, she had climbed into her jeep, driven out the two miles west on 340 to the gas station and convenience store, and met her fate at the hands of a seventeen-year-old drug addict. Murphy had seen the security film. The blotches on the boy's face must have been dirt or something, because they were gone at the trial. Unkempt hair, pale skin. Rail thin. Too many late nights, Murphy guessed. Too much drugs. He made off with fifty-three dollars, too strung out or stupid to look under the plastic cash drawer, where three hundred dollars in twenties lay.

It was almost ten minutes before the next customer came in, saw the bleeding woman writhing in agony on the floor, and called for an ambulance. Martha's telephone sat on the dashboard in the jeep. Murphy had tortured himself for months wondering why she hadn't carried it into the store with her, why she hadn't used the compact 9mm pistol he'd taught her to use.

Walter died instantly, a survivor of a brutal war in Southeast Asia fated to die at the hands of a teenager in his own place of business. Martha might have made it, had she not lost so much blood lying on the floor for ten minutes, and then the ten more before the rescue helicopter showed up to take her to the county hospital. She'd been in emergency surgery for hours; they just couldn't revive her. She died, leaving behind Murphy, their two children, and their life together.

Sometimes Murphy thought he was dead too. The other times, he wished he was.

Chapter Five
May 31

Captain Mike Morris stood, almost asleep, in the slow moving chow line, holding a foam tray soon to be covered in unrecognizable food. The chow line for the battalion headquarters was set up behind an olive drab tent, in the shadow of a badly damaged building. He looked up when he heard a shout.

"Mike! Mike Morris!"

An Army major in combat fatigues and flak vest, helmet askew, so tall he seemed to perch over the other nearby officers, approached from the shadows across the street. With a face covered in dark, coarse hair overdue for a shave by a day or two, Morris almost didn't recognize him. It was Cory Avedis, his college roommate.

"I'll be damned," Morris said. "Cory! When did you make major? What are you doing here?"

Avedis bared his teeth and growled, then grabbed Morris in a bear hug. They laughed; it had been three years since they'd last seen each other.

"Mike. I didn't expect to run into you here, I thought you were in Korea. What are you doing these days?"

"Company commander—Bravo Company First of the Fifteenth Infantry. Believe it or not, I just took command the same day all this went down. What about you?"

"Oh, you know, same old thing. Skulking around in closets, reading other people's mail. Some timing you've got. I guess you get to see your new unit perform in real life, huh? One Fifteen Infantry—I heard you guys had an injury. Some guy lost a leg or something?"

"Yeah," Morris said. "Not in my company, in Delta. One of the car bombs. He'll live; they've got him up at Walter Reed. So what's the intelligence perspective on this mess? Any clues on who's responsible?"

"Officially it's the DHS's ball, not Northern Command. Zero evidence to conclude this was a foreign attack—the news is saying it was some lunatics up in West Virginia, but I've got my doubts. Professionals, if you want my opinion. Guys who used to work for our side."

Pretty much what Morris already thought.

They left the chow line with full—if unappealing—plates, and swept the soot and debris from a low wall about a hundred yards away and sat on it.

"It's funny, I was thinking about you the other day," Avedis said. "I was down at Fort Irwin last summer, and you're not going to believe who I ran in to."

"Who?"

"Karen Greenfield. Captain now—at least she was last summer."

Morris squinted, an odd twist in his stomach unsettling him. *Karen*. He hadn't thought about Karen in a long time.

That was a lie. He thought about Karen most every day. "How was she?"

"Her battalion was down there for training. Would you believe her weekend warrior tank company knocked off a good chunk of the opposition force? I mean, nobody beats them, but her unit gave it a good try. She's in the National Guard now, works as some kind of computer engineer in her regular job."

"National Guard? Karen?"

"Yeah, it surprised me, too. Bunch of good-old-boy tankers with your old girlfriend as their commander. What do you know?"

Morris grimaced at the words "old girlfriend." Avedis homed in on the expression. "Still got a thing for her, huh? Figures; she still looks pretty good. Man, if we hadn't been all smelly in the field for two weeks, I might have tried myself."

"Cory, Alicia and I have been happily married for years."

"Yeah, whatever you say. I never understood why you broke it off with Karen in the first place, but none of my business. Hey man, I know how it goes. Just because you're on a diet doesn't mean you can't look at the menu, right?"

Morris chuckled and his friend burst into laughter. He had heard this particular aphorism from Avedis too many times to count when they were in college. But then, Morris and Karen Greenfield had dated the entire four years of college, while Avedis was busy working his way through the entire female student body.

"Seriously though, how are things, Mike? You getting along okay?"

Morris looked at his old friend and didn't know what to say. Where the hell did you start, when your whole life wasn't yours anymore? When it hadn't been for years? When you just closed your eyes and stepped off the ledge and hoped for the best when you got to the bottom. He should be grateful for his life. His career was going well, he had a beautiful wife, a wonderful daughter. So why the hell wasn't it enough? Too much to say to an old friend out here.

"I'm fine."

They exchanged current contact information, and Avedis excused himself to head back to his unit. Morris threw his tray in an overflowing garbage bin placed by the food contractors, and walked back toward his company.

He and Karen were together four years. The wedding was planned; the invitations mailed. Then everything changed. During an all-night party Morris and Alicia Skaggs got a little too close. Well, a lot too close. Pregnant close.

It happened just before spring break their senior year. The weather was warm, almost balmy. Some of the guys from the ROTC detachment rented a small house off campus, and that weekend they held a long drunken party. Karen was out of town that weekend—she had studied computer engineering her last two years of school, and that weekend attended a manufacturers' conference in Atlanta, passing out resumes and interviewing with different companies. She had already decided well before then she wouldn't apply for Regular Army, even though she was one of the top ROTC students.

The party got way out of hand. Loud music, wild drinking. Late on Saturday night, Morris and Alicia sat out on the tilting back porch of the house, each of them drinking a beer, when Morris said something stupid, something like, "You know, I've always been attracted to you."

They slept together. The next morning both of them were embarrassed and apologetic, and promised that would be the end of it. He would never have guessed that night would derail his entire life.

For two weeks Morris quaked with fear. He suffered a long bout of diarrhea and stomach pains, and jerked every time the phone rang. How would Karen react if she found out? It had been the stupidest thing he'd ever done, but that didn't mean he didn't love Karen. He couldn't imagine life without her. After a couple of weeks, he began to calm down. In the excitement of preparing for final exams and graduation, Karen hadn't noticed his apprehension. It looked like he was safe. He'd screwed up, and it would remain a secret, and that was the end of it, forever.

But of course, it wasn't. Because four weeks later, Alicia appeared on his front step, eyes red from crying. She was pregnant. *Pregnant. Christ.* What were they going to do?

"I won't kill my baby," she said. No surprise there; she was the leader of the campus "Right-to-Life" organization. He'd always suspected in her case there was more of the politician there than the moralist—her father was a powerful congressional representative from Kentucky, and she had plans too, plans that needed her future husband to not be in the Army.

"You like the Army don't you, Mike?" her father, the son of a bitch, had said. "You want a career." He then proceeded to lay out the new rules, starting with the fact that if Mike didn't marry Alicia, Skaggs would intervene in his branch assignment. Instead of infantry or armor as he'd requested, he'd find himself a finance officer or worse.

In hindsight, of course, Morris couldn't imagine if Alicia had done it. An abortion would have meant they'd killed Savannah before she'd ever had a chance to live. His daughter, the best and sweetest little girl in the world. There was little else to be done but tell Karen the truth: he was to be a father. Of another woman's child.

So, on a Sunday afternoon in the beginning of May, about two months before their planned wedding, Morris called Karen and asked her to meet him at the diner next to the college. Morris got there early and sat, fidgeting, a golfball in his throat, his bowels on fire, waiting for twenty minutes.

When she came in the door of the diner, the bell rang above her head. She looked as beautiful as she ever had, in a light blue sleeveless sundress that highlighted her blue eyes, red hair loose and hanging over her shoulders. She wore the silver chain he'd given her two years before, with a tiny heart-shaped locket. She smiled when she saw him, sat down at the battered table, reached out and touched his hands.

"Hey, baby," she said.

Morris opened his mouth and found he couldn't speak. He blinked back a tear.

Her mouth opened in surprise. "Honey, what's wrong?"

"Karen…" he said, his voice low, his eyes on the stained Formica table because he couldn't bear to look at her. "I've got something I need to talk to you about. There's no easy way to say this, and I don't know what it means to us… and our future."

He looked up at her, then back down at the table, unable to meet her eyes.

"Karen, when you were in Atlanta I did something stupid. I was drunk and stupid and I … I…" He stopped, unable to continue.

He looked at her. She leaned close, her head tilted a bit to the left, and a single lock of hair fell over her forehead.

"I slept with someone else. I regretted it, and it was the most idiotic thing I've ever done and I'm sorry."

Her face froze, and the smile disappeared forever.

"But that's not all, Karen. She's pregnant. She's going to have the baby. My baby."

He looked up from the table and met her eyes, and shivered. They were wide with shock.

"I am so—so sorry. Karen—I love you more than anything else in the world. I would never do anything to hurt you. I am so sorry."

"What can't the bitch get an abortion?" she said, her voice on the edge of vicious. Several of the other people in the diner looked over at them, startled.

"She…thinks it's murder. She won't consider it." He didn't say that her father was a deeply conservative congressman. A congressman with the power to abort Mike and Karen's careers into oblivion. Mike was too ashamed to admit that. Karen would never have given into Skagg's attempt at intimidation; no matter how much harm it did their future. But the Army didn't mean to her what it did to him, never would. And he wasn't ready to give that up.

Her eyes filled with tears, looking at him as if she didn't quite know what to say, and Mike thought his heart was going to break. "Well, I guess that's the end of it," she said, her tone cold. She got up, turned around and started to walk away.

"Karen," he called, desperate.

She paused, almost as if she were about to turn around. His breath caught, he watched her take a deep breath, and just for a second he thought she really was going to turn. Then she straightened her back and walked away, out the door and out of his life. The bell rang over her head, and he never forgot the sound. The two of them hadn't spoken since.

Thinking about it now, seven years later, wouldn't do him any good. He had more important things to worry about now. Like keeping his company safe. Like keeping his marriage together, when there wasn't anything left to keep it that way.

All the same, as he tried to go to sleep that night, he still saw her in the summer dress, her blue eyes and the way they'd made him shiver, her white teeth shining… even her back as she walked away. He could still hear the bell ringing.

Chapter Six
June 7

The key was stiff in the lock: it hadn't been opened in nearly three years. Finally, the bolt drew back, and Murphy opened the door to the shop and stepped inside, the real estate agent behind him.

"Sorry about the dust," he said. "I haven't been in here in a long time."

Inside, Martha's florist shop was largely empty. Display tables had been cleared of flowers three years ago, and everything lay under a quarter-inch of dust.

The agent looked around, leaving footprints as she walked to the back. Murphy stood at the door and watched her explore, strangely unwilling to go any further. He owned the building outright, had been unwilling to sell it after Martha died. Before her death, she'd had a thriving business here.

The agent said, "Everything seems to be in good shape. You'll need to have it cleaned and repainted, and I'll need to get an inspector in here to make sure nothing's been chewing on the wiring. Has the power been turned off? The water?"

"That's right. You can take care of the painting and whatnot. I can't spend much time here."

She nodded. "I understand. You know, it's really too bad you didn't sell it last year, when we talked. I could have easily gotten you four hundred thousand, then. Now, it won't be so easy. Not unless those union folks manage to get the plant back open somehow."

"Is it that bad?" he asked.

"Yes, I'm afraid so. Worst it's ever been, at least since I've been selling in the county. Lot's of houses on the market, and no one buying. I think we can probably get a hundred, maybe a hundred-fifty thousand for the shop. I wouldn't recommend listing it for any more than that, not if you want to it to sell this year."

The statement hit him like a blow. *One hundred thousand dollars.* He'd finally received the paperwork from Saturn for continuing Kenny's health insurance. That would run him over five thousand a month alone. His VA disability check was less than ten percent of that, and unemployment, when it started, wouldn't make much of a dent either. He'd run through a hundred thousand pretty quickly, especially if there was another trip to the hospital.

No choice. "Do what you need to do. I'm going to need every cent I can put my hands on."

The agent left soon afterward, leaving him to think about the town meeting to be held tonight, wishing he could be two places at once. The crowd that had been talking about purchasing the plant was meeting at the high school gym, but he'd be in Washington by then, preparing to testify in front of a Congressional committee at the request of his daughter. He must be getting old. It was too much change, too fast.

Too fast. He looked around the shop where Martha had made her life and fought to hold back tears.

༄

Karen Greenfield arrived twenty minutes early, but still ended up parked almost a quarter mile away from the high school, on the shoulder of the road behind a long line of vehicles. Cars and trucks jammed the parking lot and the shoulders of the road for a fair distance.

After she parked and began walking up the crowded street, two unfamiliar men in grey suits caught her attention. Both carried digital cameras and walked from vehicle to vehicle, taking photographs of the license plates. Karen stared in disbelief as the couple walking ahead of her noticed the two men and crossed the street to avoid encountering them. She stood watching the men as they went from car to car. Who the hell were they? Corporate security? Some kind of paid informants? With a burst of anger, she walked toward them.

The short one, no older than twenty-five, looked up at her approach with a frown. He tapped his partner's shoulder and pointed, just before she reached them.

"Excuse me. What are you doing?" Karen demanded.

The older one, a balding man with a bushy mustache, said, "I think you need to mind your own business, lady. This ain't it."

"All right," she said. She opened her purse and both men straightened. One of them slipped his hand into his jacket. She tensed; she hadn't thought corporate security would be armed. She took out her phone and dialed 911.

"Hey, lady. What are you doing?"

"I think you need to mind *your* own business."

Two rings, then she heard, "Jefferson County Emergency."

"Hi, I'm calling from outside Highview High School, on Route 340. I'm on my way to the town meeting here, and there are two suspicious men walking from car to car with cameras. I think they may be trying to steal something."

"Hey, lady, you can't do that," the younger one said, his face red.

The older one shook his head, then took a wallet-sized folder out of his coat pocket, opened it, and held it out to her. She glanced at the folder, and felt her frown deepen. Department of Homeland Security.

"We'll send a patrol car out there," the dispatcher said on the phone. "Can I have your name please?"

Should she tell the dispatcher she'd made a mistake? No. Better have the cops come; these guys might not be legitimate anyway. She gave the information to the dispatcher as the older of the two agents stood, arms crossed over his chest, looking at her with lips curled up in amusement.

After she disconnected and put her phone back in her purse, the older of the two agents said, "You didn't want to do that. We're not people you want to piss off."

"Is that so? Well, maybe I'm not a person to piss off, either. You want my license plate number? Since when did coming to a town meeting become suspicious behavior?"

"Look, lady, as a matter of fact we're on the trail of a suspected terrorist. You are in our way, and I suggest you move on and mind your own business."

The younger one wrote in his notebook, then looked up at her. "You told the dispatcher your name was Karen Greenfield? Is that spelled how it sounds? We'll need it for our report."

"Yeah, it is. G-R-E-E-N-F-I-E-L-D. I'm in the phonebook. How do I spell your name?"

A sardonic smile on his face, the older one handed her a business card. Lawrence Harris, it said. Special Agent. She put the card in her pocket, and, with exaggerated motion, walked around the men and continued toward the high school.

She walked into a wall of sound when she entered the gym. It looked like two thousand people were jammed into the room, employees at the plant and their families. She climbed to the top of one of the bleachers, sat down and started shaking. Who the hell did those guys think they were? Why would the DHS be interested in a town meeting?

Below, she saw something more chilling. Two more men dressed in dark suits, taking photographs of the crowd. The men and women nearest them recoiled, dread and anger on their faces.

Too bad Murphy wasn't here. She'd met him for lunch earlier that day, and they had discussed the upcoming meeting, but he was driving to Washington tonight. In the morning, he would be testifying before a Congressional hearing. *We need him here,* she thought. She thought of him as a father, certainly more of a father than her drunk of a real father had ever been. He'd be furious to know there were federal agents stalking around taking pictures of everyone, making notes on who attended a town meeting in a small town in West Virginia.

What were they doing here anyway? Terrorist, hell. She knew what it was. Saturn's CEO, Nelson Barclay, was a high-dollar campaign contributor for the President.

He'd probably picked up the phone and called someone at DHS to suggest that the people whose livelihoods he'd stolen were potential terrorists. Bastards.

The meeting started late. About fifteen minutes after her arrival, three vaguely familiar men walked to the stage at the front of the gym. A podium stood at the head of the room. One of the men spoke into the microphone.

"Testing." The noise of the crowd abated somewhat, and he spoke again. "Okay everyone, let's go ahead and get this show on the road. Most of you know me, but for the federal agents in the room, I'll introduce myself." The room erupted in laughter, and one of the agents flushed red. "I'm Tim Wagner, and I've worked at the Saturn plant since the day it opened just after the turn of the century. In the last couple weeks, I've been working with a number of the other folks here in the room to put together a union, so we can deal with the plant collectively and maybe get ourselves out of the situation we're in."

"Let me tell you the way I see it. Highview is a small town. Our population at the last census came in at just under six thousand people. The single biggest employer in town is Saturn: eight hundred people, not to mention all of the businesses supported by the plant. Folks, this is a full-fledged disaster. If we don't come up with a way to respond, we can just forget about our homes. Highview will be a ghost town in six months. If you got equity in your house, forget about it. Who's going to buy your house if there're no jobs here?"

The crowd roiled. Karen had been thinking the same thing for some time, but it was clear from the reaction that not everyone in the crowd had been.

"Now, a few of us got together right after the plant shut down, and we worked with an attorney, who put together the legal documents for us to put together a company. And we got agreement from the Bank of Jefferson County to provide us with a loan to buy the plant outright. The bank sure sees the value in operating it independently. Here's what we were thinking. The plant is profitable. Let's buy it from Saturn, license their chip designs and operate it as our own company. We can diversify as we go along. We could be independent, run our own company. We don't need any outside company to come in and run things for us. So, we put together a proposal and last week we drove down to Virginia to meet with Mr. Nelson Barclay. Do you know what he said? Do you know what he told us when we made our good faith offer?"

Someone in the crowd shouted, "What did he tell you, Tim?"

"I'll tell you what he told us. He told us he could make more from the plant by selling it as scrap metal, and he planned to auction everything off. He'd rather scrap it than risk having us do better without him. He said he wouldn't sell it at any price. He'd rather kill our town than give us a chance to move forward."

The noise level in the room rose as the crowd shouted. Loud catcalls rose from the back of the room.

"That's not the worst part, folks. The son of bitch—excuse my French—had the gall to tell me he might have been more considerate of our needs if we'd listened when the company endorsed President Price during the elections, since our precinct voted almost seventy percent for Senator Wilson. So I ask you, Highview, what are we going to do? What are we going to do?"

A man she'd never seen before, about halfway toward the back of the room, stood up and shouted, "I'll tell you what we can do, Tim!"

That was staged, she thought. The man who had stood and spoke sat conveniently next to the aisle, and the reply was too polished to be anything other than rehearsed.

"I'll tell you what we'll do, folks," he shouted as he walked forward. "We'll just have to convince Mr. Nelson so-high-and-mighty Barclay we mean business. We'll tell him it's better for him to work with us than work against us."

He reached the stage, took the microphone from Wagner and spoke. She got her first good look as he reached the stage. An older man, possibly in his fifties, in jeans and a flannel shirt. He had mud on his boots, and his graying hair was cropped close.

"Folks, most of you know me. My name is Dale Whitt. My father lived in Highview, and my grandfather lived in Highview. My great-grandfather lived down in Logan County, and moved up here after the Army shot him. See, back in 1921 my great-grandfather was crippled courtesy of a gunshot from the United States Army, when the coal workers in southern West Virginia saw fit to ask for better working conditions. Instead of living in a dump and dying down in those mines, they wanted to earn a decent wage. And you know what happened? The coal companies sent in their own private armies, backed up by the good old US of A.

"This is my town, not Nelson Barclay's. This is your town. Not Saturn Microsystems's. My family paid in blood for the right to live and prosper here. So did yours. Are you going to let some outsider from pointy-headed Vienna, Virginia tell you your livelihood is worth more as scrap metal? Or are you going to stand up for yourselves?"

A roar rose from the crowd. Some yelled and waved their fists.

"I'll tell you what you're going to do. Tomorrow morning, you're going to show up for work. You're going to break the locks off the gate, march in there, and start making chips. And they aren't going to turn you out until you get a fair deal."

The crowd went wild with shouting, excitement, and the bleachers under her feet shook as the men and women around her pounded their feet. The enthusiasm swept over Karen. Why should these people who had put their entire lives into this company—into this town—give up everything because the company wanted to save a little more money and pay a bigger dividend?

Whitt spoke again. "See, unlike a hundred years ago, we'll have the press on our side. We'll have the whole country watching when you go back into that plant. They won't be able to send in a private Army to take us out. They won't be able to send in thugs to shoot at working folks. They'll have to let you do your jobs in peace, so we can make our own way. *Our own way!* Do you hear me, Highview?"

Shouts came from the crowd in response.

"Are you going to take back your jobs, Highview? Are you going to take control of your destiny?"

The crowd went wild with excitement.

"That's right, we *will* do it. And we will win, because right is on our side. We will win, because we are the sons of liberty. We will win because God is on the side of the meek and the poor!"

The room broke up into loud cheers and applause, and everyone stood. For almost five minutes no one could hear a word Whitt shouted over the noise of the crowd. Karen stood and shouted with the rest of them. Whitt made sense, damn it. Why should one person be able to make a decision that ruined hundreds of families' lives? Why should one person be able to determine the fate of an entire town?

Then she glanced back toward the doors, where four men in dark suits and ties stood, each of them with a camera. They stood there, the only people in the room not clapping.

Chapter Seven
June 8

The chair of the House Health and Welfare Committee called the hearing to order at five minutes after ten in the morning. The room, one of the largest and most ornate hearing rooms in the Rayburn Building, held at least a couple of hundred people, and from his seat just behind the witness table Murphy could see that all the seats were filled. Men and women stood in the back of the room, and the area between the witness tables and the raised semicircular dais where the twenty-five committee members sat was crammed with reporters and cameramen, who sat on the floor. Behind the witness tables were thirty rows of chairs, the first row reserved for witnesses.

Sitting on the dais facing the audience, Representative Clark sat toward the left side of the room, near the windows. The other members of the committee were arrayed in a semicircle on either side of him. Valerie was just to Clark's left, in a row of chairs behind the members of congress, reserved for aides. She looked pensive as she leaned forward and said something to the Congressman.

Murphy was as uncomfortable as he'd ever been. He wore his dress uniform today, with all his awards and decorations, and sat stiffly, waiting for the hearing to begin. He hadn't expected this hearing to gain so much attention, and wondered again if he should really be here. He wasn't political. He hardly voted, except for Presidential elections. Martha would have laughed at his discomfort. Her self-confidence would have propelled her through any situation, but for Murphy, the politics and intrigues of Washington were too treacherous.

At the head of the room, Clark seemed tense, his back ramrod straight, and looked straight ahead as Valerie continued speaking in his ear.

A few minutes after nine, every member of the committee was seated. Valerie had once told him that for most hearings, only a few representatives showed up, and they rarely stayed for the entire hearing. But this one was getting a lot of attention from the national press, and he supposed most congressmen and women couldn't pass up the opportunity to get some free ink. Murphy looked around the room, wishing he could make for the exit.

Too late. The chairman slammed his gavel into the table and called the committee to order.

"All right, Ladies and Gentleman, let's call this hearing to order. We are meeting today to conduct our review of H.R. 172, the Fiscal Responsibility Act, introduced by Representative Mark Skaggs of Kentucky. Now, there is a great deal of in interest in this bill, so I would first of all like to ask our spectators despite the crowding to please stay quiet and not disrupt the proceedings. We'll start with the gentleman from Kentucky, Mr. Skaggs. You have five minutes, sir."

Mark Skaggs sat to the right of the dais, almost directly across the semicircle from Clark. Skaggs was a slight man with a narrow face, high cheekbones and blonde hair. He looked younger than his nearly fifty-five years, and Murphy caught himself wondering if Skaggs had undergone cosmetic surgery. He began his statement and Murphy leaned back, barely following his convoluted argument. He seemed to go on interminably, droning about the fiscal status of the country, deficits and trade balances, welfare statistics and God only knew what else. Murphy looked down at his hands, folded in his lap. It was long past time for him to leave, but he couldn't go.

The audience and the reporters in the room stirred as Skaggs completed his statement.

The chairman said, "Thank you, sir. The Chair recognizes the gentleman from West Virginia. You have five minutes, sir."

Clark leaned to his microphone and glanced down at Murphy, meeting his eyes.

"Thank you, sir. I shall be brief. Ladies and gentlemen, when I think about this question, I have to think about the people who elected me to come to Washington to represent them. I have to think about the coal miners, and the factory workers, and the engineers, and the farmers, the mountain folks of my home. I think about the many, many poor people who have struggled for what is theirs, only to see staggering tax rates that no one could have believed a generation ago.

"I have to think about the men and women of my district, such as the eight hundred families in Highview, West Virginia, who lost their jobs and their livelihoods three weeks ago. I might add they lost their careers as well. There are no more computer chip manufacturers left in the United States of America, which means there is nowhere left to ply their skills. Eight hundred families in my district were given a simple choice: change careers, start over from scratch and maybe lose everything, or leave the country. Come to Jakarta, they were told, to the workers' paradise, made so on the backs of hardworking Americans who lost their livelihood."

"Ladies and gentlemen, these are not crack mommies or drug addicts. These are not the liars and cheats my esteemed colleague Mr. Skaggs speaks of. No, these are hardworking Americans, who have served their country in wartime and served their communities in peacetime. And yes, most of them are going to need a little help. A little help starting over in their devastated community. Maybe a little help paying for medical care for their children. Until they can start over. This bill will take that helping hand away and replace it with a fist."

Clark let out a sigh and took a drink of water.

"Mr. Chair, I'd like to request unanimous consent to revise and extend my remarks."

"So be it, Mr. Clark, and thank you."

Murphy stretched. He was on the second panel—still a long ways away. The Chair introduced the first panel, a passel of government beauracrats who were going to talk about numbers and policies far removed from reality. Murphy leaned back in his chair and prepared for a long, dull morning.

⌁

It was quiet in Highview. Too quiet, as far as Karen was concerned. She had arrived at seven that morning, as agreed. About half an hour later, they made a great ceremony of using bolt cutters to shear off the padlock holding the new gates shut, and the workers began to stream in, preparing for the day. As she passed the gate, she saw the Sheriff and one of his deputies, leaning against their cars and watching the employees stream past. They did nothing to stop them.

No reporters or news vans in front of the factory. That surprised and troubled her. She would have expected eight hundred workers marching back into their closed factory to at least make the local news, but the press was nowhere to be seen. Maybe they would appear later, but that seemed doubtful. The dramatic moment to air on TV would have been the cutting of the locks.

In any event, she went to the lab in the Quality Assurance department, where her job was to select random samples and perform a variety of tests to ensure the chips met performance standards. The familiar white, carpetless room with wide counters, bright lights and large workbenches made coming back to work feel almost like coming home. At least all the home she had.

Karen has grown up in Hardburly, Kentucky: coal country, way the hell out in the middle of nowhere near the junction of West Virginia, Kentucky and Virginia. Her dad, chronically unemployed, spent most of her formative years mean and drunk. Right after the turn of the century, before Karen was even twelve, the son of a bitch began to eye her in a way that scared hell out of her.

One late winter night he'd arrived home drunk and beaten Karen's mother to death. Karen might have been next, had the neighbors not heard the screaming and called the county Sheriff. The Perry County Child Welfare Department placed her in a foster home, her dad went to prison, and that would have been the end of it except that sometimes she could still hear her mother screaming, though it was half a lifetime ago.

If nothing else, her dad taught her one thing—to never depend on anyone but herself. In high school, Karen joined the wrestling team and Junior ROTC, and the first time one of her foster brothers touched her the wrong way she broke his arm. Nothing made her happier than the day she left Hardburly behind forever, on an Army scholarschip at Bowling Green.

Now, for the first time since Mike Morris had suddenly dumped her before graduation from college, she felt lost, directionless. Maybe Murphy was right, and she should try to get transferred to the regular Army. Somehow she had the feeling that despite the plant takeover, this would be a temporary thing.

Temporary or not, she had a job to do now.

She sat down and logged into her computer, and then checked her email. Nothing but junk had come in since the plant had closed; no workers, so no one to send mail. She had received one note from the Bowling Green Alumni Association, asking for money. Delete that one.

About twenty minutes later, David Firkus showed up at the door with a cart full of chips. "First load of the day, Karen."

"Hey, Dave. It's good to see you."

"You too, Karen, you too. I'm very happy to be back at work."

With an IQ of 68, David had grown up in nearby Harpers Ferry, attending a school for disabled children, which had placed him in the job here at Saturn almost fifteen years ago. He had a simple job: take the loads of freshly manufactured chips from the line up to Quality Assurance, then pick them up later and take them to packaging. He made a variety of other deliveries around the building, as well. It did take a great deal of care, as the equipment was delicate. So far as she knew, he had never damaged one. His job could probably be automated, but management had been happy with his work and happy to provide the job.

She had not thought about him since the plant closed. Realizing that was like an accusation. She wondered what he had been doing.

"How've you been, Dave—you know, since the plant closed."

"Oh, pretty good. I had to move out of my apartment. I wasn't too happy about that. I moved back into my old room with my Mom. But that's okay, I like to watch her fish, and I might be able to get a new job at Al's Pizza. Except I don't need a new job now."

"Well, don't put all your eggs in one basket," Karen said. "We don't know for sure if the plant will stay open, so you might consider taking the job at the pizza place."

"Yeah. That's what my Mom said. But I missed everyone at the plant. And you." He blushed, right to the roots of his hair, and started to back out of the office. "See you later, Karen," he called. He stumbled as he backed up.

"Careful, Dave." She paused, and then called, loud enough to be heard in the hall, "I missed you, too, Dave."

It was the truth, too. She wasn't the most social person on earth, but being at home all day... not her cup of tea. Dave was a nice guy, and he cared about people. She felt bad she hadn't checked up on him at all.

Karen reached for her jeweler's glasses. There was a small microscope mounted on the left eye. By changing the focus on the lens, she could examine objects as small as five microns and see if there were any obvious blemishes on the chips. Picking out a dozen or so, she examined them, placed them on a small plastic tray, and then carried them over to the testing station, where they would be inserted into a socket and tested for functionality.

She looked up when she heard a low rumble outside. It was a sound she'd heard a thousand times in the Army: the tracks of an armored vehicle, very faint. She shook her head. Her imagination was way too vivid. It must be a bulldozer. Except she knew for sure there was no construction anywhere around here now that the fences were all finished.

And there was no question now: a low diesel thrum, tracks banging on the road. Not the distinct whine of a tank's turbine engine. Possible a Bradley, or a personnel carrier. She set the tray of chips down and walked, very slowly, toward the window, which overlooked the parking lot.

Remembering the words of one of the speakers last night, Dale Whitt, something about his grandfather being shot by the Army during a strike, it made her shudder, and even feel afraid. But only briefly. What was she thinking? This was the twenty-first century, not the nineteenth. His story probably wasn't even true.

The outer wall began to shake and a shadow passed overhead, followed by the overpowering sound of more than one helicopter. The window rattled in its frame. Karen looked out in disbelief.

Four military helicopters landed at the far end of the parking lot. Their tails swung around in unison, their miniguns pointed at the factory, and they disgorged black-clad riot troops: all wearing black combat gear and helmets, and carrying rifles. Many had plastic shields as well, labeled the same as the backs of their flak vests: DHS.

She ducked away from the window. *What the hell?* Occupying the factory might be illegal, but it wasn't like they were a bunch of armed crazies. They were civilians, workers with families, not terrorists. She was an officer in the goddamned National Guard. Who the hell would send in antiterrorist troops for something like this? She reached for her phone in a panic, her hands shaking. If nothing else, she had to call Murphy. He needed to know what was happening here. She didn't want to think about what might happen if anyone in the factory was armed.

Murphy heard the beep of his phone and cursed under his breath, just as he sat down at the witness table. He pulled out his phone. Karen Greenfield. She could wait; he would call her after the hearing. He hit the power button and tucked the phone away.

The chairman said, "Please rise and raise your right hand."

Murphy and the other two witnesses stood.

"Do you swear to tell the truth, the whole truth, and nothing but the truth, so help you God?"

"I do," Murphy responded with the others.

"You may sit. I believe the gentleman from West Virginia would like to introduce our first witness."

Murphy sat and laid his hands flat on the burnished table. A pitcher of ice water sat at the center of the table with several short glasses. He poured himself a glass, and then glanced up at his daughter, still sitting behind Clark. She looked cool and competent up there. Martha would have been proud.

Albert Clark sat up and said, "Thank you, Mr. Chairman. I would like to introduce to the committee an upstanding resident of my district. The witness, Lieutenant Colonel Kenneth Murphy, is a former Director at the Highview manufacturing plant of Saturn Microsystems, which, as some of you may know, shut its doors three weeks ago in order to squeeze more profit out of a factory overseas. As you can see, he is a serving officer in the West Virginia National Guard and is commander of the Second Battalion, Four-hundred and thirty-second Tank Regiment. He has served in two wars for our country, the first as a young enlisted man and later as a company commander. During his tour in Iraq, he lost his left leg below the knee, but pushed himself until he was again able to meet the physical training standards and remain in the National Guard.

"He is the recipient of a Bronze Star for Valor and the Purple Heart. This man is one of the heroes of my district: a loving husband to a wife who was murdered three years ago, a loving father of two children. One is a Harvard graduate, the other six years old and suffering from a degenerative nerve ailment for which there is no cure. Colonel Murphy has come here to tell us about Highview, West Virginia, and what the impact of the so-called Fiscal Responsibility Act will be on the people who live there, and I thank him for being here."

Clark finished, and the chairman spoke again. "Thank you, sir. Colonel Murphy, I'd like to welcome you before the committee, and may I say it is an honor to have you testify here. You have five minutes to make your statement, and you are welcome to also submit written testimony. We will then ask questions. Go ahead, Colonel."

"Thank you, Mr. Chairman. First off, allow me to begin by stating as a matter of principal that I'm not happy being here. I'm not someone who feels comfortable asking anyone for help, as I'm sure my daughter could tell you. But all the same, I find myself in an unthinkable situation.

"For the last twenty years, I worked with Saturn Microsystems in Highview, West Virginia. I've worked in just about every position in the company, working my way up to become one of the two directors at the plant. In that role, I was responsible for four hundred men and women who reported to me or one of my managers."

"Those men and women are now all out of work. Saturn decided to move their manufacturing operations to Indonesia. Never mind that the plant and its operations were profitable. They weren't profitable enough. I read an article in the Wall Street Journal last week indicating that Saturn expects to make an additional two hundred fifty million dollars a year from this move. These profits will be on the backs of eight hundred families who now have nowhere to go.

"My story is simple. I loved my wife, more than you can imagine. Three years ago, a drug addict from Charleston robbed a convenience store and murdered Martha. I thought my life was going to end when that happened, but Martha and I had two children who needed taking care of. My daughter Valerie is a Harvard graduate—something Martha and I put our life savings into. Our son, Kenny Jr., is six years old. In the last year he has been in the hospital several times, averaging about twenty thousand dollars a month in medical bills.

"My family faces complete destitution. With our savings poured into college, and with no medical insurance, I will be unable to pay Kenny's medical bills and he will… die. I am seeking new work, with no luck so far. That will take some time. I have twenty years' experience, but the only places left still using my experience are all outside the United States. In the meantime, Kenny qualified for Social Security Disability, which isn't even enough money to pay for his medical insurance. The only reason we're making it at all is my VA disability, which, since it is rated at less than forty percent, I will lose because of this bill.

"I ask myself, is this why I paid taxes all these years? Is this why I served in two wars? Is this what I paid in blood for? What happened to the seventy percent of my income that has gone to taxes for the last few years? None of it will come back to my family. Is this what it was all for? So my company could take its jobs to Indonesia, so you people could deny my son the medical care he needs to live? I don't matter, Mr. Chairman, but that boy is the future, and if you go forward with this proposal you'll abandon the future to a horrible death. Save my son. Save my town. You can't just cut off millions of hardworking Americans from the only safety net they have. Save our future. Don't turn your back on the children, whatever else you do."

※

Damn! Karen disconnected the phone and stuffed it back in her pocket. Murphy's phone had switched over to voicemail after one ring.

The sound of the helicopters still shook the walls, but now she heard a new sound: shouting, then a woman screaming. The agents must be in the main factory floor.

Karen jumped at the sound of a shotgun blast. It was followed by a dozen more shots from a higher pitched weapon. Sounded like an M16. Somewhere downstairs, a woman screamed. *Oh, Christ.* Someone had shot at the feds!

A noxious smell hit her, and tear gas drifted in through the open door. Karen ducked down to look for shelter, a place to hide. Behind the desk. She moved that way.

Too late. The door burst open, and a young man armored in a black flak vest and riot gear charged in, rifle aimed in her face.

"Get on the ground, get on the ground! Now, *now!*" She hesitated as another, older man charged in, this one armed with a pistol. She recoiled in shock. This was the man she'd confronted the night before, Agent Lawrence Harris.

"Get on the goddamn ground, hands behind your back," he shouted.

She froze. He ran forward, stuck the pistol against her forehead and yelled, "Get on the ground!"

He grabbed her hair and yanked her to the ground.

"Fucking hillbillies," the younger one cursed and shifted around on both feet, too excited from the adrenaline rush. "They shot Dylan. I can't believe they shot him!"

The other did not speak until he hit her on the side of the head with his fist, raising stars.

He leaned his head down close enough that she could feel his lips against her right ear and growled, "What is wrong with you people? I hope they roast all of you in the goddamn electric chair."

Rage struck, and she arched her back and pulled at the cuffs.

"Keep your hands to yourself, you fucking thug. You're talking to an officer in the United States Army."

"Officer, huh," he said, low in his throat. "Well, fuck you, officer cop-killing bitch."

She saw stars again as he hit her again on the side of the head. The two of them dragged her out into the hall.

She heard a scream. "Karen!"

She looked up, startled and still disoriented, to see Dave Firkus charge at them, his face almost purple with rage, a bear protecting its cub.

"Take your hands off her. Let her go! *Let her go!*" he shouted as he charged.

"Stop," shouted Agent Harris, as the other agent raised his rifle. They dropped Karen to the floor with a thud.

"No," she screamed. "David, stop!"

The young one shot a burst from his M16. The first bullet struck David square in the chest, the next two though the neck. Blood spattered across the hallway and he fell to the floor. Blood from an artery poured out onto the carpet and stained it black.

"*No*, God damn it!" she screamed. "You killed him! What is wrong with you people? *Murderers!*"

Harris shouted. "Idiot, put that rifle down."

Karen shrieked again, struggling. "Let me go! Bandage him! *Do* something, goddamn it!"

"Shut up, bitch," the young one shouted, still rocking back and forth on his feet. He kicked her on the side of the head. The third hit on the head in five minutes, this one knocked her out cold.

Chapter Eight
June 8

Murphy knew it was bad when he saw his daughter hunch over and whisper into her phone. Her face twisted with shock, fear and grief all at once. What could be wrong? Murphy's heart thumped as he watched her lean forward and whisper to Clark.

Clark's face went pale, and he quickly wrote a note and passed it to the chairman. The chairman nodded to him, and Clark and Valerie moved toward the exit. Clark pointed to Murphy and crooked his finger. Murphy stood and pushed his way through the crowd, which largely ignored him as they listened to the final panel of witnesses, the first of whom had been answering questions for twenty minutes.

Outside, Clark spoke first. "Colonel Murphy, I've got some bad news. A gun battle of some kind took place at the Saturn plant this morning."

Clark's statement was so far from anything Murphy had expected that it took him a moment to respond.

"How many people were hurt? What did you hear?"

"No details yet, I'm afraid."

"I have to go home, immediately," Murphy said.

"Actually, Colonel, I suggest we all go together, in your vehicle. Valerie and I can rent a car to come back."

Murphy thought about it half a second, and then replied.

"All right, that'll work. Let's get rolling." He turned and led the way toward his car.

As they walked, Valerie called instructions back to the office to have a rental car made available in Highview later in the day. Murphy dialed Karen's number. No answer for six rings, then a rough male voice.

"Hello."

"Hello, is Karen Greenfield available?"

"No. Who's calling?" a man asked, tone brusque.

"This is Colonel Murphy, her battalion commander. Who are you, and why do you have her phone?"

Murphy heard the guy on the other end call out, "Sir? It's some person says he's a Colonel something-or-other. Wants to talk to the woman who had this phone."

Murphy heard a rustling, and then someone came on the line. "This is Special Agent Hagarty. Who's speaking?"

"Hagarty, this is Colonel Ken Murphy of the West Virginia National Guard. I need an explanation right now for why you have the telephone of one of my company commanders."

He heard an intake of breath. "Colonel, it's funny to hear from you again. In fact, it worries me to hear from you again. I don't know about any company commanders. This phone belongs to someone we arrested, who aided and abetted the murder of two of my men. If you know anything about this, sir, I suggest you come here now to speak with us. If you don't, we'll want to talk to you anyway."

"I'll be there soon enough."

Murphy hit the off button and put away the phone. Hagarty's tone reminded him too much of the Cold War movie portrayals of the KGB.

"Hagarty, huh?" Clark said, after Murphy relayed what he had heard. "Isn't he the guy who threatened you after the bombing? I still haven't gotten a reply from DHS about the incident."

"It was him, all right. They did let Ahmed and his son go, about a week ago."

Murphy unlocked his truck and they climbed into the vehicle. He had to move a pile of books off the front passenger sear in order to make room for the Congressman.

Murphy drove a little too fast as they left town via I-66 and the Dulles Toll Road toward Leesburg, then north into West Virginia. Traffic was still light in the middle of the day and they made good time. They dialed through the radio, trying to find news of events in Highview. Murphy tuned the radio to the all-news radio station and they listened. Less than two minutes passed before they heard about the plant.

"Two federal agents were killed today in a raid gone bad," the radio announcer said. "The Department of Homeland Security raided a closed computer manufacturing plant in Highview, West Virginia, after the plant was seized by a group accused of being anti-government terrorists. In the raid, two agents and five of the suspected terrorists were killed, and more wounded."

Murphy and Clark met each other's eyes. Seven people killed. *Christ.*

"Anti-government terrorists? Where do they get this crap?" Valerie said. "If you hadn't been testifying, you would have been there, wouldn't you, Dad?"

Murphy didn't reply. He felt as if someone had punched him in the stomach. This was far worse than he had imagined. Five people dead? Was Karen Greenfield one of them? She didn't have her phone anymore. That fact alone was ominous. Five so-called "radicals" dead.

"Listen to this," Valerie said. She read from her handheld computer. "'Radicals kill federal agents.' That's on CNN. The Washington Post says 'Suspected terrorists kill two agents, five civilians.' Who wrote these articles, the DHS Public Affairs office?"

Clark looked back at her. "I think that's the way it's been for a long time. The Pentagon or DHS puts out a press release and the media just spits it back out; they don't even rearrange the words half the time. It's like reading Pravda during the Cold War. You know, we're going to have another problem. A serious one."

"What's that?" Murphy responded.

"If the DHS frames this as a bunch of 'anti-government' activists, you can bet they'll prosecute the rest of the employees, maybe as accessories to murder or manslaughter or something like that. They'll move quick to cover their asses."

Murphy's knuckles went white on the steering wheel. "What were they thinking? Why would you send in the DHS with guns blazing before finding out what the situation was?"

Clark shook his head. "They're covering themselves. Except for the Pentagon, the DHS is the single biggest government agency and money-waster, and they couldn't even stop the bombing in Arlington. Now they can demonstrate they've done something: they've stopped a cell of potential terrorists. If any DHS agents were hurt, it'll make it that much easier to wave the flag and get people to ignore reality. On top of that, Nelson Barclay is one of the big contributors to the President; they go way back. You know the Vice President used to sit on Saturn's Board didn't you? Nelson Barclay has access like you wouldn't believe. My guess is he asked the President to make the problem go away. The President delegated the whole issue to one of his aides, and this is the result."

Murphy didn't like the way that sounded. "You really think President Price authorized this?"

"Maybe not directly," Clark said, "but Price is owned by people like Barclay."

They drove in silence through Harpers Ferry. After Harpers Ferry, Route 340 was still lined on both sides by dense, dark woods. Twenty minutes later they pulled up to the gates of the plant.

A crowd of reporters and news vans were parked on the drive approaching the plant, along with fifty or more cars belonging to employees and their family members. Murphy carefully drove through and around the crowd and pulled up to the gate, which was blocked by two police cruisers.

Paul Machen, one of the Sherriff's deputies, stood in front of his car. He approached as Murphy drove up. Behind him, inside the fence, Murphy could see armored vehicles and helicopters scattered about the parking lot.

"I'm sorry, Colonel," he said as Murphy rolled down the window, "'Fraid I can't let you any further."

Murphy leaned out and looked up at him. "Afternoon, Paul. Now listen, I've got Congressman Clark with me, we're here to see what happened today and how bad it was. What can you tell me?"

Machen almost stood at attention when he realized the Congressman was in the car.

"Yes, sir, Mr. Clark, I didn't realize it you was in there, I'm sure you can go in. The Feds told me to keep everyone out, but I don't suppose they meant you. Hey Valerie, it's good to see you again."

She gave him a weak smile. The two had dated briefly in high school. It hadn't gone well at all.

Machen looked over his shoulder, and leaned close to the car. "It was pretty bad, Colonel. They come storming up here with tanks and helicopters and about a hundred troopers come a-charging out and into the plant. Never even a by-your-leave to the Sheriff, who is mighty pissed right now."

The Deputy looked over his shoulder again and lowered his voice to a stage whisper. "You want my opinion, they was looking for a fight. And they sure found it. Somebody in there had a shotgun, took out one of the agents, and that started a gunfight right there on the plant floor. Way I was told it, people was screaming and jumping under tables and desks while Rob Bailey and Phillip White shot it out with the agents right there on the floor. Course Bailey and White both got themselves blown away."

Murphy closed his eyes. He couldn't help but imagine the scene, on the crowded, open factory floor. "I knew those boys would cause some kind of trouble one day, but I never imagined this. Who else is hurt?"

"Why, fifteen or twenty people got shot, they had to be taken to three different hospitals. Mandy Blankenship's dead, she got hit in the crossfire. And Dave Firkus."

Valerie gasped. "Dave! Oh, no! What happened?"

"Way I heard it, he charged two of the agents, attacked 'em."

"No way," Murphy said. "I don't believe it. Dave wouldn't hurt a fly."

"Well, this whole thing is screwy; it never shoulda happened. You'll want to be looking for this Hagarty fellow, he was over near the helicopters last I saw. He's a little funny turned, if you know what I mean."

They drove into the compound, past three parked armored vehicles and onto the area near the four helicopters. In the chaos of the site, no one had secured the front gate. A cluster of men stood near the helicopters. Murphy parked near them, and the three got out of the car.

"Special Agent Hagarty?" Clark called in a commanding voice.

"Right here. I believe I know Colonel Murphy. Who are you?"

Murphy recognized the man who turned toward them. Even in his field gear, the balding Hagarty had more of the look of an accountant than a federal agent. But the other men gave him a wide berth as he turned and walked toward Murphy and Clark, shading his eyes against the glare of the sun as he walked.

"Are you in charge of this... incident?" Clark asked.

"I am. This is a crime scene, sir. I'll need you to identify yourselves immediately."

"Agent Hagarty, I am Congressman Al Clark. This is my assistant, Valerie. We're here to find out what happened here today. I need some explanations and I need them fast."

Hagarty rolled his eyes. Murphy glared at him, angry at the outright disrespect of Clark's congressional authority.

"Sir, you'll have to talk to the Secretary to get the details, I'm sure they'll be happy to make a report to Congress when the time comes. I can give you a quick overview. A large group of armed men took control of this building this morning. They were sent here by a known anti-government activist, Dale Whitt. Mr. Whitt is under investigation on a variety of charges, including weapons violations. Our people arrived on site to assist the local sheriff's office, disperse the crowd, secure private property and to insure there were no weapons. On our arrival, the suspects opened fire on my teams, killing two officers and wounding another. We secured the building and we are securing the crime scene now. And that, sir, is all I can say. You'll need to discuss anything further with the Secretary."

Clark frowned. "I take it, then, your officers arrived in tanks and armed helicopters in a sudden raid."

"Sir, I'm afraid I can't answer any more questions. You need to leave the area immediately. As I said, this is a crime scene, sir, and we can't have any non-law enforcement personnel on the site. You might damage evidence."

"You work for the citizens of this country, who I happen to represent. You will answer some questions. Where have the wounded been taken?"

Hagarty put his hands on his hips. "Look, Congressman. I'm don't want to get in your way, but I've got a job to do, and it's one I take very seriously. Our job is to protect the American people, and if you don't like our methods then I suggest you take it up in Congress. Here and now is not the time, sir. Let me make one thing very clear, however. The criminals inside that building shot and killed two of my men. You understand me? They fired on federal agents and killed them. Think on that, sir. I'm afraid I won't be able to answer any more questions. Henry! McClain! Get over here!" He shouted the latter at two agents still in riot gear and armed with rifles, and the two ran up. "I want you to escort these gentlemen and this lady off the site right now. If they resist, place them under arrest."

Clark said, "Agent Hagarty, are you aware it is a felony to interfere with a United States Congressman in the commission of his duty?"

"Sir, you have no duties here. I'll risk it."

"Answer my goddamn questions now, or I will be on the phone with the Secretary in about five minutes to have you fired!"

Hagarty crossed his arms over his chest. "All right, you get three questions and then I want all of you out of here."

"Where are the wounded?"

"They've been taken to a variety of hospitals in the area."

"I want a list. Names, and the locations they went to. Have it faxed to my office, by four p.m. today. Second, where are the people you apprehended?"

The demands and questions were issued like bullets.

"They are en route by bus to Charleston where they will be held until their arraignment. That will be handled in the federal court; I don't have any control over their procedures."

"Last question. Who authorized this operation?"

"Sir, the President of the United States authorized it. Now, I am going to ask you to leave one more time, or I will have you arrested for obstruction of justice."

Clark turned and walked away without another word, and Murphy and Valerie followed him.

Murphy glanced behind them as they reached the car. Hagarty had already turned aside and was shouting at two of his agents.

"I don't get it, sir," he said to Clark. "How can they think they'll get away with this?"

"They might," Clark replied. "We don't have a lot of oversight authority over DHS. If the President did authorize the operation, all the machinery of our government will be flying to back him up. Valerie, call the office. Let them know we're headed to Charleston, and see about that rental car; I don't want to take any more of your father's valuable time."

"Right on it," she said.

"I'm clear until morning, sir," Murphy said. "I have a sitter available overnight; we didn't expect that I would make it back here today."

"Yes, but I have the feeling there's a lot of very worried people in Highview today. Mothers and wives and husbands and children. Someone needs to talk to them. I think you've been been handed that job; I would suggest you talk to the mayor, see if you can get together another town meeting right away. Let them know I am working on the release of all those arrested, and we will have status soon on the wounded. Do you mind taking that on?"

"Not a problem, sir," Murphy said as he waited for an opening in traffic.

"Dad, the rental car was dropped off the house about an hour ago."

Murphy took a left turn, and headed toward his home.

✧

As people streamed into the high school gym, Murphy spoke to those he knew, many of them wives and husbands of employees at the plant. Murphy was surprised to see Vince Elkins. A family practitioner in Highview, he had referred Kenny to the specialists when the boy's symptoms began to crop up. On the occasional weekend and summer training, he served as executive officer of Murphy's battalion. Elkins was anything but political, and typically didn't get involved in the town's public life.

"Tell me the Russians didn't take over while I had my back turned?" Elkins said. "The feds are out there taking pictures of everybody who comes in the building. What the hell is going on up there, Ken? Were you there when it happened?"

Murphy shook his head. "I'll be talking in just a minute, Vince. It's been pretty crazy, today."

"I'd say so. All afternoon I had a stream of people in the office, hysterical, suffering from anxiety and ulcers and God all knows what. The whole town is wild with rumors. Next time the feds come in to round up half the damn town, they should round up everyone. That way families can stay together."

Murphy looked around the room. The families of the arrested employees were here, as expected, crowding the room. A large number of others were here as well: folks from town, what looked like the entire Chamber of Commerce, and two or three members of the clergy. Only twenty-four hours had passed since the last town meeting, when the employees decided to take the plant back. What a difference twenty-four hours made. Murphy looked around the room at the angry and frightened townspeople, and knew something fundamental had changed here today.

The Mayor, George Machen, walked to the front of the room and stood in front of the crowd. He bore a strong resemblance to his son: stocky, thin hair, even the swagger that had so turned off Valerie in high school. He walked to the podium and held his hands out. The audience quickly quieted down.

Machen spoke, not quite projecting to the back of the room. Just quiet enough that most of the crowd leaned forward and listened close in order to hear him.

"All right, folks. I think everyone knows we had us a bit of a disaster today. I've got Colonel Ken Murphy here; he was out at the plant this afternoon with Congressman Clark. He's going to tell us what he can."

As Mayor Machen spoke, half a dozen cameramen lit up the bright lights of their video cameras. Murphy felt lead in his stomach as he walked to the podium.

He spoke quietly, describing what they had seen this afternoon: the helicopters, and the executor of the operations, Special Agent Hagarty. As he finished, a dozen people stood to ask questions. Murphy pointed to the first, Amy Hillerman. Amy's husband was an employee at the plant; the couple had two small children.

"Colonel Murphy, do you have names—do you know exactly who was killed up there, who was arrested?"

Murphy shook his head. "Not yet. Representative Clark's office is compiling a list, ma'am. I think it'd be most appropriate to let the families of the dead be notified privately, don't you?"

An overweight woman in a faded dress stood up. Murphy recognized her. Shannon Firkus, Dave Firkus' mother. She used to come up to the office and have lunch with Dave every Thursday. Her eyes were red-rimmed with grief, dark circles under them.

"Mr. Murphy, I already know they done killed my boy. What I want to know is what are we going to do about it? We can't let these deaths go in vain. They was working for our survival!"

Machen approached the microphone again, Murphy stepping into the background. His part was done.

"Ma'am," Machen said, "I can't tell you how sorry I am about your loss, but what exactly are you suggesting?"

The shout came from the back of the room.

"She's suggesting we go back up there tomorrow!"

Everyone turned and looked. It was Dale Whitt. Not an employee at Saturn, he had not been among those arrested, though his voice has been loudest among those calling for action the night before.

The cameramen hustled to get a good shot of him speaking. "Mr. Mayor, with all due respect, all the congressional inquiries and lawyers in the world won't put food on the tables of the families of Highview. Nothing but getting our families back to work will do that."

He stood to the side and spoke to the crowd. "Folks, a hundred years ago Old Mother Jones was arrested for reading the Declaration of Independence out loud, right here in West Virginia. Today, the Federal Government spent your tax dollar to send in soldiers to shoot at your loved ones. Think about it, folks. You pay sixty or seventy percent of your family income to the government, and for what? So you can subsidize the companies that are screwing you over? So you can subsidize rich playboys like Nelson Barclay? He doesn't pay one red cent in taxes, but he can call in his government thugs and goons to beat up and shoot our families for trying to work for a living! Thugs and goons we paid for with our tax dollars."

Murphy watched and wondered where this was leading. As uncomfortable as he was to realize it, Whitt had a point. Murphy vividly recalled reading an article not two months ago about the sweetheart tax deals corporate executives were making. Barclay had been one of those profiled. The reporters looked excited as they jockeyed their cameras around to Whitt. This was turning out to be a much more interesting story than they had expected.

The Mayor spoke into the microphone, "All right, folks, this isn't getting us anywhere. Thank you for having your say, Mr. Whitt, but we need to move—"

"Shut up, damn politician!" someone shouted. Machen stepped back in shock at the blatant discourtesy.

"Let the man speak," said one of the men at the back of the hall.

"Let Dale have his say," called another man.

Machen's face went pale at the strong response. He motioned at Whitt to come to the podium. Whitt walked to the front of the room and stood next to the Mayor in front of the podium and spoke again.

"Folks, I only see one clear path ahead of us. Only one path that will do honor to David Firkus, who gave his life on your behalf. Only one path that includes honor and dignity. Tomorrow, all the citizens of Highview must march to the Saturn plant and take possession of it. Every last one of us. Because it does not belong to some rich son of a bitch who cares more about Jakarta than he does about West Virginia. It belongs to us, to our town, and to our people, who built it!"

The crowd erupted in loud applause.

Whitt turned to Murphy, a gamble in his eyes. "What say you, Colonel Murphy? Tell us what you think."

He stepped away from the microphone. *A gamble,* Murphy thought. A very smart gamble. Whitt knew Murphy tended to be very conservative, and had a great deal of influence in the town. Murphy walked forward, very conscious of the uniform he wore. Damn it, if there was ever a time to speak up, this was it. He would just have to live with the consequences. He leaned into the microphone and spoke.

"This morning I testified in front of a congressional committee that was deciding whether to take away the medical benefits my son needs to live. Folks, all it took was the greed of one man to destroy our economic life. You understand what I'm saying? One very powerful, very rich man makes a decision for his benefit, and the lives of everyone in this town are twisted out of control. I'm sorry, folks, this isn't the America I fought for in two wars. This isn't the America I swore to defend. It's not right. Some might disagree with what I say, but… I believe we don't have any choice. We *must* go back to the plant."

He turned away from the microphone, a sinking feeling in his stomach, knowing he had just crashed a torpedo into whatever was left of his military career. *Screw it.* He was close to retirement anyway—not that his retirement from the Guard would amount to much. There was a hushed silence after he spoke. Then the crowd burst into applause.

Machen shook his head. Murphy met his eyes, but the Mayor looked away, contempt on his face. Murphy grimaced. He and Machen had been friends for twenty years. But Murphy had to tell it the way he saw it. To shoot and kill someone like Dave Firkus and call him an anti-government activist was ludicrous—and criminal.

The gathering broke up soon afterward, with most agreeing to meet in the high school parking lot at six the next morning. Murphy wondered how many would show up—and whether or not Dale Whitt would be among them. He pushed his way out at the end of the meeting, threaded his way between the cameras and refused to answer any of the reporters' questions.

It was time to go. He'd pick up Kenny; they could have a quiet dinner, and get the boy to bed in his own home.

The old grandfather clock Martha bought at the antique fair in Winchester was ticking, and Murphy knew he needed to get to sleep. Tomorrow was going to be a long day. All the same, he sat there, holding a picture frame four years old. In it was a picture of Martha and Kenny, the last one he had of them together. They sat side by side on the bench in the back yard, each holding an apple. She had a subdued smile on her face as she looked at the camera, and Kenny a wide grin.

He started when the phone rang, glanced up at the clock. Quarter to eleven.

He reached over and grabbed the phone, then set the photograph on the coffee table.

"Hey, bro, I saw you on the TV tonight." It was his younger brother Tom.

Murphy smiled, "Tom, how you doing?"

"I'm all right, Ken. I was a little worried about you. You want to tell me what's going on?"

Tom Murphy was thirty-five, and had followed his brother into the military, but unlike Murphy, Tom had stayed Regular Army, and was now a colonel, a brigade commander down at Fort Campbell, Kentucky.

"Tom, you wouldn't believe it. These folks were making what amounted to a political protest, going back into our old factory, and the DHS attacked them—they had Bradleys out there, and helicopters. It was crazy."

"The news says they were armed."

"Well, it turns out a couple of hotheads were. But it wasn't what the news said, anti-government activities, or suspected terrorists, or whatever the hell they were saying. It was nothing more than the employees of the plant. Had I not been testifying in Washington this morning, I would have been there, Tom."

"News says you're going back tomorrow."

"That's right. The whole town is."

Tom didn't reply right away. Then he said, "You might want to think about that a little harder, Ken. Folks are pretty pissed in the DHS. And not just there. They put us on alert, Ken."

Murphy frowned. "I'll tell you what, Tom, there's something seriously wrong if an air assault brigade is being put on alert because of a labor dispute. You ever think of that?"

At the other end of the line, Tom sighed. "You're right, Ken. You are right. I just worry about you, you know. You haven't been yourself… well, in a long time. Just take care of yourself, okay?"

Tom might as well have shouted the unsaid words: *you haven't been the same since Martha died.* What the hell did he expect? Everyone seemed to think he was just going to pick up again, as if she'd never been there.

None of the anger came through in his voice. "I will."

"How are Kenny and Valerie?"

"Valerie's doing well. You should see her at work, Tom. Looks like she's running the whole show up there."

"Good, good. And Kenny?"

Murphy shifted his position, glanced down the hall to Kenny's room.

"Well—you know, Tom. Kenny's doing the best he can. I don't know how much time we have."

Tom let out a sigh. "I know. Take care of yourself, Ken, and be careful. I don't want to be seeing you on the evening news again, all right?"

"You got it, Tom. Love you."

"You too, bro."

Murphy hung up the phone, looked at the photograph again, and closed his eyes.

Chapter Nine
June 9

When Murphy awoke and rolled out of bed early the next morning, the unseasonable chill startled him. His breath appeared in a mist, and he hurried to dress in stout jeans and heavy flannel shirt. Half a dozen old, ignored pieces of wood lay in the steel basket next to the cast-iron wood stove in the living room. He hadn't used it in almost two months. He hurried to get a fire going.

His leg ached below the knee; where by rights he shouldn't feel anything at all. He wasn't usually bothered by phantom pain, but sometimes, when it was cold, it was bad enough to wake him up in the middle of the night.

After he had the fire going, he had his coffee alone at the kitchen table, and stared out the window into the darkness. As usual, he thought of Martha. Once, it would have been the two of them drinking coffee together before the kids woke up and the day started. Not long ago, Valerie suggested the time had come for him to think about moving on. As if he knew how to do that. How could he move on when all it took to see her was closing his eyes? Or looking at Valerie, who looked so much like her mother it was breathtaking?

Sometimes it seemed only yesterday the Sheriff called and told him. When he thought of her on the floor of the convenience store, her lifeblood pouring out as the son of a bitch stepped over her to take a pathetic sum of cash out of the register, his fingernails bit into his palms. When he thought of her dying alone, he wanted to howl.

We were supposed to grow old together, he thought. *Now I've grown old without you.*

A car approached outside, tires crunching on the gravel driveway, slowed down, and the newspaper thumped against the side of the house. He stepped out into the cold and brought it in.

The center of the page above the fold displayed a color photograph of him in front of the podium the night before. The lurid headline said, "DHS Raids Computer Plant, Seven Killed." The caption under the photograph read, "Lieutenant Colonel Ken Murphy of Highview speaks to demonstrators."

Murphy scanned the article, and then wished he hadn't. Filled with inaccuracies, it portrayed the people of Highview as a group of anti-government ideologues, lumping them in with white supremacists and the militia movement. But these folks weren't political at all—or, more accurately, they fell all over the political spectrum. He'd spent much of night after the town meeting, on the phone with Valerie and the Mayor, trying to determine the whereabouts of the employees who'd been injured or arrested. The injured were all accounted for now—and the dead. Those arrested had been bussed the several hour drive to the Charleston federal lockup—among them, Karen Greenfield. God only knew what he was going to do about that.

Murphy finished his coffee, rinsed the cup and put it in the sink, then laced up his work boots. He woke Kenny and got him ready to go, and then they drove into town. On the way to the town square, he passed the high school. Cars already filled half the lot.

The lights were on downstairs at the Al-Khoury grocery, but the doorknob wouldn't turn. It was still two hours before opening time. Murphy rang the bell and Samira answered the door. She was a petite girl and a stunning beauty, with luxurious black hair, pale brown skin and green eyes. In high school she'd been a solid student, but just missed being part of the popular crowd because her family didn't have a lot of money.

She smiled when she saw them.

"Hey, Kenny, how's it going?" She ruffled the boy's hair. Sleepy, he hugged her.

"Ken." Ahmed bounded down the stairs. "I wanted to say thank you, my friend. I think the calls from Congressman Clark helped free me and Hayder so quickly."

"I'm glad. Are you okay? Any problems in town since then?"

Ahmed and his daughter met each other's eyes, then looked back at Murphy.

"As good as can be expected. You know how it is—every time something bad happens anywhere, it is the fault of an Arab. This is how some people think."

Samira spoke to the boy, breaking the awkward moment. "Hey Kenny, why don't you come on up with me? Want some breakfast?"

"Yeah!" Kenny said.

Murphy held out a stuffed backpack. "Here's his bag. The autoinjector is in there, along with an extra change of clothes. Thank you."

She led Kenny upstairs.

Murphy turned back to Ahmed, reached in his pocket and handed him an envelope with writing on the back.

"Listen, if anything happens to me today, this is my parents' number. They know there might be a problem. If need be, call them and put Kenny on a plane down to Georgia. There's enough money for a ticket in there."

They said goodbye, and Murphy backed out the door. He got back into his truck and drove over to the high school. The sky was an unforgiving grey above the trees. He hoped it wouldn't rain.

Forty-five minutes later, Murphy saw that most of the town had gathered in front of the high school, including, to his surprise, Mayor George Machen and Dale Whitt.

Murphy didn't hem and haw. "I'm kind of surprised to see you up here, George."

Machen grimaced. "I am, too. I don't approve, but the whole dang town is out. I won't sit on the sidelines while women and children are out here fighting for their livelihood. If we all go down, we all go down."

A line of about two hundred cars stretched down the street. The television vans were back, and bright lights shone in the semi-darkness as the cameramen filmed the gathering. A group of reporters started to approach the three who had, by virtue of speaking the night before, become the leaders of this gathering.

"Looks like it's time for us to get rolling," Murphy said, watching the reporters.

"Let's not run off just yet," Whitt said. "The press may be annoying, but they can also be our best allies."

"Or our worst enemies," Murphy said. "Won't take much to make the media turn on us. You read the Gazette this morning?"

"I did," Whitt replied. "The media will get it wrong, but the more you talk, the more chances they have to get it right. Besides, unlike yesterday at the plant, the media is here. I asked around—Barclay apparently called in a bunch of favors, told the networks there was no story in Highview. Given what happened, I expect he's burned some bridges—the reporters aren't happy they weren't here when things went south yesterday. It will be harder to distort what they see with their own eyes; they won't repeat what the DHS tells them if their own cameras show something different. It's not all about politics—this is beyond politics."

Murphy glanced sidelong at Whitt. From what he'd seen of Whitt, everything centered on politics.

The reporters immediately began asking questions, which were quickly dispensed with. But Murphy gained one valuable piece of intelligence from them: the armored vehicles were now brazenly parked at the front gate of the plant. He didn't know whether to take the implied threat seriously or not. Were these people idiotic enough to attack unarmed townspeople with armored vehicles? On television, no less? Before yesterday, he wouldn't have thought it possible. He shrugged and got behind the wheel. He would find out soon enough. He drove out of the parking lot slowly, a long line of vehicles forming up behind him.

From the high school it took about five minutes to reach the closed, locked gates. Murphy pulled to the side of the road and parked. Behind the gates were two Bradley fighting vehicles. The turrets were turned backward, with the main gun away from the crowd. At least they had that much sense.

Four agents from the DHS stood behind the gate in full combat gear, carrying rifles with grenade launchers slung under the barrels. A fifth stood to the side, digital camera in hand with a telescopic lens. He began shooting photographs of the townspeople as soon as they parked. Murphy ignored them, his face impassive. He stepped out of the truck, walked around the back where the agents couldn't see him, and lifted an old pair of bolt cutters he'd thrown into it the night before. The officers appeared to become very agitated when he appeared again, bolt cutters in hand. One spoke into a cell phone while the others backed away from the gate, toward the armored vehicles.

Behind Murphy, a crowd gathered as townspeople parked in a line behind his and got out of their cars. The mayor and Whitt both approached him. At least two or three hundred others approached as well. Three television vans had parked to the side of the two-lane road, with cameras mounted on tripods. A reporter stood in front of the CNN van, making what appeared to be a live report. Two more reporters crouched down close to Murphy, filming him and the others as they made their approach.

"Sing. The National Anthem." Whitt said.

"Do *what?*" Machen replied.

"We're going to start singing now."

Mayor Machen looked at Whitt with contempt. "I don't think that's necessary—"

Whitt, ignoring the Mayor, turned around and walked backwards beside Murphy. "Men and women of Highview, this is our plant," he shouted. "This is our town. Federal police stand on the other side of the gate, but they cannot stand against the people. They cannot take away our rights as Americans. Let us now go forth."

Whitt started singing the Star Spangled Banner.

The crowd followed Whitt's lead, slowly at first, then more enthusiastically as they fell into the rhythm. Glancing back, Murphy saw tears in the eyes of some of the men as they sang. "… by the dawn's early light.…"

Murphy approached the gate with the bolt cutters as the men and women behind him sang. "…What so proudly we hailed… at the twilight's last gleaming."

"Sir," called one of the black-uniformed agents, "if you do that I will have to place you under arrest. Please put down the bolt cutters now."

Murphy ignored him. The cameramen jockeyed for position against the fence, trying to get the best shot as Murphy positioned the bolt cutters.

"Careful," he said, glancing at the closest cameraman. "You don't want to get a fragment of this in your eyes."

He placed the lock between the blades and squeezed. It didn't break, so he squeezed harder, veins popping out on his forehead. The padlock snapped with a loud crack, then clattered onto the pavement. Murphy pulled the chain loose and threw it to the side, then opened the gates.

The townspeople continued to sing. "And the rocket's red glare... the bombs bursting in air... gave proof through the night... that our flag was still there."

The singing sent chills down Murphy's spine. He walked forward. The federal officers backed away and put on gas masks.

Oh, no. He'd been through the gas chamber three times in his military career. Riot gas made you choke and puke and gag, made your eyes hurt like hell. They wouldn't be singing much longer.

He walked forward anyway, with the town behind him. "Oh say does that Star Spangled Banner yet wave...."

The feds fired three, then four gas grenades with a low-pitched pop. The grenades landed amidst the feet of the townspeople. Smoke started to billow up and someone screamed. The singing abruptly stopped. The newsmen rushed to the side with their cameras and continued to film.

Someone threw a gas grenade back at the feds. It came down behind the line of riot troops who marched forward, carrying plastic shields and batons. They moved in a phalanx and shoved the crowd back. Another scream, as a fed hit someone on the head with a baton. They fired four more grenades into the crowd.

An agent stood right in front of Murphy now. Murphy looked at the man's face behind the plastic visor and saw fear. The agent slammed his shield into Murphy, then reached out and cracked him over the head with the baton. Murphy's prosthetic leg slipped out from under him, and he fell back to the ground with a grunt. He felt blood in his hair and on the side of his face.

"Disperse and return to your homes," someone called over a megaphone. "Disperse and return to your homes."

Many in the crowd were running away now, and the line of troops had forced most of the people outside the gate. Murphy looked up, saw David Firkus' mother. She lay on her side, her face bright red, mouth open. The tear gas rolled over her in a great cloud. Murphy crawled toward her.

"Get out of here," one of the agents yelled. Murphy felt a kick in his side.

Murphy stood and pointed at Shannon Firkus. "She needs help." Then he doubled over and vomited. Tears ran down his face from the concentrated smoke.

Vince Elkins had showed up at her side just as Murphy had. Mucus and tears poured from his face as he took her pulse, then cursed.

"God damn it," he shouted at Murphy. "She's got no pulse. She's had a heart attack. I told her not to come out here today."

Murphy felt the crack of a baton against his back and stumbled.

"I'm a doctor," shouted Elkins. "This woman needs—"

The black-clad riot policeman silenced him momentarily, cracking a baton over his head. The two agents shoved Murphy and Elkins.

"That woman needs help!" Elkins screamed in the face of one of the agents. Blood ran down the side of his face. He pointed at Shannon Firkus, who still lay on the ground. This time, the officer listened, dropping to his knees beside the woman, but it was too late. Shannon Firkus, like her son the day before her, lay dead.

Chapter Ten
June 17

A week after the events at the plant, Murphy was still reeling in shock. Somehow he'd never expected the violent response, the ready deployment of paramilitary forces. He moved through his days, mailing resumes, filling out job applications, playing with his son, feeling something akin to grief. He'd spent his life in the military. He never thought he'd see its agents used against their own people.

The town was as quiet as a funeral. The plant employees had been released, but the streets were still hushed, some businesses closed. Nine people had died by violence in two days, unheard of in a town only a few thousand people. Murphy and others from the town had driven a convoy to Charleston to bring back the workers who'd been arrested; they returned with horror stories of being crowded into both the county jail and the federal lockup, packed in ten to a cell with drug dealers and murderers. Everywhere he looked, smoldering rage was just under the surface. He'd never seen Karen Greenfield so angry—during the drive back she'd described the cell, with twenty women packed into a ten by ten room with nowhere to sit. One of the women, a junkie, had gone into convulsions, but it still took twenty minutes to get the attention of the guards to get her medical care.

The rest of the country, by contrast, seemed to have gone off the deep end. Stories about anti-government movements and militias flooded the media, focusing on the Sons of Liberty in Baughman Settlement, thirty of whom had been detained by the DHS during their raid the previous week. A tremendous amount of coverage was also devoted to Oklahoma City and the bombing twenty years before. Now that the federal government had squarely pointed the finger at a domestic group, the previous weeks' violence and suspicion against Middle Easterners passed from the consciousness of the nation, or at least of the national media. Reporters crowded Highview: satellite vans still sat beside the town square, and Murphy's home phone rang off the hook for three days after the town had tried to take the plant. He'd finally unplugged it. Valerie had his mobile phone number if she needed to reach him.

The DHS and their armored vehicles still occupied the plant. It was an uneasy standoff, and small groups of townspeople, by ones and twos, made their way to the entrance of the plant and put flowers next to the gate, in a makeshift memorial to Dave and Shannon Firkus, Mandy Blankenship, and the others who had died there.

Murphy's somnolence came to an abrupt end one afternoon a week after the violence at the plant, with a phone call from Dale Whitt, who insisted on meeting in person. The next day, Murphy arrived at Sally's Diner at noon, irritated that the noxious smell of tear gas still permeated his car. At least he wasn't planning on reselling it.

When Murphy arrived, Whitt was already there, sitting at a table in the back, hands cradling an oversized mug. The room was not well illuminated, but it was clean and not too crowded today. Folks were staying home and saving money, and all the local businesses were feeling the pinch.

Murphy sat across from Whitt. In the last few days, Whitt had gained celebrity status in Highview. Murphy had seen it in the way people talked about him, in far more respectful terms than they spoke of the Mayor.

"Ken. I appreciate you coming." Whitt smiled as he spoke.

"Thanks, Dale. You were awful mysterious on the phone."

Whitt took a sip from his steaming mug, and then replied. "You'll understand why soon enough, but I'd like to discuss it all together. Can we wait until the Mayor arrives?"

They talked of other things for a few minutes: mostly bad news, businesses that had closed in the county, the string of funerals, and the suspicion they were drawing from the rest of the country.

Then Murphy heard the Mayor's voice behind him. "Well if it isn't Mr. Whitt and Colonel Murphy. I didn't realize you were involved in his scheming, Colonel. How are you two doing today?"

Murphy stood, as did Whitt. They shook hands all around.

The Mayor sat, looking at the two of them with frank curiosity. The waitress approached and they ordered without looking at the menu.

"Well, Dale," said Machen, "you was pretty hot to talk right away. You want to clue me in?"

Whitt sat back and studied the two of them.

"Mr. Mayor, Colonel, I'm going to ask you both to keep what I have to say mum, understand? Until I can make my announcement in public."

Murphy shrugged, and the Mayor answered. "Well, I'd have to know what you had to say to make a hard promise. But a man's only as good as his word, so you've got mine."

Irrationally irritated that the Mayor had managed to give two opposite answers at once, Murphy replied. "I don't have any problem with that, Dale."

"I appreciate that. Gentlemen, I'm here to ask for your support. I plan to run for the state Senate in November."

Murphy and Machen looked at each other. The Mayor spoke first. "Well, Dale, I appreciate you asking for my support, but I have to admit, your candidacy... well, it ain't earth shattering. Old Man Davidson has been in that seat—God, I don't even know. Thirty years, at least. You don't have a chance against him."

Whitt grinned. "I know. My daddy lost an election against him in 1984. But the way I see it, things is different now. Davidson may be a long term incumbent, but he doesn't have any passion. The voters vote for him 'cause there isn't anyone else on the ballot, or they recognize his name or some such. I plan to give them a reason to vote for me."

They stopped speaking, and there was an uncomfortable silence as the waitress brought their drinks.

After she left, Machen asked, "And what would that reason be, Mr. Whitt?"

"Gentlemen, I plan to run on a platform proposing that West Virginia secede from the United States."

The silence after his statement was long. If it hadn't been for the banging of pots and pans in the back room, you might have heard the wind whisper outside. Murphy brought his water to his lips, leaned back in his chair, and studied Whitt in a very different light. That neither he nor Machen burst into laughter was a measure of just how angry they—and the rest of the town—were.

Mayor Machen was the first to recover. When he spoke, his tone had an edge. "Are you out of your mind? They'd tear you apart. This is a very patriotic town and you're talking treason."

Whitt gestured with his hands as he replied. "You're right, and you're wrong, Mayor. Folks are patriotic. They're patriotic for what they know—for their town, for their families, even for West Virginia. They love America. But what do they know of the federal government of the United States? Bunch of foreign wars, no one was sure what they were about? Peacekeeping duty in some half-baked mud puddle half way around the world? Sixty percent of their money supposedly for social security spent on something else? Forcing them out of the plant at gunpoint? Shooting our neighbors and friends and husbands and wives?"

Machen turned red. "Well, I never... I ought to have you arrested, you son of a bitch."

Murphy raised a hand, palm up. "Let him have his say, George. You may not agree with him, but he's got a right to speak."

"Not to me, he don't. Get the hell out of here, you red son of a bitch."

"Mayor, don't you even see how disconnected you are from your own people? This is what the voters want. They've had enough. Only thing the federal government ever did in West Virginia was send in the Army to back up the coal company thugs. Look at this situation down in Baughman Settlement—you ever heard of those folks down there, before the feds said they were behind the Arlington bombing?"

Murphy said, "No."

"Well, I'll tell you what, I know those people, and I've been down there to their compound." He looked around and lowered his voice. "They're not political; they're isolationist, religious folks. They've got their little compound in the mountains, and they just want to be left alone, understand? I tried to get them hooked up with the Libertarians down there about two, three years ago, and they just weren't interested in politics. Now why would they go blow up a bunch of defense contractors? It doesn't make any sense."

Machen looked at him with contempt. "Next you'll be saying the federal government bombed their own people, won't you?"

Whitt shrugged. "I don't know who did it, Mr. Mayor. I do know it wasn't the people the DHS said did it. But they sure were easy pickings, weren't they? Just like we were in Highview. Send in some combat troops against unprepared civilians and tell the public you've got yourself a bunch of terrorists. Shows they've been doing something about terrorism, doesn't it?"

Machen stood up. "I'm not listening to another word out of you. Not only that—you ain't gonna run against that old fool Davidson. You'll run against me. I'll be damned if I'll have some red traitor son of a bitch as my senator."

Whitt held his hand palm out. "It doesn't have to be this way, George."

Machen spat. "Mr. Mayor to you. You coming, Colonel?"

Murphy pursed his lips. "I'll hear him out, Mayor."

Machen's eyes widened. "For God's sake, Ken. You of all people—you fought in two wars for this country!"

"And I would do so again. I fought because I believe people should have their say. I'll respect Dale's right to have his."

"Well you can both go to hell then," Machen said. He turned and stalked out of the diner.

"I was hoping he wouldn't react like that," Whitt said.

"You must be out of your mind, Dale, to think you can get elected on that platform. He's right, you know."

Whitt responded, "No, he's not. Colonel, think about what you said the other day. Is this what you fought in two wars for? How about having your tax money used against you right here in Highview, not halfway around the world on some peacekeeping operation, enforcing corporate policies for the oil companies, or subsidizing sons of bitches like Nelson Barclay. Christ, Ken, *you* probably paid more taxes than Richardson did last year. Not to mention the Purple Heart you earned protecting our oil supply."

Murphy took another drink, unwilling to commit to an opinion. "I'll think about it, Dale. That's all I'll promise. It's a little different for me, you know. You can talk about something like that all you want, and it's just a lot of hot air. I'm an officer in the National Guard. If I start talking like that, it really is treason, and I could go to jail, or lose my command."

Whitt frowned. "Would you rather lose your command or your dignity? Your freedom? How much is too much, Ken? As far as I'm concerned, they crossed the line when they started shooting civilians during a political demonstration. That just doesn't fly. Not with me, and not with most folks around here."

"It's not just my dignity or freedom we're talking about, Dale, it's my kids too. It's not that simple."

The problem was that to some extent Whitt was correct. You couldn't have the federal government shooting civilians. But this wasn't the way to deal with it. There had to be another way to improve the situation. A way that didn't involve violence. And for damn sure, no independence move by West Virginia could result in anything but more violence.

"Ok, Whitt. Let's talk this all the way through. Let's say by some miracle you get yourself elected. What happens when you get to the Senate?"

"Well, first off, there are some folks who feel the same way as I do already in the Senate, and more running for seats around the state. I'm not operating in a vacuum; I fully expect to get some support once I'm there. I'm taking two steps. I'm running for the office, and I'm starting a petition campaign to amend the State Constitution so that it's legal to secede. Right now the Constitution explicitly rules that out. Once I'm in office, we'll propose a bill to act on the amendment."

"You can't win this one, Whitt."

Dale smiled. "You're probably right. But if I can get a legitimate debate going, that's something. The government is out of control, Ken. Way out of control. But if I can get even a few votes—do you have any idea what kind of a political firestorm we'll create?"

Murphy shrugged. "What happens if you succeed? Do you think the President will just let it go? Before your bill ever passes, you'll have the Army right here in Highview, and all over the rest of the state."

"It won't come to that, Ken. You yourself said it—this one would never pass. But we can make a strong as hell argument for reform. We have to make the point, Ken—both to the government and to the rest of the country."

"What point is that, Dale?"

"They can't bleed us dry. They can't take all the coal and natural gas and oil—they can't take the fruits of our labor while our people struggle in mines, and not give anything back."

Nothing left but ice in Murphy's glass. He raised his hand to catch the attention of the waitress, pointed to the empty glass.

"I still think you're crazy to be pursuing this. I hear what you are saying—and I agree with some of it—but I can't support you, Dale. I just can't do it."

"I understand. If nothing else, I appreciate you listening, not charging out of here like the Mayor."

Murphy shrugged. "Man's got to have his say. I wouldn't mind hearing more of your plans, anyhow. If nothing else, it'll be an interesting election for a change this year."

"That it will, Colonel. That it will."

Chapter Eleven
June 20

Valerie opened the door a few inches and knocked. Clark was on the phone.

"Hold on please," he said to his caller, then covered the handset with his left hand.

"Al, I've got good news. Your appointment with the President is at three."

"Great. Can you pull together a quick briefing packet?"

"It's already done."

"Thanks."

He smiled, went back to the phone.

Valerie hurried back to her desk. She had prepared an information packet targeted at the media, but had hoped they would be called on to meet with the President. The information in the packet was targeted to put as much pressure on Saturn as possible. First, a brief on the workers of the Highview plant and quotes from past Saturn press releases that highlighted the engineering and technical advances made by the employees of the plant. Economic data: out of a population of less than five thousand, Saturn had provided eight hundred jobs. With the plant closed, the town would be devastated. Next, a list of those killed in the violence. Not extremists or anti-government activists, as the Secretary of Homeland Security claimed, but good, hardworking people.

"Hey, Valerie," one of the other aides called. "Did you see this?" It was Megan McClain, one of the interns, annoyingly cute and incompetent. She held a magazine up in the air.

Valerie did a double take. Standing up, she marched over and snatched the magazine out of the intern's hand.

The dramatic photograph of her father was splashed on the cover of Newsweek, tear gas roiling around him, giving CPR to Shannon Firkus. It put Ken Murphy in an almost heroic light—something he would not appreciate. Across the bottom of the page were the words, "Violence in West Virginia."

Opening the magazine, she saw another large photo of him, this time in uniform, testifying before the House. *Dad is going to be so pissed when he sees this,* she thought. She read through the article, which described the events of the last two weeks in Highview in significant detail. Photos of David and Shannon Firkus, when David was a baby. A sideline article on Nelson Barclay highlighting the fact that the plant was profitable, just not profitable enough for one of the richest men in America. The article also pointed out that due to an accounting anomaly, Saturn had not paid a dime in federal taxes in the last three years, despite how profitable it was. Saturn issued a brief statement expressing "regret" for the deaths, but of course denying any responsibility for the chain of events that led up to them.

The County Prosecutor in Harpers Ferry had called a grand jury to investigate a charge of excessive force in the raid, indicating that homicide charges against the federal officers might result. She would have to check into that. If charges were brought against the DHS by the local jurisdiction, it would bolster their argument.

She thought about copying the article and placing it in the packet for the President. It painted a far different picture of the situation than the DHS did. *Why not?* She made a copy of the article, then returned the magazine to Megan, thanking her. The article, with its dramatic cover photo, should help set the impression.

She checked her watch. Noon. Two hours before they would leave for the White House. She paced across the room, then back, and looked out the window. The sky over the bare courtyard was tinged brown with pollution. Another code red day. They were becoming more and more common every summer. Last summer half a dozen deaths in DC were attributed to heat and pollution.

She looked across the room. Megan sat at her desk painting her nails. For God's sake, couldn't she find a better place to do that, or something more productive to do at work? Valerie started in her direction, scowling.

Ambrose Hall stepped in front of her. "Hey, Valerie, no point in sitting around here getting nervous. Let's grab some lunch."

Valerie stopped and demanded, "Who's nervous?"

Ambrose gave her a wicked grin. "Maybe not nervous, but you were about to bite someone's head off."

Valerie closed her eyes. "You're right. Let's go."

"It's on me."

"No way. You bought last time."

As they walked toward to the door, Ambrose leaned over the intern's desk and said in a stage whisper, "Honey, you better put the nail polish away. You don't want to cross Valerie. She'll be writing your recommendation letter at the end of the summer. Maybe."

Valerie waited until they were outside, then punched Ambrose in the shoulder. "You jerk! I'm not that bad."

"Don't you remember Mike Wilson? He used to look like a deer caught in the headlights when you got to work."

"That wasn't my fault. He was just horny and afraid of girls. Kid needed to get laid is all."

Ambrose laughed.

In a few minutes, they reached the cafeteria in the basement of the Rayburn Building. After retrieving their food, they sat and talked about Hall's partner, who had been offered a spectacular job with a prestigious law firm in Los Angeles. A benefit of moving there, of course, was that California recognized same-sex marriages. Of course, the DC government had voted to recognize them years before as well, but Congress had intervened and reversed the decision. Either way, Hall wasn't ready to quit his job. He loved working on the Hill and didn't want to consider giving it up. But the two of them been together nearly ten years, and were struggling over what to do.

Valerie was grateful and somewhat distracted when they returned to the office. She sat down at her desk, tinkered with the briefing packet and fidgeted nervously. Half an hour. She spent the last few minutes checking the latest news, scanning for information about DHS, then got up and knocked on Clark's door.

"Time for us to get going, sir."

"Great. You have the briefing packet ready?"

"We're all set."

They walked out the sizeable entrance to the office into the hall. With wide marble floors and high ceilings, ornate stonework and graceful columns, the buildings on Capitol Hill always made her think of the ancient Roman republic and its timeless institutions—timeless until, after hundreds of years, it lost its checks and balances and the republic became a sham.

On to the front entrance, they walked down the steps at the Independence Avenue entrance and Valerie stood on the curb and stuck out a hand. Three minutes later they were in the back seat of a cab on their way to the White House. When it stopped at 15th and New York Avenue they climbed out at the corner, next to the Treasury building. From there, they walked to the west wing entrance and showed their identification to the guards. After fifteen minutes of security checks, they were led upstairs by one of the President's aides and into the Oval Office.

"You sit here," the aide said. "The President will be back shortly."

They sat on the uncomfortable antique couch. A matching one faced them across the coffee table, both couches sitting near the Seal of the President emblazoned across the floor. Against the wall, halfway between the desk and the table and chairs where they sat, stood a gangly man in a black suit and tie. Secret service. He didn't acknowledge them, but Valerie knew he was acutely aware of them.

Minutes later President Wendell Price walked into the room, his presence immediately filling the space. They both stood at the entry of the unusually tall man.

"Representative Clark? A pleasure to finally meet you in person. And this is your assistant?"

"Valerie Murphy, Mr. President," she said. Valerie and Clark shook hands with the tall, florid faced man. Valerie thought his voice was even more engaging in person than on television. His meaty hands engulfed hers when they shook.

"Please have a seat," he said. "I have to tell you up front, I've only got a few minutes before my next meeting, but we felt this was very important and we should meet. The situation over there is pretty grave, isn't it?"

"Yes, sir," Clark said. "We're hoping to discuss two things with you today, sir. The first, as you may know, is that the County Prosecutor in Harpers Ferry is investigating charges of excessive force and homicide during the DHS raid. I wanted to make sure you were aware of this, and to ask you to ask the Justice Department to also investigate. The charges are quite serious, sir—a DHS agent shot and killed at least one unarmed bystander, and the team assaulted a number of others."

The President arched his eyebrows. "I know the DHS has a bad reputation, but they are not bad people. I find these charges difficult to credit."

"Sir, that's why we are asking for an investigation. I know some of the people involved, Mr. President. These are not criminals; some of them are pillars of our community."

The President tilted his head to the left. "Then why were they trespassing on private property?"

Valerie spoke up. "Sir, that's the other issue we'd like to discuss with you. As you may know, the Saturn Microsystems manufacturing plant in Highview closed a month ago, laying off all the workers. The plant moved to Indonesia, where the company can exploit cheap labor. Again, the entire workforce was laid off without notice."

"Well, I'm sorry to see jobs leave the United States, but I hardly see where the federal government comes in to this."

Clark replied, visibly struggling to keep his tone level. "Sir, the federal government came into this when it started shooting the citizens of my district. The federal government is in this thing up to its neck, Mr. President. It was a simple labor dispute before the DHS stepped in, called my people terrorists and attacked them with a large combat force. Now, this was a profitable plant. Saturn shut the plant down and moved it not because they were losing money, but to increase their margins. This will economically devastate the town. The workers met with attorneys and banks, and then made an offer to Saturn to buy the plant and license the technology. Saturn would get pure profit. Unfortunately, they turned the workers down."

Valerie watched the President as Clark spoke. Something about his expression just wasn't clicking Maybe it was the makeup he wore; he must have been on TV this morning.

"What can we do about it?" President Price asked.

"Two things, sir. First, federal prosecutors are harassing the townspeople and hitting them with outrageous charges, accusing them of being anti-government conspirators and worse. Second, even though the federal government can't do anything to fix the situation, you know Nelson Barclay and have some influence with him. Sir, you can ask him to allow the workers to buy the plant. Allow them to have their economic lives back."

By this time, the President had leaned back in his chair and rested his chin in his hand. Valerie tensed. The President looked almost sympathetic as he stared at Clark, but it seemed disingenuous to Valerie. She didn't trust him, and the sympathetic look turned on and off like a light switch whenever he wanted it to.

Abruptly Price narrowed his eyes, and then shook his head in the negative. "Mr. Clark, I'm surprised at you. If I were to interfere in an ongoing investigation being conducted by the Justice Department, you and your friends on the Hill would be all over me with ethics investigations. I most certainly will not do that, nor will I pressure a private company—*private*, mind you—to change its policies to suit your needs. Now, I will take what you have said into consideration, but I must say, Mr. Clark, I am disappointed."

Clark's face was wooden, and Valerie was stunned. She had not known what to expect—a noncommittal answer maybe. "I'll think about it." Something like that. Not this outright refusal.

"Now," the President said, "if that is all, I have to go on to my next meeting."

"Mr. President, please hear me out. This is a critical issue."

President Price shrugged. "Mr. Clark, I don't see anything further to discuss. I appreciate your concern for your constituents, but it just wouldn't be ethical for me to intervene. You must understand. It was a pleasure meeting both of you."

The President turned and walked out of the Oval Office. Clark and Valerie looked at each other, downcast. And then they were escorted out of the office by the silent Secret Service agent.

※

"All right," Clark said. "What do we have today?"

Valerie handed out copies of the schedule to Clark, Ambrose and Dan Harris, Clark's Press Secretary. The sun had not been up long, and the pale dawn shone in through the windows. The treeless courtyard looked desolate in this light. The air conditioning was broken again; it was going to be another hot day in the office. Ambrose, Clark, and Dan had already doffed their coats and ties and rolled up their sleeves.

"Meetings this morning," Valerie said. "Plastics Association at nine o'clock, Veterans for Justice at nine forty-five, you get a break, then the Airline Pilots Association at ten thirty."

Clark rolled his eyes.

She continued, "A tour group from Morgantown is coming through at eleven thirty. You're scheduled to shake hands and take a group photo on the capitol steps with them."

"And when do I get to do some real work?"

"Afternoon is a little better, sir; we've got a meeting with Senator Parkinson and his staff to talk strategy on the Skaggs Bill. We're holding back a tidal wave on this bill; Skaggs has more than a hundred co-sponsors now."

"We'll keep trying. Anything in the news?"

"Three major items," she said, and handed out another sheet. "Last night in Morgantown a white police officer shot and killed a twelve-year-old black boy—the kid was walking home from the grocery store, his mother was sick. Apparently the kid ran when the cops tried to stop him, so they opened fire. It looks pretty clear cut to me, based on the media coverage, but Mayor Scafella hasn't taken any action on similar incidents in the past, and the all-white City Council hasn't either. Expect demonstrations."

Dan, the press secretary, spoke up. "Al, we should work out a statement on this right away."

Clark assented. "Work out something this morning and let me see it. What else?"

"Second, the Grand Jury in Harpers Ferry has subpoenaed two DHS agents—a Lawrence Harris and a Ben Matley—in connection with the Highview shootings. DHS says they don't have to honor the subpoena. They're appealing. The attorney general was on Washington Talk this morning and announced that not only won't the Justice Department investigate the shootings, but they consider any similar claims to be frivolous and unpatriotic."

"What?" Clark cried. The others in the room gasped.

"I'm quoting him, sir. 'Anyone who says Homeland Security overstepped its bounds is making a frivolous and unpatriotic gesture.' He then suggested similar incidents would merit a stronger reaction."

"Dan," Clark said to his press secretary.

"Yes, sir."

"I want something on this today."

"Last item," Valerie said. "Y'all remember Dale Whitt?"

"He's kind of a crackpot, isn't he?" Ambrose said, raising his eyebrows as he looked at the papers Valerie had handed him. Whitt was well known in the office from his almost weekly letters and phone calls offering his perspective on every issue.

"It all depends on your perspective," Valerie answered. "Six weeks ago I would have said yes, but things have changed a great deal, and his perspective just became a lot more mainstream. He's putting out a petition to get a referendum on the ballot to amend Article I of the state constitution, and make it possible for us to secede from the United States."

"He's crazy," Dan said.

"Maybe," Clark said, "But this article is sympathetic."

"Exactly," Valerie said. "The Sunday editions in six newspapers ran long, detailed and sympathetic articles on him. Six of them. Not one critical comment. Look at this one in the Charleston Gazette. Front page center. Good photo of him. It makes him out to be a folk hero."

Dan smirked. "Valerie, that one's not worth wasting your time on. It's just a flash in the pan."

"We'll see," she said. "I think it bears watching. He's holding his first rally this weekend—in Highview, of course, because of the shootings. I would expect a huge turnout. Sentiment against the federal government runs pretty strong there now."

"Can you blame them?" Clark asked.

No one replied.

※

Murphy wasn't one for rallies, but he had to admit, his curiousity had gotten the better of him. It was Saturday morning, and there was nothing to keep him from having breakfast with his son at Sally's. Nothing except the fact they were broke, a nagging voice kept telling him. All the same, they had arrived early enough to get a booth next to the front windows, where Murphy could see across the street to the town square. He came armed with his pocket computer for Kenny—he would get restless soon—and a newspaper for himself.

Across the grassy square, two black Ford SUVs sat, their windows tinted almost black. Not far away from the vehicles, two men in suits stood in the shade of a tree, one shooting photos of everyone walking through the square with a high quality camera. Interesting, and very disturbing.

A few minutes before nine, Paul Machen drove up in his deputy sheriff patrol car and parked directly across from the diner. That could be trouble; the Mayor was pretty pissed with Dale Whitt. Murphy had gotten word that Whitt had been unable to procure a permit for his rally this morning.

Machen stepped out of the car and ran across the street, straight toward the diner. When he got inside, he walked to the counter and ordered a cup of coffee, then looked around. Murphy nodded, and Machen approached.

"Morning, Colonel. How's Valerie doing?"

"Morning, Paul. She's okay... Very busy, up on the Hill."

"Suppose so. You're here early, ain't you?"

Murphy shrugged and grinned. "Thought it might be interesting in the square today, Paul."

Deputy Machen scowled. "Ain't nothing happening in the square today, Colonel."

Without a word, he turned away and paid for his coffee, then walked out the door.

Murphy took a sip of his coffee and kept watching the square, as Kenny played a video game on the handheld. Dale Whitt's ancient brown pickup truck, loaded high with equipment, was pulling into the square. Voices in the restaurant dropped. Looked like Murphy wasn't the only person who had positioned himself to see events unfold.

Machen sat on the trunk of his patrol car and waited for the ancient pickup, which came to stop right behind him. Whitt stepped out of the truck, nodded to Machen, climbed into the bed of the truck and began untying equipment. Murphy could tell the Deputy was saying something angry from the expression on his face. Whitt looked up from the speaker he was working on, and said something to Machen with a winning smile, which seemed to infuriate the Deputy. The spectators in the restaurant gasped when Machen pitched his coffee cup at Whitt, narrowly missing him and the equipment. The Deputy stomped to his vehicle, a scowl on his face, then got in and sped off.

Whitt shook his head and continued his work. After a few minutes, apparently finished, he spread a campaign banner across back of the truck: "Whitt for Senate. Give me Liberty or Give me Death."

Murphy groaned. That was too much. Way too much.

Moments later Whitt made his way into the diner. He spotted Murphy on entering. "Morning, Colonel. Can I join you?"

"Only if you tell me what it was you said that sent Paul Machen off sulking like a two year old."

Whitt chuckled and sat down, then said hello to Kenny. The boy nodded, not looking up from his game.

"I just asked him if the sheriff knew he was here, or was he visiting on behalf of his daddy. Sure pissed him off. What do you think that means?"

Murphy nodded. "Probably means you're going to have some trouble with him before the day is out."

"I expect so," Whitt said.

The waitress approached.

"Can I get a cup of coffee?" Whitt asked.

"Only if you promise not to throw it at me," she said, her voice low and sly.

Murphy and Whitt laughed, then talked for a bit about local politics. These were dangerous times, but there was still local business to worry about, crops to bring in, coal to bring out of the ground.

Every time someone entered the building, the little bell over the swinging door chimed, and Murphy glanced up. So he saw the federal agents before Whitt did. Whitt went on talking about the latest news from Charleston until Murphy held up his hand, palm forward, signaling him to stop.

Two men, both in black suits and dark ties entered the restaurant. Both had the seasoned look of long-time DHS agents: well muscled, a little bit menacing. Earpieces in their right ears were connected to barely visible wires that led under their shirts. Both had bulges under their coats. Dark sunglasses made it impossible to see where they were looking. Their overall appearance was so stereotypical it might have been funny if hadn't been so menacing. Murphy reminded himself that just a few weeks before, he might not have thought of them as menacing at all. A lot had happened since then.

One of the agents went to the counter and ordered two cups of coffee. The other stood in the center of the room and scanned it, turning a full circle in the room, then stopped and seemed to fixate on the table where Murphy and Dale Whitt sat.

Everyone in the diner was silent as the two men stood there, one waiting for his order. Murphy's skin crawled; the fear in the room was palpable, the only noise coming from the cook behind the counter, and from his son's video game.

These are the men who are supposed to be protecting us, Murphy thought. *They've twisted that beyond all recognition.* Instead of protecting Americans, they watched them. Instead of guarding the nation's liberties, they were steadily eliminating them.

It turned his mind back to the Esther Rosen case, a few years back. Rosen was a private attorney, and something of an eccentric. She had taken on Hamas as a client in a federal lawsuit challenging their designation by the DHS as a terrorist organization, arguing that their humanitarian activities were separate from their militant ones. Rosen disappeared in the middle of the lawsuit. Media speculation had been rife: had she been kidnapped or murdered? Had her terrorist clients gone crazy and done her in?

Then she turned up in Australia, of all places, and told a story that should have been instructive to all Americans. She had been arrested by the DHS, and in a secret tribunal stripped of her American citizenship in the absence of counsel or any contact with her family. After four years, she'd finally been released and put on a plane out of the country, stateless.

The citizenship provision, passed in the early part of the century, had rarely been used, but it allowed for the government to strip someone of their citizenship involuntarily if associated with terrorist groups. Had anyone imagined it would be turned against attorneys in the middle of a lawsuit?

What struck Murphy about the case was that there was a temporary splash in the media, a small scandal, but one that wasn't that juicy—no sex, no murders, just a plodding beauracracy rolling over someone's life. He didn't know how it had turned out, what had happened to Rosen in the end. Was she still in Australia? Sitting here now, with this menacing federal agent staring at him in a public restaurant, he desperately needed to know. Murphy was no fan of anyone who dealt with terrorists like Hamas—he'd served in one too many combat zones dealing with car bombs and suicide bombers to have any sympathy for her. At the same time—secret tribunals and midnight arrests? That wasn't the country he'd grown up believing in.

The moment passed, and the agents got their coffee and left the hostile restaurant. Conversation resumed, though hushed; as if some residue from the DHS remained.

"Dale," the waitress called. "Isn't that your truck over there?"

"Hmmm?" Whitt said and looked up. A bright red tow truck had parked in front of Whitt's pickup, and the driver was jacking it up. Murphy shook his head. He'd known the thrown coffee cup wouldn't be the end of it.

"Oh, damn," Whitt said, and stood. "Heather, can I come back and settle up in a little while?"

"You go on."

Whitt stepped outside and trotted across the street. Murphy stood and leaned down to his son. "You stay here," he said. Kenny nodded, and Murphy stepped outside the front door.

Machen stood across the small street, writing in his citation book.

"Deputy, I suggest you stop this game right now," Whitt said, his voice pitched just a little too high.

Machen grinned. "What game is that, Mr. Red Communist? Is this your truck?"

"You know it is."

"Well, I'm afraid I'm having it impounded. As you can see, it is not displaying license tags, and it is parked illegally. You can pick it up at the County impound lot on Monday morning."

"God damn it, Machen," Whitt shouted. "You know this truck is licensed. What'd you do with the plate? Is it in your goddamn car?"

"Mr. Machen, you are dangerously close to obstructing an officer. I'm not going to have to take you in, am I?"

"I'll have your badge for this, you son of a bitch."

"Mr. Whitt, I'm afraid I'm placing you under arrest. Please hold your hands out to your side."

Whitt's face flushed. "I'll do no such thing," he shouted, inches away from Machen's face.

The younger man shoved Machen back, then reached for his belt and pulled out his baton.

"Sir, please place your hands behind your head, right now."

That was enough. Murphy stepped into the street and approached the scene. "Paul Machen, you know as well as I do this is wrong."

The deputy glanced over at him, his face red with anger. "I don't know any such thing, Colonel."

Whitt had stepped back from Machen, apparently realizing events had turned a dangerous corner.

"Deputy, you need to rethink this," Whitt started. He did not finish, because Machen cracked the baton across his chest.

"Hands behind your head, *now*. Lace those fingers together."

As Whitt complied, Murphy noticed a large crowd was gathering from around the square, watching the situation. They were folks early for the rally scheduled to start in a little over an hour. They did not look happy as Machen grabbed one of

Whitt's wrists and twisted it around behind his back, cuffed it, then pulled the other one down.

"Dale Whitt, I'm placing you under arrest for assaulting an officer, obstruction of an officer conducting official business, and for resisting arrest. You have the right to remain silent. You have the right to an attorney. If you cannot afford an attorney, one will be appointed for you. Do you understand these rights?"

"I also have the right to sue you for violating my civil rights. Do you understand that?"

"Personally," Machen answered, "you can kiss my ass with your civil rights."

Murphy spoke urgently. "Deputy Machen, you're making a big mistake."

"You want to shut the hell up, Colonel?"

Someone in the crowd hissed.

"Deputy's gunning to be a DHS agent," someone said.

"You gonna arrest us too?" a young woman shouted.

"Come on, Deputy. Why don'tcha arrest all of us. I'm sure you can make up something to charge us with."

Machen flinched back from the menacing crowd and shoved Whitt ahead of him, toward the patrol car. His eyes cut over to the federal agents across the square taking pictures with a telescopic lens.

"What you looking at them for, Machen? You gonna be a fed? Think they're going to come help you out?"

Machen shouted at the growing crowd, his face red. "Y'all go on home now. Ain't no permit to demonstrate. Ain't gonna be no rally anyhow, not with this scumbag in lockup. Go on home."

A burly man in jeans and a red t-shirt pushed his way to the fore of the crowd, his face almost as dark as the shirt, his expression murder. He spoke in a low, dangerous tone. "Why don't you make me, Mr. Deputy? Why don't you make us all?"

Machen turned his back, shoved Whitt into the patrol car, and closed the door. The speaker was Joe Blankenship, whose wife had been killed at the Saturn plant.

"Come on, Mr. Deputy. Looks like you belong over there with the feds, shooting up people who are just minding their own business. You going to shoot me? You going to throw me in jail?"

Machen looked around. His left eyebrow started to twitch. At least thirty people surrounded him now. He stood with his back to his patrol car.

"Y'all go on, now," he said, his voice no longer so confident as the townspeople—his lifelong neighbors and friends—surrounded him, angry. He got in the car and slammed the door. Joe Blankenship said something to the others near him, and set the others laughing as they looked in at him. Inside the car, Machen's face flushed. Blankenship pointed at him, made his fingers into the shape of a pistol, index finger extended, then pulled the "trigger." Inside, Machen looked bewildered, almost as if he was going to cry. He put the patrol car in gear and jerked forward too fast for such a crowded situation. A young woman barely had time to jump out of the way of the car as he sped up the street, away from the town square.

Murphy glanced back at the diner. Kenny still sat at the booth facing the window, playing his video game. He'd keep for a few more minutes. A few yards away stood Joe Blankenship, face still flushed. Murphy approached him, held out his hand.

"Joe," he said. "I'm so sorry about Mandy."

Blankenship took the hand and pulled Murphy toward him, grasping his shoulders. His face was twisted in anguish. "Thank you, Colonel. You know she loved working up there, always said you were a good boss. Look, we got to do something. Whitt's done nothing but the right thing, standing up for our rights. Now they've gone and arrested him. What the hell is wrong with the Sheriff?"

Murphy grimaced. "Somehow I doubt the Sheriff knew what was going on. Machen's daddy gave him his instructions on this one. What you need to do is talk to the press when they get here for the rally. Tell them what happened, and hold the rally without Whitt. You can get up there and speak as easily as he can."

"You think so, Colonel?"

"Sure, why not?"

"I didn't figure you would support this."

Murphy frowned. "I don't. But I'll be damned if I'll see Americans arrested because they have the wrong political opinion. Spits in the face of everything we are."

Blankenship clapped his hand on Murphy's shoulder, and his face screwed up, on the verge of tears.

"Mandy would want me to speak up. I'll do it, Colonel."

Chapter Twelve
June 27

A drop of sweat crawled down Morris' back as he stood in front of his assembled company. At 0800 hours, the sun already beat down on them mercilessly. It was going to be a hot day, over a hundred degrees. They stood on the edge of a parking lot, close to where their tents had stood for the last four weeks, next to the ruins of the shopping center. Damaged buildings and debris still scattered the area, but the Army's job was over.

"You've done a good job out here. We came into a dangerous situation a month ago, and each of you has seen things we'd have rather not seen. We'll talk more on that subject, quite a bit, but in the meantime, I want you to remember a couple of key points here. Because of your work, the Department of Homeland Security has been able to collect the evidence they needed to identify the terrorists, and yesterday afternoon they filed charges against those who were responsible for this terrible crime. Because of your work, the site was secured and civilians were protected. You can all be proud of yourselves for the outstanding jobs you've done. First Sergeant."

At his order, the first sergeant marched back in front. The men and women noticeably straightened as the no-nonsense NCO walked to the front of the formation. Morris might be the commander of the unit, but he knew that the enlisted men and women tiptoed around the first sergeant. In their lives, he was the one with the real authority. Though gruff and almost aggressive in his manner, he sometimes seemed like a mother hen clucking over a brood of chicks. The troops didn't know how good they had it.

"Load them up, First Sergeant," Morris said.

"Yes, sir."

Morris walked away, leaving the first sergeant to direct the company onto buses for the ride back to Fort Meade. Small puffs of ash and debris rose around his feet as he walked. He paused, squinting from the glare, and stared up at the still damaged mall. Workers had built scaffolding, and were replacing the blown out windows. It would still be weeks before the area was cleaned up, and probably years before the buildings were rebuilt or repaired.

Lieutenant Colonel Barksdale was talking on the phone when Morris approached. Morris stayed back a respectful distance while Barksdale finished his phone call.

"Sir, my company is loaded. We're ready to move."

Barksdale studied Morris, eyes squinted, like a teacher examining a problematic student. His comment came as a surprise to Morris. "Well, Captain Morris, despite first impressions, you've done a solid job out here. You should be proud of your company."

"Thank you, sir. They were well tuned when I arrived."

"All right, then. We'll see you back at the post. When you get back, have your folks clean and turn in their weapons, then send them home for three days. I'll plan to meet with you and the other company commanders at oh seven hundred hours tomorrow morning to go over next week's training schedule."

"Yes, sir," Morris said. Alicia would be thrilled.

Barksdale turned and walked away without another word, and Morris was left to wonder whether he was expected to follow the Colonel or if he'd been dismissed. Barksdale continued marching away without looking back, so Morris shrugged and headed back to the company. It was already turning out to be a scorcher.

Today Morris had completed his first month in command. Some month. He had wanted to be an officer in the Army ever since, as a fifteen-year-old kid growing up in Kentucky coal country near the border of West Virginia, he had seen his cousin come home from Afghanistan. Lucas Morris had been nothing but a lanky kid when he left for the Army. When he came home from Afghanistan, he'd become a man who commanded respect.

The military became a lifelong fascination for Morris, driving him to college as an ROTC cadet at the top of his class and on to the Regular Army. What was the alternative? Coal mining? He'd seen enough of that life.

Well, here he was, the tip of the spear, in command of a line infantry company, and half the time he didn't know what was coming next.

On the drive back, Morris and his driver didn't talk. Instead, he worked on notes for the upcoming weeks, including training plans and leave for the men and women in the company. He found it difficult to concentrate. He'd not seen Alicia since their last conversation, which hadn't exactly gone well. They had not written, only had a couple of brief telephone calls.

Not like the old days, he thought. Five years ago, they phoned every day when he was in the field. Hard to imagine what it must have been like in the military in the days before satellite phones and advanced communications. Two or three decades ago troops went overseas for years at a time without any contact with their families other than letters. During Morris' overseas deployments he was able to call home inexpensively on his personal satellite phone. Substantial communications power was now within the reach of lowest ranking private soldier. The world had indeed grown smaller. The hard part now was keeping the troops from taking their phones with them on guard duty, though being caught with one while on duty was treated as severely as falling asleep or drinking would be. Wasn't anything much worse than being in a concealed observation post and having your phone ring—except maybe losing your buddy because of it. Soldiering was serious business, and with a dozen or more combat deployments in the last two decades, it had become deadly serious.

But when he thought of home, a cold lump of anxiety twisted his stomach and stiffened his neck. No question she would lash out at him when he got home. Might be a day or two, or even a week, but within ten days at the maximum he would feel her fury. When it came, her verbal tirade would cut to the soul, and it always came back to the same thing: leave the Army, leave the Army. Live a normal life. Go be a lawyer or a CPA or a teacher or anything—anything other than a soldier. Be a congressman, like her father.

If he had a dollar for every time she'd suggested his military experience could help a political career, he'd be able to afford to buy his own election. He always wanted to point out that his military experience would help him where it mattered most: with his military career.

Ah, well, he thought. *Enough self-pity.* He would be home soon enough, and in a few days it would come, and then it would be over. Except every time it happened he wanted to go home a little less. *Let's face it.* If it wasn't for Savannah, he would have left her years ago. But even that was based on a false premise. If it weren't for Savannah, he never would have married her in the first place.

What a crummy thing to think. But sometimes he felt that cold. He tried to go back to his notes, but no luck. He just stared out the window. He'd be home soon enough. He brushed sweat out of his eyes and wished he were happy about it.

જ

Monday morning dawned unusually cold and wet in West Virginia, but that didn't stop the crowd gathering around the ramp in front of the Jefferson County Sheriff's Department. Karen tried to count. There must have been five hundred people out there, maybe more. Not much light yet, but not too dark to see the signs that read "Free Dale Whitt," "Recall George Machen," and one, "Give me Liberty or Give me Death."

She looked around, but did not see Murphy. Of course, he had a six-year-old son to take care of. Given the way things had gone recently, this demonstration was likely to be shut down by the police in a hurry.

The media was out in force, including the nationals like CNN and MSNBC. Good news. At least somebody was taking them seriously. Traffic was completely blocked: it was a two-lane road here in front of the Sheriff's Department, and the people spilled out into the street. She pulled her raincoat tighter as the water poured down.

Another look around, and there they were. The ubiquitous federal agents and their cameras stood across the street in the lee of the city government building. Every time she saw someone taking pictures now it turned her stomach. Were they building a file? Preparing for prosecutions? Karen had never attended a demonstration in her life; would this one be enough? *Bastards.*

At the door, Joe Blankenship shouted into a megaphone.

"Citizens of Jefferson County, hear me speak. Less than a month ago my wife was murdered, along with several others, by federal agents claiming we were terrorists, we were unpatriotic. Now, the man who stood up for us and spoke out for us is in jail. Why? Because he was foolish enough to speak out loud, and try to stand in front of a crowd and tell us what he thought. Is this the America you want? Is this the America you believe in?"

"No!" the crowd shouted back.

"You know, it was right there, at the courthouse on the corner, that the miners from the Blair Mountain rebellion were tried for treason. Sixty years before Blair Mountain, old John Brown was tried for treason in that very building, after trying to free slaves in Virginia. He was fighting against tyranny. The miners were tried and some hanged because they fought against tyranny. Because they asked for the right to speak for themselves, to vote the way they wanted, to live their lives not under the thumbs of rich men with guns. And you know who came out to fight against them? You know who came out to defend the gun-thugs and the dictator of Logan County? The United States Army, that's who. The very same federal government that murdered my wife last month. The very same men who stand across the street in their black coats, taking pictures of you right now."

Blankenship pointed his finger at the two men across the street. "That's right, I'm talking to you. Murderers!"

The crowd murmured, a dangerous tone, and the two men backed toward their car.

"Don't worry about them, they'll get theirs, one way or another." Blankenship said. "Today we're here for one reason. Dale Whitt was assaulted by a sheriff's deputy and thrown in jail, for nothing more than speaking out. It's unconstitutional, and it's wrong. I won't stand for it. Will you?"

"No!"

"Free Dale Whitt!" Blankenship cried.

The crowd responded with the chant. Karen was crowded in now; more and more people were packed onto the slippery sidewalk, possibly two or three hundred, the rest blocking half the street. She brushed the rain off her face and stared up at the steps of the building.

A ripple moved through the crowd, and Karen saw a man in a black raincoat walk up next to Blankenship. Sheriff Watson. He took the megaphone from Blankenship and held it to his lips.

"All right, all right, everybody pipe down a second and listen."

Tom Watson was popular in the county, and even in this circumstance the crowd listened.

"Folks, I know what happened. Here's the deal: Deputy Machen has been suspended until we can complete our investigation, and all charges have been dropped against Mr. Whitt. He'll be released in a matter of minutes. All I can say is I didn't know Machen had done this, but I accept full responsibility. First I learned of the arrests, unfortunately, was when I was called at home about an hour ago."

The crowd broke into loud cheers and applause. Karen clapped too, elated.

"Now," Watson said. "As soon as Mr. Whitt comes out, let him say his piece, and then I'm going to have to ask you to move on, because you're blocking traffic and it is Monday morning, all right?"

The crowd cheered even louder, until, five minutes later Dale Whitt walked out to the front steps of the jail. His eyes widened when he saw the crowd, and even more so when the loud cheer reached a crescendo. Someone in the back of the crowd began chanting his name, and the crowd picked it up.

Two television cameramen scrambled unsuccessfully to get around the crowd and talk to Whitt. They held their cameras high over the heads of the crowd to get a shot. The lights glared in Karen's eyes, and she shifted her position next to the wall, squinting.

Blankenship smiled and handed the megaphone to Whitt.

"All right, all right. Thank you so much everyone for supporting me. We're going to win this thing, you hear? We're going to win!"

The crowd continued chanting his name, and Karen realized Whitt had become a celebrity, a symbol for all the pain and anger these people experienced. It wasn't just about Saturn and the plant. It was about every time they looked at their paychecks and saw the federal government had taken half; every time they looked at the crumbling high school and the potholed roads, every time they sent their sons and daughters off to fight wars halfway around the world for vaguely defined principles that always seemed to come down to the corporate good, not the common good.

That was it. Damn the consequences, she was going to throw her support behind Whitt.

Chapter Thirteen
August 4

As the newest member of Harpers Ferry's small police force, Antoine Jackson's most frequent contribution to law and order was writing traffic tickets. But with Sergeant Teags out sick today, and Wilson still on crutches from the night he lost control of his vehicle in the rain and slid into a ditch up in Bolivar Heights, Jackson was the only officer available. Jackson suspected Wilson had a load on when he crashed his patrol car, but as the junior officer on the force, there were things he just couldn't say.

The result was that he was to be the "ride-along" for a federal bust this morning. As the agent from the DHS said, he was here merely to observe.

"Your assistance will not be necessary. This is a federal investigation, not local. You've been invited as a professional courtesy only. We're arresting a suspect in one hour, one Mark Wheatley, believed to be a dangerous anti-government terrorist."

The DHS agent went on. The suspect was under surveillance, on his way to work as a volunteer for Dale Whitt's senatorial campaign. Expected to be armed and dangerous. The DHS has the operation well in hand, thank you, but we'd like an officer from your department to be present for the proceedings. But only as a professional courtesy, you understand.

Jackson understood he was wanted here about as much as an IRS agent on April 15. The requirement for a local "ride-along" had come from Washington after a series of botched arrests and the violence at the Saturn plant in Highview at the end of May. The county prosecutor had subpoenaed some of the agents, and that had tied them the courts for weeks. Even though DHS won their appeal, they were trying to play a little softer now. So here he sat, in an unmarked car in the alley. It was only 9:00 in the morning, but the August sun glared in the curved glass windows. Perversely, the DHS agent who had retrieved him, Richard Whitcomb, kept the windows raised. Whitcomb wore a flak vest, and a helmet with a plastic shield rested on the seat beside him.

"You think you can maybe lower the windows a little? Or run the air conditioning?"

Whitcomb glanced at him with contempt, then looked back out the window without a word. They waited.

⁂

Though they lived in the same small town, no more than two miles apart, Dale Whitt had never met Karen Greenfield. Now that he had, he was enchanted by her. She was an extremely intelligent woman, assertive, and quite attractive. She was also half his age.

Romance had never worked out for Whitt anyway. He'd been married once, but Sarah had long since divorced him and moved to California with a new husband. Just as well. Didn't mean he couldn't think about it.

"Tell me about this Blair Mountain rebellion," she said. "I keep hearing about it from you guys, I don't know the story."

She sat across the desk from him in his new campaign office in Harpers Ferry, a grey, dark office in a second-floor walkup above a day care center. The hardwood floors were scuffed and scratched and had been painted grey by a previous tenant. The office seemed quiet—a few volunteers were working at computers or talking on the phone, but the level of activity they'd had just a few weeks before was diminished. Whitt looked into Karen's eyes and wished he were twenty years younger.

"Well, about a century ago down in Logan County a man named Don Chafin ran the county. They used to call it the 'Kingdom of Logan.' He ran the county, ran the polls, manipulated elections through violence. Back then you couldn't even get into the county except by rail, and he'd have his men at every rail station, and they would stop and interrogate anyone who came into the county. He was mean as a snake, and he had three hundred paid gunmen. It was brutal for the miners."

One of the volunteers, Mark Wheatley, approached, holding a chart with a pie graph.

"Sorry to interrupt, just had a quick question. Is this what you were looking for?"

Whitt examined the paper. "That looks perfect. Thanks, Mark."

"No problem," Mark said, and walked back to his desk. He was quiet, but a workhorse, and had handled most of the computer presentation work for the last several days.

"Mark's been with the campaign for about a week," he said to Karen. "Sharp kid, from down near Baughman Settlement and Front Royal. Anyway, all through 1920 and '21, there were bloody strikes and battles all over the state, particularly down there in Logan and Mingo. The miners were mostly homeless during that time, thrown out of their camps; whole families, thousands of them, lived in tents. Some bloody shoot-outs happened—in fact, there was a massacre down there in '20 or '21, and the governor announced martial law in Mingo County. In the summer of '21 an army of about 5,000 men marched on Logan County. Their goal was to throw out Chafin—or hang him—and unionize the mine. Two or three bloody battles—no one knows how many people were killed—and the Army was called in to deal with it. The miners were tried for murder and treason."

"Wow," she said. "I've got some reading to do. I'd heard a little about it, but not much. I didn't realize it was so... well, large scale." She looked at her watch. "I appreciate the history lesson... and here I am, supposed to be volunteering for you, keeping you tied up. I'll get going, and get these flyers out this afternoon. I have a job interview this morning."

"Well, good luck, and thanks, Karen. It's been a pleasure having you here."

She flashed him a winning smile and stood up. Waving to the others in the office, she walked out.

Whitt pulled a sheet of paper from his desk. Back to cold calling potential major supporters. Talking to a beautiful young redhead was much more pleasant.

He'd been sitting at his desk all day yesterday, calling a list of potential supporters to ask for their support and their donations. Cold calling was discouraging work under the best of circumstances. The surroundings did not help; the office was dingy, the windows were dirty, and it was time to do something to reenergize his campaign.

He needed to motivate people—both the volunteers and the donors. In the initial anger after the incident at the Saturn plant, folks were outraged and gave freely. The first four weeks of his campaign were exhilarating: large rallies all over the state, with tremendous response. As more time went by—almost three months now—the outrage waned. The DHS wasn't in the news any more, and Whitt had difficulty getting coverage as a third party candidate. He still had many supporters, but they weren't winning over converts.

Highview had just about dried up and blown away the way Tim Wagner had said it would in the last three months, as trucks came through, carting away all the property from the now empty plant. No one seemed to care. It was hard to tell how many people had left town—unemployment checks still came in for most of the workers, and most wouldn't leave until those checks stopped coming, if then.

But what could he do? It was sad that it took some monumentally stupid act by the federal government to get people to look beyond their personal circumstances. Or maybe it was the opposite: it took making those stupid acts personal for it to interest people. Well, if he knew the federal government, it was a matter of time before they would provide the motivation he needed.

One thing at a time. It doesn't pay to get sidetracked. Right now it was time to focus on running his campaign, which meant more phone calls. He picked up the phone and dialed.

A loud bang on the front door interrupted him, and he looked up from the phone startled. One of the volunteers nearly jumped out of her seat. Door wasn't locked; who the hell would bang on it like that?

※

The back door of the building opened and Officer Jackson sat up. A young red-haired woman walked down the alley and unlocked a car. Antoine studied her face. She looked familiar.

"Hey, I know her," Antoine said. "The redhead. She worked at the Saturn plant—filed a complaint against you guys after the raid."

Whitcomb glanced over at him, then lifted his camera and shot several pictures of her as she got into her car. She backed up, then drove out of the alley and turned down the street.

"Remember her name?" Whitcomb asked.

"Yeah, it was Greenfield. Karen Greenfield."

A drop of sweat rolled down Jackson's forehead. *Arrogant DHS agents.*

Five more minutes passed in silence. Jackson shifted in his seat as sweat dampened the back of his neck, and he told himself that if God wanted him to be cool, he would have been born with an air conditioner.

"All units, we go in thirty seconds. Countdown."

Jackson and the DHS Agent, Whitcomb, reached for their door handles.

"Positions."

Doors opened. Jackson followed Whitcomb and they met two other agents who had just exited their own vehicle at the back door of the building. More prepared to enter the front door, and two were even now entering the High Street Day Care to evacuate the kids if it became necessary.

The order came over the radio: "Go."

Whitcomb opened the door and the three agents burst upstairs, Jackson following. At the door on the second floor, they paused and waited to hear the other agents pound on the front door. As soon as the sound came, two agents forced open the back door and they charged in, weapons ready.

It happened too quickly for Jackson to follow. In one corner, an agent yelled "Get on the floor, get on the floor!" to the terrified volunteers. At the opposite side of the room, two more agents grabbed Dale Whitt. Jackson recognized him from television. Agents ran everywhere brandishing weapons.

And that was when everything went all to hell.

※

At the sound of the pounding on the office door, Mark Wheatley, the new volunteer, ran for the bathroom. Whitt watched him go, puzzled, then turned, shocked as armed men burst into the room, weapons raised, shouting "Federal agents. Get on the floor, now!"

Whitt jumped to his feet and found himself flanked by two men in black body armor. "Get on the floor."

Whitt got down on his knees and started to lie down on the floor when he remembered Mark, who had run for the bathroom as the agents arrived. What the hell was he doing? The bathroom door opened and a small olive green cylinder rolled out to the middle of the floor.

"Run!" shouted an agent. "Grenade!"

The thermite grenade ignited with a roar and bathed the room in intense white light. Whitt ignored the agents as he jumped up and ran for the door, slapping at burning hair on his head as he ran. He heard gunshots behind him, didn't know if they were aimed at him. At that point he didn't care.

֍

Officer Jackson felt the blast of heat through the back doorway as the grenade went off. The floor caught fire, along with a volunteer, who shrieked. He also caught a good view of the son of a bitch who'd thrown the grenade. Instinctively, Jackson raised his service weapon, a 9mm Beretta. He paused to breathe, and then fired three rounds through the door of the bathroom. The room was a conflagration, and Dale Whitt, the remaining agents, and volunteers all fled except one volunteer who rolled, screaming and burning, in the middle of the floor.

Jackson was forced back by the intense heat. The thermite grenade, still shining like a white-hot road flare, had burned a tight orange-white circle into the floorboards. A fraction of a second later, the hole burned all the way through and the grenade fell, out of sight. Into the day care center down below.

Jackson howled as he ran down the back stairs, two at a time, racing for the day care entrance.

֍

When Dale Whitt reached the ground floor he saw the DHS team already evacuating the day care. The entrance was a logjam, with DHS agents all over the place, screaming children streaming out of the day care. Other agents were trying to get back into the building, and now smoke poured out of the second floor windows. In the chaos, he'd lost his two handlers. Whatever the agents had planned, they'd clearly bungled it. Had they evacuated the kids?

The door to the day care at the bottom of the stairs that led to his office stood open. Whitt pushed past two agents, went inside and shouted, "Is anyone still in here? Hello?"

No response. He ran through the room; no one was there.

On the way back to the front door, he saw the darkening spot in the ceiling. The grenade burning through. Without a word, he ran for the entrance as the grenade fell through the ceiling and ignited the carpet.

An agent nearly shot him as he burst out the now cleared front door, covered in smoke and soot. One of them shouted, "DHS, arms up! Get over here."

He complied—no point in doing anything else. As he reached the appointed location, he said, "Someone want to tell me just what the hell happened in there?"

An agent, his face covered in soot, approached. "Dale Whitt?"

"That's correct. And your name?"

"Mr. Whitt, I'm Special Agent Aaron Madison. I'm running this operation."

"Well, Agent Madison, you really screwed up. You've got a whole hell of a lot of explaining to do. What the hell was this about?"

The agent responded as they heard the first sirens from approaching fire trucks.

"Mr. Whitt, we had information leading us to believe one of your volunteers, Mark Wheatley, was involved in a terrorist incident within the borders of the United States. He has been under surveillance for some time, and we moved this morning to place him under arrest."

Whitt answered, voice cold. "And what the hell were you thinking doing it here? Couldn't you have arrested him at home, or on the street or something?"

Madison shifted on his feet. "We are very interested in your connection to him, Mr. Whitt. We'd like you to answer some questions."

A shout interrupted them, as one of the agents ran up. "Madison, sir! The day care teachers just did a headcount; they're missing one of the children."

Madison blanched and ran away from Whitt. "*Oh, shit!* Can we get somebody in there?"

ॐ

Officer Jackson was trying to figure out how to get out. After seeing the grenade go through the second floor, he had run down the back stairs, then slammed open the back door of the empty day care. Doing a sweep through the now burning building, he found a four-year-old girl crouched in a fetal position, screaming, against the wall in the bathroom.

"Hi, honey. I'm Officer Jackson, I'm a police officer. We need to leave the building now."

She kept screaming.

Jackson walked to her and picked her up, gripping her by the arms as she struggled. "Listen to me, little girl. I'm a police officer; I'm here to protect you. We have to leave now. Understand?"

She nodded frantically. "Okay," she whispered. "I'm scared."

"Don't worry, honey, God is watching out for us both."

Carrying her, he walked to the door, which had closed behind him. It was very hot to the touch. He couldn't open it. The only window was a tiny thing near the ceiling, about thirty inches wide and maybe... maybe sixteen inches tall.

Only one thing for it. He walked to the wall and stood on top of the radiator, trying to open the window. It was coated with many, many years of old paint. He took out his baton, and hit the window, hard. It shattered. He scattered most of the glass away from the window, and shouted, "Hey, anyone out there? Anyone out there?"

He heard shouts outside.

"Listen up. This is Officer Jackson, I'm passing a little girl out. She's coming out right now. Help me."

He glanced back at the door, sweat dripping from his face. The door changed colors before his eyes, the paint darkening, swelling. He could hear a fierce roar outside the door as the fire consumed the main floor area of the day care.

He picked up the girl again; they were both slick with sweat in the intense heat. "What's your name?" At first his voice rasped from the smoke, then cleared.

"Melissa." She quivered in his arms, and he almost dropped her. He glanced back at the door, black now, the paint peeling off and flaking to the floor. Black smoke poured in around the edges. Oh Jesus, he wasn't going to make it.

"Melissa, I'm going to pass you through the window to the folks out there. I want you to listen up to whatever they say, got it?"

"Got it."

"All right, watch the glass."

He lifted her to the window, and a prayer coursed from his lips. His eyes watered from the smoke and sweat stung his eyes; he had to blink to see.

He heard more shouts outside. "There she is," someone said, and then he felt her weight lifting from his hands. *Thank God, at least she was safe.*

The door was now shrouded in smoke. Heart pounding in his chest, he jumped on the radiator and grabbed the edge of the window sill, slicing open his hands.

Behind him, the flames roared as the door burst.

※

Whitt reached the corner of the building a step behind Agent Madison, just as the little girl was pulled free. The fire trucks roared up the street behind them.

Two hands gripped the edge of the windowsill, and a police officer got his head and shoulders through. Two DHS agents ran to him as he struggled to boost himself through the tiny window. Then he disappeared, replaced by flame that burst out the window. The agents jerked back, one of them shouting in pain. Whitt cringed when he heard the officer scream. Then the screaming turned into an animal howl.

"Get back from the building," shouted a fireman who came running up the alley.

"There's somebody in there, in that room," shouted Whitt. "A police officer."

"We got it. Now get back, get back." He turned away from them and spoke into a radio. Whitt backed away, and so did the DHS agents. Several more firemen ran around the corner, and he watched as they took to the wall with axes, but it was too late. No one could be alive in there.

※

Five hours later, Whitt sat in the field office of the DHS, after interviews with a team of agents. In direct contrast to his own dirty, now nonexistent office, this small field office was well appointed, with fresh paint and an expansive view of the confluence of the Potomac and Shenandoah rivers a mile away. Sitting at a highly polished desk, drinking fresh coffee, Whitt waited to find out just when the hell he was going to be allowed to go home.

The questioners turned him over to the Special Agent in Charge of the Harpers Ferry field office, Justin Hagarty, after their interrogation ended.

The stereotype of a DHS agent was a well-built white male, tanned, with dark sunglasses. Hagarty was short, balding, and looked more like an accountant than an anti-terrorist agent. All the same, there was a conspicuous bulge under his navy blue blazer, and the other agents treated him with a level of deference Whitt found surprising.

Hagarty said Whitt was not under arrest; he was merely being detained for questioning. When asked how long he would be so detained, Hagarty did not respond. Instead, he put on a pair of reading glasses, opened his desk and began shuffling through paperwork. Whitt's eyes narrowed. It was a game, one Whitt did not feel like playing. He didn't care how long Hagarty could make him wait. The game simply proved what Whitt already knew: the man was drunk on his own power. After a moment looking through the papers, Hagarty picked up the phone and dialed. *Screw him.*

The room was small, but did not feel cramped, with the view of the river valley on one side. The floor was carpeted, the furniture expensive. It did not feel like a police station or a government office to Whitt. More like the offices of a high-flying corporation. *So this is where all the tax money was going.*

After a long wait, Hagarty finished his phone call, looked up from his papers and removed his reading glasses. He folded them and placed them in a leather case that he put in his coat pocket.

"Mr. Whitt, first of all I want you understand you are not under arrest, nor are you in any way a suspect in any investigation we are conducting. You can choose to get up and walk out of here right now. However, I'd like to talk with you, if you are willing to be cooperative."

Whitt shrugged.

"You have the right to remain silent, or to speak to an attorney. As I said, you can get up and walk out of here right now if you so choose. If we genuinely suspected you were involved in terrorist activities, we have the authority to hold you up to a year while we investigate. However, at this time the attorney general has not made that determination."

"I get it, although you know as well as I do holding anyone for a year without charges is unconstitutional. Still, I'm happy to cooperate, but I want an explanation from you. Your men killed one of my people this morning, and you are very lucky none of those kids got hurt today."

"Sir, if your volunteer Mark Wheatley hadn't been carrying explosives, we wouldn't have had that problem now, would we? He was the murderer here. That's what we'd like to discuss with you."

"You said something about him being involved with a terrorist incident. Are you saying he was responsible for that thing in Arlington in May?"

"I can't say, but I'm going to be straight with you, Mr. Whitt—you seem to be a straight shooter yourself. It's my job to protect our country from people like Wheatley, from terrorists, whether foreign or domestic. Understand that first. I'm not here to harass you. I'm here for your safety."

"That's why I've spent the last several hours being questioned."

Hagarty ignored the comment. "Now, since May we've been investigating this bombing in Arlington. The bombing got in under the wire—we didn't even have a whisper about it beforehand. However, as you know we recently made some arrests: a radical anti-government group operating out of the mountains of West Virginia. These are not nice people, Mr. Whitt. Mr. Wheatley was closely associated with some of them, and we became very interested when he showed up in Harpers Ferry."

Whitt interrupted. "You know, I've been curious about that. Did you know I've been down to Baughman Settlement? Did you know I know some of those folks?"

"We did, Mr. Whitt, which makes you of significant interest to us. Even more so, with Wheatley dead. How long had he been volunteering for your campaign?"

"Just a week, actually. Most of the new volunteers had pretty much dried up about three, four weeks ago. He was an exception—started last Monday. Just strolled in, said he wanted to volunteer, he was between jobs. Lot of folks in that boat right now."

"What skills did he have?"

"He knew his way around a computer. We had him doing cold-calls, asking for contributions and supporters. He helped put together some flyers and such, nothing too complicated."

"So why did he volunteer for you?"

Whitt answered, somewhat defensively. "I had to assume he shared my political views about the future of West Virginia."

Hagarty looked at Whitt, his face impassive.

"Can you just briefly outline those?"

"I think you know the answer to that," Whitt responded, bristling.

"Let me make sure I understand them. You advocate amending the West Virginia Constitution such that the state could become an independent country. Is that correct?"

"That is correct."

Hagarty leaned forward with a deep frown. "You know, Whitt, you don't strike me as the type to delude yourself. What makes you think anyone would go for this idea?"

Whitt leaned close to him and responded. "You and your pals are the reason they will."

Hagarty's lips curled up in an unpleasant smile. "I'm not here to argue with you. Whether or not you agree with our methods, I can't address that right now. Here's my problem. We've had a number of indications the same group has additional attacks planned, and we're trying to wrap them up before that happens. They have half a dozen people loose, absolute religious fanatics, and those people very much support your political agenda. But they aren't getting out the vote. They're killing people. Get the picture?"

"Look, Hagarty. I know those people. They aren't the types to be blowing up buildings. Hell, I couldn't get them interested in politics at all when I was down there—they just wanted to be left alone."

Hagarty leaned back in his chair. "Maybe they just didn't trust you, Mr. Whitt. You do have a reputation as a loose cannon. We've had our eyes on the group at Baughman Settlement for a while. At least two of their members are convicted felons; both were involved in assaulting a US park policeman on the National Mall eight years ago under somewhat bizarre circumstances. Circumstances that led us to put them on our potential terrorist watchlist."

Whitt sneered. "Am I supposed to be impressed? Nowadays if you buy the wrong groceries you get put on the watchlist. I bet I'm in your database. One week I bought falafel and ammonia and chlorine all at the same time."

"Don't be an ass. These people really are dangerous. You probably heard about the park policeman—apparently something in his mannerisms caused them to think he was homosexual. They tied him up and tortured him." Hagarty replied.

Whitt rolled his eyes. "Yeah, I know about the case. It's hideous, I agree. But a couple of bizarre crimes doesn't justify turning into a police state. Don't you get it, Hagarty? I'd like to have a safe society too. But the more you guys tighten your grip, the more you spy on people, the more you set people against each other, the more likely you make it so people will lash out. Terrorism doesn't happen in a vacuum, it happens as a response to intolerable conditions."

Hagarty spread his arms. "What, you think it's okay to blow up buildings?"

"Hell, no. But I'm also not stupid enough to think people do that sort of thing just for the hell of it. You guys are creating the desperation. Holy Christ—you took a loyal, hardworking American town and turned them into a town of people who hate the federal government. Innocent people were gunned down."

"Some of my agents were gunned down too, Mr. Whitt. I got pictures right in my desk." Hagarty reached into his drawer and slapped a photo on the table. "Here's Charles Dylan. He was married, two kids. Got blown away by some redneck with a shotgun at that plant of yours. I had to tell his wife afterward, and hand her a flag at his funeral. Yes, mistakes were made, but tell me, why the hell did your loyal hardworking Americans go to work carrying shotguns?"

Whitt leaned back in his chair, took a deep breath to calm down. "Look, Hagarty, when I look for who did something, I look for who benefited the most. And you know what? The way I see it, ever since Arlington, the DHS is getting new powers, more free reign. Nobody even questions the fact that you guys rounded up hundreds of American citizens after the bombing—for 'questioning'—and didn't allow them access to attorneys. Now Congress is talking about a new bill to make DHS even more powerful. Give me a break. If I wanted to look for a smoking gun, I'd look there."

Hagarty stood up, face red, and stepped back from the table. "I'm not going to debate with you. I've got a war to fight, and you don't fight wars by screwing around. I go home every night wondering if we go too far, if we harm the Constitution. But I'll tell you what, the Constitution isn't a suicide pact."

"You're wrong, Hagarty. That's exactly what it is. It's real Americans saying they'd rather die than give up liberty. That's what the Constitution is."

Hagarty stood at the window, looking out, shoulders slumped.

"Mr. Whitt, you are free to go. We'll call later this week with more questions, most likely. Please keep yourself available."

⁂

The sun had nearly set when Whitt walked out of the building. As he approached the glass doors of the exit, he was surprised to find bright lights and a knot of reporters. He stepped out and they clamored to get the first question in, shoving microphones in his face.

"Mr. Whitt, the DHS says you are not a suspect in the Arlington bombing. Can you make any comments about the incident today?"

"I certainly can," he answered. "Today is a perfect example of why West Virginia must be shed of the federal government. The DHS came into the office of a political campaign today with weapons drawn. Instead of making their arrest at the suspect's home, or on the street, they chose to do so in an extremely dangerous situation. They killed one of my staffers and endangered the lives of twenty children in the day care in our building. One of our brave police officers gave up his life to save the life of one of those children. As always, the federal government has shown a callous disregard for state' rights and the safety of citizens, and disrespect for local law enforcement."

"Did the DHS ask you about the Arlington bombing?"

"No, ma'am. I wouldn't have any information for them. They wanted to know about a volunteer, a man who showed up at our office just a week ago."

"So there is no connection between your organization and the Arlington bombing?"

"Of course not. Good God, those people, whoever they are, killed civilians. That's what we're trying to get away from, is the feds coming in and hurting our people. That police officer, and the children in the day care, and my co-workers and volunteers—*they* are the victims here, caught in the crossfire between a mass murderer on the one side and an overbearing federal government on the other."

"Will you continue your campaign to have West Virginia secede from the United States?"

"Absolutely. You know, when the United States was founded there were less people in the entire country than there are in West Virginia today. Democracy on this scale doesn't work any more. Not when the automatic response of the federal government is to shoot first and ask questions later. Not when our basic, fundamental freedoms are trampled on. Not when the government takes out far more in taxes than it gives back in services. And especially not when the government protects the very corporations that own and exploit ninety percent of the land in West Virginia while taking all the wealth out to New York and Los Angeles."

Another reporter jumped in, one he recognized: Maria Chase from the Charleston Gazette. Her articles had tended to be sympathetic to his campaign to date. "Mr. Whitt, were the petitions for the ballot initiative located in your headquarters?"

Whitt caught a breath, stopped short. "Yes, ma'am, they were. We're going to have to start over."

"You've only got a month to get the required signatures. Will that be long enough?"

"We will, of course, press for an extension under the circumstances. But it will have to be enough."

※

How the news reported the events of the day depended a great deal on where the reader or viewer was. In many ways, the reporting showed the growing gap in political beliefs among the editors rather than a divergence in the news.

For example, the evenings news out of Harpers Ferry's NBC affiliate opened with the statement, "A rookie police officer and college intern were killed in a bungled DHS raid today," then proceeded to give an account of the events. The camera lingered several seconds on the late officer's fiancée as she described their wedding plans, now cancelled.

In Washington, DC, Channel 9 News opened with, "A suspected mass murderer was cornered today in Harpers Ferry, West Virginia, where he was killed in a gun battle with the DHS. More news at eleven."

The Charleston Gazette, West Virginia's biggest daily newspaper, ran coverage sympathetic to Dale Whitt's campaign and the family of the slain officer, and excoriated the DHS for needlessly endangering the lives of children. The one-inch black headline on the front page read, "Officer killed saving child during DHS assault." A second article, also above the fold, said, "Petition signatures destroyed by DHS; Whitt reopens campaign for West Virginia Independence."

The DHS had provided just what Whitt needed. His movement had now become mainstream.

Chapter Fourteen
August 15

A grey squirrel perched, swaying on a branch, not far outside Ken Murphy's window. It looked around, alert, then ran down the branch and disappeared, leaving behind an unbroken view of trees. In a few more weeks, they would begin changing color, with the slow transition to another cold winter.

Summer had almost ended, and Murphy had been out of work for three months. Money wouldn't last much longer either, though the cash from selling Martha's flower shop would help him hold the line through the fall. He'd made ten cold calls this afternoon, after a frustrating morning interviewing with a defense contractor in McLean, Virginia. It was a long hike from Highview, but a job was a job. The manager who interviewed him was younger than Valerie and had dismissed Murphy's three decades of work experience as irrelevant.

He stared out the window at the evening twilight, eyes unfocused, his thoughts on the summer he and Tom found the holed boat in Peachtree Creek. Murphy was sixteen, his little brother six, the same age as Kenny. The creek was sluggish, swollen from rain, the air thick with mosquitoes. The summer had been sweltering, and some time in cool water seemed to be just the thing. He'd swum out and flipped the boat over after a struggle to get it out of the mud, then lifted Tommy over the side and climbed in.

Tommy had screamed and laughed excitedly as water started to pour in through the softball-sized hole in the bottom. The boat sank before they'd floated more than fifty yards, and they swam ashore and lay there in the sun.

Thirty years gone, and he still remembered his mother's biting lecture. Ten years older than his brother, and he'd risked that little boy's life—and lost one of Tommy's shoes in the bargain. It had been worth every minute of the lecture; they hadn't had so much fun all summer. Tommy still remembered it too; it was one of his earliest memories.

It was hard to believe the hardcore commander of the First Brigade, 101st Infantry had once been a laughing little guy who screamed and cheered as their boat sank in the muddy water. Christ, his blonde hair had turned grey, his face careworn and rough.

Where did the time go?

A scream jerked Murphy back to the present.

"Daddy!" The word trailed off into a wail.

Murphy ran to Kenny's bedroom. Kenny lay curled up in a fetal position on the floor, plastic army men scattered on the floor around him. His arms and legs twitched uncontrollably, knocking the plastic men about on the floor. His face was white, eyes wide and terrified. Tears ran down the boy's face as he clutched at his left arm.

Murphy gathered his shaking son into his arms.

"Daddy, it hurts, it really hurts."

He cried out again, jackknifed almost double.

Murphy held onto him and whispered urgently, "I got you, little guy, I got you. You'll be all right. We're just going to take a trip back to the hospital, okay?"

Kenny shook, and a moan escaped his lips. "Why don't it stop, Daddy? Please, make it stop. Please."

His face turned even more pale, and sweat ran down his forehead in tiny rivulets.

Murphy stopped a sob. "I'll do my best, little guy." He picked the boy up in his arms and carried him to the front room. "Kenny, I've got to set you down while I get my keys and stuff. Can you hang on until then?"

"Okay."

Murphy set him on the couch. He hurried into his office, gathered his wallet and keys, and the folder containing Kenny's medical records.

When he came back outside, Kenny gasped for breath, his face pale, eyes wide.

Murphy ran to him. "Kenny?"

"Daddy, I can't breath," he whispered.

At least he can breathe enough to talk. It would have to be enough. "We're leaving right now, little guy."

Murphy lifted the boy in his arms, then struggled to open the door. He left it open behind them, ran to the truck and loaded Kenny in. The sky was streaked with red. Murphy buckled the boy in, then climbed in the driver's seat and started the car.

He drove as fast as he could on the twisting, curving roads. After twenty years he knew the way well, and he pushed the bounds of safety as he raced around hairpin curves and over hills.

Kenny sat in his booster seat, curled up, leaning his head against the window. Every once in a while he would moan from the pain. The headlights from approaching cars lit up his face in a pale, washed out light. Each time, Murphy glanced over, straining to hear—was he still breathing? He would never, ever forget the sight of his son, then five years old, on a respirator, unable to breathe without a machine. *Please*

God, he thought, *just let me get him to the hospital in time. Please. Don't take my son. Take me, but not my son.*

The sky was dark when, tires screeching, he pulled into the turnaround at the emergency room entrance to the county hospital. He jumped out of the car and called out, "Please help," to the hospital workers who stood smoking at the entrance.

He lifted Kenny out of the car and hurried in through the automatic doors, brushing off the workers at the door who were only then putting out their cigarettes. The doctors met him at the door and lowered Kenny into a gurney. The emergency room doctor fired off a series of questions at Murphy, who handed over the folder with the medical records.

"It's all in there. He's been in here a couple times before, he has adrenoleukodystrophy. I'm worried about his breathing, he said he's having trouble."

They hurried into the exam room. "Does he take any medication?"

"He takes lovastatin daily, sometimes Tylenol with codeine for the pain, but not in the last couple weeks. Also dilantin, to control the seizures."

The doctor went back to work. Murphy stood, arms folded, and watched, aching to do something, anything to help.

He was helpless and it was killing him.

༄

Two hours later, Murphy stood riveted outside the intensive care unit, watching his son through a glass door. Kenny was breathing with the assistance of a respirator, and the rasping noise filled the room. He looked tiny under the weight of the wires and equipment piled around the room. The nurses and doctors in the ICU stepped around him with care, and lowered their voices as they spoke. *They must think he's not going to make it. It's a blessing he's asleep and can't see all this stuff. It would scare hell out of him.* Murphy wondered if it was time to call Valerie. With a quick intake of breath, he dismissed the thought. He couldn't give in so easily.

He felt a tap on his shoulder and looked around. Hal Perkins, Kenny's neurologist, had arrived. Respected as one of the top neurologists in West Virginia, he had still been unable to help Kenny.

"Dr. Perkins," Murphy said.

"Ken."

They stood together in silence, and looked at the boy. Ken could hear the monitors beep quietly.

"Ken, I think it's time we had a talk about long term options."

Murphy felt heat rise to his face. What was that supposed to mean?

"What I mean is... It's a matter of time before Kenny has a seizure and you won't get him here in time. He'll stop breathing and won't be able to start again. Kenny is a strong little boy, but this thing is destroying his nervous system. You saw his last set of test results. He's losing control of his extremities, and he's starting to get Addison's Disease—that's the increase in pigmentation; have you noticed how much he tanned this summer? His vision is also failing; he'll almost certainly be blind within a matter of months. Those are the beginning signs that the last stages of illness have been reached. In a few months he may lose the ability to walk. Do you understand the seriousness of this?"

Murphy felt his eyebrows twitch and his jaw tense. He spoke in a low, sharp tone. "Dr. Perkins, this is what I live with every day. I've been asking you and every other doctor on the planet for answers for the last two years. Don't tell me it's time to get goddamn serious."

Perkins held his hand up, palm toward Murphy. "Ken, you misunderstand. What I'm saying is, I... I don't have any answers for you. All I can do is watch him deteriorate, same as you. I do have a recommendation, however. Last month a team of doctors at Cincinatti published a paper describing an experimental treatment. They've only tried it with a dozen or so of the worst cases, but in at least a few of those cases results have been positive."

"How positive?"

"Don't get your hopes up; treatment failed in half the cases they described. In the other cases, the treatment arrested further deterioration, and the children have been able to continue normal lives, within limits, and with continued treatment. So far the oldest is fifteen. Understand: none have improved. No one is getting better, and you need to get that hope out of your mind. However, in some cases the deterioration was arrested."

It was something.

"Okay, how do we get signed up? I'm unemployed anyway, I might as well be in Ohio as here if it will help Kenny."

"Why don't we go down to my office and call them right now. I took the liberty of sending an e-mail with a summary of Kenny's case to the head of the program. We'll see what the situation is. I think your son will be a good candidate for the new trial. He's progressing... well, very quickly. It's a federally funded study—it may be we can get you in at no cost."

Murphy took a last look in at his little boy. The monitors were still running, and he was still breathing. Maybe there was some hope. Just maybe.

On Wednesday they left for Cincinnati.

BOOK TWO

Chapter Fifteen
September 12

Things just weren't coming together for Brian Ibrahim. For the second week in a row, he was working third shift, when there wasn't another soul in the Charleston Federal Building, and he could hear his steps echo on the marble floors as he walked his rounds, checking the empty offices, the parking lots, and the lobby.

He hadn't done anything to get the assignment twice in a row. But the new Security Chief, Ralph O'Malley—he was something else. Said he didn't like "towel heads." His brother had been a New York fireman, and lost some friends in the World Trade Center. O'Malley thought all the towel-heads should go back to their own countries.

Brian thought his new boss needed to take his foul attitude and shove it where the sun didn't shine. Brian had been born in Dearborn, Michigan, played on the football team, and then served as a Ranger and bomb disposal specialist in the United States Army. This *was* his country, whether that Irish bigot liked it or not.

The elevator reached the ground floor. Brian told himself for the hundredth time he needed to chill out. He was a student at Marshall University on the GI bill, and worked nights as a security guard at the Federal Building to help cover the bills. Normally—at least until the last couple weeks—he worked second shift only. Now he was suffering in school, just trying to stay awake.

As he stepped off the elevator into the cavernous lobby, he froze. The service door stood wide open, and the acrid smell of smoke drifted from the hall beyond.

Slow and calm, he unsnapped his holster and raised his pistol, a black .45-caliber Glock, and engaged the slide to chamber a round. He held the heavy pistol in front of him, the plastic-and-rubber grip warm in his hand. His heart pounded in his chest. Except for target practice, he'd not held a weapon in earnest since he left the Army. He walked toward the open door, keying the microphone he wore at his shoulder.

"Base, this is Unit Three. We've got a possible burglary in progress at the Federal Building, with an open utility door and smoke. I'm investigating at this time."

A tired voice issued from the speaker.

"Roger, Unit Three. I will alert the police and fire department and get them en route to your location."

Brian stepped into the dark doorway. Beyond, the normally brightly lit hall with grey painted walls and scuffed floor lay shrouded in darkness. Flashlight in one hand and pistol in the other, Brian stepped forward. He passed the light across the hall. No one. He took another step. His shoe squeaked as he stepped forward. This part of the building stank with a slight odor of garbage; just at the end of the hallway, the exit to the back parking lot opened beside the dumpster. Not so pretty in here: the marble floor of the lobby gave way to concrete, the walls unpainted drywall, grey and dingy.

"This is security. I'm armed. If you're there, come out now!"

His voice echoed. He leaned to his left and peered around the first corner into an open doorway. No one. Christ, why didn't he take the job at the college bookstore?

The DHS had shown up on his doorstep a week after the bombing, and he'd even been taken into custody briefly when they found his military records and realized he knew a hell of a lot about bombs. Brian almost lost his job over that one. The feds let him go—there was no reason to hold him, no connection at all, and he was, in fact, an American citizen, whatever the DHS might think.

Who the hell knew who was a terrorist? What if there was a bomb or something in the building? What if some redneck decided to get rid of the local IRS office to save himself from writing a check? A coal miner, pissed because the Bureau of Mines had turned down a complaint, ready to do justice to those government pissants? Time to find a new job. This one didn't pay worth a damn anyway.

He moved on to the next doorway. No one. Then he froze. What the hell was that?

In the utility closet, tucked behind the mop buckets, a cube the size of a cinderblock lay wrapped in burlap. Crude wiring ran to a cheap timer fuse. It was piss-poor work—whoever did this was a rank amateur. No question what it was though. The timer was counting down, already too close to zero.

He didn't have any tools, but his pocketknife would do, if he was careful. He wiped sweat off his forehead, suddenly hot, though it was only sixty-five degrees in the building. He'd done this a hundred times in the Army—in practice anyway. He examined the wiring, loosely wrapped around two posts on the timer. Brian held his breath and unscrewed the posts, then pulled the wires loose. His radio crackled again and he jerked.

"Unit Three, this is base. The police are arriving at your location. Switch over to their frequency at this time."

Brian keyed the mike at his shoulder. "Roger, base. Tell the police there's a bomb in here. I disarmed it but they'll need to call the bomb disposal team."

He reached down to his belt to change to the local police frequency, but he was too late. When the first police officer reached the front door of the building, the car bomb just out front exploded.

ॐ

Dave Hansen was the unfortunate officer who picked that moment to approach the front door of the Federal Building on Virginia Street. A rookie officer, his wife was at home asleep—or more likely awake—with their six-week-old daughter. His wife and daughter would never see him again, because the force of the explosion drove him through the plate glass windows, already disintegrating, fifty feet through the lobby of the building. Seconds later two hundred tons of steel, glass and concrete crashed down on top of him.

Dave's partner, Clinton, didn't live any longer. He had no family in Charleston except an Irish setter who would shortly find herself in the city animal shelter.

A third casualty, eventually identified from his military DNA records, was Scott Heuser. Scott was homeless, and slept on a bench at the corner of the building when he and the bench were thrown two hundred yards and slammed into the marquee of the Charleston Players Theater.

ॐ

Charleston Fire Engine 12 was speeding up Main Street, lights flashing, when the car bomb exploded. Just far enough away they weren't killed, the truck screeched to a stop when a flying concrete block slammed into the front and smashed the radiator.

"Holy shit!" screamed the driver. "Call the Chief, we're going to need some serious backup."

From there, the alarms went out, alerting the country that yet another terrorist incident had occurred on American soil. It would be some time before anyone realized these were the opening shots of a new war.

ॐ

The phone rang at 2:00 a.m. Slowly, Mike Morris rolled onto his side, reached out to the table and lifted the phone to his ear. Any call at this hour had to be bad news.

"Morris," he said, voice rough, disturbing the silence.

"Captain Morris, this is Sergeant Wilson. We're being alerted, sir. I've been instructed to inform you this is not a drill."

Morris grimaced. *Not again, so soon.*

"Thank you, Sergeant."

He hung up the phone and sat up, then opened the drawer of his bedside table. The alert list was folded in the side of the drawer. Each soldier on the list had another one to call, to ensure the entire company got the word quickly. Morris made his calls, then turned to Alicia. She was already awake, blanket pulled up to her neck, watching him.

"Hey, hon. We're being alerted again."

She was silent.

"Alicia?"

She rolled over and turned her back to him.

Morris sighed. "Hon, I have to go. I wish I had another choice."

He stood, switched on the bedroom light, then walked to the closet and pulled out his camouflage uniform.

Very quietly she muttered, "Bullshit."

He lowered the clothes he had in his arms and said, "I'm sorry? Didn't quite catch that?"

"I said bullshit," she responded, louder. "You have a choice. You could resign your commission. You've done your time playing boyscout. Mike, you've spent half our marriage out in the field or on deployments. I'm tired of it."

"Alicia, this is what I do. It's who I am. I won't resign my commission."

"If you leave now, don't come back. I've had it. I'll divorce you."

Morris did not answer. He pulled his pants and t-shirt on, and then buttoned his camouflage blouse.

"Did you hear what I said, goddammit?"

He glanced at her. She still lay there, flat on her back now with the blanket pulled over her body, the narrow vertical line between her eyebrows demanding a response.

He shrugged.

"Do what you have to do, Alicia."

Morris walked out the door of the bedroom and down the hall to Savannah's room. She lay in her bed, curled under the blue-and-white quilt Morris's mother made her last year for Christmas, the one with the pictures of queens, stars, and princesses all over it. Her mouth was slightly open as she slept—her nose was always stuffy from the ragweed this time of year. He could just hear her breath whisper through the gap between her two front teeth. One of the teeth was loose; it would be gone in another week.

It would be easy to walk away from Alicia. Impossible to walk away from Savannah. Looking at her, he thought about turning around, apologizing, trying to smooth it over. What would it be like for Savannah to grow up in a home poisoned by resentment and anger?

No. Time to move. Very quietly, he leaned over and kissed her silky, cool cheek.

His always packed field gear sat in the closet, ready for deployment. He slung the pack over his back, then walked out the front door. The light in the bedroom went out as he drove away.

༄

The phone next to Karen Greenfield's bed rang three times before she woke up. Foggy, she rolled over and put the phone to her ear.

"Karen, this is Vince Elkins," said the voice at the other end. The tone of his voice jerked her awake. She sat up in the darkness. "We've been called up by the Governor. Some son of a bitch blew up the federal building in Charleston."

"Oh, God, no," she said.

"We're on duty, Captain. Now you can say, 'Oh, God, no, sir.'"

"Roger, sir," she said, and wondered how he could make jokes in this circumstance. "I'll get my company moving. What time do we roll?"

"Zero-eight-hundred. I'll be in command; Colonel Murphy is out of state for a while. We'll be truck mounted for the time being—infantry. This job is going to be guard duty."

"Yes, sir."

"All right, get in as soon as you can and get your company moving."

He hung up without a further word. She switched on the light, walked to her desk and picked up the cordless phone. Even as she pulled out her field equipment, she started making calls. She didn't have much time.

༄

Even as the military geared up to surround and protect the now demolished building, civil authorities had arrived at the scene—a scene of chaos at this point as dozens of fire trucks, ambulances and police cars descended on the area. Three helicopters from the 130th Airlift Wing at Yeager Field circled over the site, warning away civilian and news choppers. High above, two fighter jets arrived on station to fly combat air patrol. Air traffic into and out of Charleston was grounded. The local emergency personnel had been first on the scene, and worked to define the extent of the damage.

Just as with the Murrah Building in Oklahoma City twenty years ago, the entire front of the building was sheared off, with most of the top three floors crashed down into those beneath. Downtown Charleston lay under a blanket of smoke and dust.

Across the street several partially vacant office buildings were seriously damaged, but no one had been present in the building at the time of the explosion.

Twenty minutes after the blast, fire department and rescue workers started to clear a path to the Federal building and cordoned off the area directly surrounding it. Urgent calls went to the various agencies to determine who might have been in the building at 3:00 a.m. Initial returns indicated the only individual expected to be there was the security contractor, Armor Security.

The name of the employee on duty? Brian Ibrahim. An Iraqi-American.

⁂

Unaware of the feverish activity taking place a few dozen yards away, Brian lay on his back and prayed he would have the opportunity to escape.

The tiny cavity he occupied was too small to sit up. He couldn't move—in fact, he couldn't feel anything below his waist. Couldn't see either; he was in absolute darkness.

Very slowly, he stretched his right hand and arm. He was unable to touch a wall to his right, but to his left he could feel a wall. A pillar of concrete lay across his waist. He could feel it with his hands, but not where it rested across his waist and legs.

Brian knew what that meant: it had crushed or severed his spine. Which meant, if he got out of here alive, he would be in a wheelchair.

Better a wheelchair than dead. The real trick would be to live through this. Rescue workers must be looking for him by now, but Brian forced himself to be serious. They'd never even found all the bodies in New York, and Brian couldn't help but wonder just how many people there were here like him, crushed but alive, lying there for how many days before they suffocated or starved or burned to death, with months to go before the rubble was cleared.

Christ, what the hell was he thinking? *The radio!* He reached for the radio handset at his shoulder.

"Anyone out there? This is Unit Three. Base? Can you hear me?"

No response. He waited, then sighed. Either the radio couldn't work under all this rock, or it was damaged. Or the dispatcher was off taking a piss at the worst possible time, who the hell knew?

He tried to reach for his cell phone left-handed, and gasped at the sharp pain. Arm might be broken, or at least strained pretty badly. Could he reach across his body with his right arm? He reached across his chest with his right hand, trying to find it. No phone. It might be just two feet away, but might as well be two miles.

He was stuck.

⁂

Though Brian didn't know it, things weren't going any better for him on the surface. Ralph O'Malley, his boss, stood at his front door three miles away in a stained white t-shirt, talking to a DHS agent who was beginning the already fast moving investigation.

"I'll tell you what I think," O'Malley said. "I'd bet it was that Ibrahim guy. You haven't found him yet, have you?"

"I can't answer that."

"Yeah, I bet you won't, he's probably long gone now. I never trusted that guy. Understand, I don't have nothing against towel heads in general, but it'd be nice if they'd stay in their own countries, if you know what I mean. Anyway, this guy Ibrahim had a bad attitude. Always kept to himself, real loner type. I'll bet he blew up that building for Allah then hauled his ass back to Egypt or some place. You should round up some of those folks in Little Cairo or whatever the hell they call it. Someone there will know what happened, that's for sure."

The agent nodded, then said, "I'd like to get Ibrahim's personnel file, if that's possible. Can we drive to your office?"

"Yeah, just let me get something on, all right?"

The agent nodded and took out his phone and made a report.

༄

Murphy watched the news in his hotel room as the sun rose outside. Images of the collapsed building flashed on the screen as the commentators discussed the "Middle Eastern" connection.

As bad news frequently does, word of the bombing spread quickly. Before the sun came up, DHS already had a prime suspect and a leak to the media: one Brian Ibrahim, a security guard who had access to the building, a loner from out of state who kept to himself, an Iraqi who had a high degree of expertise in explosives.

Murphy had received the alert call at three in the morning. Three months ago, he would have welcomed the chance to have some income, put his unit to work, to make something out of a disaster. Now… Kenny was in the hospital, seeing some progress. Murphy didn't want to leave, no matter what the circumstances were.

But he had a job to do. His mother was already on a plane from Atlanta, and would watch over Kenny for the next two or three weeks, the longest period the alert could be expected to last. Once she was here and introduced to the hospital staff, Murphy would drive to Charleston.

The good news was Kenny was responding to the therapy. They'd been in Cincinnati for three weeks, and no attacks since then. Not even a muscle spasm. Kenny was happier and more playful than he'd been in over a year.

The phone rang, and he almost pounced.

"Murphy," he answered.

"Colonel, Vince Elkins. We're at seventy percent now, just a few stragglers. We're not going to get 'em all—several people were on vacation; no one was expecting a call-up order. We've also half a dozen people who moved away, no one seems to know their whereabouts. Probably left the state looking for work."

"I figured as much."

"Yeah. Well, get this, sir. I got a call from Charleston about an hour ago; the initial order was go deployed as infantry, but now we've got orders to load up half a dozen tanks as well. What the hell are we going to do with tanks in Charleston? It sends the wrong message, sir. Anyway, I assigned that one to Captain Greenfield's company."

"Good."

"I also had Corporal Adler go to your house and break in, sir. He got your uniforms and field gear, so you can meet us in Charleston, no need to drive all the way hell out here. He says he didn't do any damage or steal much else."

After a brief pause Elkins said, "I didn't press him for details."

Murphy had to smile. "Well, Major, I will hold you responsible if he did. Fair?"

"Sure, Colonel: but only if you can prove it. We'll meet you in Charleston."

Chapter Sixteen
September 12

Agent Justin Hagarty scrambled his team from Harpers Ferry and arrived by helicopter in Charleston at 5:30 p.m. Despite the urgency of the situation and the desctruction across the street from the command post, they'd been standing around for an hour, waiting for the Charleston Field Office to get in gear.

Hagarty had offered his help, but Aaron Manning, an outsider from Chicago and the local Special Agent in Charge, refused it. Hagarty had worked with Manning before, and he knew that as an out-of-stater, Manning didn't get how West Virginia worked. They'd been at loggerheads ever since June and the Saturn Microsystems screwup anyway. Manning had insisted they go in there in force, whatever the consequences, and left Hagarty holding the bag. What were they, Nelson Barclay's personal police force?

Now this. What a mess. At least the building had been close to empty: the Charleston Field Office, located on the third floor of the federal building, had been completely destroyed. On top of that Manning had ordered that DHS deploy in combat gear with helmets, as perfect a case as Hagarty had ever seen of closing the bard door after the horse escaped.

Aaron Manning came into the musty tent they were using as a temporary command post, followed by two other agents. Rain rattled against the canvas. Electronics gear in an armored personnel carrier provided communications to the outside world.

Twenty-five agents from both the Charleston and Harpers Ferry field offices—all of them wet from the rain—crowded the tent. A layer of steam floated near the ceiling.

"All right, listen up," shouted Manning over the rain. "We're going over this quickly, we've got a lot to accomplish in a short time. Here's what we know. At approximately 1:00 a.m., the night security guard for the federal building called into his dispatcher that he was investigating smoke and a possible burglary. A few minutes later he called back, just as the first emergency personnel arrived on the scene. He indicated to his dispatcher that he had found a bomb. The dispatcher received no

138 | Republic

further transmission. Less than a minute later a car bomb killed the first responders and destroyed the front of the building."

Manning gestured to another agent, who handed out color-copied photographs of an olive-skinned man in an Army uniform.

"This is our prime suspect, gentleman. His name is Brian Ibrahim. He is a US citizen of Iraqi descent and an explosives expert, thanks to training provided by Uncle Sam. Mr. Ibrahim worked for a local security contractor, and was on shift at the time of the explosion."

Hagarty glanced over at Larry Harris, one of his senior special agents. They'd known each other five years, and didn't need to say the words. It figured he'd been trained by the Army.

"Now," Manning continued, "we have some other people we're looking into."

The other agent passed out another sheet. This one held two smaller photographs.

"The woman on the left is Sasha Zana, Ibrahim's girlfriend, of Kurdish descent. The man is Mahmoud Kamel, a Palestinian. All three of them recently made anti-American statements at a pro-Palestinian rally just two weeks ago."

Manning turned and pointed to a map attached to a tripod, already marked.

"Okay, here's the plan. First, the Charleston office. Wilson, your team will cover the main site, work with the forensics and rescue teams to look for evidence, or for Brian Ibrahim if it turns out he stayed in the building when the bomb went off. Don't assume he left—these people do suicide bombings all the time. Marcus, I want you to split your guys up, follow up with Ibrahim's past employers, with the University, all the local police departments. I want to know everything about his movements in the last three months, as well as the movements of Zana and Kamel. Hagarty, how many men did you bring from Harpers Ferry?"

"Eight."

"Okay, good. You'll cover Little Cairo. You know the area? This whole part of town was flooded by immigrants, mostly from the Middle East, around ten, fifteen years ago, about six square blocks. You've got two missions: first, find any of our suspects, and second, look for targets of opportunity. Anyone you think might be an illegal, or might know something, detain as a witness. We'll sort them out later this week. We've borrowed a couple of buses from the Department of Corrections."

Hagarty grimaced. "You're kidding, right?"

Manning frowned. "No, I'm not. The Secretary has authorized a house-to-house search."

"All right. The civil libertarians will go bananas on this one. Do we have a warrant?"

"Civil libertarians, my ass. Anybody notice the pile of smoking rubble across the street? This is the second terrorist attack in six months, and we know there's a Middle Eastern connection this time. Anyway, the Secretary is working on a warrant, don't worry."

"All right, we're on it. I'll need some bodies to contain the area; I can't do it with eight guys."

"There's a National Guard unit detailed to provide perimeter security when you start. Until they arrive, just post your men at the intersections and watch for the prime suspects. Once you've got your perimeter, proceed with the rest."

Hagarty shoved his hands in his pockets.

"We're on it."

A few minutes later they broke up, and Hagarty stepped outside into the rain. Carefully shielding his lighter under his helmet, he lit a cigarette.

Seconds later Larry Harris joined him. Harris had seen better days. There were dark circles under his eyes now, and unusual stress lines split his forehead.

"Hey, Harris. How's it going?"

"Not good, boss. Not good. We don't need any more screwed up operations. Manning… He doesn't get it, does he?"

"Yeah, I know. This is going to piss off a lot of folks."

Harris lit his own cigarette, took a deep drag, then exhaled. "I need to take some time off, and soon. Sarah says I keep waking up the kids at night."

Hagarty looked over at Harris. "Nightmares?"

Harris shrugged. "It's been a really bad year. That guy Matley shot, then the godawful mess in Harpers Ferry last week. You weren't there, boss. When that asshole threw the grenade, the volunteer who got it went up like a torch. I never even saw her before she went up in flames. And the cop—man, he was right out of college, very young. Said he'd been with the force about eight months. What a waste."

Hagarty put his hand on Harris's shoulder. "Look, Larry. How long you been doing this? Seven years? Maybe you do need a break. It's been pretty bad lately."

"Yeah, it has. Seems like it's getting worse. We've had—what, ten, fifteen incidents in the last two years? I just don't know if I can take it. Seems like every step we take, the terrorists get smarter and more dangerous."

Hagarty squeezed his friend's shoulder. "Larry, stick with me through this one. Do that, and I promise I'll get you a leave of absence, six weeks or something. Can you do that?"

Harris bounced his head, took another drag. "Yeah, that sounds about right. Six weeks away from all this."

"Just remember," Hagarty said, gesturing at the smoking pile of stone and steel, "Every day you do your job, you're keeping your family safe from that. You know we got a confession from the leader of those people at Baughman settlement?"

"Yeah? I hadn't heard that."

Hagarty nodded. "Just yesterday—it's being kept under wraps until they have the case ready for trial. Fucking religious nuts. It was all about gays, believe it or not."

"*What?*"

"Exactly my reaction. You remember about fifteen years ago, that Baptist church that was going around picketing soldier's funerals during Iraq? *God hates fags?* This guy was one of their converts, and he decided to go a little further than insulting people."

Harris shook his head. "Jesus Christ. What happens next? Will the confession hold up?"

Hagarty caught the subtext of his question. "Yeah – this one was by the book—no coercion involved. He practically dictated a manifesto."

They looked at each other, and Hagarty grinned. "We'll get the folks who did this one, too. Don't worry."

Harris shrugged. "All right." He shook his head. "Wonder if this was some of the same folks."

"Could be," Hagarty replied. "Could be."

ॐ

By the time the sun rose, a torrent was pouring down on West Virginia.

Surrounding the chaos around the federal building were dozens of emergency vehicles from as many jurisdictions, in some cases blocking streets and preventing access to others. Over a hundred people were working on the site now, searching for survivors. A massive plume of smoke filled the already dark grey sky, even as the rain poured down.

Despite the rain, spectators crowded the streets for three blocks beyond the police barriers, watching the disaster unfold so close to their homes.

Brian Ibrahim remained unaware of the rescue efforts above as he lay in the darkness, succumbing to shock and fever. He'd been thinking about Sasha. He closed his eyes and it was like she was really there with him. Sasha was… amazing. Long black hair, full figured, red lips, beautiful. Her family was Kurdish, but she was mostly punk rocker. He hadn't seen her in a couple of days, and found himself regretting it now. Of course, even if he got out of here, she probably wouldn't have much to do with him anymore. She wasn't going to push him around in a wheelchair at the club; that's for sure. And he knew nothing down below was going to work anymore.

He sighed, stretched out his right arm for the hundredth time, trying to find the phone. What if nobody found him? He didn't know how long he'd been here. Couple days, maybe? His stomach was in an agony of hunger, but worse, he was parched, as much as he'd ever been in his life.

Wait—a noise. Then he heard them more clearly: voices, faint.

"Hey!" he tried to shout. Nothing came out but a faint rasp.

Dammit! He tried again. "Hey! Is someone there? Hello. Hello. Help!"

He couldn't get any sound out. Bang something. He grabbed one of the many pieces of broken concrete with his right arm and banged it on the column resting across his body. "Hey!"

He banged a few times, then waited. He heard shouting. "We found somebody." The voices were still very faint, but it was clear they knew he was here. He'd been found. Thank God. He'd been found. A tear rolled down his cheek. He'd been found. He would see that beautiful girl again. He would have a life. Oh, thank God.

♫

Fifteen feet away, rescuers were trying to clear the rubble near the back entrance of the federal building. This side of the building was surprisingly intact. In fact, the first fifteen feet of the service hallway lay virtually untouched, except by dust. Slightly further in, the walls and ceiling had collapsed. Somewhere under the pile, they could hear tapping.

"Careful," one of the men said. "We don't want to shift the rubble and kill whoever's in there."

Slowly, carefully, they worked, joined by another group of firemen, along with one man in a DHS windbreaker, who stood back near the entrance, not helping. The firefighters carefully avoided him.

"Found him," someone shouted. What they had found was a main support column with two blackened feet sticking out from under it. The legs were crushed. The DHS agent, Bob Horvath, grimaced: the legs looked like the Wicked Witch of the East's did after Dorothy's house fell on her. With any luck, Brian Ibrahim wouldn't get off so easily.

Quickly, they cleared the rubble on the other side, lifted a collapsed wall and there lay Brian Ibrahim, the security guard and probably the bomber. Brian's face was washed out, and he was clearly in shock, but his eyes were open and alert.

Even as the firemen worked feverishly to lift the column, Horvath came forward and knelt beside the crushed man.

"Brian, it looks like you're going to be okay. These guys are going to get you out of here and take you to the hospital. You'll be as good as new."

The pale young man looked up at him, eyes wide. "My legs?" he whispered.

Horvath frowned. "They're hurt pretty bad, but you'll be fine. You'll see."

Brian sighed in obvious relief and closed his eyes for a moment. "You got any water?"

The agent leaned close and looked Brian in the eyes. "In just a minute. I need to ask you something first. Do you know who did this?"

Brian's eyes opened. "No. Do you have any leads yet?"

"Well, we've got a pretty good idea. That's why I'm talking to you."

Weight shifted on the heavy column and Brian cried out in pain.

The agent took his chance. "You did it, didn't you? This was supposed to be a suicide bombing, right?"

Brian looked at him, his face contorted by pain and sudden anger. "What are you talking about?"

"Come on, man. We know all about you, we've dug up your entire background. We know about your friends. You can go ahead and tell me."

"Are you crazy? Get away from me."

"Look, we already know everything, and it's not going to go well for you. Better you tell me now. Who were you working with?"

Brian grimaced. "Just get me out of here. I didn't blow up shit, asshole, and if I wasn't stuck under this pillar I'd jam my foot so far up your ass, your eyes would bug out. Get away from me!"

The agent shook his head and sighed. Nobody was going to just go around killing people and blowing up buildings in this country. Not any more. Not if he could help it.

※

Two hundred miles to the north, Karen Greenfield stood in front of her company. The wind and rain whipped against her plastic olive raincoat, and water streamed off the front of her helmet.

"Men, I want to impress upon you the seriousness of this situation. West Virginia has been attacked by terrorists. In Charleston right now the federal building lies under thousands of tons of rubble, and no one knows how many people may still be in there. Our job in this is to provide security. The Department of Homeland Security will conduct the investigation, with assistance from other federal agencies."

Some of the men in the ranks stirred at the mention of the Department. They weren't exactly that fond of the DHS. Not any more.

"Couple of guidelines. Unless your life is in imminent danger, you will not lock and load your weapon. Platoon sergeants will issue ammunition, but there are to be no incidents. It's highly unlikely there will be any need for any of us to do anything other than stand around and look mean. I want to keep it that way. We are going to instill confidence, bring calm to the situation. Investigations and whatever else will be the job of the federal authorities.

"Now, one final comment. I am all too aware many of you—many of *us*—have very intense personal feelings about the DHS. Set them aside. We have a job to do, and we have a common mission. I don't want to hear a peep about it. Got it?"

The men were deadpan, but she knew anger lurked just under the surface. A dozen of these men had worked at Saturn, and had seen firsthand the senseless brutality.

"First Sergeant," she called, and stepped back. The first sergeant dismissed the formation and directed the men onto buses, except the tank commanders. They would be accompany their tanks, loaded on flatbed trucks, to Charleston.

As the men boarded the buses, Major Elkins approached Karen. She saluted, and he returned it.

"Sir, we're at eighty percent now. Best we can do. I've got six men who have moved away in the last six weeks to look for work."

"It'll have to do."

"Any news, sir?"

"Not much. The radio said they know who did it, some Iraqi student."

She shielded her eyes as a gust of wind sprayed icy cold drops of water at them. "Seems pretty early to say who did it. It's only been a few hours. I don't trust the DHS, sir."

"I know what you mean. You're not old enough to remember Oklahoma City, but everyone assumed it was a Middle-Eastern terror attack then, too. Pretty big shock for everyone when they caught Tim McVeigh."

"Well, I'll make sure my guys know to keep their opinions to themselves. Charleston has a pretty big Arab community. I don't want us making the situation worse."

"Good deal, Karen. Let's get this show on the road."

"Yes, sir." Karen saluted.

He returned the salute and walked away. She stayed and, for just a moment, watched the dark clouds roil over the mountains, then walked to her HUMMWV.

Corporal Stanson, her driver, sat behind the wheel, rocking his head and slapping his hands on the steering wheel, the tune of music inside his head.

"Let's go, Corporal."

"Yes, ma'am," he replied, and put the vehicle in gear. Once they were moving, he tapped the steering wheel again. She wondered what the song was.

⌘

"Watch out, watch out!" shouted one of the firemen as they struggled to lift the rubble from Brian Ibrahim.

Brian's vision faded as he watched them, long since gone into shock. He'd been there for hours by the time they found him, and two more passed as they tried to remove the crushed steel and concrete without killing him. Soon, he thought, it would be too late. Everything seemed so fuzzy, he hardly cared. Only real problem was the cold. But at least he couldn't feel any pain. One of the feds took great pleasure in describing Brian's blackened and crushed feet and legs to him. *Son of a bitch.* How could they think he would do something like this? A wave of darkness washed over him and his already grey world went black.

From deep underwater he regained consciousness to see two doctors at his feet. He heard a whine, like a dentist's drill. What was that?

"What's going on?" he asked groggily. "Am I going to die here?"

."We're trying to get you free—we have to get you to a hospital now. Try to stay calm," said one of the doctors.

Suddenly it hit him: they were preparing to amputate his legs.

"No way. Get… get away from me." His voice weak, he said, "I want to talk to a priest. Let me see a priest."

Brian saw blood splash on the concrete and he started to cry. His vision went black.

Five minutes later Brian Ibrahim made it to the ambulance, but it was too late. He was dead.

෴

The rain was really pouring down now, and Murphy had to slow down to a crawl. The Secretary of Homeland Security was holding a press conference live on the radio. The threat of terrorism was still out there. DHS needed more domestic powers to do their duty.

Murphy gripped the steering wheel tighter as he listened to the words on the radio. As if they didn't have too much power already. How dare they use a tragedy of this magnitude to advance their political agenda? He'd had it up to here with politicians.

His car slid as a giant truck thundered past in the rain, throwing water off the highway in a great wave. In a moment it was gone, taillights fading into the distance.

He glanced at the clock. Another hour at this rate before he reached the Capitol. Maybe two. He'd hated leaving Kenny behind, even with his grandmother. The boy had been better since they'd arrived in Cincinatti—better than he had any right to expect. Murphy knew as well as anyone that no recovery was possible, but if they could just keep the goddamn disease from progressing, that would be enough. It had to be enough—he didn't have any other hope.

෴

Captain Karen Greenfield's HUMMWV rolled into Charleston at fifteen minutes before noon. The convoy, including two buses of men, the supply truck, the first sergeant in his Humvee, and the four very large trucks with tanks on their flatbeds, followed her. As they drove into town, people stopped and stared at the camouflage painted behemoths. Even on the back of a truck, with its 120mm cannon locked over the rear deck, an Abrams tank was a frightening machine.

After the events of this morning, Karen thought it ominous to come into an American city with tanks. Who was this designed to frighten? The terrorists or the citizens? Or did the DHS not make a distinction any more?

Fifteen minutes later she stood with Major Elkins and the other company commanders in Elkins's temporary headquarters, a basement office in the State Capitol.

She took notes in a pocket-sized green notebook as Elkins laid out where each company's positions would be.

Karen's team was split: the tank platoon would be positioned around the state Capitol, a highly visible protective force. The platoon, armed with four cannons and twelve heavy machine guns, seemed a remarkably heavy force to protect a building from what was an unknown threat.

It didn't make good tactical sense, but just as much, it didn't make good political sense. As a citizen, she was concerned about the idea of tanks patrolling an American city. As an officer, she was appalled by it. But those were her orders.

The other part made more sense, at least. Her second and third platoons—twenty-four of the thirty-two men there would have been at full strength—would provide perimeter security to the Little Cairo neighborhood, only twelve blocks away. One violent incident had already occurred, when someone threw a brick through a plate-glass window in a Lebanese bakery. Her orders were to maintain calm, protect the civilian residents and prevent further incidents.

"You may have some other tasks, Captain Greenfield. My understanding is that DHS will conduct some interviews in your area of operations today, and we've been asked to provide some support and security for them as well. This will be escort duty. A couple of your men will accompany the DHS teams. According to my orders, they have some suspects who may still be in the area."

Karen looked up at him as she wrote. "Yes, sir."

"One other thing," Elkins said. "Make sure you drive it home to your men: we are here to protect the citizens and calm the situation down. I want everyone to proceed with absolute caution and calm. I don't need to say this, I know, but just remind your people. Last thing we need is an accusation that we trampled on people's civil liberties. I'll be around to each of your positions later today. We'll be setting up the battalion command post here; the radios should be up shortly."

Elkins dismissed the four captains and they went their separate ways.

※

Rain stung Morris's face as he leaned out the doors of the helicopter. He glanced at his watch. Almost noon. Even in this lousy weather, he could see the plume of black smoke that rose from the center of town. The choppers—six of them—circled around the south side of the demolished federal building. Morris could see vehicles below, small as matchbox cars, many of them with emergency lights flashing. To the west, in front of what must be the State Capitol Building, he could see a group of tanks offloading from trucks.

Tanks. Holy Christ. This was as serious as could be, but who the Christ would think of deploying tanks around the State Capitol? What kind of threat were they worried about?

He lost his view of the tanks and the destruction around the federal building as the choppers came in to land beside the river, two at a time. He jumped off first, followed by his headquarters team. The second chopper contained part of Sergeant Kathleen O'Donnell's First Platoon.

"First Sergeant," called Morris.

The first sergeant approached.

"Gather the men in formation over there," Morris said, pointing to a spot some distance away from the landing zone. "As soon as we've got all the men, we march to the federal building."

"Yes, sir. You mean the men and the ladies, sir." The first sergeant grinned as he spoke.

Morris rolled his eyes. "Whatever, Top."

A brown Crown Victoria drove up, headlights shining, wipers on high, and a man with a black windbreaker got out. The letters DHS, 18 inches high, were emblazoned on the back of his windbreaker.

"You Captain Morris?" the man shouted over the noise of the incoming choppers. He held up a hand to shield his eyes from the rain.

"That's right."

"I'm Agent Wilson from the Charleston Field Office of Homeland Security. They sent me over to show you the way to the Federal Building."

"All right, Agent Wilson. We've got a couple more choppers coming in, though. You'll have to wait a few minutes. What's the situation over there?"

Wilson shouted over the noise. "Could be worse, Captain. It was a car bomb for sure, pretty damn big one, but almost no one was around, went off in the middle of the night. Security guard was the only person in the building. Towel head—we think he's the one who did it. A couple of cops got killed, they were entering the building when the bomb went off, and at least one homeless guy got killed, possibly more. We don't know if anyone was in the offices yet, but it's unlikely given the hour."

Morris grimaced.

"I guess that is lucky. Wonder why they set it off in the middle of the night?"

Wilson shook his head. "Don't know sir. Maybe a mistake?"

"The next load's just about it; we'll be ready in fifteen minutes."

☙

Several blocks away, in the small enclave known as "Little Cairo" for the last decade, four unmarked sedans pulled to a stop in the middle of the street. Justin Hagarty stepped out of the car and looked up and down the street. The block was lined with two- and three-story shops with flats above them. Even as he looked around, the street cleared: the shop owners closed and locked their doors, men and women practically ran to get out of the area. There was no use, though; two platoons of National Guardsmen blocked the intersections. No one would be coming or going for some time.

Larry Harris approached from his vehicle.

"Why do you think they're running away? Looks suspicious."

"It does, doesn't it. Well, let's get this show on the road."

He turned around and looked at his men. "Listen up! You know what to do. Men who meet the suspect profile are to be detained; we'll gather them over here to put them on the buses. Make sure you explain that if they cooperate they will be quickly released. If you find our actual suspects, they go in a patrol car for immediate questioning. I want everybody in helmets and flak vests, understand? No exceptions!"

Chapter Seventeen
September 12

The rain rattled against the canvas roof of Karen Greenfield's HUMMWV like popcorn, loud enough that she couldn't hear the radio. The air had turned cold from the rain, and the inside of the humvee smelled like sweat and mildew. Her soaked Kevlar vest didn't help, as moisture seeped through it and her olive-drab raincoat.

The tanks were in position, four of them stationed at the intersections around the Capitol Building. A few blocks away, her executive officer was positioning the remainder of the company in the Little Cairo neighborhood.

Since she'd been with the company, they'd been activated three times. The first two didn't require weapons, they were to deal with floods. Then, last year, they briefly deployed to Morgantown after a riot. In that case they stood around and did guard duty, much as she expected to do here. In no case was the use of main battle tanks required.

The men inside the tanks would be miserable; unable to cover the tank with a tarp, they'd be sitting inside what amounted to great, leaking tin cans, getting soaked. She'd never understood how they could make a tank that could survive the direct hit of a 125mm sabot round, but couldn't design one that didn't leak.

"Let's head over to Little Cairo," she said to her driver.

Corporal Stanson, who sat behind the wheel blowing on his hands to warm them, bobbed his head. "Yes, ma'am." He put the vehicle in gear and drove, faster than she liked; it was still light, but with the rain, visibility was down to less than fifty meters.

In Little Cairo, the twenty-four men were positioned at eight intersections. As she approached the position closest to the federal building, she saw two of the men setting up shelter halves against the wall of a building as the third stood guard duty in the driving rain. The one on guard duty was Private Campbell, from up the road just outside Highview. At seventeen, a senior at Highview High School, the Guard required him to get permission from his parents before he enlisted.

Damn. She couldn't stay inside, not when the guys were outside in the rain.

"Stop here."

She stepped out of the somewhat warm HUMMWV into the icy downpour. It didn't soak through her plastic wet-weather jacket immediately, but it would soon enough. She walked through the rain to Campbell.

"Ma'am." He was shivering and his teeth chattered.

"As soon as they've got that shelter up, you get under it, okay, Campbell."

He nodded vigorously, and little droplets of rain flew off his chin. "Yes, ma'am."

She started to turn away, but he spoke again. "Ma'am, can I ask you a question?"

"Sure, Campbell," she replied.

Lightning struck nearby, and the light flashed in their eyes, followed by a loud crack.

"Ma'am, in your briefing you said we was here to protect the Arab folks here against being attacked and stuff, right?"

She braced herself, half expecting to hear an argument against the mission of protecting the neighborhood. "Yes, that's right."

"Well see, that's the thing, ma'am. When you go around that corner, you'll see what I'm talking about. Bunch of guys in sunglasses and whatnot are rounding up a lot of folks. Banging down doors and stuff, ma'am."

He looked away, and then steeled his resolve. "I know we're here to support the DHS, but it just don't look—it don't look *American* to me, ma'am, if you take my meaning. Looks like more of the same as the Saturn plant, ma'am."

Her eyes narrowed. "Thanks. I'll have a look, Campbell."

Bracing herself, she walked on through the rain. As she reached the corner, Stanson followed her in the humvee.

Sitting in the open rain, soaked and miserable, hands cuffed behind their backs, a group of fifteen men and boys who appeared to be Arabs sat with their backs against a shop window. A man with an automatic rifle stood guard over them. He wore a black raincoat with the letters DHS emblazoned on the back.

Two other men kicked in a door about fifty feet away. They were covered by a third, this one armed with a rifle. A woman screamed in a foreign language, and then she heard indistinct male voices shouting. One of the agents shoved a woman out of his way, roughly. A moment later the two armed men came out, dragging a fourteen-year-old boy between them. He struggled, terror on his face. They threw him to the ground and one knelt on the boy's back while the other cuffed him with plastic ties. They unceremoniously dumped him with the other prisoners.

Her face tightened. It was him. The son of a bitch who killed David Firkus, Agent Ben Matley. He was one of those under investigation by the Harpers Ferry DA, and they had the stupidity to bring him here and allow him to treat American citizens like cattle. Shoving women and kids around like they didn't matter.

Not on her goddamn watch.

She marched back to Corporal Stanson, who still sat in the humvee. He unzipped his plastic window and leaned out to hear her.

"Call the platoon leaders; have them move the men to the edge of the intersection where they can see. I may need some backup; I'm putting a stop to this. And call Major Elkins right away. Tell him what's happening, then catch up with me."

"Ma'am, I don't think that's a good idea." His eyes were wide.

"When the Army wants your ideas, Corporal, they'll promote you to Captain. Until then, you follow orders."

"Yes, ma'am."

He scrambled for the radio.

She turned around. Half a block down, parked in the center of the street, sat two bland-looking sedans; lights flashing behind their grilles. Two men stood at the cars, one talking on the phone. She recognized one of them: Agent Lawrence Harris. He'd been at the Saturn Plant as well.

She walked toward the cars as lightning struck again, bathing the entire scene in garish white light.

"Who is in charge here?" she demanded.

The man on the phone lowered his handset. Short, in his late forties, he dressed in the same black raincoat as the others, his head covered by a black baseball cap, and a small earpiece in his ear. He looked up at her and eyed the railroad track insignia on her helmet.

"I am, Captain. Special Agent Hagarty. I was told to expect a National Guard company to assist our efforts. I've already seen the men on the perimeter. Good job."

"I'm Captain Greenfield. Those are my men on the perimeter. What's going on here?"

"We're gathering material witnesses in our investigation of the bombing this morning. They'll be taken into custody and questioned."

"Material witnesses? Looks to me like you're grabbing every male over fourteen!"

"That's right. Anyone who meets our profile. They'll be released once we've established they're clear."

"Mr. Hagarty, this has to stop right now. What you're doing isn't right, and it's not legal. You can't just round up people and cuff them and carry them away."

Hagarty frowned at the challenge and his chin jutted out. "I most certainly can, Captain. I strongly urge you to mind your own business and leave me to mine."

Karen clenched her teeth and fists.

"Hagarty, I don't care what your business is. Mine is to protect and defend the Constitution of the United States, and you are treading all over that. I want you to do three things right now: release those men and boys over there, gather up your men, and get the hell out of here. Someone else can deal with investigation, someone who understands this is still America."

He approached until they stood a foot apart.

She glanced back. Six of her men and two of her lieutenants approached, along with Corporal Stanson. All nine of the men were armed. They gathered in a loose group between her and the humvee. Just twenty feet away, they were difficult to see in the driving rain.

She heard another door crash in, screams from inside. Agents came out with two men between them, a teenager and his father. Both were handcuffed. Karen signaled to Lieutenant Carson to approach. He ran up to her, and she pointed directly at the agents who had just exited the building.

"Lieutenant, I want you to take three of the men, go over there and free those two men, then the others lined up on the sidewalk. If necessary, you are authorized to take these so-called federal agents into custody."

Carson looked stunned by the orders.

Hagarty spoke. "Lieutenant, this operation was authorized by the President of the United States, who I believe you swore an oath to obey. If you follow that order you will suffer the consequences. I'll see you both court-martialled."

"Hagarty, you have no legal standing to round up people in the streets and arrest them, nor to threaten an officer under my orders. You are committing a grave crime here, sir. I won't stand for it and neither will my men."

Lieutenant Carson nodded, swallowing. For just a second he appeared to waver, then his jaw set.

"I got it, ma'am." He turned back to the men. "Billings. Cole. Wilson. Over here, on the double."

The Lieutenant and the three soldiers approached the stunned agents, weapons ready. The agents looked back and forth between the approaching soldiers and Agent Hagarty, jaws slack.

"Lay your weapons on the ground right now."

One of the agents started to raise his hands in the air.

Hagarty screwed his face up, red with rage. "Goddamn it, don't listen to them." He reached out and shoved Karen.

She fell back a step, then straightened. By the time she regained her balance, Hagarty was staring down the barrel of Corporal Stanson's M-16A2 rifle.

"You better keep your hands to yourself, Mister." Stanson's voice was steady.

She took a breath, adrenaline pumping into her system. They were at a stalemate, as her men and the federal agents stood with weapons leveled at each other. She had to calm the situation down before it got out of control.

"All right, let's keep it cool. Everybody lower your weapons." She raised her hands in a gesture to stop.

Unfortunately, that was when lightning struck with a crack and a flash of light. It only took that moment for the whole thing to go to hell.

She didn't know who fired the first shot, but heard it clearly, the crack of a rifle, immediately after the lightning strike. The second bullet hit Karen square in the middle of her Kevlar vest. She spun to the ground, her vision going black. Above her, she heard a burst of shots.

"Oh, no." She struggled to her feet. Her hands were scraped bloody from her landing. She pushed herself up and her vision cleared. Rainwater poured off her helmet.

Hagarty lay on the ground, blood pumping out of a hole in his neck, mixing with the half-inch deep water on the pavement. One of her men writhed on the ground, screaming, his knee shattered by a bullet.

"Cease fire, goddammit," she tried to shout, but she couldn't get her breath. She tried again. "Cease fire! *Cease fire!*"

She tried to make sense of the situation. Two or three DHS agents were crouched in the doorway of an apartment building, rifles out. They huddled down, trying to stay out of the line of fire. She saw a muzzle flash. The air stank of the acrid smell of gunpowder.

The men and boys apprehended by the DHS were still on the sidewalk. Bound by plastic cuffs, they tried to get out of the line of fire as small arms continued to go off around them. One boy, who couldn't have been older than fourteen, squirmed underneath a car, and the plate glass window behind the men shattered from a bullet. The man guarding them ducked behind the car, little more than his rifle showing.

Behind her, her own men fired from behind the HUMMWV, and several more ran forward from their positions on the perimeter. Corporal Stanson lay on the ground, and a pool of blood stained the rainwater around him. Blood pumped from the center of his chest—he wasn't wearing his vest.

His face was white and his arms flapped around.

"Mama!" he screamed.

"Cease fire!" She waved her arms. "Cease fire! Cease fire *now!*"

Her head jerked to the left as a bullet glanced off her helmet. It knocked her to the ground again. Then, miraculously, the firing stopped, and she could hear nothing but the rain slap into the pavement.

She took a breath, then another. The DHS men stared out from their positions, shock on their faces. She glanced behind her. Her own soldiers were just as bewildered.

Oh, God, her head hurt. She stood, one hand on her neck, where sharp pain radiated from a pulled muscle.

"You." She pointed at Larry Harris, one of the only agents she recognized. "Take your men and move over to the other side of the intersection. I don't want any goddamn arguments. And call for ambulances, right now."

She turned around. "Lieutenant Carson, call the medics. Lieutenant Gavin, pull our men on a line behind the position of the humvee. And have someone cut those men loose." She pointed at the prisoners.

She dropped to her knees and crawled over to Hagarty and ripped open her first aid pack, removed a bandage and placed it on his neck. The bandage instantly stained red, the blood seeping through the cloth and between her fingers and out onto the pavement. Her hands shook as she tried to stop the blood. God, she could smell the blood, there was so much.

"I need help here."

Two of her men ran up, as well as Agent Harris. She glared at him, then looked away.

"Help Stanson," she told her men. Corporal Stanson had stopped moving.

"You," she said to Harris. "Lift him up enough so I can get this bandage around him."

He nodded, his face pale. Quickly, she wrapped the tails underneath the opposite armpit from his wound and tied if off as tight as she could. It might as well not have been there; blood still poured steadily from the wound.

"Best I can do. He won't make it if we don't get an ambulance right away."

Harris looked up and spoke.

"I know you, don't I?"

She glared at him.

"Yeah, you do. You killed my friends and neighbors in Highview."

Confusion clouded his eyes, and then he recognized her. His eyes widened. She stood up and walked away. As she approached her humvee, she shook.

Stanson lay there, the medics trying to save him. They covered the sucking chest wound with a plastic bag and wrapped him with bandages. Blood had splattered six feet away from him as he struggled.

What had she done? Oh, God, look at him. She could hear an echo in her mind: *When the Army wants your ideas, Corporal, they'll promote you to Captain.*

Those were just about the last words he'd heard.

The rain continued to fall.

Chapter Eighteen
September 12

Morris found the battalion headquarters, in a tent across the street from the collapsed federal building. He took a deep breath, then pushed his way into the dark tent and took off his helmet, rainwater splashing to the ground. Barksdale stood in front of the map with three other officers; they turned to Morris as he entered.

"Morris, come on over. We're going over the dispositions." Barksdale said, waving Morris over.   The officers looked up at the sound of small-arms fire, faint, but clear, a group of high pitched pops. Morris thought it sounded like a mixture of pistol shots and automatic rifle fire. Given the rain, it couldn't be more than a few blocks away. Barksdale actually ducked down a little at the sound, and his eyebrows squeezed together. Morris reminded himself Barksdale had served in combat three times.

"What the hell is that?" one of the officers said.

More shots, a lot of them. Sounded like at least a dozen people with automatic weapons. Most of the shots came in the clear, almost signature three-round burst of an M16A2 rifle.

"Those are M16's," said Barksdale. "Morris, is your company close or did you come ahead of them?"

"Right behind me, sir; they're less than two minutes away."

"All right, then, you get the assignment. Find out who's shooting, and deploy your platoons across this area to screen the federal building. It's close, whatever it is. Remember, we can't arrest anyone. Just assess the situation and report back."

※

Morris, winded from his sprint back to his company, laid a laminated map on the hood of a car and motioned for his platoon leaders to gather around.

"All right. Fourth and fifth platoons, position yourselves here and here. You will provide a screening force for the area around the federal building."

He pointed out the positions on the map and gave the platoon leaders time to mark their own maps with grease pencils.

"First, second, and third platoons come with me; we'll split into three columns. Advance on these three streets, and stay on line with each other. Find out where the shots came from. As soon as we find it, we assess the situation and report in. Again, stay on line as we move forward, but move quickly. Brief your squad leaders; we go in two minutes. Rules of engagement: lock and load, but fire only if you have been engaged and cannot withdraw. If you are fired on, hunker down and we'll assess the situation. Questions?"

The platoon leaders looked unhappy with the rules of engagement, but didn't ask any questions. Morris didn't like them either, but no one got to pick their mission. They weren't in some third world city: they had to be extra careful of the civilians in the area. Two minutes later the company broke up into platoons and advanced rapidly through the city. The rain continued to pour down.

Morris scanned doorways and windows, accompanying second platoon. The streets were quiet—most of the downtown businesses were closed today because of the bombing. The gutters rattled and rain ran down them into the sewers below. His men ran up the street as in a combat zone, covering each other carefully. Each fire team covered its counterpart as they sprinted forward, leapfrogging each other.

Halfway up the second block, a woman in a suit stepped out of a door and saw a group of soldiers bounding toward her. She screamed and ducked back into the doorway.

Morris' radio let out a burst of static, and he heard Sergeant Miller's voice.

"Black six, this is red four."

"This is black six, over."

"Black six, you better come to our position. We've found where the shooting came from. We've got wounded over here; there's been a pretty nasty firefight."

"On the way. Has your platoon taken fire?"

"No, sir."

Morris turned to his second platoon leader. "Lieutenant, form a perimeter at the next intersection and wait for my orders."

He relayed similar instructions to third platoon, then jogged eastward to Miller's position. Despite the cold and rain, sweat rolled off him. At sixty pounds, he carried a light load for an infantryman, but it was still pretty damn heavy, and he wasn't twenty-two any more.

He was winded when he reached Miller's position. Sergeant First Class Kevin Miller was his most experienced sergeant, and had served multiple combat tours in Iraq and Afghanistan, among others. Six foot three, with a shrapnel scar across his forehead that stood out against his dark brown skin, he was an imposing man who kept an incredibly tight platoon.

Miller's men were in positions on either side of the road, covering in all directions. A block ahead, a HUMMWV and a Crown Vic with a nest of antennas blocked the street, facing each other. A second Crown Vic, pockmarked with bullet holes, sat at the curb about thirty feet away. The whine of approaching ambulances could be heard over the rain. As he approached the scene with Miller, two soldiers immediately broke away, a female Captain and a sergeant. From across the street a man in a DHS raincoat also approached.

Morris came to a dead stop when he realized that the woman who walked toward him, blood stains spattered across her uniform, was Karen Greenfield, whom he hadn't seen in seven years. Even covered in blood and sweat, a scarred helmet on her head, she still looked beautiful.

"Jesus Christ," he murmured to his XO, Derek Hutchison, "What the hell happened here?"

As she approached, the officers exchanged salutes. It felt strangely formal.

"Karen." For some reason, saying her name made him want to cry.

When she looked back at him, her face was so impassive he didn't think she recognized him at first.

"Mike Morris." She spoke in a monotone when she said his name, but became more animated when she continued.

"Look, we need your help right now. Ambulances aren't here yet; we've got several wounded up here. Can you send up your medics?"

Morris turned to Sergeant Miller. "Sergeant, send Corporal Woods up, and Hall from first platoon."

"Yes, sir." Miller turned away and shouted to his platoon.

"What happened here?"

Karen shrugged. "The feds were rounding up people on the street, knocking down doors house to house. It was a gross violation of civil rights. We ordered them to stop, but it turned ugly."

"Jesus, Karen. You got in a firefight with the DHS?"

She nodded slowly.

"I never would have guessed, not in a million years. Jesus, did you get hit? You've got a hole in your flak vest. And your helmet—"

He pointed to the deep furrow carved in the side of the helmet, above her right ear. "God, if that had been an inch to the right it would have killed you."

She shrugged. "I've got wounded men over there; I don't have time to worry about myself."

"Karen—how have you been?" He spoke in a low tone, not quite a whisper.

Her response was cold. "Captain, I've got work to do. Why don't you look me up in a day or two?"

Without waiting for an answer, she turned and walked away.

Hutchison spoke. "You know, sir, that's what happens when you put women in the combat arms. Gets to be their time of the month, and they go crazy. Can you believe that? Shooting at the DHS—they must be crazy!"

Morris turned and looked at Hutchison. "Shut up, Lieutenant."

Hutchison froze. "Yes, sir."

༄

Minutes later, Major Vince Elkins roared up in his Hummer, sending a wave of rainwater splashing up onto the sidewalk. The vehicle had barely stopped before he jumped out and marched toward her.

"Captain, I need a report, right now."

"Sir." She paused, almost stumbled from exhaustion. "I observed a serious crime: federal agents were assaulting the civilian residents, rounding them up and arresting them. I ordered them to stop, and the situation got out of control. I… I take full responsibility, sir."

Elkins's eyes flicked across the street to the DHS men, back over to the wounded National Guardsmen, then to the bullet hole in her flak vest and the scar on her helmet. It took him about five seconds to make the decision she expected.

"Captain, you are relieved of your command. Wait for me in the Hummer while I sort this out. Where is your executive officer?"

"Right over there, sir." She pointed, hating the tremor in her voice.

"Lieutenant Britton, report to me this instant!"

Karen sat in the back seat of the Hummer and rested her head in her hands. What could she have done differently? *No.* No matter what happened in the end, whether this ended her military career or landed her in prison, she'd made the right decision. She'd had to stop them.

Karen's conviction wouldn't be much consolation to Sherry Stanson when she found out her husband was dead. She stifled a sob.

Outside, Major Elkins spoke with Morris and another Lieutenant Colonel, probably Morris's battalion commander, along with Agent Harris. Elkins was waving his hands as he spoke. She supposed they were working out a new security plan—for sure the National Guard couldn't stay here.

God damn it. Was she supposed to just stand there and let it happen?

No point in wasting any more time. She pulled out her pocket computer and unfolded the keyboard. Time to compose her report.

The rain continued to pour down.

༄

An hour later, Karen stared straight ahead as she gave a more detailed verbal report to Elkins and Colonel Murphy at the makeshift battalion headquarters in the basement of the State Capitol. Murphy, still wearing civilian clothing, stared intently at Karen as she described the day's events. As she spoke, part of her felt like the little girl she'd once been, explaining a mistake to her unpredictable and dangerous father.

Then his phone rang. He examined the number it displayed, flipped it open and answered.

"Murphy."

Karen heard a panicky voice on the phone, though she couldn't make out the words. Whoever it was sounded hysterical, and Murphy's response was forceful.

"Slow down, Valerie, there's no need to get excited at this point. Yes, it's true. I'm in Charleston now; I just got in a few minutes ago. Actually, you can do something for me. Talk to Representative Clark. My understanding is that the DHS was going house to house, kicking down doors and arresting all of the teenagers and men, with no regard to whether or not they had anything to do with anything. My men got caught in the middle when they intervened."

Murphy paused to listen, and then spoke again. While he spoke, Karen looked down at the scuffed tile floor and wondered, again, if there was any way she could have handled the situation without betraying her principles.

Face it. She hadn't done it on principle. She'd done it out of anger. It was her first gut reaction on seeing the bastard who'd killed Dave Firkus. Now two men were dead.

"He's a lot better, hon. Better than he's been in a long time. I really think this treatment is helping. Your Grandma's with him, she's going to stay in Ohio while I'm on alert. Listen, I'm in a meeting, hon. Let me know what you find out… Love you too."

He folded up the phone and looked at Karen, his expression kind.

She met his eyes and her stomach twisted. It was like looking at her father, except she had far more respect for Murphy. What the hell was he going to say? The irony was, never in her life had she cared about her father's approval. The thought of Murphy's disapproval—that terrified her.

"Am I going to end up in prison because of this?"

"Not if I can help it," Murphy said. "Captain, your actions were rash, and you should have consulted with me or Major Elkins before you acted. That's where you went wrong. Very wrong. You may lose your command because of this, maybe your commission."

She held her breath.

"The fact is, though you acted without authority, I believe you took the correct action under the circumstances. What happened at the federal building this morning not withstanding, this is still America, we still have a Constitution and you've sworn to defend it. I'll back you up, Captain."

Tears clouded her eyes, but she blinked them back savagely. She wasn't going to cry in front of them. Not a chance.

"Thank you, sir." Her voice was almost a whisper.

Thank God. But, blinking her eyes, she could still see Corporal Stanson on the ground, the blood pumping out of his chest turning the rainwater red, screaming for his mother as he died.

"Here's the bad news. I want to get you out of the line of fire immediately. That means that, temporarily, I'm going to relieve you of your command."

Karen's stomach twisted. It must have shown, because Murphy spoke quickly.

"Captain, look at me. I meant what I said. I will back you up. But we need to get you where you won't be in everybody's line of fire, because I guarantee you before the day is out, the federal government will come gunning for you. I've got to move quickly if we're going to be able to protect you. In the meantime, you'll move over to the battalion S-3, which will be some good staff training for you anyway, and for the duration of this deployment to Charleston, Lieutenant Antal will take over your company."

Trying to hide her disappointment, she replied, "Yes, sir."

"Vince, where are my uniforms? I have to go see General Peak."

As Murphy walked away, Karen stared at the floor, wondering just what the hell she was going to do.

Chapter Nineteen
September 12

Representative Albert Clark tried not to squirm as the woman applied foundation to his forehead. He sat in a barber's chair, weaving a little from exhaustion, bright lights trained on him as she worked. She was approaching sixty, about ten years Clark's senior, with long gray hair parted in the middle and down behind her shoulders. She wore a wicked grin as she spoke.

"Congressman, you've aged since last time you were on. Everything all right?"

"I'll be just fine if you run away with me," Clark grinned.

She laughed and slapped him on the shoulder. "You congressmen are all the same, always thinking in your pants. Get on out there."

He thanked her and stood; then an aide led him into the studio. Mark Skaggs was already there.

Skaggs stood when he saw Clark. They shook hands, and then sat down facing each other on opposite sides of a small coffee table. Skaggs wore a custom-fit suit with a bright red tie. Very slick. Clark knew others didn't share his view: Skaggs had won lopsided victories in his district, and was well respected on the Hill.

"Mark, how are you?"

"I just keep on keeping on, Albert," Skaggs replied. "It has been quite a year, hasn't it?"

"That it has."

"Sixty seconds," someone shouted.

Bill Warner, the moderator for Washington Talk, charged onto the set. Clark and Skaggs both stood. "Good afternoon, gentlemen. Are we ready?"

They shook hands all around and sat. Warner's aftershave was so strong it made Clark's eyes itch, and he wore so much makeup he looked like a corpse, though that wouldn't show up on screen.

The lights came up and washed them in light bright enough that Clark wanted to shade his eyes. He could just see Valerie through the studio window, pacing back and forth, talking on the phone. A young man, twenty or so, approached Clark and stumbled into his chair.

"Sorry," he muttered, then pinned a wireless microphone on Clark's lapel.

Someone counted down from ten. When they reached one, the studio went silent, and then Warner spoke.

"Hello, America. This is Bill Warner with Washington Talk. Today we have with us representatives Albert Clark of West Virginia and Mark Skaggs of Kentucky. We're talking about the Fiscal Responsibility Act today, but first, the news on the forefront of everyone's mind: After a terrorist bombing in West Virginia; this afternoon saw a violent shootout between the National Guard and the Department of Homeland Security. Gentlemen, thank you for being on the show today."

Clark and Skaggs nodded.

"Early this morning terrorists destroyed the federal building in Charleston, West Virginia. Now, the federal authorities say they have a suspect, one Brian Ibrahim, a 25-year-old Iraqi American. Are there any updates on this, Mr. Clark?"

"Well, Bill, I have to correct you on one thing. The DHS is investigating, but they haven't named Mr. Ibrahim a suspect. My office has done some checking: Mr. Ibrahim was a decorated veteran, and worked as a security guard while going to college on the GI Bill. All that makes him a suspect is the fact he was in the building."

Skaggs interrupted. "He was from Iraq; that makes him a suspect right there."

Clark shook his head. "No, he was not from Iraq, he was from Detroit. He was born in the United States and was a US citizen, and our understanding is his parents fled Iraq because they were supporters of the failed rebellion against the Iraqi government. All I'm saying, gentlemen, is that we need to take our time and not prematurely point fingers. This man wasn't allowed to see a priest before he died, even though he specifically asked for one. Is this who we want to be? It is this very kind of speculation that fueled the stupid move by the Department of Homeland Security today, which is an irredeemable tragedy."

Warner moved to take control of the conversation again.

"Gentlemen, let's turn to our second topic. In a second incident today, Homeland Security officials were fired on by members of the West Virginia National Guard. Two men were killed and another four injured. We've just gotten word the attorney general plans to prosecute Captain Karen Greenfield, the commander of the National Guard unit. Any comments on this incident, Mr. Skaggs?"

"Yes, Bill. If the incident occurred as the media has reported, Captain Greenfield ought to be given a medal. It's a terrible thing people died in this incident, and I lay the blame for that squarely on the DHS."

Warner raised his eyebrows, and his face turned a shade of red under the makeup. "But isn't it a crime to interfere with federal officers conducting an investigation?"

Clark leaned forward to listen closely. He and Skaggs were so often on opposite sides of every issue, he found it hard to imagine they agreed on something.

"Sure, it is, and she'll likely be charged with obstruction of justice and murder, as well. But think about it for a second. The reports so far indicate the DHS was kicking in doors and dragging men and teenagers out of their homes. None of this was based on an investigation, they just went down there because the suspect was Iraqi and lived in that neighborhood. At the least, we need to have an independent investigation."

Warner took that moment to jump in. "I think many people will disagree with your point of view on this, Congressman. The Department of Homeland Security is our defense against terrorism, and according to the latest polls, most Americans agree they are willing to trade some of their civil liberties for security. What say you, Representative Clark? It's your state that was hit by terrorists."

Clark leaned forward. "I think most Americans would disagree if the polls didn't ask questions in a very limited way. In West Virginia, people have been very unhappy with the long reach of the federal government in recent years."

Warner responded, "Are you suggesting this Dale Whitt person has the correct answer? Secede from the United States? Most Americans think he's a crackpot."

"Of course not," Clark said. "I've served the United States my entire adult life. But it would be foolish to dismiss him out of hand. What I'm suggesting is, he has tapped into a strong current of dissatisfaction on the part of ordinary people. Americans may be afraid, but not just of terrorists. They are afraid of their own government."

Warner raised his eyebrows in an exaggerated look of surprise. "You mean to tell me you both agree on this?"

Clark looked at Skaggs and they both chuckled.

Skaggs spoke. "Apparently we've found some common ground, Bill. Mr. Clark is right—at least about this. We've abandoned some of our fundamental principles. Dale Whitt may be a fruitcake, but he's awakened a lot of very angry people."

Warner interrupted as Skaggs took a breath. "Well thank you, gentlemen. Our regular viewers will recognize we have a first today: Mr. Clark and Mr. Skaggs agree. The question is: are they both right, or are they both wrong? When we come back, we'll talk about something they won't agree on: the Fiscal Responsibility Act, scheduled for debate in the House tomorrow."

"Three minutes," someone called.

Skaggs leaned back, a grin on his face. "You know, Al, we should consider a bill to cut DHS's funding, or cut their activities way back. We could introduce it together. That would turn some heads."

Clark nodded. "Not bad. Let's get our folks to set up a meeting."

"Sixty seconds."

As they spoke, Warner shouted at one of his assistants. Clark and Skaggs ignored it and continued talking—Bill Warner was jovial on screen, but well known as a terror for his staff.

"You know they're going to crucify that Captain," Skaggs said. "If the Justice Department doesn't get her, the Army will."

Clark bobbed his head. "Didn't you hear? The attorney general is calling for the death penalty. It's appalling."

"Ten seconds."

They were silent as the lights came back up.

"Welcome back, America, this Bill Warner with Washington Talk. We're here today with Mark Skaggs of Kentucky, and Albert Clark of West Virginia, who are behaving with unusual harmony this afternoon. Gentlemen, you'll hurt my ratings if you keep this up."

Clark and Skaggs chuckled politely.

"Now, for the big issue. The Senate passed, fifty-four to forty-three, a companion bill to the Fiscal Responsibility Act last Monday. Here we have the original author and sponsor of the bill, Representative Skaggs. Mr. Skaggs, the house is scheduled to debate this tomorrow morning. What are the prospects for it?"

"Well, Bill, we're pretty confident. I don't expect the debate to be much fun, but we'll get there—despite all the special interest money that's come into this debate, we'll do the right thing and pass the bill."

"Mr. Clark?"

"Bill, this is the same-old same-old. We've passed massive corporate tax cuts, to the tune of tens of billions of dollars, in the past few years. At the same time we've fought half-a-dozen foreign wars. Now, big surprise, we're on the verge of bankruptcy. So we're going to go after the weakest parts of our society. We're talking about cutting many benefits for the disabled, for wounded veterans, in fact for just about everyone who is not a multi-millionare."

Warner spoke. "But it isn't it true the General Accounting Office investigation you requested found many of the programs are rife with abuse?"

"No, that's not true. It did conclude there was some abuse—as there is with any government program. The vast majority are people who will be in serious trouble without some assistance. Families will become homeless. People will die from untreated diseases. This won't just be a problem for those individuals—it'll be a problem for our entire society."

Warner grimaced. "Dire predictions, Congressman. Do you offer an alternative?"

"I do. For the last four years running I've been introducing a bill that will make measured cuts in defense, means test social security, cut corporate subsidies, and ensure the poor children in our society don't get left behind."

"Mr. Skaggs, what say you?"

"Bill, Congressman Clark is well intentioned, and I'm sure he's sincere, but he misses the point. Social Security is not some government program you can use to hand out benefits willy-nilly, based on your preferences. People pay into the system. They get money out. Simple. Second, he suggests the tired old mantra of the Democrats: raise taxes. We can't raise taxes anymore, the backs of our people are broken."

Warner interrupted. "According to yesterday's Washington Post, over two million layoffs have been reported this year. Are we headed into another recession? Mr. Clark?"

"Did we ever leave the last one? We've gone off the edge of a cliff and we're busy cutting the strings off our parachute."

"Mr. Skaggs."

"I don't know you can call it a recession yet. I do know in my district we've got rising unemployment. The people in my district are worried, and that is why I've made many of the proposals included in the Fiscal Responsibility Act. If we can't get the federal government's house in order, how can we help the economy?"

"That's all we have time for, gentlemen. You've got ten seconds to get in the last word. Mr. Clark."

"We'd be crazy to pass this so-called Fiscal Responsibility Act, especially now. It's going to hurt a lot of people."

"Mr. Skaggs."

"Government spending must be brought under control."

Warner looked at the camera. "And that's it for Washington Talk. Join us next week for more discussion of current Washington events. This is Bill Warner, your host, with our guests Congressmen Mark Skaggs and Albert Clark. Thank you for joining us, and have a great day. That's all."

The lights dimmed, and Clark and Skaggs stood.

"Should be an interesting day tomorrow, Al."

"I think it will be."

They shook hands with Warner and with each other; the production assistants removed their microphones; then they parted in opposite directions.

As Clark walked away, Valerie approached.

"The White House called. The President wants to see you at six tomorrow morning."

༄

Murphy arrived at the Governor's office at 7:30 a.m. the morning after the bombing. He wore his dress uniform, with rank and insignia displayed. After twenty years in the West Virginia National Guard, he had never met the Governor in person, much less been asked to breakfast with both the Governor and the commanding general. At the door he paused and adjusted his tie—except for the hearing in early summer, it had been a year since he'd worn his dress uniform, and the collar was too tight.

He opened the door. Inside was a spacious entry, with rich dark paneling and a polished marble floor. A brown leather couch and chairs lay off to the side. The Governor's secretary was behind a maple desk, talking on the phone and typing at the same time. She looked up as he walked into the room and asked her caller to hold.

"Colonel Murphy, the Governor is expecting you. You can go on back." She indicated the door next to her desk.

"Thank you, ma'am."

Murphy walked to the door, knocked once, and then opened it.

Major General Harris Peak and Governor Frank Slagter sat at a small polished table to the side of the Governor's office, eating breakfast next to a window that overlooked downtown. Unfortunately, the window perfectly framed the devastated federal building and its surroundings.

The Governor, still chewing, waved with his knife for Murphy to sit.

General Peak spoke first. "Good morning, Colonel Murphy."

"Good morning, sir; Governor." Murphy sat.

Slagter belched into his fist, then spoke. "Colonel Murphy, it's a pleasure to meet you. General Peak has spoken well of you for years; I'm surprised we never had the opportunity to meet in person. Here, have some coffee."

"Thank you, sir."

General Peak put down his cup.

"Murphy, we called you here for two reasons. We'll take care of the easy one first, how does that sound?"

Murphy smiled, not knowing what to say.

The Governor called out, "Sophie, send in the photographer please." He then stood, and waved at Murphy. "Come on over here."

A young man in his early twenties entered, high-end digital camera in-hand. Murphy recognized the model; it was one he wanted to buy a couple of years ago to help feed his photography hobby, but the price had been too high.

General Peak walked around the table. "Let's do it against the wall over here. You'll get the best light for the photo that way."

Slagter agreed. "That sounds good."

Murphy was bemused.

"Stand at attention, Lieutenant Colonel," Peak said.

Murphy did.

"Colonel," Slagter said. "I'd like to be the first to congratulate you on your promotion."

Promotion! He hadn't even been on the list. All the same, Peak pulled from his pocket a small plastic bag containing two silver eagles of a full Colonel, and pinned them on Murphy's lapels, removing the leaf of a Lieutenant Colonel.

"This nice thing about being in the National Guard, Colonel," Slagter said, "is that you don't have to wait for the Army or Congress to approve your promotion. I can do that. We need more men of courage like you in the top ranks, Colonel Murphy. I'm certain you will do credit to the Guard."

As General Peak was pinning the silver eagles the photographer took a photograph, and then another as Slagter shook Murphy's hand. Murphy had to stop a wave of sudden sadness; at his last promotion, Martha had been beside him. God, would it never stop hurting?

General Peak followed Slagter back to his seat. "Now, down to business. We're making a couple of organizational changes. Colonel Wilkins has retired, effective immediately, and I'd like you to take command of First Brigade, reporting directly to me."

Brigade Commander. The Brigade headquarters was in Morgantown, about an hour's drive from Highview.

"Sir, isn't that a full-time position?"

"It is. Do you want it?"

Murphy took a deep breath, his mind racing over the implications. A full-time position in the Guard meant health insurance again, it meant help for Kenny. And, everything else aside, he loved being an officer. The chance to command a Brigade... He'd have never thought it would happen. "Yes, sir, I do."

"Good, good. Governor, I told you, Colonel Murphy is just the man for the job. Do you know during his battalion's rotation to the National Training Center, they did as well against the OPFOR as any active duty unit ever does? Remarkable, when you consider how little time they have to train."

"Indeed." Slagter took a sip of coffee.

"You'll have to call your brother and brag. Now he's not the only brigade commander in the family."

Murphy smiled. "Tommy is too humble for bragging to do any good, General."

Slagter looked at them, his head cocked slightly, and Peak explained. "Colonel Murphy's brother Tom commands a brigade of the 101st Air Assault at Fort Campbell. Didn't they just get back from the Middle East?"

"About six months ago, General, in February."

Murphy's gaze slipped from the white table cloth, the bright orange juice, the coffee, to the devastation just outside the window. A plume of smoke still rose from the scene of the federal building, and from here he could see the flashing of hundreds of lights down there, the area still surrounded by emergency vehicles. Something about sitting up here in this rarified atmosphere, chatting and looking at the destruction below—it just didn't seem right.

"Well Colonel," said General Peak. "That brings us our second task. We have to decide what to do with that Captain of yours. I've got some ideas, but I'd like to hear yours first."

Murphy looked first at the General, than at the Governor. He had known Peak for years, but he couldn't predict what the General would do in this situation. Murphy would have only one chance to persuade them not to abandon Karen Greenfield.

"Sir, I don't believe we have a choice. The way I see it, Captain Greenfield had two imperatives. First, her standing orders, which were to maintain law and order in her area of operations. We explicitly gave her that order. Second, she operated under her oath as an officer, sir, which requires her to protect and defend the Constitution." Murphy took a deep breath. "I suspect I may lose this discussion, but my opinion is we must back her up. She did the right thing, by protecting the rights of the civilians in the area. If she hadn't, she would have been complicit in a serious crime."

Peak frowned and spoke, his voice sharp. "Colonel, are you suggesting that a firefight with federal police in the street is maintaining law and order?"

The Governor held his palm out to General Peak and said, "Wait, please. Colonel, please go on."

Murphy cut his eyes to General Peak, whose face was tense.

"Sir, I would recommend you take two steps. First, acknowledge in public she did the right thing. Second, I'd order an investigation into DHS. I'd refuse to turn her over to the federal government until that investigation is complete."

Slagter and General Peak glanced at each other.

Governor Slagter spoke first. "That's close to my own opinion, Colonel. General Peak sees things differently. Let's hear your reasoning."

Murphy took a deep breath. "Sir, you've got a couple of issues to think about here. The first one is that it's clear to me that the Department of Homeland Security is way out of bounds—you've had several West Virginia citizens killed in the last few months, none of them in clear or clean arrests. They sent in armored vehicles and helicopters to deal with a labor dispute—this in a case where the owner of the plant was a personal friend of the President. Now this, smashing in doors and dragging kids out in the street to be tied up and left in the rain. Sir, it's not just inappropriate, or unconstitutional. It's repressive. It's like something you would have heard about in Iraq or Jerusalem ten years ago, sir, or Russia thirty years ago. If you don't speak out, who will?

"People outside West Virginia look at Dale Whitt and they see a crackpot, sir. But he has touched on a level of anger and frustration I would never have guessed at, and I don't know if it can be kept in hand. But sir, you can keep this from going too far, by insisting constitutional limits still apply. If people see you going out on a limb to protect them from the federal government, they are far less likely to follow a radical path like Whitt's."

Slagter grunted and frowned at the mention of Whitt. "My advisors tell me there is no chance Whitt's measure will make it on the ballot. What do you think?"

Murphy answered. "Sir, I think he's already got enough signatures. The question in my mind is whether or not it will actually pass. If it does, sir, you'll have a very serious problem to deal with."

"It's inconceivable to me. The citizens of this state wouldn't vote for it. It's insane."

"Sir, it seems to me if many more incidents like yesterday occur, they just might. Look out your window. Do you really believe some college kid on the GI bill did that? Someone who was conveniently Iraqi? I don't. No offense to anyone, but if this was a serious attempt at a major terrorist incident, they would have done it in the day and killed a few hundred people. Instead, it was in the dead of night. The federal building was destroyed, but there were very very few casualties. I think this was done by a local who wanted to hurt the feds only. The DHS is barking up the wrong tree by rounding up Arab families."

Slagter grimaced and nodded.

"I believe you're right, Colonel." He paused and looked out at the plume of smoke rising from the center of the city, then spoke again, his gaze far away. "We need to get on top of this. If we can just keep the feds from doing anything else really stupid between now and election day."

Murphy nodded. One more incident might push them over the edge.

General Peak spoke. "Well, Colonel, tell Captain Greenfield we won't hang her out to dry."

"Yes, sir."

Slagter stood. "Murphy, be prepared to come back here for a press conference later today. I'll send someone around to get you."

"Yes, sir." Murphy stood when Slagter did. It was clear he was being dismissed. "And sir—thank you."

"All right, Colonel. You can get back to your troops, we won't keep you any longer."

☙

The ride back to the State Capitol and Murphy's battalion headquarters was quick. Now it would be Major Elkins's battalion. Picking up his pace, he walked to the headquarters and entered.

Corporal Harris stood guard outside the door, holding an M16 rifle.

Harris came to attention as Murphy approached, then reached to his side and opened the door.

Someone called out "Attention!" as Murphy entered.

"As you were," Murphy said.

Everyone returned to what they were doing. At the map table, Karen stood with Lieutenant Antal reviewing paperwork. Dark circles framed her eyes.

"Sir." Karen paused and took a breath as she noticed the silver eagles on his lapels. "Congratulations."

"Thank you, Captain. Do you have a moment?"

"Yes, sir."

"If you will excuse us, Lieutenant."

"Yes, sir, and congratulations." Antal walked away.

"Karen, I wanted to let you know I just met with the Governor and with General Peak."

"Yes, sir." He saw a tremor in her hands, very slight. She clenched her hands into fists and the tremor vanished.

"The Governor says he'll back you up."

"Yes, sir."

"This doesn't mean you are out of the woods yet, but it's a lot better than I expected. We'll just have to see it through. Have you had any sleep?"

"Sir, I keep asking myself if… if there was something else I could have done… *Something.* Corporal Stanson is dead, sir, and it… It was my fault."

"Cut the crap, Captain."

She jerked at the harsh words, looked at him startled.

"Karen, part of being an officer is you have to make the hard decisions. The kind of decisions civilians wouldn't dream of making, the kind that can save a life or take one. And you have to live with those decisions. I'll tell you now, if you make a lifetime of this, it won't be the last time you'll have to make this kind of decision. Do you understand? You could tear yourself up with doubts, wondering what you could have done. Learn from the mistakes you make, and move on. The fact is you made your decision to protect innocent bystanders. You did your job. You can't spend your life second-guessing what might have been if it had gone differently; you'll drive yourself crazy. Trust me on this—I know what I'm talking about."

She nodded, her eyes watering. "Sir, I was up all night, working on a letter to his wife. Stanson… He's got a two-year-old daughter, sir. They came to the company picnic last spring, right before all this started. I don't know… I don't know what to tell her."

"Tell her the truth. Her husband died defending the citizens of this country. She has every right to be proud of him."

She nodded, but he could still see the doubt on her face.

"You don't look convinced."

"I'll be all right, Colonel."

"Make sure you are more than all right, Captain. Your men depend on you when you get out there. Doubts are natural, and the fact that you have them makes you a better officer. But remember, it can be more dangerous for you to hesitate than to make the wrong decision. You're a good officer. All right?"

"Yes, sir."

"Good. I need to take a walk around and talk to the troops."

"Yes, sir."

He turned and walked to the door. At the door, he paused and spoke to Corporal Harris.

"Listen, Corporal. If any federal agents show up here—FBI, DHS, whatever—you are to refuse them entry. Make it clear I gave the order and have me notified immediately."

"Yes, sir."

"All right, I'm depending on you."

༄

Corporal Harris, still standing guard duty at the door, stuck his head in.

"Ma'am?" It was clear who he was asking for, because Karen was the only woman in the headquarters. "You've got a Captain Morris here to see you."

Just what she needed. Mike Morris.

She turned around. "Send him in, Corporal."

"Yes, ma'am."

Harris stepped back from the door and Mike Morris entered. He wore his camouflage uniform and web gear, with a pistol at his hip and his k-pot under his arm. He looked at her, his expression unreadable.

"Hi, Mike." She realized the headquarters had become unusually quiet. She was subject to scrutiny of everyone in the room.

She looked at the others, eyes narrowing. References to her being a woman were off-limits. Her first year in the unit she'd been besieged by requests for dates from the other officers. She had fended them off, and after a few months the pursuit was called off. It had been a long time since anyone had treated her differently because of her gender.

"Lieutenant Antal, this seems like a good time to grab some lunch. I'll meet you back here at 1300 hours."

"Yes, ma'am," the Lieutenant answered.

She walked out of the headquarters with Morris behind her, and led him down a dim basement corridor.

"I can't go outside, the press is out there, and probably the FBI, so we'll have to make do here. How are you, Mike?"

"I've been worse. It looks like I'm in for a career, I've got an infantry company now, First of the Fifteenth."

"And your family?" She hoped her tone wasn't too stiff.

"Savannah is a wonderful little girl—she's the light of my life."

"Well, good for you."

"What's happening with you, Karen?"

"Well, until recently I was working for Saturn Microsystems. But I've been laid off, and relieved of my command. The justice department just announced they're going to throw the book at me—capital punishment, no less. It's been an interesting summer."

He looked at her, eyes wide. "I hadn't heard about the Justice Department."

"It was on the radio a little while ago. The attorney general himself made the announcement. 'We're going to catch that rogue National Guard captain and try her for capital murder while committing a felony.' The felony is obstruction of justice."

Her tone sounded bitter, even to herself. "They are actually charging *me* with obstruction of justice. Like the DHS was doing anything resembling justice."

"Jesus, Karen. What are you going to do?"

She laughed sadly. "I guess I can't stay in the basement forever. I'm told that in a little while the Commanding General of the West Virginia Guard, as well as the Governor, will go out there and refuse extradition."

"What a mess."

"Yes, it is."

Mike stared at her, and his expression softened. *Asshole.*

"Don't look at me like that, you son of a bitch. You made your goddamn choice. You're married now."

"Well, not exactly."

"What the hell is 'not exactly' married? Is that like 'almost pregnant?' 'Sort of' dead?"

He looked away. "Karen, would you believe me if I told you leaving you was the biggest mistake I ever made in my life?"

She grimaced. "Of course leaving me was your biggest mistake, bonehead. I could have told you that."

"I've always loved you."

"Oh, Christ. You show up now after seven years and look at me that way? You can't do that, Mike. I've got my own life now; I don't need you."

He closed his eyes and nodded.

"Look. I don't need to complicate my life. I've got more than enough problems of my own. I could really use…." Her voice broke, and she savagely blinked back tears, then spoke again. "I could really use a friend right now." Then she laughed. "Well, that and a good lawyer."

He reached for her and they embraced. It had been a long time, and having his arms around her felt right. *This is a mistake.* She shouldn't be standing here with Mike Morris, of all people. But back when she'd first started college, a lost and confused almost-orphan, he'd been there. Enough of a similar background that he wasn't alien—after all, he'd grown up less than a hundred miles from her. But completetly different from her father and most of the other men she'd known in her life. Self-centered, yes, but never aggressive or angry. They'd clicked, and had a wonderful four years together.

Then he'd dropped it like a bomb that he was leaving, breaking her heart. Right now, she didn't care. It felt so good to be held for a change, she just didn't care.

Chapter Twenty
September 13

Al Clark drove his ancient Ford through the gate at the south entrance of the Ellipse after the military police completed their search. He drove to the designated spot, and then walked to the iron gate of the White House, where the guards searched him again. Inside, he was X-rayed. This was Clark's fifth visit to the White House in ten years, though the first three were to this President's predecessor. Each time the security was a little tighter, and the perimeter of restricted areas around the White House a little wider.

He still remembered when people held demonstrations—or walked their dogs—in Lafayette Park or on the Ellipse. When they could stand outside the fence of the White House and take photographs from three or four hundred yards away. For that matter, when he'd first come to Washington as a twenty-two-year-old Senate aid during the Clinton administration, Pennsylvania Avenue was still open to vehicular traffic. Oklahoma City stopped that. Today, it would take a telescopic lens to shoot the same photograph, the parks on both sides were closed, and Pennsylvania Avenue was closed from 14th to 18th streets.

At least the Secret Service agent who escorted him into the official residence above the West Wing was polite, commenting that Clark was very early; the sun wasn't up yet.

Clark's answer was quick. "You don't turn down a breakfast invitation from the President."

Though Clark had visited the White House before, those were official visits in the West Wing. He'd never seen the inside of the residence upstairs, and was impressed with its size and spaciousness. Any sense of opulence was offset by the lack of privacy, however. Even in sleep, the occupants of this residence were never alone, never unwatched.

The agent escorted him to a small room. President Wendell Price sat at a table, along with Congressman Mark Skaggs. Clark thought the two of them couldn't contrast with each other more: Price big and tall, his presence filling every room he entered; Skaggs slight, thin and reserved. They sat at a table overflowing with food. In the corner of the room stood a large man, 250 pounds or more, in a black suit. It must be like living in a fishbowl, surrounded by the Secret Service twenty-four hours a day. Or was that one more sign of power for Price to relish?

"Come in, Mr. Clark. Sit down, have breakfast."

"Thank you, Mr. President," Clark responded, and sat in the third chair.

"You should try this orange juice, Mr. Clark. Do you know these oranges are grown in my hometown, Land-o-Lakes, Florida? Someone actually ships them up here regularly so I have a taste of home every morning. It reminds me it's only two more years and I'll be free."

"You'll be reelected for sure, sir."

"We'll see. This is the worst job in the world, Al. Can I call you Al?"

"Of course, sir."

"You can call me Mr. President." Price and Skaggs chuckled.

Clark forced a polite laugh. *All right,* he thought. *You've had your little joke, Mr. President.* Like a couple of little piglets oinking at each other. There was no such thing as a purely social visit for the President, and Clark wished he would get down to business.

"Mark here tells me the two of you agreed on something on television yesterday. I was shocked. That's why I invited the two of you to breakfast—I figured if both of you agree on something, it must be exciting news. This is a first, so far as I know. Is that right, Mark?"

Skaggs nodded, wiping his mouth with a napkin, then spoke. "Yes, sir. I believe Al and I have been on opposite sites of the fence of just about every vote we've ever had. Although there have been some unanimous votes."

"Well, those don't count. Let me guess—one designated March 14 as National Spelling Bee day?"

Clark pretended to laugh again, in spite of his discomfort.

"So tell me about this thing you agree on, Mr. Clark."

Back to Mr. Clark now. Clark took a deep breath, then spoke.

"Sir, somehow I expect you won't like what I've got to say."

"That's all right, Mr. Clark; if both you and Mr. Skaggs agree, it must have some merit. Besides, this is a democracy—all our opinions are equally important."

But some are more equal than others, right, Mr. President?

"Mr. President, I'm sure you've been briefed on events in Charleston."

The President nodded and shoved a forkful of eggs into his mouth.

"Sir, the attorney general announced he is planning to prosecute the National Guard captain involved in that incident. His decision is misguided, sir. The DHS team broke the law. Captain Greenfield responded as her training and professionalism dictated: she acted to protect the citizens in her area of responsibility. My understanding is she tried to talk it out with the head of the DHS team, Agent

Hagarty, but he refused to listen and physically shoved her, which escalated tensions between the two groups."

Price scowled. "You understand they killed a federal agent."

"Yes, sir. And you understand your agents killed a National Guardsman, a young man from my district? Let me be clear, Mr. President. I did a little bit of digging recently. In the last year the DHS has been involved in over 30 incidents in which people were killed, and not one of them verifiably involved a terrorist. Four of those occurred in my state, sir. We've got a situation of seething discontent in West Virginia, sir, discontent over the federal government's involvement in people's day-to-day affairs. Discontent over lack of privacy, and especially over regulation of everything under the sun. You need to understand, sir, most West Virginians are ready to vote for that idiotic referendum. This is as serious as it can get, Mr. President."

Price rolled his eyes. "Come now. The last reports I have is they can't even get many signatures, and the ones they had were destroyed in a fire."

"Mr. President, it sounds like your intelligence may not be up to date. The signatures were destroyed in the fire, but that event was a catalyst. I'm told they already have enough signatures to get it on the ballot, and will deliver them today. Understand, sir—a local police officer was killed that day saving a little girl's life, because the DHS stormed in and conducted a raid the floor above a day care center. If you had planned it, sir, you couldn't have found a way to infuriate the citizens of West Virginia more."

The corners of Price's mouth twitched—he must have been annoyed to be reminded of DHS's spectacular screw up. "I'm well aware of the incident, Congressman. The Department is conducting an investigation."

"Sir, are you aware of any incident—ever—when the Department has investigated itself and found anything wrong? Sir, if you prosecute Captain Greenfield—especially if you try to have her executed—it will push the state over the edge. Nobody wants that, sir. Nobody."

Skaggs leaned forward, his eyes rapt.

The President spoke again. "Mr. Clark, whatever does that mean? Will West Virginia declare its independence? That's impossible to believe in this day and age."

Clark shook his head. "Sir, I can't imagine it would go that far. But it's only unthinkable today because the Civil War was so brutal secession became unthinkable. To the voters in my state, that's beyond ancient history. It might was well be something that happened in Rome two thousand years ago."

"Don't you people see the benefits you get from the federal government?"

"Sir, with all due respect, what benefits? We've run the statistics. For every federal tax dollar that leaves West Virginia, we get fifteen cents back. For the last three years—ever since the latest economic slide began—our newspapers have been full of stories covering these issues. My people are boiling, sir."

The President shrugged and put up his hands in a surrendering gesture. "All right, Mr. Clark. I get it. What do you want me to do?"

"Reconsider the decision to try Karen Greenfield. Or at least take the death penalty off the table."

Price shook his head just slightly. "You know I can't do that. The Justice Department is an independent agency."

"Sir, you know as well as I do that's been a fiction for decades."

Price looked at Clark, his brows creased. "Let's just say you're right, and I can drop the prosecution. I've got big problems too, Mr. Clark."

Here it comes, Clark thought. *What's the tradeoff?*

"I'll give you an example, Mr. Clark. I run a government bleeding red ink right now. We're in debt up to our ears, the deficit is getting worse, and it's getting to a point where we can't even pay for our national defense. You're well aware we've pulled most of our troops out of Central Asia in the last couple of years. We make a big show about that being a strategic decision, but it's not. It's a financial decision. It costs too much to maintain bases all over the planet."

Price paused and took a sip of his coffee, set the cup down with a clink, then took another forkful of eggs. He chewed thoughtfully for a moment, followed it with a sip of orange juice—home grown in Florida, as he'd pointed out. It was all a charade to show Clark who was running the show. He was surprised they hadn't left him cooling his heels outside when he got here.

"Where was I? Right. We're bankrupt. Now we're spending millions to investigate this bombing in your state, because some terrorists decided to take out a federal building. Half the reason DHS is so screwed up is we had to cut their training budget. So, we've got a bill on the floor that will cut the red ink, it's in danger of not making it through the house, and you are the biggest roadblock."

Oh, crap! Clark glanced out the window, tinted blue from the unusual thickness of the bulletproof glass. Beyond, the sky was just growing pale.

"You want me to drop my opposition of Mr. Skaggs's bill."

Skaggs and the President nodded. Price gave him a friendly smile.

"You do that, Mr. Clark, and I'll see to it your National Guard captain doesn't go to jail—or to the electric chair."

"Sir, you are going to hold that woman hostage to this bill? Is that what this is about?" Clark's voice held enough of an edge that the Secret Service agent stepped away from the wall and caught Clark's eye in a silent, menacing warning.

The President leaned forward in his chair, a frown on his face. "Mr. Clark, politics is about compromise. You ask me to compromise on something I feel strongly about. I ask you to do the same."

Clark's felt his face getting hot. "Mr. President, with all due respect, it is *not* the same. You are holding a woman's life hostage to your political goals. It's despicable!"

Skaggs sat up straight, his mouth open. No one talked to the President of the United States that way. Clark told himself to calm down and shut up.

"It is you who are despicable," the President said, voice laden with contempt. "You expect everyone else to compromise, but you won't do it yourself. You hold your pride and your career above everything. That's what this is about. You'll lose face if you back off your opposition to the bill, won't you? You'll lose your election, too. Is that what this is about, Mr. Clark? Is this some overblown plan for you to win reelection?"

Clark closed his eyes and took a deep breath. This had to stop. The discussion had already gone far enough—too far. *Too far.* His fingernails bit into the palms of his hands.

"Sir, I... I apologize. Feelings run very strong on this issue. I'll need to think about it, sir."

The President leaned forward like a predator sensing weakness.

"Mr. Clark, I need your answer now. Debate starts on the bill in three hours."

Clark looked at the floor. Beautifully polished oak planks, laid down before his great-grandfather was born. If he abandoned his position on the Fiscal Responsibility bill he'd betray his constituents, he'd betray everything he'd ever stood for. If he stuck with it, Karen Greenfield might go to the electric chair. *God damn it!* He was going to lose this battle whatever he did.

He shook his head.

"Sir, I can't abandon my principles. Thank you for reconsidering, but I can't take you up on this."

Skaggs muttered under his breath. The President sat back, solemn, betraying a twitch at the corners of his mouth. Son of a bitch was enjoying this.

"Mr. Clark, I can't fault you for sticking by your guns—just like your young National Guard captain. We'll see her in court."

Clark placed his napkin on the table and stood. There's wasn't much left to say, and he couldn't take another minute here anyway. Protocol said he should stay until the President dismissed him. Damn protocol.

"Good day, Mr. President. Mr. Skaggs—I'll see you in the House."

He turned and walked out, the watchful eyes of the Secret Service on him all the way.

༄

The briefing room on the first floor of Charleston's capitol building was packed with journalists. This had all the elements a television producer would kill for: tragedy, terrorism, conflict. The room was awash in pale, bright light from the television cameras, giving the entire place an unhealthy pall. It was hot and damp in the room.

Murphy arrived in the small antechamber next to the briefing room several minutes early. A few minutes later, the Governor arrived, with Major General Peak in tow, as well as two other men. Governor Slagter introduced them as the State attorney general and the secretary of state. They'd arrived together, as if the four of them had just come from breakfast together. *What had they been discussing?*

Murphy dismissed the question as petty, but he couldn't shake the feeling something was wrong. General Peak he had known for many years, but he had no reason to trust the others. Late the previous night, Peak had called him and explained the promotion, both on the grounds that he felt Murphy was the best available candidate, and also due to his concern that, with the loss of his job, Murphy might leave the state soon. That made sense, but he still couldn't bring himself to trust the Governor.

Introductions over, Governor Slagter preened himself in the small mirror near the door. "Let's get this show on the road. Colonel, you might be called upon to answer questions about the incident; your response should be that we're investigating, and Captain Greenfield has been relieved of her command."

"Yes, sir."

"All right, then. Let's go."

Slagter walked into the briefing room, followed by the other men. Murphy filed in last. He rocked on the balls of his feet and wished he were just about anywhere else; he still didn't trust the press.

Slagter walked to the podium and spoke without introduction. "We're ready to get started. I'll make a brief statement, followed by the attorney general."

The lights turned up brighter. For two full minutes the only thing Murphy heard was the clicking and whirring of cameras; flashes illuminated the room.

"Yesterday, in the space of fourteen hours, two tragedies struck West Virginia. First, a terrorist bomb struck the federal building and killed several people. At this time we have confirmed nine dead. Search and rescue efforts are continuing, and we are cooperating with federal authorities in this investigation. We ask anyone with information to come forward.

"Several hours after the bombing, an incident took place between agents of the Department of Homeland Security and the West Virginia National Guard. This occurred while federal agents were conducting an unconstitutional search and seizure in a Charleston neighborhood. In short, the DHS agents were banging in doors and rounding up the residents, arresting them, handcuffing them and leaving them to sit in the street in the rain. We have no indication that any of these individuals had any involvement or knowledge of the car bombing earlier in the day. The only reason they were arrested was the fact they were male, Arab, and in most cases—not all—between the ages of fourteen and forty. At least one of those detained was a twelve-year-old boy."

"Folks, this is the United States of America. We will not tolerate activity more suited to Stalinist Russia. As you will shortly see, a courageous National Guard captain, Karen Greenfield, risked her life to intervene in this unconstitutional activity.

The DHS agents responded with deadly force, and in the ensuing firefight one DHS agent and one National Guardsman were killed. Several others were wounded."

Murphy's ears perked up. *As you will shortly see?*

"Now Mark Brown, the attorney general, will brief you on several items."

Brown stepped forward on the podium. A short, balding man in a brown suit, he looked confident, almost aggressive, as he adjusted the microphone.

"Thank you, Governor. Yesterday our state police polled the neighborhood and discovered DHS personnel confiscated the security tapes from the three stores in the neighborhood that may have had a vantage point to record the incident. We are working on obtaining those tapes, and we are considering obstruction of justice charges against those who seized this evidence. However, a concerned citizen did videotape the entire incident, from beginning to end. In a moment, I will play that tape, and copies will shortly be distributed to you."

Murphy took a breath as the reporters started buzzing. *A tape.* That was a revelation, and was guaranteed to change the dynamic of this discussion.

"I have consulted with the secretary of state and the governor, and we made two initial conclusions. "First, as to the federal indictment of Captain Karen Greenfield on capital charges, we refuse to honor the extradition request, and explicitly deny the right of federal agents to arrest her or take her out of the state. Captain Greenfield operated under State authority at the time of the alleged incident, therefore it is a matter for which the State of West Virginia will conduct the investigation. That investigation will be handled by the State Bureau of Investigation in cooperation with the National Guard's Inspector General's office. In the meantime, Captain Greenfield has been suspended from her command until our investigation is complete."

"Second, as to the incident in which federal agents violated the rights of West Virginia citizens by rounding them up like cattle and tying them up in the street: we are convening a grand jury to investigate the issue. Subpoenas will be served to the individuals involved, as well as the Secretary of Homeland Security and the United States Attorney General."

The reporters looked stunned. None of them expected anything like this. Neither had Murphy. Not in a million years had he expected this in-your-face confrontation with the federal government. Dale Whitt must be jumping up and down in his seat and cheering.

"Now we'll watch the video, and then you can ask questions."

The attorney general waved a hand to signal a young man standing in the doorway, who rolled in a cart carrying a large television. They quickly had the large screen adjusted, and the aide placed a disk into the player.

The video began as whoever shot it rushed to a window, and then angled down, apparently from a fourth or fifth floor window. Murphy saw the DHS staff cars, and a dozen men walking around, carrying assault rifles. In teams, they walked house to house, smashed in the doors and marched inside. After a few moments each team appeared again, dragging men and boys, who were deposited in the street. Another DHS agent stood guard over the prisoners. At one point one of the men on the ground twisted his head around and his mouth moved, and the agent shoved him over with his boot.

The video quality was high, but sound was terrible, just the sound of rain and sirens and the occasional wail and scream.

Then the camera focused in on a Hummer, and two soldiers walking toward the DHS staff car in the center of the area. Murphy recognized Karen as she approached the agents and began talking with them.

As the scene unfolded, it became clear that both Karen and the DHS agents were angry. Other soldiers approached from the sidelines, as did DHS agents. Then the man Karen argued with—Agent Hagarty, Murphy supposed—shoved her and shouted something. Men on both sides raised their rifles.

The attorney general slowed the video. "I'll slow this down, so we can watch it frame by frame."

What happened next wasn't clear. A flash of light—maybe lightning—just as four of the agents ran out of one of the buildings, weapons at the ready. After the flash, one of the agents fired. Maybe he stumbled, or thought the flash of lightning was a gunshot. In any event, he pulled the trigger and his rifle fired. As the video advanced, one frame at a time, the muzzle flash was clear. DHS fired the first shot.

Men on both sides returned fire, and several went down, including Karen and Manning. She'd broken two ribs, he knew, when the bullet slammed into her Kevlar vest. Even with the lousy sound quality, the shots were clear, as were her shouts to cease fire. One of the agents in a doorway fired another shot at her, which glanced off her helmet and knocked her back to the ground. *Christ*, she was lucky to be alive. Then the firing stopped as quickly as it had started.

She immediately shouted orders. Murphy was impressed watching the scene. Karen had performed better than he'd realized, immediately reasserting control over the situation, and directing medical care for the wounded on both sides. The sad part was, it didn't matter whether or not she was cleared. It didn't matter whether or not the DHS was wrong. She would forever be the officer who had killed a federal agent. Her military career was over.

The governor returned to the podium and someone raised the lights. He looked back at his prepared statement. "Since the passage of the 1970 Drug Control Act, the 1972 Clean Air Act, the 1996 Anti-Terrorist Act and the 2001 USA Patriot Act, we have seen the federal government take greater and greater authority from traditionally state and local jurisdictions. The federal government has for fifty years asserted its right to continually expand its mandate, to override local statutes, to practice double jeopardy by trying in the federal courts people who were cleared of the same crime by state courts. In the last two years alone, the United States government imprisoned 75 West Virginia citizens for actions that are not criminal under West Virginia law. Further, in the last two years, the United States government shot and killed 17 West Virginia citizens in a dozen incidents, not one of which resulted in a conviction." He jabbed his index finger at the cameras as he spoke the last few words.

"Ladies and gentlemen, after review of the constitutional issues, we have concluded the federal government has no law enforcement authority within the state of West Virginia except for those crimes defined in the Constitution of the United States: treason, counterfeiting and piracy. Since we have no oceans here, it would seem the third is also ruled out. In any event, we will challenge the right of the federal government to come into a neighborhood in one of our cities, gather up citizens and arrest them with no cause. We will also not allow the federal government to conduct a politically charged trial of a young woman who did nothing more than defend her neighbors as was required by her orders and her oath of service. Questions?"

For twenty long seconds the room was near silent as the journalists absorbed the full weight of what they'd been told. Then the dam burst, and questions poured out in a torrent. Slagter pointed at a woman at the front of the crowd.

"Governor, Dale Whitt has announced he will deliver signatures for the independence ballot initiative to the Capitol today. Does this statement mean you support the independence measure?"

The governor shook his head. "Of course not. I am a loyal citizen of the United States of America. I do believe Whitt has a core of truth: the federal government has gotten out of control in the last fifty years. You there, in the back."

"Governor, how will you prevent the DHS from arresting Captain Greenfield? Will you use force to keep her in the state?"

"Captain Greenfield will remain on active duty and under state authority until this issue is satisfactorily resolved on all sides. You saw the video. It's clear she intended no crime. We will conduct a state investigation—and, if necessary, a state prosecution—to deal with her. Next."

"Governor Slagter, how will this impact your chances of reelection?"

"That's irrelevant. Next."

"Governor, have you made any special security preparations to deal with Dale Whitt when he arrives with the petitions?"

Slagter shook his head. "Mr. Whitt is a private citizen exercising his democratic rights. We are open for business, and will welcome him and anyone else with business at the Capitol."

"But is there a concern for security?"

Slagter's frown deepened.

"Ma'am, in case you missed it, what used to be the Byrd Federal Building is lying in ruins right down the street. Of course there is a concern for security. However, I don't see a need for special precautions to deal with a private citizen exercising his constitutional rights. Is that clear? Next."

"Governor, most of America is in a rage over what happened here—both the destruction of the building, as well as the shooting of federal agents while they were investigating a crime. It's hard to imagine you'll have any support among your fellow governors, or from President Price."

Slagter frowned. "Is that a question or an editorial?" With a pause for effect, he went on, "You've asked me to react to a situation that doesn't exist. The American people will see the justice of the situation, especially when they see that tape."

"Governor! Are there any leads in the investigation other than the ones the DHS and FBI produced up until the shooting incident? Haven't you derailed a terrorism investigation by interfering?"

"No, we haven't. The DHS had no leads, nothing at all that would point them to the Little Cairo neighborhood except for the fact that one of the victims of this attack was an Iraqi American."

"Isn't the fact he is Iraqi enough to warrant further investigation?"

"Certainly. Do you think we should also round up all the Army rangers in the region and arrest them as well? Or all the college students?"

Another reporter shouted, "Governor, how will you respond if the FBI or DHS uses force to apprehend Karen Greenfield?"

Murphy met General Peak's eyes. Peak was worried, Murphy thought. Force, under these circumstances, was absolutely the last thing anyone needed.

"I'm confident Secretary Stevenson has more sense then that. Any use of federal agents to remove someone from this state by force would be a severe escalation of an already tense situation. What we need right now are cool heads and calm counsel. I would ask the President to recognize that, and in fact, I will be calling him today to discuss this very issue."

Another reporter raised his hand. Murphy recognized this one, an ABC News reporter.

"Governor, do you believe you have popular support in your own state for this action? Considering there is a giant burning pile of rubble right here in the city, it's unimaginable that people would support this."

"We'll see about that," Slagter answered. "I am confident that the citizens of West Virginia support justice, and want to find the truth of what happened. Jumping to conclusions is not the way to get there. I'm more than a little bit annoyed. You are the second reporter in here who has determined what people's reactions will be without asking them. Why don't you go out there and ask our citizens what they think, instead of telling them? Last question, then we're done."

"Sir, we have unofficial reports from the DHS they have arrested another suspect in the bombing, someone affiliated with Brian Ibrahim. Can you confirm that?"

"I'll have to direct that question to the Department of Homeland Security. I'm not aware of any arrests. Thank you, ladies and gentlemen. We'll continue to conduct regular briefings with my staff as the investigation continues."

The men filed out of the room, with shouted questions raining down on them. Murphy breathed a sign of relief.

Slagter paused. "All of you to come with me, please."

Murphy followed as Slagter quickly made his way to the elevator and they rode upstairs in silence.

Slagter marched into a large office on the top floor, his back straight, tense, angry. He closed the door behind them. His voice had an edge to it when he spoke.

"Colonel Murphy, I want you to keep a guard on that Captain of yours twenty-four hours a day. I don't want one pretty little hair of hers hurt. If you've got one guy watching her, make it four. Understand? And if the feds come for her, you do two things. First, you call me. Then you do whatever it takes to keep their hands of her. Don't let them get her."

"Yes, sir."

Slagter walked to the window and stood, looking out at the smoke plume, still rising into the sky twenty-four hours after the bombing.

"And one more thing, Murphy. Can you quietly deploy some additional men around the entrance to the Capitol and all the approaches to it? The last thing we need is something happening when that lunatic Whitt shows up." He took a deep breath. "*Goddamn it!*" he said. "Mark! How soon can you have that Grand Jury rolling?"

"We've got the initial work in place sir, but jury selection will take some time."

"Make it fast. I want the Goddamn Secretary of Homeland Security indicted, and soon."

"Yes, sir."

Slagter turned around, his face still flushed. "All right, back to it. Thanks for sitting through that damn circus."

Murphy filed out with the others.

The situation was out of control.

Chapter Twenty-One
September 14

Valerie Murphy sat in her seat and looked out across the House, half full now with members who milled around, chatting with each other. She had a stomachache, and wished she'd stayed back in the office. Not today of all days, with the vote imminent.

The Speaker pro tempore introduced the debate, giving thirty minutes to each side, with an interminable, droning discussion of the rules. After what seemed an eternity, he said, "The chair recognizes the gentleman from Mississippi."

Clark sat beside her studying his notes, no sign of tension on his face, though today might be the most important of his career. *Good.* He needed to stay focused for this. She heard a faint tone, and looked down at the screen of her handheld. A message from the office. Did Clark want to talk to the *Washington Post* after the vote ended? She sent a response.

Joseph Maginnis from Mississippi stood. A Democrat, former Air Force pilot and NASA astronaut, he'd been injured when the International Space Station was punctured by a tiny asteroid. He'd patched the hole and saved the lives of the other seven crewmembers from five different countries, making himself an international celebrity. Most of the members had never served in the military, never done anything more dangerous than buy a drink after finishing their bar exams, so a genuine hero was hard to argue with. A corpulent man with pale blonde hair, he'd once been the picture of a fighter pilot, but since retiring he'd become not only one of the most respected members of the House, but also one of the largest. Valerie was glad he was on their side.

"Mr. Chairman, I yield myself such time as I may consume. Today is going to be a long debate, and one of the most significant ones of this congress, in my estimation. Few bills this House has considered have had such a wide-reaching effect on so many people, and we must remember the human impact as we discuss these very important issues."

Maginnis went on. Valerie looked away as she heard another tone in her ear. She looked down again. David had sent her a popup message.

In bold red letters on her handheld, the question: *Are you ever going to call me back?*

She sighed, looked back up at Maginnis speaking at the floor. What was she going to do about David? He seemed so far away now; it was easier to just put it off. This weekend. She'd call him then, maybe catch the shuttle up to New York.

Even as she thought it, she didn't really believe it. She closed the computer with an audible snap and put it in her purse.

Maginnis went on, arguments she knew because she'd helped write many of them in the last week. It was hard to listen to him go on—even when the issue was critically important, sometimes house floor debates could be dull as dirt. Positions were already staked out, and nothing they said would persuade anyone else. The speeches weren't for the House, they were for the TV cameras, and the voters who would see their representatives debate on the Hill. In the end, the vote would be what it would be, regardless of all the talk on the floor.

She told herself not to be so cynical and pay attention.

Maginnis was wrapping up, and Clark would be next. "Mr. Chairman, I ask unanimous consent that the gentleman from West Virginia may control twelve minutes of the time allocated to me and that he may yield such time."

Members of the House were milling about the room. Less than two-thirds of their compliment was actually here, though in truth that was unusually high. The biggest charade of all was the days Congressmen came in here and made speeches to an empty room, all the while their images were beamed back home. To have this many people in here—easily four hundred—it was remarkable.

Skaggs sat across the chamber from them, and nodded at Clark. Cool as always, Clark smiled and nodded back. After what had happened at the White House this morning, she was amazed he was able to maintain his composure.

Clark stood and spoke. "Mr. Chairman, I rise today in opposition to the Skaggs Bill. Now is the time for us to do what is right. It is time to stop taking money from poor working class families and giving it to the wealthy living out their retirements in the Bahamas and Belize. Here we are in the worst recession since the turn of the century—two million jobs lost since January 1st. Let me repeat: two million jobs. Mr. Skaggs correctly believes we must cut expenses at the federal government level, we must pay down our debt, we must even consider balancing the budget for the first time since the turn of the century. But not on the backs of the unemployed working class people who lost their jobs in this recession. Don't wipe out the last bit of social safety net just so you can get reelected."

Skaggs stood up. "Mr. Chairman, will the gentlemen yield?"

Clark replied, "I yield to the gentleman from Kentucky."

Skaggs spoke. "Mr. Chairman, with all due respect to the gentleman from West Virginia, he couldn't be more wrong about this bill. This bill won't cut unemployment benefits for the men and women who have worked and paid for it. It cuts the benefits for the people who refuse to work for a living, the lifelong welfare recipients, and the people who suffer from nonexistent legislated invisible syndromes."

"Mr. Chairman, reclaiming my time," Clark interjected. "Mr. Skaggs would like to portray this as a responsible bill, but it is not. I have many men and women in my district who will be left out in the cold, possibly homeless, as a result of this bill. Working men and women who have fallen on hard times. Isn't it interesting the strongest supporters of this bill are in the states with large populations of wealthy retirees? This is all about getting votes!"

Bob Robinson of Florida stood, face red, and called out, "Mr. Chairman, I have a Parliamentary inquiry."

"State your question."

"Is it permissible for members of the House to cast aspersion on others' motives in this debate?"

Clark rolled his eyes theatrically, spread his arms wide and shouted, "Mr. Chairman, this is bizarre!"

The chair banged his gavel and shouted back, "This House is out of order, and in particular the gentleman from West Virginia is out of order. We will refrain from personal attacks and emotional diatribes and we will conduct this debate in a calm fashion. In answer to the gentleman from Florida's inquiry, no, it is not permissible. Now, we will return to the gentleman from West Virginia. You have seven minutes, sir, and I ask you to refrain from attacking the motives of your peers."

"I promise to be more sensitive, Mr. Chairman. I didn't realize my fellow representatives had so much to be sensitive about."

Laughter spread across the floor of the house, and Robinson glared at Clark. Valerie made a note to talk to Clark about that. He couldn't afford to make enemies.

☙

It didn't matter to Murphy whether the tanks were under his command or not. The sight of a main battle tank at an intersection in an American city made his skin crawl. He had a visceral reaction to the sight all too common in other cities in his lifetime: Beijing, Gaza, Moscow, Baghdad. Not in America. He made up his mind to talk to General Peak about removing the tanks today. They sent the wrong message, and were useless in an urban environment besides.

At the bottom of the steps, pairs of additional soldiers stood guard. More stood in the shade between the towering columns on the front of the building. Murphy didn't expect any problems, but if they came, he was prepared to deal with them. Captain Wilkinson of Alpha Company commanded the security detachment, a mix of his own Alpha and Captain Greenfield's Bravo companies. This had visibly disappointed the ambitious Lieutenant Antal, acting Commander of B Company, but Antal just wasn't ready for this mission. He was a good staff officer, but needed more seasoning before he commanded this type of sensitive detail. And he couldn't very well put Karen in charge of security when she was the object of most of the security detail.

As Murphy watched from his spot about a hundred feet from the main entrance to the State Capitol, Wilkinson stood at the foot of the stairs with the platoon leaders and platoon sergeants of his company, the wind buffeting them. He was a good officer, and would give them appropriate instructions. Murphy frowned. As Brigade Commander now, he was further away from the troops. Even standing here was not a good idea. He had given his instructions to the Battalion's new commander, Major Elkins, and should trust his subordinates to do the right thing.

He walked toward the front entrance, but stopped as Dale Whitt's red pickup drove past one of the tanks, headed toward him, easily recognizable with its rusted body.

Maybe Murphy would stick around and watch after all.

The pack of reporters who stood near the entrance realized the old beat-up vehicle belonged to their quarry. They moved down the stairs almost as one unit: half a dozen cameramen, plus many more print reporters and photographers. This was probably the best-covered petition that had ever made its way to the West Virginia Capitol, but then again, the reporters were already here from the press conference, so it was convenient.

A cold breeze blew by, and Murphy wished he had on his field jacket. The clouds were dark grey—it looked like the rain was going to start again soon.

At the bottom of the steps to the Capitol, Whitt stepped out of his car on the driver's side. Murphy grimaced when he saw Joe Blankenship step out of the passenger side. At Saturn, Mandy Blankenship had been a reserved, deeply religious woman who leant an air of formality to their usually relaxed workplace. God, what a tragedy. It was absolutely absurd to think the Secretary of Homeland Security dared to call her a terrorist. One more indication they had gone around the bend in Washington.

Joe didn't look any better than he had last time Murphy had seen him, some months before. His face was pale and drawn, lips tight together, dark circles under his eyes. His dark hair was greasy, almost black, and stood up straight in the wind.

Whitt, on the other hand, looked elated, confident, almost bouncing on his feet. He chatted and joked with the reporters, though after the press conference, Murphy doubted the questions were friendly. All the same, they treated him as a man to be respected—a far cry from the Dale Whitt he had known in Highview, seen as a local eccentric until this summer had changed everyone's lives.

Whitt said something and the reporters stepped aside. He and Joe Blankenship climbed the steps, each carrying a cardboard box. As they walked up the steps, they were flanked by reporters and cameramen shouting questions. Whitt continued to talk to the reporters as Joe Blankenship walked beside him, frowning, a line down the center of his forehead. A few paces behind, they were flanked by two soldiers from A Company, both armed with M16 rifles.

As they neared the top of the steps, Whitt saw Murphy in the shadows and called out, "Colonel Murphy, hello!"

Blankenship looked up and saw Murphy as well. His eyes widened, but he didn't smile.

Murphy raised his hand to wave and heard the thump of the bullet hitting Dale Whitt before he heard the crack of rifle fire.

The front of Whitt's face exploded and blood and brains splashed across the ground, the petitions and the reporters. A second shot hit him in the back and drove his body to the ground.

Blankenship spun around, dropping his box to the ground, and shouted, "*No!*"

Most of the reporters scattered, screaming. One of them ran straight into Murphy and knocked both of them down, as a third shot blew a hole through the center of Jim Blankenship's hand.

"Get off me!" Murphy shouted, struggling to his feet. He could hear the very distinctive sound of turbine engines turning over—both tanks were firing up their engines. Soldiers ran from all points of the compass and surrounded Blankenship, Whitt and the remaining reporters.

Murphy reached for his phone and keyed the command channel.

"Cornstalk Six, Cornstalk Six, this is—"

He stopped, realizing he didn't have a new call sign. "Elkins, get your battalion deployed ASAP. We've had shots fired out here."

Elkins voice came back quickly, "Already got reports, sir, I will keep you informed."

By now, a dozen soldiers lay deployed, prone with rifles pointed in almost every direction. Three more soldiers grabbed Blankenship and the boxes and pulled them inside the building.

Murphy looked at the blood-soaked mass that might have been his friend, at least for a short while. *Christ,* what was going to happen now?

Chapter Twenty-Two
September 14

"Turville, let me check your gear."

Turville stood uncomfortably as Meigs checked him over. "Gas mask? Got your bandages? Ammo? Good, good. See, you're not such a screwup after all."

Turville looked back at Meigs, too tired to respond. They stood in a loose formation outside their tent near the ruins of the federal building. A light drizzle came down, just enough to soak through their combat gear and set them shivering. That's the way things were in the Army. They waited.

After twenty minutes, a seeming eternity in this drizzle, Sergeant O'Donnell ran over, followed by the lieutenant.

"Fall in," she ordered.

"All right men," said Wingham. After five months with the unit, his manner was much more confident than it had been during their deployment in Arlington. "Here's the deal. About thirty minutes ago someone murdered some local activist right in front of God and everyone, while the National Guard stood around and watched. We're going to assist the local police in canvassing the area while they look for the shooter."

"Rules of engagement are simple: you don't. Unless someone takes a shot at you, you do not respond. You will not lock and load your weapon. Squad leaders, I will hold you responsible for ensuring this. We are not here to arrest anyone, we will simply escort the police and secure intersections as they perform the search. Questions?"

This didn't make any sense at all. Who the hell calls in the United States Army to deal with a local murder? Turville swallowed, and then spoke tentatively.

"Sir? Is it even legal for us to be doing this? I thought the Army couldn't perform law enforcement activities or something."

Wingham rolled his eyes.

"I don't know, Private Turville, I'm not a lawyer, I'm an infantryman. These are the orders Captain Morris gave me, this is what I will do. Got it?"

"Yes, sir, sorry sir."

"Any more questions?"

No one had any. "Okay, Sergeant O'Donnell. Get them loaded up, we'll be heading over shortly."

The Lieutenant marched away, back to the clump of officers surrounding Captain Morris. O'Donnell said, "Everyone on the truck. Fall out."

The platoon broke and ran for the back of the two and a half ton truck that sat idling nearby. As they boarded the truck, a couple of the sergeants laughed at Turville.

"Hey, LT? Is it legal for me to take a crap?" Loud guffaws followed the question.

Meigs leaned over, his face close to Turville's, and said, "Hey, asshole, when the LT says 'any questions,' you're not supposed to have any. Got it?"

Turville leaned back. "Whatever, Meigs. I just didn't get it, is all. Why is the Army on this mission? Doesn't make any sense."

Meigs laughed. "You are something else, Turdville. Nothing the Army does makes any sense. When are you going to figure that out? You just do what you're told and keep your nose clean, okay?"

"All right, Corporal."

Turville leaned his head back against the side of the truck. A few minutes later the truck moved out.

෴

Turville wasn't the only one asking questions. Already at their destination, ten blocks from the State Capitol, Lieutenant Colonel David Barksdale had grouped his officers and three Hummers in a temporary command post. His company commanders stood in a loose circle around him.

"Each company will secure one sector; your positions are marked on the map here. Vehicles are to be allowed through only after you have recorded the identification of the driver and the license plates of the vehicle. We may be asked to assist the local police with sweeping some buildings. Our people will make no arrests; that's up to the locals."

The officers nodded.

Morris, his face pale, dark rims around his eyes, spoke up.

"Sir, I'm a little concerned about this mission. This place is already nuts over use of force by the federal government. I didn't think it was legal for the military to participate in law enforcement activities."

Barksdale nodded. "I asked the same questions, Captain. First, on the local politics: this is a Black neighborhood we're operating in. Most of the African Americans in West Virginia are dead opposed to this stupid secession measure: imagine West Virginia independent, run by a bunch of hillbillies. These folks will be happy to see the federal government around. Second, we cleared this through the Judge Advocate

General in Washington. As long as we don't participate in any arrests, we should be okay. There are precedents."

"Thank you, sir," Morris said. He looked relieved, not so much at the answer, but that Barksdale didn't bite his head off for asking it.

Barksdale had told himself to let up on Morris for a while. He didn't want his officers too afraid to make decisions. Morris was a good officer, but sometimes he seemed to lack confidence. The question was actually a good start—it showed he was thinking ahead.

"Any more questions?" Barksdale asked.

None of the officers responded.

"All right, move out."

The officers turned and walked back to their companies, leaving Barksdale standing with his battalion operations officer.

Gooding, the operations officer, said, "You know, sir, Morris is right. The Posse Commitatus Act clearly forbids this."

Barksdale nodded and sighed. "Major, this is a stupid mission I know, but the city police asked for assistance, and our orders came straight from the top. Remember, we're not reporting to the Army, we're reporting to Homeland Security, at least while we're on this mission. We'll do the best we can."

"Yes, sir."

Barksdale didn't tell them what he really thought. No one cared if they found anyone. This was nothing more than a show of force. Someone wanted to remind the West Virginians that the U.S. Army was around, in advance of their stupid referendum. Idiots back in Washington. Idiots.

⁂

Edmund Wilson, Speaker pro tempore, spoke again. "The third reading is done. The question is on the passage of the bill."

Clark gripped the seat of the chair in front of him, then glanced over at Valerie. Not for the first time, his eyes caught the curve of her leg. He looked away. He'd managed sixteen years in Congress without succumbing to those kinds of temptations, and he wasn't about to start breaking the rules now. Besides, Valerie would just tell him to go to hell if he made that kind of advance. Al Clark's mother hadn't raised any fools.

Distractions over. He looked back at the chairman.

The clerk counted the house members, and then said, "The ayes appear to have it."

"Mr. Chairman, I request a recorded vote," Clark called out.

Wilson nodded, expecting the request. "The gentleman from West Virginia wishes a recorded vote. We will vote using electronic device. Please proceed."

Clark indicated his vote, and then sat back and looked at his watch. "Any more news?" he asked Valerie.

She looked anxious, and shook her head in small, rapid jerks. "Nothing. All they have is the approximate part of town they think the shot came from. The police are looking, but... I don't know how they'll find anyone. Al, apparently the Army is helping the police search the neighborhoods. Can they do that?"

He frowned. "That's the last thing we need happening right now. Folks are going to go nuts seeing Army troops in the city."

He sat forward and looked around. Most of the house members were already here—they would know the results of the vote in a few minutes. He checked his watch again. Three minutes had passed.

Valerie touched his wrist. "Stop fidgeting, boss. It's out of your hands now."

"I know, I know." He reached into his coat pocket, took out his computer and surfed restlessly to the Washington Post, CNN, and other news sites. The exploding violence in West Virginia had all but pushed the vote on the Skaggs bill out of the news. What in God's name was going on there?

"Al," Valerie said, squeezing his arm a little too hard.

He looked up. The count stood at 199 to 195, with only three minutes left for the vote. Still thirty-six votes left to count. The numbers crept up – 210 to 211. Another vote for, then another.

Clark stared at the count as it ticked upward. Skaggs only needed four more votes in order to win.

Then it happened. The count crept up, and the voting stopped. 220 for, 214 against, one abstained. The bill had passed.

Clark closed his eyes and leaned his head in his hands. *Christ.* The most important vote in his life—possibly the most important in recent history—and he had failed.

༄

Turville flinched when he heard the shout.

"Get down, get down! *Gun!*"

Turville slammed himself against the wall. Across the narrow street, Leo and Gomez, the other members of the fire team, crouched behind a car. In the window above them, Turville saw Halloween decorations. *What the hell were they doing?* The four of them—one of the fire teams in third squad—were on a small side street packed with cars.

"He went down the alley!" Leo's shout was so high pitched his voice almost cracked.

"Chill out, stay cool guys," Meigs said. He keyed his radio as he crouched against a car just in front of Turville. "White Six, White Six, this is White Three Leader. We have an armed individual, heading down the alley next to our position, over."

Lieutenant Wingham replied immediately. "White Three, this is White Six. You are to proceed with extreme caution. We will dispatch local police to your position to make the arrest."

"Leo," Meigs whispered. "I want you to lob some tear gas down the alley. Go high so it comes down on the other side of the dumpsters, got it?"

The eighteen year old, just across the narrow street, nodded. He trembled as he loaded a grenade into the fat tube of the launcher slung under his rifle. All four of the men put on their gas masks, and then Meigs nodded to Leo.

Turville heard a low thud, and the grenade flew into the alley. His heart beat so hard he could feel it in his ears. Why did they gas the alley? What if someone came out with a gun—came out shooting? What if the killer was in there?

Turville slowly pulled back the charging handle on his rifle and chambered a round. The sound was muffled from inside his gas mask and hood, and his vision was constricted. He could hear himself breathing fast. Better this than the damn tear gas.

The smoke puffed out of the alley, and then Turville heard a loud clang. Holy shit, what was that? Another bang, then someone came running out of the alley, straight at them. Short black guy, hard to see, his body silhouetted in the billowing smoke. He had something in his hand—a pistol.

Leo shouted, voice muffled under the mask, "He's got a gun!"

Turville raised his rifle, flipped the thumb safety forward, and aimed.

"Turville, *no!*"

He squeezed the trigger and the rifle jerked back against his shoulder. The running man screamed and fell to the ground, then slid to a stop ten feet away. The other three soldiers ran to him and stopped, staring down. Turville hung back, afraid to look for a moment. Then he took a step forward. The teargas was already dissipating, and he pulled his mask off.

It was a kid, maybe fourteen years old, maybe younger. He stared up at the four men in their combat gear and gas masks, eyes wide. He opened his mouth to speak, and a line of bright red blood ran out of the corner of his mouth. He didn't have a gun—he had a video camera gripped in his right hand. A small hole had punctured the front of his chest, but it must have made one hell of an exit wound, because blood soaked the ground. Meigs leaned over the boy.

"Oh, shit," Turville whispered. He could still smell the acrid gunpowder and teargas.

Meigs turned to him in a rage, ripped off his mask and threw it at Turville. The mask bounced against his chest, but Turville hardly noticed.

"You *motherfucker!* What the *hell* were you thinking?"

Turville stared back at Meigs, eyes unfocused, his mouth open. The corporal shoved him back against a wall, his face swollen with rage. He grabbed the rifle from Turville and shouted, "I ought to shoot you with this, you stupid cracker!"

In the background, a thousand miles away, Turville heard their platoon leader on the radio. "White Three, White Three, we heard a shot, what's going on, over?"

Meigs turned his back to Turville, then keyed his microphone. "White Six, this is White Three Leader. We have a civilian casualty. I repeat: we have a civilian with a gunshot wound. We need a medic right now, over."

"Roger, civilian with a gunshot wound. I'll be there ASAP. I need a full report. White Six, out."

A civilian. I shot a civilian.

Meigs crouched over the boy and broke out his field dressing, and then looked back up at Turville.

"Turville, you're going to fry for this. I told you not to lock and goddamn load! I checked your weapon! Even after that you loaded your goddamn rifle and pointed at someone and fired? What the *fuck* is wrong with you?"

The blood covered the street.

Turville shook his head and started to cry. "Oh, shit. Oh, shit."

Gomez, his squad automatic rifle slung over his shoulder, looked at Turville with contempt. "Go ahead and cry, you stupid fuck. You killed a fucking *kid*, Turville. And you screwed us all. *Motherfucker.*"

Turville sank down to the ground and watched as Meigs and Leo tried to save the boy's life.

It was too late.

Chapter Twenty-Three
September 14

"Black Six, Black Six, this is White Six. Contact report, over."

Morris winced at the sudden pain in his right ear. Lieutenant Wingham's voice sounded high pitched, almost at a squeal.

"Hold on a second, sir," Morris said to Major Simone Gooding, the operations officer.

He keyed his microphone. "White Six, you need to calm down and give me your report in a professional manner, over."

"Black Six, we have a civilian down. I repeat we have a civilian down with a gunshot wound, at my platoon's position. I need an evac, sir."

Morris looked at Major Gooding, held his breath, and then keyed the radio again. "White Six, did our people fire on this individual? Over."

Major Gooding's face paled at Morris's words.

"Affirmative, sir."

"Damn it, I'm on my way. What's your position?"

Lieutenant Wingham gave him the position, and Morris replied, "Black Six out."

"Major, we've got a problem. One of the men in my first platoon shot a civilian. I don't know the circumstances yet. Can you get an ambulance and let Colonel Barksdale know? I need to get to my company."

Simone frowned. "Oh, God, that's just what we need. You go deal with it, Captain. Get the situation calmed down. I'll get the ambulance on the way."

"Yes, sir."

Morris spun around and called out, "Watson, let's go, right now. We need to get to first platoon's position yesterday."

"Yes, sir." Specialist Watson, Morris's driver and radio operator, had the HUMMWV rolling as soon as Morris got into his seat. Two minutes later, as they raced toward the position, Morris received another call from the first platoon leader, Lieutenant Wingham.

"Black Six, this is White Six. Please be advised we have civilians at our position. The situation is getting ugly, over."

Watson turned the corner and drove into the intersection of Eagan and North Rand. A crowd had gathered thirty feet from the intersection, on a narrow side street. Morris could see half of first platoon, plus four civilian men and one woman. More men and women crowded the opening to the alley, staying well back from the soldiers. As Morris jumped out of his vehicle, sized up the situation and approached quickly.

"Okay, folks. An ambulance is on the way, we need to make some room."

"Who the hell are you, motherfucker?" shouted one of the men. His face was swollen, angry.

"I'm Captain Michael Morris. I'm trying to get an ambulance in here to the victim. Who are you?"

"That's my son, you son of a bitch!"

Morris sized up the scene. A boy who couldn't have been older than fifteen lay on the ground, blood spread in a pool all around his body. Bandages were scattered about, some of them tied around the boy's midsection. Some of the blood was dried, crusted on the bandages, and the medics had stopped working on him. Morris' shoulders slumped.

A woman was crouched over the boy, wailing. Her clothes were soaked in blood. At the head of the intersection, nearly a dozen people watched the scene, and more looked down from windows above.

Morris turned and looked the man in the eyes. "Sir, I can't undo what happened, but I'll make damn sure the person responsible is arrested immediately. We'll do whatever we can, I promise."

"You've already done too goddamned much."

The father swung and punched Morris in the face. His vision went black, and he fell backwards to the ground, stunned.

Soldiers grabbed the father and restrained him. Lieutenant Wingham helped Morris up.

Three soldiers dragged the father away from the scene as he shouted. Morris put a hand up to his nose. Blood came away on his hand.

"Who did this, Lieutenant?"

"Sir, it was PFC Turville in my first squad."

Morris looked around. Turville leaned against a wall, his face red and bloated.

"Turville, get your ass over here," ordered the lieutenant.

Turville looked up; saw Morris, and his eyes widened. He jumped to his feet and ran over, then stood at attention and saluted.

Morris did not return the salute, but stared at Turville, his eyes cold. Turville held the salute. Morris did not return it, and hated himself for what he knew he had to do. Turville was just a kid, and had screwed up badly. Now he'd have to pay adult consequences.

"Put your arm down, private. As of now you are a prisoner and are no longer entitled to salute. Do you understand me?"

Turville's face worked and his reply was a whisper. He dropped the salute. "Yes, sir."

"Where's your team and squad leader?"

The lieutenant yelled, "Sergeant Roy, Corporal Meigs. Get over here!"

Both men ran up and stood in front of the CO, then saluted. He returned their salutes.

"Meigs, Roy, because of your negligence one of your men shot and killed an unarmed civilian. Do you have anything to say for yourselves?"

Sergeant Roy shifted his feet and frowned. "Sir, we made the orders clear, and I personally checked everyone's weapons to make sure no one was locked and loaded, just like the LT said."

Morris frowned. "Lieutenant Wingham, I want both of these men to report to me once we're done with this operation. In the meantime, Corporal Meigs, I want you to escort PFC Turville to battalion headquarters. Do you understand?"

Meigs nodded. "Sir, what should I do with his weapon?"

"Give it to the MPs, and make sure they sign for it. You've had it in your possession since the incident? Has anyone else touched it?"

"Just me, sir, I took it from Turville right after it happened."

"Good job. Get going, I want this—person—out of my sight."

"Yes, sir."

Meigs grabbed Turville and led him away.

"Hey, that's the motherfucker shot my son."

Morris turned around at the shout. The crowd at the corner had grown larger—and angrier. Two of Morris' soldiers still held the father off to the side of the alley.

Three of the men from the crowd—teenagers—approached Meigs and Turville.

"Meigs, Turville, get back here. Belay that order. We'll send you to battalion shortly."

He turned to Wingham. "We need to get control of this situation now. Post some men to block anyone coming down here."

"You," he shouted to the three approaching teenagers. "Stop right there!"

One of the teenagers looked at Morris with disdain, then at the body of the boy, then back at Morris.

"What if I don't? This is America. You gonna shoot me, too?"

"No, in fact I just arrested the stupid son of a bitch who did it. You want to get in the way of that?"

"Bunch of white folks shooting up the town, from what I can see."

As they spoke, Lieutenant Wingham and Sergeant O'Donnell placed men at each corner of the side street as security.

Someone called from the intersection, "Why don't you go shoot some rich white folks instead!"

Morris ignored the shouts and catcalls and called Lieutenant Colonel Barksdale on the radio.

"This is Colonel Barksdale."

From the background noise it sounded like he was in a vehicle.

"Sir, this is Captain Morris, with a report."

"Proceed, Captain."

"Sir, I am at the position of my first platoon. One of my men, PFC Turville, shot and killed a civilian. Turville has been placed under arrest. I've got men securing the perimeter of this position, and a growing, very angry crowd. A civilian ambulance has been called, but it's too late to do anything. That's it, sir."

"Can you maintain your situation there?"

Morris glanced at the crowd. "I think so, sir, but if this crowd gets more belligerent I may have to disperse them. These folks are very angry."

"I got you, Captain. Try your best to not to have to do that."

Morris flinched at a loud crack. A small rock bounced off his helmet.

"Yes, sir, I will."

Morris marched toward the edge of the intersection, which four of his men were blocking. Morris guessed there were now about twenty men there, most of them teenagers, really. Morris could see the anger in their eyes. The rest of the crowd looked to be just gawkers, onlookers, but not people he needed to worry about.

"Listen to me," he shouted. "I understand you are angry about what happened here. So am I. I have placed the individual who did this under arrest, and he will be tried for what happened. But I need you to disperse and return to your homes or wherever else, now. An ambulance is on the way to pick up the victim."

A young man of maybe sixteen looked at Morris with contempt. "This is my home, and that's my cousin you shot. I need *you* to disperse, motherfucker."

Morris heard a shout behind him. "Sir, we got dismounts up on the roof."

Morris stepped back and looked up. The apartment building next to the alley stood four stories, and someone stood there, silhouetted against the sky. Something flew off the roof.

"Ah, shit!" shouted one of the soldiers.

One' soldier had to jump out of the way to avoid the object, which shattered onto the pavement. A brick.

"Lieutenant Wingham, get some tear gas on top of that building."

He turned back to the crowd and called out, "Please disperse at once. We will deploy tear gas in thirty seconds."

He heard an ambulance approach with a wail. Another brick crashed into the ground near him. Morris put on his gas mask as the men did the same. The mask still smelled acrid from the last time they'd used it in the gas chamber.

"Fire," Wingham called. Four tear gas grenades fired in an arc: two of them landed on the rooftop, the other two fell back to the ground. The noxious smoke drifted toward the now shouting crowd.

Wingham shouted to his men to reorient and target the crowd. The four men calmly reloaded their grenade launchers. One of the teenagers pulled out a gun.

"*No!*" Morris shouted.

"Fire," Wingham said at the same time, and the four grenadiers launched tear gas grenades at the crowd.

The teenager shot a soldier in the face. Morris ran forward and heard a rifle fire. The kid with the gun fell to the ground, shot in the gut.

Morris screamed, "*Cease fire! Medic!* We need a medic right now!"

The people in the crowd screamed and scattered at the sound of gunshots. The kid on the ground raised his weapon again to fire, and one of Morris' men kicked the pistol away from him.

Morris reached the man who'd been hit—Specialist Jack Frazier. "*Medic!*" he shouted.

Another brick crashed down and hit a soldier, who screamed and fell to the ground.

"Lieutenant Wingham," Morris called. "Get your men out of this alley and into the intersection. *Now!*"

Wingham and Sergeant O'Donnell rushed the platoon off the narrow street and into the intersection. The remainder of the crowd scattered as the soldiers ran out of the alley.

The medic, a female PFC named Hall, skidded to the ground next to Morris and Specialist Frazier.

Oh, Christ, Morris thought. Hall and Frazier had dated over the summer. *Why the hell do I have to have women in this unit?*

She looked at the body, her face frozen. Frazier had only a small hole in his cheek next to his nose, but the exit wound was gruesome and terminal: a good chunk of the back of his head was scattered across the pavement.

She spoke in a monotone. "He's dead, sir."

"Do what you can to help the kid there who shot him. And we've got another man down over there; he was hit by a brick."

He paused, wondering if he should say something to her… No. He turned away.

"Wingham, deploy your men to secure this intersection, and clear those rooftops. I don't want any more goddamn casualties!"

As the men spread out into the intersection to comply with his order, Morris followed, going to the center of the intersection. One of his platoons had split up into squads to occupy the nearby rooftops. He cracked open his gas mask. The air was mostly clear of tear gas now. He pulled off his mask and called Barksdale again.

"Barksdale."

"Colonel, this is Captain Morris. Our situation is rapidly deteriorating. We were assaulted with bricks thrown off the top of the buildings at our position, and then someone in the crowd shot one of my men. I have one killed-in-action, sir, and one seriously wounded. He was hit by a flying brick, plus there's one more civilian down with a gunshot wound. I've got men securing the perimeter now."

As he spoke an ambulance came screaming into the intersection. Lieutenant Wingham ran to meet it and led the paramedics to the wounded. As they did so, Morris heard another shot fired, this one distant.

Barksdale spoke. "Between the DHS and your man, we've stirred up a goddamned hornets' nest. There's been another shooting incident, this one not involving our troops, but the locals are pissed. Just hunker down and keep your position secure. I'm working on getting us pulled out of here."

"Roger, sir."

༄

Morris heard the thump of another tear gas grenade, this one to the south of the intersection. Twenty tense minutes had passed since the ambulance left, and his company had now linked up in one location. Then men were hunkered down, hoping to avoid any more trouble. Periodically one of the grenadiers fired a tear gas grenade to prevent the crowd from reforming, but otherwise it had been quiet since the initial disaster.

Morris's nose was red and swollen. He tried not to touch it—felt like it might be broken. What the hell had Turville been thinking? Now two people were dead, and Turville was sure to face a general court-martial on their return to base.

Turville wasn't the only one facing a court-martial. Morris knew he would be held responsible for what happened. He was in charge; he was the officer who had allowed one of his men to blow away a kid on an American street. *Goddammit.*

"Black Six, this is White Six," he heard Lieutenant Wingham call over the radio. "We have a TV satellite truck approaching the position at this time, over."

"Stop them," he ordered. "Don't let them in the position."

Morris stood and saw the van approaching from the south. Two of his men stood out in the intersection, rifles slung over their shoulders, waving the van to a stop.

The van pulled around them, tires squealing, and pulled directly into the middle of the intersection. What the hell was wrong with that driver, he could have run over one of the men! Morris marched toward the van, a scowl on his face.

A cameraman was already out of the van, filming in a circle, capturing the smoke and the men huddled around the intersection, staying low behind cars. A second man set up a tripod and sound equipment, while a blonde woman stepped out of the passenger side of the van. She wore a red coat and a gold pendant in the shape of a hawk. Her hair was platinum blonde, not quite shoulder length, and her blue eyes flashed at Morris as he approached. She reminded him of Alicia.

He already hated her.

"What the hell are you doing driving around my men like that? Didn't you see them wave at you to stop?"

The man with the tripod stopped what he was doing and approached Morris from the side, hovering protectively over the reporter. The cameraman, meanwhile, turned his lens to Morris and the blonde woman.

"We're filming here, and I didn't see any police," she said. "I'm Sarah Davis from NBC Channel Four. Who are you?"

"Ms. Davis, this area has been secured by my men, who you almost ran over. I'm going to have to ask you to stop your filming and go somewhere else, immediately."

Morris could sense the camera closing in on him, and he felt his stomach clench as he realized the situation he'd gotten himself into.

"You don't have any authority to tell me to go anywhere, soldier. We're not in some Pentagon-controlled foreign war where you can order the press around. This is America, and I am filming right here." As she spoke the last sentence she pointed her finger straight at the ground for emphasis.

She turned away from him and spoke to the man with the tripod.

"Set up the camera with those soldiers as a backdrop." She pointed across the intersection to indicate the direction.

Morris clenched his teeth and kept his arms straight at his side. "You may not film my men, do you understand me?"

She rolled her eyes and turned away.

Morris turned, walked away and called Barksdale on the radio.

"Sir, this is Captain Morris. We have another situation developing. A news satellite van just drove into my position, and they are planning on filming my men and this position."

Barksdale cursed. "Don't let them film your troops! Understand me, Captain?"

"Yes, sir. I'll probably have to use force to take the camera from them."

"Understand, but this is a U.S. Army operation and I won't have damn reporters wandering around filming the troops."

"Yes, sir."

They hung up, and Morris called out. "Lieutenant Wingham!"

The Lieutenant ran over. "Two men. I want that camera disconnected and the film removed and destroyed, right now."

Davis primped herself in the mirror of the van as the cameraman filmed the activity of the men. The cameraman started to back away as two of the soldiers approached, rifles slung over their shoulder.

"Sir, please stay right where you are and turn off that camera."

The cameraman looked at Morris, then the approaching men, then at Sarah Davis. He shook his head and continued to film the approach of the two soldiers.

One of the soldiers spoke, his voice firm. "You are going to have to give that to us, sir."

One of the soldiers grabbed the cameraman from the side as the other grabbed the camera.

"I'm not giving you the camera! What the hell is this?" The cameraman struggled, his face red.

The other man came at a run, but Morris and Lieutenant Wingham stepped in his path.

"Don't do it," said Morris. "Look, my men were called in to help the situation, and we have been shot at and attacked and I won't have their faces on the evening news, do you understand me?"

The cameraman shouted as one of the soldiers got the camera away.

"How do you work this thing?" the soldier said, trying to figure out how to remove the tape.

"There's no tape," the cameraman said. "It's on a satellite uplink. Your whole Gestapo act was filmed live, asshole," the cameraman said. "I hope you enjoy watching yourself on the news."

The contempt in the reporter's voice turned Morris's blood to ice.

"Wingham. Tell your men to mask. I want four tear gas grenades under this truck in thirty seconds."

"Yes, sir."

Morris spoke to the two soldiers. "Give him back his toy and get your masks on."

"Gas!" In addition to shouting, Wingham made the hand signal for the troops to mask.

The soldiers put on gas masks, and panic appeared on Sarah Davis' face.

"Go, go!" she shouted and ran for the van. The film crew rushed to get back in the van as four tear gas grenades flew into the center of the intersection.

Smoke billowed up from underneath the van. The reporters sped off, a cloud of smoke trailing them.

Ten minutes later Morris got the call from Colonel Barksdale to get on the trucks and pull back to the federal building.

෴

Only a few blocks away from the developing chaos, Murphy stood with Joe Blankenship at a counter in the Office of Elections and Licensing, arguing with the police and the clerk. Their voices sounded disjointed to Murphy as a radio talk show played in the background.

"I'm sorry, sir, but those boxes are evidence in a murder investigation. You have to turn them over."

It appeared the clerk agreed. Both boxes were spattered with blood, especially the one Dale Whitt had been carrying when he was murdered.

Blankenship shook his head fervently. "No way. Don't you understand what this is? This is the petition we've been running all over the state for the last two months to get signatures for. Today is the deadline to turn it over if we want to get in on the ballot."

The police officer put his hands on his hips, anger on his face. "Sir, it doesn't matter to me what it is. I'm working on a murder investigation, and those boxes are part of the evidence."

Murphy spoke. "Officer, I'd like to talk to your precinct captain. A man died to deliver these petitions, but he got them here. For you to take them—even for one day—would be a tremendous miscarriage of justice."

The officer sneered at Murphy. "I know what this is. It's seditious crap. You can't tell me you believe what they're doing is right."

Murphy replied, "It doesn't matter what I believe."

They all looked up when they heard the radio host talking again.

"In yet another bizarre incident of violence in Charleston, the scene of several major incidents in the last three days, troops in the U.S. Army have engaged in a shooting incident with civilians in the city streets. At this time we understand there are three dead, including a teenager who was shot while videotaping the Army. According to sources on the scene, the troops were assisting local police in identifying the assassin who gunned down anti-government activist Dale Whitt on the capitol steps just this morning. All I can say is, what is going on there, folks? West Virginia is starting to look more dangerous than the Middle East. That will be our topic for the hour, and we're ready to take your calls."

The radio host moved on to a caller. Murphy, Blankenship, and the police officer looked at each other.

Blankenship's face twisted and he spoke, his voice on the verge of breaking. "Those people murdered my wife. You'll have to kill me to keep me from delivering these petitions. If you're going to do that, go right ahead. Otherwise, they're getting turned in. Understand?"

The police officer looked at him and sighed. "All right."

He turned to the clerk. "Hey, you got any paper boxes back there?"

The clerk nodded.

"Bring me one of them. You can put your petitions into the new box—I'll videotape you doing that—and I'll take the old boxes. Deal?"

Blankenship nodded. "Thank you," he said.

"I've got to get going, Joe," Murphy said.

He hurried back to his headquarters.

Chapter Twenty-Four
September 15

The next morning dawned cold and wet. Swollen creeks and rivers across West Virginia had overflowed their banks, challenging the capacity of the state's already strained emergency services far past the breaking point.

In Charleston, Morris had spent a sleepless night writing a report on the previous day's incident. . On his arrival at the temporary headquarters, the first thing he saw on the flatscreen television, always tuned to Fox News, was his own face as he ordered the reporters hit with tear gas. The media was having a field day already, and had moved quickly to condemn what the reporter had called his "Gestapo" act.

Now, as he went through his verbal report, he could feel Barksdale's cold eyes on him, and he knew there was no recovering from this They stood near the map table in a cold, damp tent. The battalion staff officers gathered around the opposite side of the tent, studiously turned away and surely listening to every word. The tent stank of mildew after days standing in the rain.

"That was it, sir. After the reporters left it stayed quiet until we received the order from you to pull out. Once we arrived back at the base camp I had PFC Turville confined to his tent until the MPs took him."

Barksdale frowned. "What's your recommendation for dealing with PFC Turville?"

"I'd like to handle it in-house, sir, with an Article 15. Turville screwed up, badly, but I don't believe it was deliberate malice. I honestly don't know what a general court-martial will accomplish other than ruining a young man's life."

Barksdale grunted. "Well, at least one other young man is dead because of your man's mistake. I understand the desire to use non-judicial punishment, and frankly, I agree. But it won't fly in this case: right now it's a question of how serious the court-martial will be."

"I see, sir."

"Instruct your men who were witnesses that they are not to discuss the incident with anyone—not even each other. I don't want to contaminate their testimony before the trial. And let's make sure PFC Turville gets good representation from the Judge Advocate General's office—I don't want some wet-behind-the-ears lieutenant, I want someone who knows what he's doing."

"Yes, sir."

Barksdale sighed. "For what it's worth, Morris, I think you are right—it would be stupid to send Turville to prison. But the political dimension of this... Captain, you have no idea. This is very likely to blow up in the Army's face. So what we have to do is work extra hard to make sure Turville gets a fair trial, and give the Army a fair chance to convict him. If he's cleared by a court-martial, the country will see we went through the appropriate steps to investigate and deal with it. Whereas, if we do an Article 15, they'll say we let him off, the Army doesn't care he killed some kid."

Some people were going to blame the Army no matter what they did. All the same, Morris agreed. "Yes, sir, I do understand. I'll do my best to make sure I do my part correctly."

"Good, good. Now, I want to talk to you about what this means for you."

Morris didn't trust himself to speak. For the last twenty-four hours, he'd assumed his military career had come to an end. All he needed now was confirmation.

"Look, Captain, I won't sugarcoat it. General Blake's going to order an Article 32 hearing for sure, and it looks to me like you will be the individual held responsible for what happened. It's likely you'll be forced out of the service, if not worse."

"Yes, sir. I've suspected as much."

"You do have an option, Captain. You can go through the investigation and the public humiliation of being thrown out. There's at least a remote chance you may go to prison. Or you could consider resigning for the good of the service. I can probably convince General Blake to close the door on this investigation if you resign and walk away."

Morris looked at the wall, his eyes unfocused. "Sir, I've never wanted to be anything other than a soldier."

"I understand, Captain. I can't even imagine what this conversation must be like for you. But you've been in the Army for a few years—I think you understand why this has to happen. What matters is what's good for the service, not for you and I as individuals."

"Yes, sir, I understand. I'm going to need to think about it."

"That's reasonable. We're returning to base in the next day or two, as soon as we get the orders. Why don't you come see me when we've settled and we'll talk about it."

At least that gave him a day or two.

"Yes, sir, I will. Thank you, sir."

"You are dismissed, Captain."

Morris stood and walked out. As he stuck his arms in the tent flaps to spread them apart, the other officers stepped away from him, as if he were contagious. They'd carefully avoided him since returning from the mission.

Outside the tent it was cold, but the rain had stopped.

Resign and walk away, he thought. He didn't know if he could do that.

Had the incident happened in an overseas deployment, the Army would likely shrug it off as a mistake, with an inquiry and disciplinary action, potentially severe. But this was different. They were deployed in an American city; the kid Turville had killed was an American citizen. Turville would be lucky to escape prison, and Mike knew it was a very real possibility for him as well.

Morris walked away from the headquarters tent. Turville, in one stroke, with one instance of supremely bad judgment, had ruined four lives: the dead kid's, Frazier's, his own, and Morris's. All because he'd loaded his weapon when he'd been ordered not to.

He walked aimlessly, and found himself down by the Kanahwa River. Funny. He'd been here for several days, primarily downtown, and in the historic district, and this was the first time he'd really looked at the place. It was a nice-looking town, especially near the river, but a biting wind blew in from its direction. November was approaching.

He stared out at the water, and stuffed his hands in the pockets of his field jacket. Why the hell was Turville such a screw-up? He'd been trouble since Morris's first day commanding the company.

But a conflicting voice asked, *If you knew that, why did you send him on the mission?* He vividly remembered Colonel Atkins, his military science instructor at Bowling Green, saying that it was unethical and bad leadership to give an order you knew couldn't be complied with.

Resign and walk away. What the hell would he do? His whole life was built around the Army. Hell, he'd have to go back to school just to become qualified to do anything else. Maybe he could do what Alicia and his father-in-law wanted all along: become a politician.

Not likely.

Would Alicia even be there when he returned? He'd called half a dozen times, but hadn't been able to reach her. Maybe he could try again.

Morris stood and kept walking. A lone phone booth stood halfway down the block. He went in and dialed the number, then keyed in his calling card.

The phone rang, and rang again, and then the machine picked up. Morris slammed the phone down in frustration. He'd already left three messages. And he already knew why she didn't answer: Alicia had taken Savannah and they were both gone back home to Kentucky, to her father. She'd made it clear she'd leave if he didn't resign.

Ironic. Now he was going to have to resign anyway, he didn't want her back. Not a chance in the world. Back to cold and bitterness? Back to the daily biting commentary? Screw that. In their seven years of marriage, he'd never once been able to make her happy, never once been able to satisfy her. She hated him for getting her pregnant, and that was the end of it for their relationship.

But what about Savannah? His daughter made his life worth living, in a thousand different ways. How could he ever leave her? Was there any chance in hell he could ever get custody of his daughter?

Probably not as long as he was in the military, that was for sure. Certainly not if they court-martialed him. Even if he resigned, he was marked for life. What kind of job would he be able to get? Sure, he could picture the job interview. Experience and skills: Rappelling out of helicopters. Assaulting a defended position. Movement to contact. Call for fire.

Give me a break. The Army sold the ability to carry leadership skills into the civilian world, but middle managers all across the country had been wiped out in two years of layoffs. He'd be like some of the other officers he'd seen, selling insurance off-post, or hawking encyclopedias to people who couldn't afford them. He'd have no money, no life, and no daughter.

Morris told himself to shut up. No point in going around in circles like this. He would find a job, then sue for custody, do the best he could. He'd be damned if that woman would take off for Kentucky with his child without even the courtesy of returning a phone call.

⁂

Karen's desk in the makeshift battalion headquarters was piled high with documents. She'd spent the last twelve hours writing the operations plan for the battalion to take over security for the federal building. In the morning they would take over security from the outgoing U.S. Army unit, which was being yanked out of Charleston after yesterday's shooting.

Morris's unit, she thought, wondering if he was okay. She had heard one soldier was killed and two more injured.

She printed off the completed plan, reviewed it for accuracy, then e-mailed it to Major Elkins for approval and shut down the laptop. It was time to get some sleep.

If she could. She'd had some lurid dreams of Corporal Stanson, lying on his back with blood pouring from his throat, screaming for his mother. If she never saw anything like that again it would be too soon. She didn't care what Elkins and Murphy said—it *was* her fault Stanson was dead. She was his company commander. It was her responsibility.

The guard knocked and opened the door. His eyes scanned the room until he saw her.

"Ma'am—someone here to see you. A Captain Morris."

Her stomach clenched. *Mike.*

"Let him in."

Morris entered the room. His brow was creased with tension, and there were angry red rims around his eyes as they darted around the room, at the on-duty NCOs and officers who worked in the command post.

She didn't smile. "Why don't we go talk privately?"

She stood and walked around her desk, ignoring the eyes she knew followed her.

Morris followed her as she led him down the hall to a vacant office. She switched on the low wattage light and closed the door.

Morris leaned against the desk.

"How are you making it?" he asked.

"So far, so good," she answered. "You've looked better."

"It's been a rough couple of days."

"Was your company involved in the shooting?"

"Yeah. One of my guys—a PFC Turville—had his weapon loaded when it wasn't supposed to be, and he panicked when he saw a kid running. Everything just went to hell from there."

"I know that feeling."

"Yeah, I guess so."

Their eyes met. Despite years of anger, she still caught her breath looking at him. The son of a bitch. For a moment she railed at herself for weakness. She'd been hopelessly in love with him in college, but that was a long time ago.

"How are they dealing with it?"

"Turville will be court-martialed, likely sent to prison. We'll probably yank a stripe from his team and squad leaders. My battalion commander tells me I can probably avoid an investigation and possible court-martial myself, if I resign for the good of the service. We're being pulled out. We go back home tomorrow."

"Are you going to resign?"

"I don't know yet. Would *you?* I mean—what the hell else am I going to do? I'm an infantry officer. What the hell would I do in the civilian world? I've never given it a moment's thought before."

He looked at the floor and laughed. His mannerisms, his posture—they hadn't changed in all these years.

"You know what's crazy? For five, maybe six years, Alicia's been telling herself it's my career she hates, and I've been telling myself the same. I don't think that's it at all. Here I am, I'm finally going to have to quit, and the thought of listening to her say she was right—it makes me hate her. Oh, God, does it make me hate her."

Karen rolled her eyes. "Join the club. I've always hated her."

"But Karen, I love my daughter so much. Savannah is everything to me. You can't even imagine—I'd live through a thousand hells to be with her, but I don't think I can go back to that woman."

Karen looked away from him. "You know what, Mike? I may not be the best person to discuss your domestic woes with. You won't get any sympathy from me."

He caught her eyes. "You know I never stopped loving you."

She felt the furrow between her brows. "Shut up."

"I mean it. I go to bed beside her and wish it was you. I wake up expecting you and it's like a kick in the gut every morning. I wish... I wish Savannah was calling *you* Mom, not her. Don't you get it? One night, it was the worst mistake of my life, and I'm still being punished for it."

"You should be punished for it, you son of a bitch. You broke my heart." Her vision blurred, and tears rolled down her face. "How can you show back up in my life after seven years without a word, and now you tell me this. God *damn* you!" She jerked her arm up and wiped the tears off her face. "You know what? You can't do this. I can already see it happening—in a couple days you'll be out of here, back to wherever the hell it is you're stationed, you'll be back with *her*. And you want to come here and screw with my mind. Well, screw you!"

He slowly shook his head. "No. Whatever else happens, I won't go back to her."

"You're not coming back to me either."

His shoulders slumped and he bobbed his head. "I guess I deserve that." Looking defeated, he sat down on the chair next to the desk and sighed.

She sat in the chair across from him.

"Mike, listen to me. I don't think you quite get it in that self-centered little head of yours. We were engaged, Mike. We'd been together four years. I bought my dress." Tears rolled down her face unchecked as she spoke. "Did you ever even once think about me? We had the chapel reserved, and my friends had their stupid bridesmaid dresses, we were done. Everything ready to go—oh, God, I was so in love with you. Do you know I would have taken you back in a second? I would have let it go. So you got drunk and slept with someone. Big deal, people make mistakes! But it wasn't one night, you son of a bitch. You came to me and said you were leaving me, that you were going to marry that horrible bitch so she could have her baby!"

Morris stared at her, his eyes wide, silent. She thought he looked like a deer, staring at an approaching car.

"I had to go to my family and friends and tell them you were gone," she whispered. "I had to cancel with the church, and fire the pianist, and give back the dress. I even had to tell *your* friends. You never even took your ring back. You were so self centered and weak you couldn't even face me. I still have the ring. And now—you selfish son of a bitch—now *you* are unhappy, now your marriage sucks and you come crawling back to me?"

He fell to his knees and put his clasped hands in her lap, looked up at her. She shied back from him. Tears rolled down his face. "I was too ashamed, Karen. I couldn't talk to you, I was just so ashamed of myself. Karen, I—I am so sorry for hurting you. I am so sorry. I loved you with all my heart and I just didn't know what to do."

She leaned forward and their lips brushed—just barely. She held that position, felt his lips against hers.

"I thought I was going to die when you left me." Her lips still touched his as she spoke.

"I did too," he replied, his hands rising up to touch the sides of her face.

Her eyes were closed as she kissed him, feeling his stubble against her face. She sobbed as she realized this would have to make up for a lifetime.

She broke away and pulled him to his feet, then looked him in the eyes.

"Now go. Don't come back. I don't ever want to see or hear from you again."

He flinched and closed his eyes. "I... I understand. I love you, Karen Greenfield."

"And I love you, you bastard. Go home to your family."

He backed away, opened the door, and stepped out. He took a deep breath, as if he were about to say something, and turned back toward her. She met his eyes and shivered. Then he closed the door.

Karen took a deep breath and stared at the closed door. Then she sat at the dust-covered desk and put her head in her hands.

Chapter Twenty-Five
October 20

Morris's key stuck in the lock just a little, and his hands shook from cold and exhaustion. He'd been up all night, as the company unloaded equipment and turned in their weapons and masks.

He had a pretty good idea of what he would find inside the house. He exhaled in a cloud of white mist and dropped his rucksack to the ground, then tried the lock again.

This time it opened and revealed the bare hallway.

Oh, man, she didn't screw around.

He picked up the heavy rucksack and slung it over his shoulder, then entered the house.

She'd taken everything. Most of the furniture, the books. With a grunt, he noticed she'd left behind his favorite chair in the living room, the brown leather two-seater easy-chair. He used to ask her to come join him on it, but after a while, he guessed he'd stopped asking.

She left a note, attached to the refrigerator door by a magnet she'd thoughtfully left behind. His eyes scanned it, but he wasn't ready to read it just yet. His breath still gave off clouds, and he realized she'd left the heat off. He switched it on as he walked toward the stairs.

Upstairs, the bed he had shared with Alicia was still there, along with his clothes. But everything from Savannah's room was gone, including her bed, and its bedstand with the sun and stars decorating it in phosphorescent paint.

Morris closed his eyes, leaned against the wall. *Come on, you knew she was gone. You've known for two or three weeks.* But ... *Oh, man.* In Savannah's closet, the low rail they'd put up for her clothes was still there, along with half-a-dozen miniature coat hangers.

He sat down to the floor. His eyes darted from place to place in the room, seeing the holes where tacks had been inserted in the wall. Somehow he'd been hoping against hope… Maybe she'd just temporarily left town, or wasn't around when he'd called, or something, anything other than this stark empty child's bedroom with a red plastic coat hanger lying in the middle of the floor.

He felt too tired to stand up. He sat there, slumped over, and stared at the dust left behind where Savannah's bed had been.

Fool. For years he'd pulled away from Alicia, always chasing another woman in his mind, a woman *he'd* walked away from. He shook his head. In all these years he'd never given up the fantasy of life with Karen, a life with her that would somehow be different: satisfying, happy, whatever. What if Alicia had loved him all along? Alicia hadn't poisoned their marriage—*he* had. When was the last time he'd touched her? When was the last time he'd looked at her with love in his eyes?

The shriek of the telephone startled him. Slowly, he got to his feet and walked to the bedroom, then picked up the phone and sat on the unmade bed.

"Captain Morris speaking, sir." The rule in the Army was to assume that your caller was higher rank.

"Morris, this is Major Ben Wharton, with the Judge Advocate General's office."

JAG?

"What can I do for you, Major?"

"Well, Captain, I think the question should be 'what can I do for you?' I understand there may be an investigation of the incident in Charleston. I've been asked to serve as your counsel, unless you intend to hire outside counsel."

Morris took a deep breath.

"Sir, who asked you to serve as my counsel? I just walked in my front door ten minutes ago."

"Captain, word came down from the Commanding General's office to expect an Article 32 hearing. Understand, at this point, there is no official investigation. It will come soon enough. But because the charges could potentially be serious, my boss thought it would be best you have someone experienced on your side. That's me."

Morris shrugged. "All right, Major, you're hired. Should we meet?"

"Why don't I come over there? I know where your place is, I'll bring some steaks. Your wife like steak?"

"That may not be such a good idea, Major. My wife seems to be out, and I don't think she'll be back in time for dinner."

The line was silent. Then Wharton spoke again.

"In that case I'll bring a six-pack. See you shortly."

The lawyer hung up before Morris could tell him no. He stood up and walked into the bathroom, looked critically in the mirror. He was filthy and needed a shower.

Screw it. He walked downstairs, picked up a discarded newspaper, and placed it in the door, holding it open. An icy draft blew through the crack. Then he went back upstairs, collected clean clothes, most of which were piled in a mess on the floor of the closet, and got in the shower.

They'd been in the field for two weeks, and it took a while to get the dirt and soot free. One of the things Morris hated, though he'd gotten used to it over the years, was the inability to get clean while deployed. Didn't matter that it had rained most of the time they were in West Virginia—he still came back filthy, his uniforms stinking of mildew, his skin tinged slightly green.

He took his shower mechanically, and then got out, not feeling any better. At least he didn't smell any more. Then he cursed. She'd taken all the towels.

He grabbed his bathrobe from the floor of the closet and used it to dry himself off, then put on clean clothes. She'd taken the clock as well. He'd need to stop by the Post Exchange and pick one up later today. If he had any money. She might well have cleaned out the bank accounts.

Enough. He walked downstairs in his bare feet. Normally he would never show up in front of a senior officer in jeans and a t-shirt with no shoes, but for God's sake, it wasn't as if Morris had invited him.

As his foot touched the worn carpet on the ground floor he heard a knock at the partially open door.

"Hello!" called a voice from outside.

"Come on in, sir. I was just cleaning up." Morris approached the door and opened it all the way.

Outside stood a very tall, barrel-chested man with a flannel shirt and jeans. He was probably ten years older than Morris, somewhere in his late thirties. A little old to be a major. In his left hand he held a six-pack of Rolling Rock.

"Mike, I'm Ben Wharton. Since I'm your lawyer, I want you to forget my rank, just call me Ben unless we're in uniform and getting ready to raise our right hands or something, got it?"

"Yes, sir, come on in."

Wharton took a look at the house, bare of furniture and decoration.

"Just like my ex-wife. Packs everything but the kitchen sink when she goes away for the weekend. You still got your sink? Good. Where's the bottle opener?"

Morris led him in to the kitchen. "I don't know if I own a bottle opener. Let's see."

The silverware drawer was empty, but the junk drawer underneath held a few useless implements. But there—at the back of the drawer was an old rusted bottle opener.

He took it out. "Funny she takes all the towels and furniture, but leaves this behind." He pulled two beers off the six-pack and popped the tops off, then handed one to the lawyer.

Ben replied, deadpan. "She probably figured you'd need a drink when you got home."

Morris grinned. "I'd invite you to sit, sir—uh, Ben—but I don't have any furniture, except the one chair in the other room."

"Right here is fine." Wharton settled down on the floor with his beer.

Morris sat across from him.

"All right, we'll skip the bullshit. The reason for the beer is, I'd like this to be an informal discussion. Tomorrow we'll meet at the office and you'll call me sir and I'll take a detailed, recorded statement. Today I want to get an idea of what happened out there, so I can understand why the Army is so pissed at you."

Morris smiled wryly. "It's simple enough, sir. We were sent to assist on a law-enforcement mission in an area already inflamed about federal involvement. One thing I want to point out: I explicitly objected to the mission to my commanding officer, Colonel Barksdale."

"Why is that?"

"Well, I wasn't sure it was legal. Posse Commitatus. The Army's forbidden from participating in law enforcement within the borders of the United States."

"I'm familiar with the statute."

"Well, Colonel Barksdale said any arrests would be made by local personnel, and these were our orders. So we moved out. I gave explicit orders to my folks not to lock and load their weapons."

"Will your lieutenants and sergeants back that up?"

"Sure, why not?"

"Okay, go on."

"We moved out into a dense urban area. The police were searching house to house, though for what reason I don't know—whoever shot that guy was long gone by the time we arrived, I'm sure of it. But the locals were very pissed to see the Army patrolling their streets."

"I can only imagine."

"So one of my squads was moving down an alley when they saw someone running. They popped tear-gas grenades and waited, then saw someone running at them out of the alley. All the members of the fire team say the same thing: they thought he had a gun. One of my men, PFC Turville, fired the shot that killed this kid. Turned out the kid had a video camera, but it was too late, he was dead."

"So what happened next?"

"Well, we converged on the scene. I placed PFC Turville under arrest. By that time the parents were on the scene, and a growing crowd, and some kid shot one of my guys, and the situation escalated. We deployed tear gas to clear the crowd and got the hell out of there."

"So you lost a man, killed, right. Any wounded?"

"One—had a brick thrown at him, he's still in the hospital with a fractured collarbone. Another civilian was shot, too, the kid who shot one of my guys. That one's still in the hospital."

"Jesus." Wharton finished off his beer. He stood and walked to the counter, popped the top off another bottle. "Ugly situation."

"Yeah."

"So, if I get it right, you are going to be the fall guy if this independence referendum passes in West Virginia."

Shocked, Morris almost shrieked his response. "*What?*"

Wharton looked at him with a wry expression. "Didn't you know what this is about? The White House needs somebody to blame. The DHS has been pissing off people for ten years, conducting unconstitutional searches and arrests, generally making nuisances of themselves. There's been half a dozen highly publicized incidents in West Virginia in the last couple years, several involving innocent bystanders getting killed. The situation there is a powder keg. So now you come along with—in their eyes—a trigger-happy company of gun toting infantry, and blow the situation all to hell."

"That's crazy."

Wharton nodded, his eyes wide, his gestures exaggerated. "It may be crazy, but I guarantee you the White House will do everything it can to divert blame from itself. I don't know if you've been paying attention to the news: there've been demonstrations in Charleston of a hundred thousand people. You are the perfect fall guy. Mike, don't let me give you any illusions here, I've been in the office the last couple days, I've heard the talk in the halls. They are out to crucify you. Don't get me wrong: the General will go out of his way to avoid any appearance of undue command influence on the investigation, or the court-martial if it comes to that. But everybody knows."

Morris sat in his empty kitchen, staring back at the lawyer, wondering how the hell he'd gotten in the middle of this. He stood and opened another beer. His hands twitched.

"What… What the hell can I do about it?" he asked.

Wharton nodded. "Bear in mind, my advice is only worth roughly what you are paying for it. But I say fight it. Don't resign. Don't give up command of your company unless they force you to. Will anyone else back you up on objecting to the mission?"

"Sure. I think so."

"Fight it, Mike. If you don't, they're going to screw you anyway. At least this way you get to take some of them with you."

"Hmm. How much am I paying you?"

"Nothing. The taxpayers have taken care of that."

Morris shook his head. "You know, you really inspire confidence."

"Look at it this way: at least you'll get your money's worth."

Colonel Murphy studied the daily reports from his subordinate units, not at all happy. He put the paper down and rubbed his eyes. His wireless phone rang. He glanced at the number. It was his mother, calling from Cincinatti.

"Hey, Mom, how's it going up there? How's Kenny?"

She spoke too quickly, her voice high-pitched. "Ken, they are shutting down the program up here. Kenny is here at the hotel with me; all the patients have been discharged."

Discharged? *What the hell?*

"Mom, what's going on? They can't just discharge him with no warning."

"Ken, they said their funding had been cut off. They had to let everyone go, all the doctors and nurses were fired, the entire wing was shut down."

"Oh, my God. But Kenny was doing so much better."

"I know, I know. I just don't know what to do."

Murphy sat for a moment, staring at the wall. This was a federally funded program. It must have been wiped out as part of the Fiscal Responsibility Act—the new budget had gone into effect this week.

"All right, listen, Mom. I'll call you back shortly. I'll make arrangements to fly up there and meet the two of you, then we'll all go back home. I do need to ask you one thing. Can you—can Kenny stay with you guys for a couple of weeks? It's going to be at least a couple more weeks before I can get away from this mess for any length of time."

"Okay, that's fine. We've been wanting him to come stay with us for a long time."

"Great, great. Listen, I'll call you back shortly."

"Okay. Ken, I'm really worried—he's twelve hours overdue for the shot, and he's already doing worse."

He closed his eyes. "All right, Mom. Maybe I can get him into Emory or something. I'll call you back."

He clicked the disconnect button. *Oh, Christ.* Even if he had the money to pay for the treatment, no one else was doing it—the program Kenny was in was a one-of-a-kind experiment, and it had been entirely federally funded. *Maybe we can get him into Emory Hospital in Atlanta.* Given the positive results he'd experienced in Cincinatti, maybe they'd take on the project. Okay, okay, there was something he could do. He'd need to track down the doctors in Cincinnati, get them to talk to the new ones at Emory.

In the meantime, he needed to get a few days out of here. A quick phone call to General Peak accomplished that. Murphy's new XO, Lieutenant Colonel Jian Chang, would act as brigade commander in his absence. He known Chang five years: an ambitious officer, almost universally called Jan because no one could pronounce his name properly, he'd probably expected to get the promotion himself. To be fair, if the governor hadn't personally intervened, he would have. Chang couldn't be happy about Murphy's promotion, but he'd done nothing to show what he felt.

Half an hour later, after making some arrangements, he left for the airport. On the way, he looked out at Charleston, the city he'd never loved or wanted to spend time in. Murphy had grown up in Atlanta, a good sized city. He disliked the crowds, the traffic, and the pretentiousness. Charleston wasn't nearly as big, but big enough to make him want to be almost anywhere else.

It was anybody's guess what would happen in the next few days. The federal building destroyed. A shootout between Bravo Company and federal law enforcement officials. Dale murdered as he walked up the steps. Then that poor boy killed by the Army.

The scary part was that at this point it looked like there was a strong chance the referendum would pass. What the hell would he do? He was a brigade commander in the National Guard, for God's sake. Would the governor activate the Guard because of the referendum? Would the assembly pass it? He would never have imagined this could come as far as it had, but regardless of his belief, the moment was here.

Murphy could not believe even as he sat here, that he was seriously contemplating treason. Because that, of course, was what it was. If he were to accept a position in the Guard reporting to a governor of a state that had decided to secede, it would be treason. No question. But would it be wrong? His oath was to protect the Constitution of the United States. Did the federal government represent that constitution any more, or operate within its bounds? After a lifetime of loyal service to his country, the question was chilling.

Murphy shook off the thought. He had a little more time to worry about that. Right now he had Kenny to take care of. At the airport he raced to catch his flight, though his uniform granted him quick passage through the security checkpoints without his having to wait in line.

Soon after the plane rose in the air, Murphy started making calls to track down Kenny's doctor. Doctor Li was the leader of the project in Cincinnati, an unprepossessing man who wouldn't be noticed in a crowd, unless that crowd happened to be made up of pediatric neurologists. In that field he'd become a giant, with several years of groundbreaking research. Murphy could see it in the reactions of the staff: they sat up straighter when he entered the room, and spoke of him in hushed tones.

Murphy's seatmates seemed unhappy with the calls. On his left, a sixty-or-so man read a novel, his brow furrowed, large rheumy eyes shifting about. In the window seat sat a women, forty-five or so, in a brown business suit, her computer sitting on the seat-back table.

After an argument with a hospital clerk, a nurse took pity enough to give him Doctor Li's personal number.

The line picked up after three rings.

"Hello?" A woman's voice, with a Chinese accent.

"Dr. Li, please?"

"Hold on, please."

Murphy waited.

"Hello, this is Dr. Li."

"Doctor, this is Ken Murphy. I'm Kenny's father. I'm on a plane on my way there now. Can you tell me what happened up there?"

"Our program was cut off. We were a federally funded project, and our funding was cut off completely. We've had to discharge all the patients and cancel the study. All the doctors and nurses are unemployed."

Murphy nodded. "Doctor Chang, can you tell me if there is anyone else doing this treatment? Anywhere? My son—he's been doing so much better since he went on the treatment. I'm very concerned about what might happen now."

"No, sir. I don't believe there is anyone else doing a similar study."

"If I can get him into another hospital—I was thinking of Emory, or Eggleston Children's hospital—would you provide me with the treatment information, and possibly they could duplicate your work there?"

Li hesitated. "Sir, I'll be happy to provide you with the information. You have one big problem though, I must be honest. Most insurances do not cover experimental treatments, and this was very expensive. We didn't bill you of course, because it was a federal research study. But it was very expensive."

"How expensive, Doctor?"

"We spent about twenty thousand dollars per month on the drugs."

Murphy frowned. "For how many patients?"

"For each patient. Each patient was twenty thousand per month."

"Oh, my God. That's obscene."

"Yes, I know, Mr. Murphy. But drug is experimental you see, protocol is experimental. All of it."

Murphy closed his eyes and rested his head in his hands.

"All right. I'd like to get the information from you anyway. I have to try. He was getting so bad before I got him into the program I thought he was going to die."

"I know, Mr. Murphy. It was an awful tragedy for us to shut down. We had fifteen patients in the program, and they are all cut off now."

"How are they doing off the treatment?"

Dr. Li did not answer.

"Doctor, how are they doing?"

Murphy heard… almost a gasp. "Mr. Murphy, one of the children, a little girl, died last night. It seems, in her case, the treatment alleviated the symptoms, but may have advanced the illness. We just don't know."

Murphy closed his eyes. *God, no.* No. He took a deep breath. "She died? How old?"

"Mr. Murphy, I think it's not such a good idea for us to continue the conversation."

Murphy raised his voice. "*Tell me.* How old was she?"

"Same age as your son—six."

"Please get me the treatment information. I'll be there today."

"I will do so. When do you arrive?"

"My plane gets in at two p.m. I'll meet you at the hospital? At three?"

"Three o'clock. I will be there."

Murphy swallowed and his voice broke when he spoke again. "Thank you, Doctor."

He disconnected the line and sat back, closing his eyes. The little girl died. *Oh, God, please no.* Emory. He needed to find out about the children's hospital there. He pulled the phone off the hook, swiped his credit card again, then dialed.

"Excuse me," the woman next to him said. "Could you maybe talk a little quieter?"

Murphy gave her an angry look and turned away. No use wasting even a second on her.

Soon he had the basic information he needed. Eggleston Children's Hospital was part of Emory University; it was a renowned children's hospital. They did not have a program for children with ALD, but did have some experience dealing with it. Would they take his military medical care? Yes, though it did not pay one hundred percent for civilian installations. Thank God he'd been activated. Without the medical insurance he might not have been able to get Kenny treated at all.

At the airport, he caught a cab to the medical center.

࿇

It was late that night before Murphy had finished talking to the doctor, collected the records, and packed up Kenny and his grandmother, but they made the last flight out of Cincinatti.

Murphy might have waited until the next morning to fly to Atlanta, but one look at Kenny had underlined the urgency of getting him back into a hospital. Kenny had severely deteriorated. Dark circles under his eyes, and his right eye seemed to wander aimlessly, disconnected from the left.

"Hey, Daddy, can I get a glass of water?" Kenny looked pale as he spoke, dark circles framing his eyes. He almost had to shout to be heard over the screaming engines.

"Sure, Kenny."

Murphy stepped past his mother, who slept in the aisle seat, and walked up to the galley in the middle of the plane.

"Could I have a cup of water?"

"Sure." The flight attendant, a young man with dark, swept back hair, handed him a cup.

"Thank you," he replied.

Because of the last-minute ticket purchases, they were seated almost in the very back of the airplane, between the twin engines. As he made his way back to their seats, he saw Kenny stiffen and cry out.

Murphy ran to the back, the water splashing. The flight attendant, who saw what had happened, followed. His face had gone white.

Murphy brushed in front of his mother and back into the middle seat.

"Daddy, it hurts. I want to go back to Ohio."

"I know, son. We're going to try our best to get your medicine again, okay? But the program in Ohio is gone, they've shut it down."

Tears ran down Kenny's face as he looked back at his father. "Okay."

"I got your water." The boy's hands trembled as he reached for the glass, and the water spilled in his table.

Behind him, he heard the flight attendant speak. "Sir, is there anything I can get you?"

"Just another cup of water, please."

Two minutes later the flight attendant returned with another cup, putting it in Murphy's outstretched hand. Murphy held it to his son's mouth, and Kenny gulped it down.

"Thank you." Kenny voice was no more than a whisper.

Murphy's mother had shaken herself awake by then. "He was doing much better, the last couple of weeks, Ken."

Two days since he's had the shots, and Kenny was almost as sick as he'd ever been.

Kenny leaned forward and vomited, the contents of his stomach splashing all over the seat, his lap, and his father's uniform. The acrid smell flooded the compartment.

He gasped, then vomited again.

Murphy heard someone two rows away say, "Oh, for God's sake, can't you take him to the bathroom?"

Murphy fought to stay calm.

"Come on, Kenny." He unbuckled the seatbelt, sticky with vomit, and froze.

The vomit was stained red with blood.

"Mom, find out of there's a doctor on the plane, right away! I'm going to take Kenny back to the bathroom."

He lifted the boy out of the seat and the stench of bile and acid scorched his throat. As he lifted him, Kenny stiffened again, almost a convulsion. Murphy fought to hold onto him and started to loe his balance as his prosthetic slipped.

"It'll be all right, Kenny. It'll be all right." Murphy said it as much to himself as the boy.

Kenny stiffened again as they moved up the aisle, and clawed at his throat. He let out a scream and convulsed.

Murphy sank to his knees as the boy convulsed in his arms, his screams caught between the engines. The altitude of the plane had shifted, and he heard the pilot speak over the loudspeaker.

"This is the Captain speaking. Ladies and gentlemen, we have a medical emergency on board and will be making an immediate landing in Chattanooga. We are already cleared for landing and will be on the ground in ten minutes. We apologize for the delay, and will provide assistance in finding alternate connecting flights to Atlanta."

Thank God, Murphy thought.

Kenny screamed again and convulsed. This time he cracked his head against the base of a seat. Murphy winced.

"Can I help?" someone said behind him.

Murphy looked up. A forty-year-old man stood behind him in a loose suit.

"Are you a doctor?"

"No, I'm a federal marshal. But I have had some first-aid training."

"Probably not much you can do. If he goes into convulsions again, maybe you can help hold him."

"Okay." The marshal stepped around him.

Kenny twisted again, and whispered. "Daddy, am I going to die?"

"No, son. You'll be fine." He knew he was lying, and he could see from Kenny's expression that the boy knew it, too.

Kenny looked back at him and started to cry. "I miss Mommy. Will I see her in heaven?"

Tears filled Murphy's eyes, and he sobbed.

"Boy, you've got to stop talking like that. You're going to be just fine."

He held his little boy to him, and thought about the other girl from Cincinatti—the one who had died.

He whispered. "Little guy, your Mommy loves you and she'll always be there. Always. So will I."

Kenny vomited again, this time more blood than anything else. His eyes had sunk into dark hollows, and Murphy held him close. *Please, please,* he prayed. *Please save him.*

The flight attendant came back.

"Sir, we're about to land, I need to ask you to get in your seat."

Murphy held his son tight against his chest.

"I'm afraid I can't do that. I'll just stay right here."

Kenny doubled over and screamed again, and more blood and vomit appeared, too much, way too much.

The marshal looked up from his position behind Kenny.

"Just land the goddamned plane, all right. We need to get this boy to a hospital right now. Go, go!"

Murphy sat there, his uniform covered in blood and vomit, his son tight against his chest, and he whispered the Lord's Prayer. *Our father, who art in heaven. Hallowed be thy name.*

Kenny shook, and stopped breathing.

"Oh, God!"

The engines screamed now as the plane came in for a landing. Murphy felt a hard bump as the plane hit the ground.

Frantically, he checked Kenny's pulse. None.

He lay the boy down and tilted his head back, then breathed twice into his mouth, the acrid taste of vomit flooding into his own mouth. Chest compressions. Breathe twice. Chest compressions. As the plane rolled to a stop, some of the people in the front stood and began taking down their luggage.

The marshal snarled at them.

"Sit down! Stay in your seats and let the emergency folks through. What the hell is wrong with you people?"

A businessman in the first class section continued pulling his luggage from the rack, and the marshal shouted. "You! Get back in your seat or I will place you under arrest. Right now!"

The man sat down and glanced back anxiously at Murphy and his son. *He thinks Kenny might be contagious,* Murphy thought.

Paramedics shoved their way down the aisle to Murphy. "Sir, can you step back please?"

Murphy did. "He's got no pulse, no breath."

The paramedics—both men who couldn't be any older than twenty-five—looked at the pool of vomit and blood with dismay, then looked at each other. One shook his head slightly.

"How long has he been without a pulse?"

"No more than two or three minutes. It's not too late. It's *not* too late, damn it!"

"All right, we're going to get him out right now, into a helicopter. Leave everything here, every second counts. Got it?"

Murphy nodded and turned to his mother. "Mom, get the bags and take a cab to the hospital behind us."

She nodded, her face twisted in grief.

The paramedics unfolded a stretcher and put Kenny on it, then ran for the entrance to the plane. Murphy followed them outside and down the stairs, where a helicopter sat a hundred yards away. The medics took off at a dead run for the helicopter, with Murphy running after them.

As he climbed aboard, one of the medics yelled, "Strap yourself in!"

Murphy did, and watched, terrified, as they tried to revive his son.

It was too late.

Kenny had gone to join his mother.

Chapter Twenty-Six
October 31

Mike Morris double-checked his uniform. Everything squared away. He wore his green dress uniform, with not very many decorations—he had no combat service to date. He did wear a ranger tab, and had done the necessary parachute jumps, though that was an experience he'd just as soon not repeat.

Wharton sat on the bench a few feet away. He looked over at Morris. "Relax, Captain. They won't start without you."

Morris walked away from the mirror and sat next to Wharton.

Unlike Morris, Major Wharton had clearly been around the block, and wore decorations Mike would not have expected to find on an attorney, including a Bronze Star with a V device for valor, as well as a purple heart and a Combat Infantryman's Badge. He wore a combat patch from the Tenth Mountain Division, which had seen combat in a dozen countries in the last thirty years. His medals included at least two campaign ribbons.

"Where did you get the Purple Heart?"

"Egghhh. It's nothing special. I was asleep in the barracks—I was a young PFC, in fact, when it happened. Some kid decided he didn't want Americans around anymore, fired an RPG into our barracks. I got beat up by some shrapnel is all."

Wharton didn't explain the V device, but Morris didn't press the issue. Wharton must have been enlisted, then gone to law school and come back into the military as an officer.

"All right," Wharton said. "Enough screwing around. You understand what this morning is all about, correct?"

"Yes, sir."

Wharton went on as if Morris hadn't spoken. "This is the Article 32 investigation. It's the equivalent of a civilian grand jury, and the investigating officer is the man who will determine your fate, understand?"

Wharton continued.

"We're dealing with a Colonel Frank Sheeman. He's old-school, very conservative, can be a real son of a bitch. But he's a combat veteran, and he understands things get screwed up. He's been there. You've got that on your side. In any event, he'll take all the evidence about what happened and make a recommendation to the commanding general."

"Whether or not to court-martial me."

"Right. It's actually pretty good. If this were a grand jury, you'd have no right to see the prosecutor's evidence, or to cross-examine any witnesses. In an Article 32 hearing, we will be there the whole time. We'll know what's being said, and by whom. We'll be able to figure out who the bad guys are."

Morris frowned. "I don't believe in bad guys."

Wharton shook his head and grinned. "The bad guys are the ones screwing you. What you have going for you: he won't recommend a court-martial unless he's pretty sure they can convict. He won't waste the Army's time on a fishing expedition. But there's a lot of pressure on this. Understand?"

Morris did. He understood he was screwed.

"When they ask you questions, I want to you to answer them fully and truthfully. But don't volunteer information. No tangents, and don't give them anything to hang you with, all right?"

It wasn't even 0730 and Morris already had a splitting headache. He wasn't ready for this. All it took was one screw-up. Even if no charges were brought, his military career was over. Didn't matter if he'd led a perfect career up until this point. One screw-up—especially one of this magnitude—was enough to end it for him. He stood again, looked out the window. It could be worse. He hadn't died in that alley, like the boy had, like Jack Frazier had. He wasn't in the hospital with a broken collarbone or a bullet hole in his gut.

Outside, a T-72 tank sat in the traffic circle in front of division headquarters, right next to the flagpole. Probably captured in Iraq, the things littered American bases, souvenirs of a series of wars.

His breakfast felt heavy in his stomach, his neck muscles tense. Normally not prone to anxiety, he didn't care for the feeling.

"Come on back over, Mike. You've got to calm down."

Morris sat. "Sorry. I'm not used to this."

"Of course not. Last thing you ever expected was to face charges in this kind of investigation. But these things happen, Mike. Accidents happen, and people get killed, and the Army has to sort it out. Look, you gave the proper orders at the right times. You set up accountability with your NCOs to ensure the orders were followed. PFC Turville clearly disobeyed those orders."

Morris shook his head. "That may be true, Major, but I was in command. I can't avoid responsibility."

"Look, Mike: it's a human reaction to feel guilt about what happened. But you're allowed to feel guilty after the investigation is over and you are cleared, not a day before. Got it?"

"Yes, sir."
"Good."

※

Colonel Frank Sheeman, the investigating officer, barely spoke a word through the hearing, preferring instead to listen carefully to the witnesses, occasionally asking a well thought-out question. Like the others, he wore his dress uniform, replete with decorations from more than one combat deployment. His mustache had grown far beyond the size allowed by Army regulations.

The hearing took place in a room in the Division Headquarters, strangely decorated with children's drawings of winter: giant, asymmetrical snowflakes and snowmen who looked to Mike like something you would see in a bad horror movie. Very suitable for a trial beginning on Halloween, and not a room where he would expect an investigation to be held.

Five tables were arranged in the room, facing each other in a U shape. Colonel Sheeman, the investigating officer, sat by himself at the base of the U shape. At the table to his right sat a court reporter.

To Sheeman's left, at the first table, sat PFC Turville and his attorney. At the second table, to Turville's left, sat Morris and his attorney.

Directly across from Morris were the prosecutors. One was a Major Collins, younger than Major Wharton, and with a lot less fruit salad on his jacket. His cheeks were bright red, eyes bloodshot. Morris knew this wasn't the young apple-cheeked look. Major Collins had the look of a heavy drinker. He was assisted by a sexy young first lieutenant named Ellis, who also had red cheeks and pretty legs, and was attractive enough to distract Morris from just about anything else in the room. *Probably a good thing,* he thought. *I've been too stressed about this as it is.*

They wore their green Class A uniforms. The one exception to the uniform was the court reporter, a PFC who wore his camouflage uniform and ignored all of them, even as he carefully took notes of the proceedings.

Colonel Sheeman opened the hearing.

"This is a formal investigation into certain charges against Captain Michael Allen Morris and PFC James Turville ordered pursuant to Article 32, Uniform Code of Military Justice, by Major General Wilson Blake. On October twenty-fourth, I informed you of your right to be represented by civilian counsel at no expense to the United States, military counsel of your own selection if reasonably available, or military counsel detailed by the trial defense service."

He went on in a similar vein for some time, then called Morris and Turville up together to sign a paper acknowledging their presence.

"Let me remind you my sole function as the Article 32 investigating officer in this case is to determine thoroughly and impartially all of the relevant facts of the case, to weigh and evaluate those facts and determine the truth of the matters stated in the charges. I shall also consider the form of the charges and make a recommendation concerning the disposition of the charges that have been preferredagainst you."

Morris signed and returned to his chair. The verbiage sounded straight from the manual. Sheeman continued reading.

"Because the charges involve a single incident, we will hold one Article Thirty-two investigation. However, multiple charges may result, and I will make a separate recommendation in each of your cases. Should any trial result, those will of course also be separate."

Morris looked down at the charge sheet and realized his teeth were grinding. Conduct unbecoming an officer, it said. Negligence and murder. He felt himself begin to tremble with rage.

Wharton put his hand on Morris's shoulder and leaned close. "Relax. You're turning red."

Morris took a deep breath, got himself under control.

Finally the hearing got underway, and Colonel Sheeman called in the first witness, Corporal Meigs. His low-quarters clicked on the polished floor as he entered the room and reported.

Looking at Meigs drove home how short a time Morris had been with the unit. He'd never seen Meigs in his Class-A uniform. It had been less than six months since he'd taken over Bravo Company, and in that time they'd been on two emergency deployments.

Meigs seemed unusually thin, and his arms and legs poked out of the uniform like sticks. He'd shaved his head down to the scalp, and his forehead gleamed under the harsh lights. Morris wondered if he had lost weight; the uniform did not seem to fit well.

Colonel Sheeman told Meigs to raise his right hand.

"Do you swear the evidence you shall give in the case now being investigated shall be the truth, the whole truth, and nothing but the truth, so help you God?"

Meigs bobbed his head. "Yes, sir."

"Please have a seat," Sheeman instructed. Meigs sat in the witness chair at the end of the table, facing Sheeman. "Major Collins?"

Major Collins, the prosecutor, spoke from his chair.

"Corporal, my name is Major Collins. First, I want to let you know you can relax. This is not a trial here; it is merely a hearing to find out as much as we can about what happened on October 19. We're going to talk, try to collect evidence, okay. I'll ask you some questions, then these other attorneys may also ask you some questions. This shouldn't take too long."

Meigs spoke, his voice a little broken. "Yes, sir."

"Okay then, Corporal. Let me ask you a couple of questions—just for the record, understand. Can you tell us your full name and rank, and the unit you serve in?"

"Yes, sir. Corporal Cantrell Meigs. I'm a fire team leader in First Platoon, Bravo Company, First of the Fifteenth Infantry."

"Can you tell me your relationship with both Captain Morris and PFC Turville?"

"Yes, sir. Captain Morris is my company commander, sir. PFC Turville is a rifleman in my fire team, sir."

"And how long have you known both of them?"

"Since… I guess April or May, sir. They both started around the same time. In fact, I think it was the same as the bombing in Arlington, sir. Captain Morris had just taken command of the unit when we were alerted. PFC Turville was outside the distance limits and came in late for the alert. Got in trouble."

Turville's attorney, JAG Captain Harris, leaned forward. "Colonel, move to strike that last. It is irrelevant and could be prejudicial to my client."

Major Wharton immediately pounced. "Sir, with all due respect to the Captain, I must disagree with the irrelevance. If PFC Turville has a history of disobeying orders, it could be central to my client's case."

Sheeman looked back and forth between them, and his eyes narrowed. He twirled the corner of his moustache between his fingers, his eyebrows squeezing together, then spoke.

"Gentleman, this is not a trial yet. Let's save our courtroom maneuverings for when and if it becomes one. The statement will stand. I'd like to clarify one thing, though, Corporal. Were you in PFC Turville's chain of command at the time he reported late?"

"Yes, sir. Then and now. He came in about two or three hours late from the alert; it caused a big fuss, sir. My recollection is he wasn't really punished by the CO. He let Sergeant O'Donnell handle it informally."

"Thank you. Continue, Major."

Major Collins nodded. "Corporal Meigs, why don't you tell us in your own words what happened on October 19."

"Yes, sir. Well, Sergeant O'Donnell, our platoon sergeant, rounded us up shortly after lunch on October 19th. We had a few people on guard duty, but most of the platoon was in our tent, because it was nasty wet. So Lieutenant Wingham called us into a formation and briefed us."

Major Collins nodded, and his red jowls shook.

"So what happened next, Corporal Meigs?"

"Well, as usual, Turville had something to say. Wanted to know if our orders were legal, said he didn't think we was supposed to be doing anything in the U.S. or something. The LT told him to shut up, and we loaded up in the truck."

Morris met Wharton's eyes. *Interesting,* Morris thought, *but what the hell did it mean?*

"Go on, Corporal," said Collins.

"Well, sir, we were set to patrol a side street. The cops were going from one apartment building to the next; it was a pretty small, narrow street. So I saw this guy running, looked like he had a gun. So we all ducked down—me and Turville squished into the wall, and Leo and Gomez hid behind a car. So this guy, right, he runs down the alley. So I ask Leo to put a couple of CS grenades into the alley."

"CS?"

"Tear gas, sir."

Morris thought he detected a tone of contempt in Meigs's voice. How could you be in the Army long enough to be a Major and not know what tear gas was. Or maybe it wasn't Meigs; maybe Morris was just putting his own spin on it. It was hard to like someone who wanted to put him in prison.

"We all put on our masks, and Leo takes the shot. It went high, but landed back in the alley. We hear this loud crash—sounded like something getting smashed. So, this guy comes hauling ass—excuse me, sir—this guy comes running out of the alley. I thought he had a gun; we all did. I saw Turville raise his rifle, and I yelled at him not to shoot. But I was too late. Turville took him right in the chest."

Morris glanced over at the young PFC, who sat at the next table with his lawyer. Turville shook, and sunk his head into his hands. His attorney placed a hand on his back.

"At that point we called for help."

Collins nodded. He sat back in his chair, his hands stuffed in his pockets, legs splayed out in what Morris thought was a very unmilitary posture. Morris glanced at Sheeman, and was delighted to see the colonel staring at Collins disapprovingly. Collins didn't notice.

"All right, Corporal. Let's move on a little. Where were you when Captain Morris arrived on the scene?"

Meigs—shaking a little, Morris noticed—answered quickly. "I was with the medics, trying to do something to help the kid Turville shot. It was too late—the kid had a huge exit wound; he bled out right there on the street. When the CO arrived—Captain Morris, that is—the mother was there, and the father, and they were both hysterical and screaming. Lieutenant Wingham and Sergeant O'Donnell were trying to keep the situation under control, and then somebody started shooting—some kid, I think. Shot Frazier right in the face."

Collins referred to his notes. "That's Specialist John Frazier, correct? He was also in your platoon?"

"Yes, sir, same squad. Jack was pretty squared away. He must have died instantly; asshole shot him right in the face. I mean—sorry sir!"

Meigs shifted in his seat uncomfortably.

Collins smiled disarmingly. "Don't worry, I think everyone in the room has heard the term before. Please go on, Corporal."

"Well, sir, someone shot the kid with the gun, right in the gut. I think it was Private Nowell, he was Frazier's buddy. So this kid goes down, he's screaming, the crowd was screaming and running, and the kid looks to fire again. Someone grabbed his gun, and next thing I know this big-ass—I mean, this brick, comes crashing down right next to me, blows up in about a million pieces. I still got a scratch where a hunk of it cut me on the hand, see?"

He held his hand up and pointed to a not-very-impressive scab. Of course, a couple of weeks had passed since the incident.

"Then another brick comes down and hits Sharp right in the shoulder, knocks him down. Sir, you have no idea how out of control it was. I mean, it's not like we were in combat; we couldn't do anything! We're stuck there in the street with the folks in the neighborhood coming down on us like a ton of bricks, and we couldn't shoot back. Jesus. So the CO, he starts yelling orders and gets us out of there."

Meigs went on, describing the scene as they moved into the center of the intersection, flooding the surrounding streets and rooftops with tear gas, then moved out of the area in what could only be described as a retreat. Morris sat looking at the table, trying not to make Meigs any more nervous than he already was. As the prosecutor wrapped up, Wharton and Turville's attorney flipped a coin to determine who would ask questions first. Finally, Wharton stood up.

"Corporal Meigs. Were you at any time given any instructions regarding your weapon and whether or not to load it?"

Meigs nodded. "Yes, sir. Lieutenant Wingham, sir, then Sergeant O'Donnell. Both made it very clear, sir, we were not to load our weapons. Sergeant O'Donnell ordered the squad and team leaders to check the weapons of our subordinates."

"And did you do so?"

"Yes, sir. I checked the team's weapons before we moved out of the launch point. All of them were clear."

"By the team, who specifically are you referring to?"

Meigs looked around, met Turville's eyes for a moment. He took a deep breath, then spoke, "Three people, sir. PFC Turville, PFC Leo, and Specialist Gomez."

"All right, let me make sure I have this clear. When you got off the truck and moved out in the area, when you first started out, all the weapons in your fire team were clear."

"Yes, sir."

"Even of tear gas grenades."

"Yes, sir. Leo had to load his launcher before he could fire."

"Okay. So, in order to fire that shot, PFC Turville must have disobeyed a direct order, and charged his weapon after you verified it was clear, is that not correct?"

"Yes, sir. I gave clear instructions not to lock and load. He must have done it while we were firing off the tear gas or something."

Wharton scribbled something on his legal pad, then looked back up at Meigs. "Thank you, Corporal. No more questions, sir."

Morris stared at his fingernails. It didn't sit quite right. His defense, as it already appeared to be framed by his attorney, was dependent on proving that a PFC under his command was guilty. Yes, Turville had disobeyed an order, but Morris wasn't comfortable basing his defense solely on that. He would have to talk to Wharton.

As they finished, Turville and his lawyer whispered urgently to each other. Colonel Sheeman flashed an annoyed look at them, then spoke to the officer.

"Captain Harris, if you are quite finished."

Harris stood. "Yes, sir. I have only a few questions for the witness. Corporal Meigs, how would you describe your relationship with PFC Turville?"

Meigs shrugged. "I wouldn't, sir. We're on the same fire team, we work together. But we don't hang together, don't have the same friends."

"I see."

Harris paused briefly and looked at the floor. After a brief, studied moment, he spoke again.

"Corporal, have you ever used the term 'honky,' or 'whitey,' when referring to PFC Turville?"

Meigs's eyes widened. "I might have, sir, but I don't recall a specific instance."

Harris nodded, his bald head flashing under the light. "You don't recall a specific instance. What about the term 'Turdville.' Can you tell me what precisely that means?"

Wharton sat up straight, a frown on his face. "Colonel, I don't know where this is going."

Harris, expecting an objection, responded quickly. "Sir, my intentions will be quite clear in a moment. I'm concerned about the objectivity of this witness and would like those concerns documented in the record. I believe there may be a level of personal antipathy between this witness and my client."

Sheeman looked at the two of them, eyes narrowed. "Proceed, Captain. Please answer the question, Corporal."

"Well, sir, it's like any other nickname for one of the new guys. There's always a little hazing with a new guy out of Basic, it's no big deal."

"I see. So what was your nickname for PFC Leo?"

"Well, I… I don't have one."

"You don't? Was Leo not like all the other new guys? He's been here for a little over a year, correct?"

"Yes, sir. But, Leo… Leo wasn't a screwup, sir."

Morris grimaced as Harris pounced. "Oh, so PFC Turville was a screwup. Can you give me an instance of his existence as a screwup?"

Meigs set his jaw and his eyebrows tightly scrunched over his eyes. "Sure, I can, sir. Like the first instance we talked about—when the CO gave us a pass his first day with the unit, and Turville goes outside the travel limit, comes back late from the alert. Or when he dropped his rifle in the orderly room a couple months ago and busted it."

Captain Harris's reply was laden with sarcasm. "So Turville's screwups were worse than other new recruits? Is that right? He screwed up much worse than Leo, or any other new recruits?"

Meigs shrugged. "I guess not, sir. All the new guys are screwups until they've been around for a while."

"Have you ever heard PFC Turville use the word 'nigger?'"

"Yes, sir, and I was right on him for that."

"Would a squared-away soldier ever use the word 'nigger?'"

"Hell, no, sir! I don't know who he thinks he is!"

"So you have a personal problem with PFC Turville's use of the word, is that correct?"

Meigs answered. "Yes, I do."

"Is he a racist?"

"Yes, sir."

"How did you like having a racist in your fire team?"

"I didn't like it at all, sir, but it's nothin' new. Leo's a hillbilly too, but he doesn't screw with people."

"Thank you, I don't have any more questions."

Morris glanced at Sheeman. The colonel's face was red, his brow furrowed, and Morris realized he was furious. He spoke, his anger barely concealed, "You may go, Corporal."

Meigs left the room, and Sheeman spoke again. "Listen up. I said this was not a courtroom and I meant it. You will refrain from cross-examining and badgering the witnesses and making arguments in this setting. We are here to determine whether or not there is enough evidence to warrant a court-martial. That is the only reason we are here. If and when we go to court-martial and you have to defend your client, you can then impeach witnesses all day. Until then, we're here only to establish the facts of what happened. You are wasting my precious time, Captain Harris, Major Wharton. Do you understand me?"

Wharton and Harris answered simultaneously. "Yes, sir."

"That's it. I expect to move expeditiously through this process so we can come to a decision. We'll recess. I want everyone back in here by thirteen hundred hours."

Sheeman got up and walked out of the room.

Morris deflated as Wharton grabbed him by the arm. "Come on, Captain."

Morris followed Wharton, his body numb. He was soaked with sweat and so frustrated he wanted to smash something.

An MP stood outside the door, as well as a young man with somewhat long, dirty hair.

"Captain Michael Morris, sir?"

"Yes," Morris answered.

The young man handed him a thick envelope. Morris took it reflexively.

"This man is a process server, sir," the MP said.

Morris looked back at the papers. He'd been served. Just great.

"Thanks." He walked away from the MP and ripped open the envelope. Divorce papers from Alicia. He collapsed onto one of the uncomfortable metal chairs in the hallway.

"What is it, Mike?"

Mike shook his head, waved the papers. "Divorce papers."

Wharton scoffed. "Not having much luck this month, are you?" He flopped down into the seat next to Mike.

"No, I guess not."

Wharton chuckled. "Look at it this way—it won't take much in the way of good news to turn things around, will it?"

✼

The windshield wipers on Karen's Hummer slapped back and forth, just enough to keep the road visible.

Nearly two months had passed since they'd been mobilized. Nearly two months of incessant rain, and remorse for Stanson's death, and agent Hagarty's. Two months since she'd been relieved of her command.

Karen had been company commander for almost two years, and had performed well during their training exercises at Fort Irwin. Now, in their first real deployment, in near-combat conditions, the only things she'd managed to accomplish was to kill one of her men, find herself under federal indictment and ignite a constitutional crisis. Some first command. On top of that, Mike Morris had to show up and profess his undying love for her, the son of a bitch. Seven years without a word. Seven goddamned years. No wonder his wife hated him.

As they approached the armory, Karen felt her phone vibrate and pulled it out. Looking at the caller ID, she saw it was Major Elkins.

"This is Captain Greenfield, sir."

"Captain, as you approach the armory, I'd like you to observe the front gate and the several vehicles parked outside."

She leaned sideways in order to see around the truck in front of them. Half a block from the armory, two cars idled: big neutral-colored, four-door sedans. Two more were at the next corner.

"Roger, sir, I see them."

"It looks like we were right—they're going to grab you if you leave the armory. Your transport awaits you, Captain. I'll see to it your company is taken care of."

"Thank you, sir."

Elkins hung up without another word, and Karen put the phone away. They pulled up to the gate of the armory, and she saw a helicopter on the chopper pad, its rotors still turning. It must have just landed. She glanced back at one of the cars and met the eyes of the man who sat behind the wheel. He jerked up, then spoke into a handset.

Karen spoke to the driver, a PFC from third platoon filling that role since Stanson's death. "I need you to drive straight to the chopper pad."

"Yes, ma'am."

Inside, he broke away from the convoy and drove straight toward the field and the helicopter.

Elkins stood away from the chopper, waiting for her.

She stepped out of the vehicle, then turned back and said to the driver, "Go ahead and rejoin the company."

"Yes, ma'am." He smiled.

She saluted Elkins.

"Well, sir. Am I going back to Charleston?"

He shook his head. "No, Brigade Headquarters in Morgantown. Keep a low profile while you are there. Not everyone on the Brigade staff agrees with the governor's decision, and Murphy won't be back for a few days."

"Oh, what happened?"

"He's taking his son down to Georgia. Apparently the treatment program he had him enrolled in was shut down."

"That's a shame. I hope it isn't serious."

Elkins frowned. "It is, I'm afraid. But enough said. Looks like those federal boys are just waiting for you to walk out, and then they'll nab you, huh?"

"I guess so. Major, I don't think I'm cut out to be a fugitive."

"Don't worry about it, Karen. We'll get it straightened out. I heard the grand jury in Charleston issued indictments against the Director of DHS today, among others. They aren't taking this lying down."

She nodded. "Well, so be it. I guess it's too late for me to get an absentee ballot, huh?"

"I guess so. It's just as well."

"Right. Which way are you planning to vote?"

He smiled. "I'll never tell. Go get on your chopper, Captain."

"Yes, sir." She stood at attention and saluted.

He returned the salute and then walked back toward the armory.

The chopper crew chief took her rucksack, then helped her into the harness.

"Captain, if I'm not overstepping my bounds, just wanted to say we're proud of you for defending your state. We all saw the video on TV. You did the right thing."

She was shocked. Opening her mouth to answer, she just couldn't think of what to say. Eventually, she said, "Thanks."

She didn't think he heard her over the rotors. He handed her a helmet and she put it on. The helicopter lifted off.

Chapter Twenty-Seven
November 1

The funeral home was in Chamblee, a suburb of Atlanta and not far from the house where Murphy had grown up and where his parents still lived. Valerie rode in the back seat next to her unusually quiet father, while her grandfather drove.

She looked down at her phone. Fifteen minutes before, she'd gotten the page. Clark had made a major speech in Charleston this morning, announcing his opposition to the independence referendum and calling on voters to oppose it.

Clark had stepped in front of a freight train, and she was terribly afraid he'd be run over. Everyone already knew he opposed the measure, but they also knew ninety percent of his constituents supported it. For him to make such a strong statement on the morning of Election Day just didn't make sense. Maybe he thought he could turn the tide.

After what seemed like weeks of constant rain in Washington, it seemed strange that today, of all days, had broken clear and warm, bright sunlight washing down on the city. As they pulled up to the funeral home—a nearly anonymous red brick building with a small portico—she found herself wishing for sunglasses.

Murphy sat, his hands in his lap, and looked out the window. He had not said a word the entire drive, and more frightening, he'd barely looked around, not really responding to their environment at all.

Her grandparents stepped out of the car, and Valerie smelled the fresh-cut grass outside. Murphy didn't move.

"We're here, Dad." Her voice was quiet.

His eyes shifted to her, and for the first time in her life, Ken Murphy looked old to Valerie.

"I'm not sure I can go in there." His voice was a whisper.

She put her hand on his back. "I know, Dad. I know."

He closed his eyes for a count of five seconds, and Valerie wondered what was going through his mind. Then, without a word, he opened the car door and got out. His back stiff, he walked toward his parents and the entrance of the funeral home, favoring his prosthetic leg with a slight limp. Valerie slipped out of the car and joined her family. Slowly, the four of them walked together inside.

After the bright sunlight, the interior of the funeral home seemed dark and small. A narrow, sterile hallway led down the center of the building, the floor a laminated imitation wood. On each side of the hallway lay dim chapels, each with a small, institutional black sign with white plastic letters. On the left, "Wilson." A few people sat in the pews on that side.

On the right side, the black sign read "Murphy." Four rows of pews, which could seat perhaps thirty people, sat empty, facing an open, steel casket at the end of the room. A man stood at the casket, hands clasped behind his back, his back to the room, head bowed. As they arrived, he turned around and approached, and she saw the Roman collar. A priest. His unruly hair was grey, his face was framed by a rough cut beard and mustache. He smiled as he approached.

"Fred and Helen. And Ken—I don't think I've seen you in thirty years. Welcome home."

Valerie thought her dad looked puzzled, and then his eyes widened and recognition dawned on his face.

Valerie's grandmother said, "Valerie, this is Father John Connelly; he's been the pastor at Holy Cross in Chamblee for—well, gosh, for forty years now. He married your father and mother, you know. John, this is Valerie Murphy, Ken's daughter."

Father Connelly smiled, and said in a charming voice, "It's a delight to meet you, Valerie. I'm very sorry about the circumstances, but it's always a pleasure to meet the grown children of my parishioners. It makes me feel as if I'm doing something right."

Valerie smiled. "It's nice to meet you."

"And you, Ken. Are you holding up?"

Murphy replied, in a voice so weary it made her heart ache. "I'm holding up, Father."

"Ken, you know you can call me, any time. I was crushed when I heard about Martha. You've had more than your share of tragedies. Please feel free to call me if you need to talk, collect if necessary."

"Thank you, Father."

"Are any other family members coming?"

Valerie's grandmother answered, "Yes, Lisa and her family will be here, and so will Tom."

Lisa was Valerie's aunt, younger than Murphy. She had two teenage children, and was married to Bobby Joe Wright, a stockbroker who gave Valerie the creeps. Most years the family gathered at her grandparents' house for Christmas, and Valerie had managed to make it even when she was at Harvard and working on the Hill. Somewhere along the road, she'd realized that Bobby Joe's eyes followed her a lot closer than she would have liked. But what the hell was she supposed to say? *Hey, Dad, your brother-in-law won't stop giving me the eye.* Murphy would have broken Bobby Joe's nose, and that would have really ruined Christmas.

Valerie hardly knew Tom, Murphy's younger brother. She hardly knew him; he was a senior officer of some kind, always on deployment in some country or other.

As the others quietly spoke with the pastor, Valerie's eyes locked on the casket. She broke away and walked to it.

The full sized steel casket swallowed up her little brother. He lay there, his blonde hair neatly combed, his hands crossed over his chest. He wore an unfamiliar black suit, but she recognized the tie. She had bought it for him last summer. It was red, with small yellow dump trucks and bulldozers crawling over it. A gasp escaped her throat as she recognized it.

"Oh, he's just a little boy," she whispered. Her hand shook as she reached out to touch his face. He was cold, cold. His cheeks were unnaturally red, as if he'd been running. Touching him, she realized his face was covered in pancake makeup. Why? It made him look like a little marionette. Or did he look so ghastly when he died that this was the only way to make him presentable?

Valerie looked up as her Aunt Lisa and her family crowded into the room. Lisa wore a black suit with a tasteless yellow shirt. Her husband looked around until his close-set eyes rested on Valerie, and he smiled. *Pig.* The teenagers—Bobby, sixteen; and Laura, fourteen—stood uncomfortably as their parents greeted her father and their grandparents. Lisa smiled as she shook Father Connelly's hand, but Bobby Joe looked at the priest with suspicion. Valerie composed herself, dabbing away tears with a handkerchief, then walked, her back straight, toward her relatives.

Lisa gripped her lightly by the shoulders and pressed her cheek to Valerie's; then she whispered, "You must be so broken up, Valerie. Please let me know if there's anything I can do."

Valerie looked her aunt in the eyes and smiled. "Thanks."

She tolerated Bobby Joe's hug though, as usual, it was closer and longer than she thought appropriate. One of these days somebody was going to hurt him.

A bass voice called out, "Well, I'll be. When did you make Colonel?"

Valerie's eyes cut to the door. Tom Murphy stood at the entrance.

Murphy smiled. "Tom."

To Valerie, the smile looked ghastly.

The two of them embraced, clapping each other on the back. Tom was also in his uniform, a sky blue braid looped under his shoulder, the silver eagles of a full Colonel on his shoulders.

Tom spoke to his brother, his voice cracking, "Ken, I'm so sorry about your boy."

Murphy didn't reply, but to Valerie's eyes, he gained strength from the presence of his brother; he stood a little taller maybe, a little more confident. They walked together to the casket, and she felt a small flash of jealousy: He was able to walk with his brother to face this, but not with her.

How petty, she thought immediately. Her father was in pain and she was thinking only about herself. She'd never know what it was like to have a brother or sister stand beside her.

Her cousins stood awkwardly as their grandparents fussed over Aunt Lisa and her pervert husband. Valerie walked over to the teens and said hello.

Bobby said, "Hi" quietly, unable to take his eyes off the coffin and his dead cousin. Despite the suit, it was impossible to erase the pierced ear and nose, and the unkempt hair, though Valerie was sure his father would want to do just that. It must enrage his father, Valerie thought with satisfaction. Her uncle was more concerned with appearances than anyone she'd ever known, and had been at war with his son ever since Bobby hit puberty.

Laura, on the other hand, was the picture of conservatism, with her brown suit and below-the-knee skirt. Valerie sensed their standing together was more of an accident than not—as if they'd been deposited in one part of the room and simply couldn't or wouldn't move.

"How are you guys doing?" Valerie asked. "School going okay?"

"Well," Bobby said, "things are okay. I mean, I don't think I'll be going to Harvard or anything."

"He'll be lucky if he can get into alternative school," said his sister with a decidedly superior attitude. She crossed her arms. "We just got our midterm report cards, and he's failing two classes."

"Shut up."

"Dad," Her voice whined at a pitch that almost hurt Valerie's ears, "Bobby told me to shut up."

Their father stalked over and leaned his face right into his son's, trying for the intimidating look of a state trooper or a drill sergeant. "I thought I told you to leave your sister alone. Have some God damned respect for your cousin and your uncle, why don't you? What's wrong with you? We're in a God damned chapel."

This caught Father Connelly's attention, of course, who looked at Bobby Joe with pain in his eyes. Bobby Joe was unaware his statement had caught not only the priest's attention, but his mother-in-law's. Lisa flushed, aware enough for both of them. More relatives—cousins of Ken's and their children—had arrived, just in time to hear this exchange. A prince of a man if Valerie had ever seen one.

"Sure, Dad. I'll try to be more sensitive." Bobby smiled as he spoke, his tone just on the edge of insolent.

"Maybe we'd better get started," Father Connelly said.

"Why don't we do that," Helen replied, an artificial smile plastered on her face.

Valerie winked at her cousin Bobby as she turned away. He smiled genuinely this time.

The mass was excruciating. Like many uprooted families, they were burying Kenny in a state where virtually no one knew him, though most of his relatives lived here. Valerie had been raised in a largely non-religious household, but she tried to be sensitive to other's religious needs, especially her grandparents, who were devout Catholics. But the mass…it went on and on, a ritual Valerie didn't understand and didn't care about. For her, going to church had been restricted to summer vacations when she visited her grandparents for three weeks out of the year. Neither of her parents had attended churches, though her mother, Martha, was raised a Lutheran, and Murphy had grown up Catholic. As a teenager she'd envied some of her friends, who'd been involved in church groups and activities. Not now though, especially not sitting through a mass for her poor brother, who wouldn't have understood it anyway.

Bobby and Laura were used to it. Their parents, Bobby Joe and Lisa, never missed a chance to sit in church: Bobby Joe was a Southern Baptist, and had pushed his wife into converting.

Afterward, they moved to the cemetery, halfway around town. Anxious motorists cut into the funeral procession several times as they drove around the perimeter highway.

Valerie sat numb, shivering from the chilly breeze, during the ceremony at the gravesite. Her only connection with reality, tenuous as it was, was her father, who sat beside her holding her hand. The coffin and two small rows of chairs were shaded by a tent stretched above their heads. The cemetery, spread across gently rolling hills, surrounded them on all sides. A slight breeze moved through her hair.

As the mechanical apparatus lowered the coffin into the ground, her father shook. Valerie looked over at him. His face was stone, his jaw set, but she could feel him shaking, his entire body, almost as if her were suffering from a seizure. The shaking became apparent to the others as his marksmanship medals, hanging on his chest below his campaign ribbons, began to rattle.

Valerie heard someone whisper behind her, and even Father Connelly looked up at the sound of the metallic rattling. Tom put his hand on Murphy's shoulder and whispered something to him. Whatever he said—and Valerie tried her best to hear, but couldn't—it stopped the shaking. Then it was done.

Her father lingered at the edge of the grave, Tom on one side, arm over his shoulder. She wanted to cry as she saw his face distort with pain, tears rolling down his cheeks. He reached into his pocket and brought out what looked like a ribbon, and she gasped when she realized what it was. Mom told her a hundred times about her senior prom, when Dad had proposed. She had carefully pressed and dried the corsage he gave her that night, eventually framing it and keeping it in her study. Valerie hadn't seen it since Mom died. He must have been keeping it with him all this time, because that was what he held in his hand, the blue ribbon trailing off in the wind. He'd tied the ribbon around his wedding ring.

His face twisted, and Tom held him close. She faintly heard the words he spoke. "Goodbye, Martha. I loved you. Goodbye, little guy."

Valerie sobbed at the words.

He kissed the corsage and then threw it in. The wedding ring bounced with a loud pop when it hit the coffin. Murphy stood over it, eyes closed, then turned and stumbled away.

Chapter Twenty-Eight
November 1

Second Brigade Headquarters was located in Morgantown, West Virginia, just outside of town where there was sufficient room for the motor pool and training facilities. A new three-story building, it had replaced the old, dilapidated headquarters three years before. Woods surrounded the facility, but a seventy-five-foot buffer had recently been cleared of trees between the fence and the woods.

Under normal circumstances, the headquarters was guarded by a bored private security guard, typically sitting in the booth at the front gate, not even bothering to walk a circuit or patrol the motor pool. Things were a little different now that Captain Karen Greenfield, a wanted federal fugitive, had arrived.

Two platoons of infantry were now assigned the task of guarding the facility. The men in the infantry company, primarily unemployed coal miners from the economically devastated Logan County, were happy to have been activated, as the work was bringing in good money for what was, in reality, not that bad a job. Guard duty might be boring, but it was a damn site better than no work at all.

First Lieutenant Austin Robear was in charge of the guard detail. He had assigned one platoon to secure the building itself, including the entrances, roof and approaches from the front gate. The perimeter, including the front gate and the motor pool, were guarded by the second platoon.

At the moment, Robear sat in the office he'd been assigned, his feet up on the desk as he listened to the game on the radio. His eyes were closed, but he was wide awake, his adrenaline pumping every time the Eagles got the ball.

"Black Six, Black Six, this is White Three, over." There was panic in the voice of the caller.

Robear jerked upright at the radio call, then keyed his own headset.

"Go ahead, White Three, over."

"Black Six, we have six unmarked vehicles approaching the facility at this time. They have extra antennas, appear to be federal vehicles. They are coming up from town, ETA two minutes, over."

"Roger, White Three."

Robear called his two platoon leaders, alerting them to scramble their off-duty people into position. He then stood, put on his helmet and web gear, and headed for the front door while making another call, this one to the acting brigade commander.

"This is Lieutenant Colonel Chang," he heard the gruff voice answer.

"Sir, this is Lieutenant Robear. My people report we have a group of what may be federal vehicles approaching. Six unmarked vehicles approaching from town, sir."

"Thanks, Lieutenant. Keep me informed, please."

"Wilco, sir."

Robear reached the front gate, which was closed and barred, at the same time that the vehicles arrived. The first of the cars pulled up to the gate. One of his men—Private Wilson—approached the lead vehicle from the tiny guard shack.

Behind the first car, the other five pulled into positions just across the street. Men poured out of the vehicles. Licking his lips, Robear approached, walking through the guard shack toward the first car.

From the passenger side stepped a large man, wearing a black suit and tie.

"Lieutenant, are you in charge here?"

"I'm in charge of the security detail, yes, sir," Robear answered. "I'm afraid you men are trespassing and must leave immediately."

The man walked closer to Robear. "Lieutenant, my name is Bob Newman. I'm the Special Agent in Charge of the FBI Field Office in Cincinnatti. This is a federal search warrant for this facility." He held up a folded sheet of paper.

"May I see it?" Robear asked, stalling for time. His could feel his pulse in his neck, an interesting sensation, if unpleasant. The agent impatiently handed over the papers, and Robear slowly and neatly took them out of the envelope and unfolded them.

Robear almost chuckled as he looked at the legalese covering the page. He'd never looked at a warrant in his life and wouldn't know whether it was valid or not. All the same, he had a job to do. He read over it carefully, and very slowly.

After a moment, he handed it back. "Sir, I'm afraid this warrant may not have jurisdiction over this facility. I'm going to have to ask you to take this to the state attorney general and National Guard Bureau in Charleston, so they can determine if you will be allowed in the facility. I can't do it on my own. Once I get an order from my commanding officer indicating I have to let you in, I will be happy to do so. Until then, I'm going to have to ask you to leave immediately."

"Lieutenant, if that gate isn't open in thirty seconds, I'll have my men place you under arrest for obstruction of justice."

"I see," Robear said, his heart thumping wildly. He keyed his radio and spoke into the handset. "Blue Six, White Six, this is Black Six, over."

Both platoon leaders responded immediately. The agent's mouth fell open as he heard the next order.

"Please make sure your men are locked and loaded at this time, over. The rules of engagement are as we discussed in our briefing. Acknowledge, over."

As he spoke, everyone within fifty yards heard the distinctive crack of M16 rifles being loaded. Much more frightening to the men across the street, however, was the appearance of a crew-served machine gun mounted on a tripod, sitting in one of the windows of the headquarters building. The federal agents across the street ducked behind their vehicles, except the one at the gate.

"Lieutenant, you don't want to do this."

"You are right, sir. I don't want to do this. May I recommend you quickly vacate the premises, before this goes somewhere neither of us want."

"Now wait just a goddamn minute," shouted Newman. "You are obstructing a federal investigation. Open this gate right this minute."

"Corporal Caldwell," Robear called into the guard shack. Caldwell called back, "Yes, sir!"

"Place these gentlemen under arrest."

Caldwell and the three other men of his fire team immediately stepped out of the guard shack, their weapons pointed at Newman and the driver of the vehicle, who hadn't spoken as of yet.

"Step out of the car, sir," one of the rifleman shouted to the driver. "Hands in the air."

Caldwell walked up to Newman. "Hands up. Now!"

Newman slowly raised his hands in the air. As he did so, five of the agents across the street broke away from their vehicles.

"Mr. Newman, tell your men to halt or we will open fire."

"Oh, shit," the driver of the car muttered as one of the riflemen took his weapon and cleared it.

"Stop!" Newman shouted. "Don't come any closer, I think they're serious."

The agents ignored him.

"Get in the shack now," Caldwell shouted, and shoved Newman ahead of him.

Robear keyed his radio set to call the machine gun team. "Max One, Max One, this is Black Six. If those agents cross the yellow line, fire a burst over their heads. Make sure you don't hit anybody, over."

"Wilco, sir."

Almost immediately, a burst of machine gun fire plowed into the hillside behind the agents, all of whom dropped to the ground.

"Goddammit," Newman cursed. "Do you have any idea what you are doing?" His face was bright red as he spoke.

"Yes, sir, I do. Now get on the ground and shut up."

Newman did as he was told.

Robear called the Colonel to report. Shortly after, the news vans pulled up to report on the latest chain of events.

The next morning, three major items were plastered over the front page of newspapers across the country. In the first, in elections across America, far-right candidates—many of them sympathetic to the West Virginian cause—had been elected, changing the majorities in both the House and the Senate. Representative Albert Clark of West Virginia was resoundingly defeated by a little-known, badly funded Republican Party candidate. Pundits on all side credited his defeat to his last minute announcement that he was opposed to the independence referendum—a referendum which passed in his district by a wide margin.

In the second item, several Federal agents had been arrested by National Guard forces in Morgantown, West Virginia. The DHS and the National Guard were at a standoff in Morgantown, with increasing numbers of federal agents surrounding the National Guard compound.

The final, and perhaps most important item was that in a landslide vote, Proposition 12 passed in West Virginia, granting the legislature the power to secede West Virginia from the United States.

The next morning, State Representative Brian Warfield of Logan County introduced a bill in the State House of Representatives calling for the immediate secession of West Virginia from the United States. Later that day, Governor Frank Slagter ordered the activation of the state National Guard.

Chapter Twenty-Nine
November 2

The military helicopter flew across the landscape just above treetop level, the turbine engine screaming. Murphy stared at the front of the cabin, and paid little attention to the shake of the chopper and the thump of the rotors.

It was interesting that in the absence of any orders, the pilot violated a number of peacetime, stateside rules about where and how military helicopters were flown. Nap-of-the-earth flight might be normal for combat zones, but it wasn't for ferrying around the brass in West Virginia. Several times the pilot took them between the mountains instead of over them, and Murphy caught his breath more than once as they flew meters over power lines. He did not correct the pilot. They weren't at war yet, but might be soon enough.

The pilot, an Air National Guard major, tried to make small talk twice, then gave up and looked away. Murphy replied in monosyllabic responses. He didn't mean to be unfriendly; he just didn't feel like talking. He found it easier to stare out the window.

After the funeral yesterday the whole family had returned to his parents' home. It was a maudlin, depressing dinner. Afterward, Valerie insisted on turning on the television, and they all learned, in the worst way possible, that she would soon be out of a job. Bobby Joe didn't let the dust settle before he suggested she move to Atlanta, and Murphy had to take a deep breath and settle down. Nothing infuriated him more than his brother-in-law's fawning attention to Valerie.

Tom scoffed at the news that West Virginia passed the independence referendum. What did they think? They'd field the National Guard against the U.S. Army?

That's exactly what they think, Murphy replied, sparking a loud and blessedly distracting discussion. He and his brother argued, in significant detail, the readiness of the National Guard compared to active duty units, especially those units—like Tom's—that had recently been overseas. By the time they finished, everyone else in the family was rolling their eyes and trying to change the subject. They all avoided the topic of whether Murphy would stay in command of the brigade, though Murphy knew full well his family expected him to resign. Some things you just couldn't talk about.

He had a job to do. Whatever the assembly decided, Murphy had to get his brigade prepared to fight a defense, in the event it did come to a shooting war. He prayed it wouldn't. Things were bad enough already.

"Sir? We may have a problem."

Murphy's eyes shifted to the pilot, and he paused, almost imperceptibly. "What is it, Major?"

"We've got an escort. Two choppers from the DHS."

"Wave to them and keep going."

"Yes, sir."

The pilot did just that: he leaned forward and waved at a chopper flying two hundred meters to their left. Murphy couldn't see the reaction of the escorting pilots, but somehow he was sure it couldn't be good. This situation had to change. They could not continue an ongoing confrontation outside his brigade headquarters. Maybe he could sneak Captain Greenfield out in the chopper. No. Anywhere he sent her, they'd be sure to find her, and at least at Brigade he had some control and could keep the feds from hauling her away.

He couldn't think of much of anything that exemplified the recent stupidity of the federal government than moving to try her on capital charges. Or cutting funding for a desperately needed medical trial when the patients were likely to die. Or sending federal agents into a city to round up people in the street. Or sending combat troops to intervene in a labor dispute. The federal government had demonstrated its incompetence at almost every turn.

Below, the brigade headquarters compound came into view. On the rooftop, he could see anti-aircraft guns and missile teams. What looked to be two platoons of infantry were dug into new emplacements all around the site, and Bradley fighting vehicles were also positioned in various locations.

On the outside of the site there were twenty-five or so police cars and vans, plus armored vehicles—half-a-dozen Bradleys and some engineer vehicles. Murphy grimaced. It wouldn't take much to turn this situation into an inferno.

After the chopper touched down on the helicopter pad, Murphy said, "Thanks, Major. Please be ready to go to Charleston later today; I'm probably going to need to meet with General Peak and the governor before the end of the day."

"Yes, sir."

Murphy stepped down from the helicopter and bent low as he walked out from under the still turning rotors. He pulled his overcoat tighter; it was damn cold out. As he walked off the helicopter pad, Lieutenant Colonel Jian Chang, his executive officer, ran out to meet him.

Chang saluted as Murphy approached, and Murphy returned the salute. Unlike Murphy in his dress uniform, Chang wore battle fatigues, complete with helmet and pistol belt. Murphy felt uncomfortable with the need for combat gear under the current circumstances, but then again, it wouldn't surprise him if whoever ran the show for DHS decided on some idiot scheme to storm the compound. They turned to walk into the building. As the door opened, Murphy felt a cushion of warm air hit him.

"Colonel, I was very sorry to hear about your son. My condolences."

"Thank you, Jan." Murphy changed the subject. "What's the situation here?"

"Not good, sir. We have a growing contingent of federal police outside, including some armored vehicles. They've periodically tried calling on our people to surrender, threatening them with treason charges, but no one is budging. I'll be honest with you, sir. I'm… very surprised; we've had absolutely no one who wanted to walk away from this situation, so far as I can see. Don't take this the wrong way sir, but I called the men together yesterday and offered them the opportunity to resign and walk away with no prejudice. No one went. In any event, we currently have three prisoners; they are being held in very comfortable conditions."

"Have they been given the opportunity to meet with attorneys?"

"No, sir."

Murphy stopped walking for a moment and turned to the other officer. "Jan, you're not going to like this, but we need to try to diffuse this situation. I want to meet with those men, and then we're going to release them. We're not going to do what they've been doing. Take me to them."

"Yes, sir."

A few moments later, they walked into a small conference room. A large man with a broad, flushed face stood as they entered. Two other men at the far side of the table remained seated.

"How long are we going to be held here?" he demanded as the officers entered the room.

"Not any longer. I'm Colonel Ken Murphy; I'm the brigade commander here."

The man facing him gave him a withering look, before responding. "Then you have a lot to answer for, Colonel Murphy."

Murphy frowned. "What's your name?"

"I'm Bob Newman. I'm the Special Agent in Charge for the FBI's Field Office in Cincinatti."

"Okay, Mr. Newman," Murphy said. "Here's how we're going to do this. I'm going to talk, and you're going to listen. Then you are going to walk out of here. Understand?"

Newman's face twisted as if he wanted to respond much more violently. Instead, he nodded.

"Good. I don't want any bloodshed, understand? In case you didn't notice by the lopsided election results, the federal government isn't all that popular around here. It's going to make things a lot worse if your trigger-happy boys start a battle against a brigade of the National Guard. Do you get that? Do you want to fire the opening shots of a civil war?"

Newman did not respond.

"I'll take that as a no. Good news is, I don't want to, either. So, here's what I want. I want you to walk out of here, and I want your people to back off a couple hundred meters from the compound. Let's ease the tension here, so no one does anything stupid, okay? I don't need one of my guards spooking at three a.m. and opening fire. Neither do you."

Newman nodded. "Anything else, Colonel?"

"Yes. I've got a pretty good feeling somewhere in Washington some bureaucrat who has never looked down the business end of a gun barrel is planning to conduct some kind of strike on this place to arrest Captain Greenfield. Newman, make sure they put that out of their minds. These aren't unarmed factory workers here; these are trained and determined soldiers, and you don't want a battle. Let's allow this thing to work its way through the legislature or the courts or whatever, and then we can all walk away from this situation alive."

"All right, Colonel. I agree with you, and I'll pass that on."

Murphy turned to Lieutenant Colonel Chang. "Colonel Chang, can you have someone escort these men out of the compound."

"Yes, sir."

A few minutes later, the men were escorted out of the building, and Ken went to look for his office.

༒

Clouds of white mist appeared around Mike Morris as he exhaled, and he pulled his coat tighter around him. Another cold spell had set in, making for what had been one hell of a cold autumn. He dreaded winter this year, if it was already this cold. The sun was just setting behind the trees on the other side of the desolate parade ground, stretching the shadows out into long, distorted shapes.

He walked across the field, head held low in the event any reporters were about, and reached the back door of the battalion headquarters. Locked. He'd forgotten they usually locked the back and side entrances at six. He walked around the side, still hunched over in his coat, and walked in the front door. A news van was parked out front. He was surprised—he would have expected them to lose interest in favor of the election the day before. No such luck, but no one got out of the van as he walked into the building.

His feet echoed on the floor with a dull, flat sound when he entered the building, crossed the empty entryway to Lieutenant Colonel Barksdale's office and knocked on the door.

"Enter." Barksdales voice was muffled by the door.

Morris opened it and stepped inside.

"Come in, Captain, sit down."

"Thank you, sir," Morris replied stiffly.

"How are you making out with the Article 32 investigation?"

"Not bad, sir. My attorney thinks there is a good chance this thing will be dropped before it goes to court-martial, and if it isn't, almost no chance I'll be convicted. It's a relief."

"Good, good. That's actually why I called you over here, Captain."

"Yes, sir." Morris straightened in his chair, his stomach tensing.

"I discussed this thing with the brigade commander, the whole issue with the Article 32 hearing, the possible court-martial. The way I see it, Captain, it's bad for discipline. This is nothing personal, but your company is suffering because of it. I don't want to see that. Especially if we end up going to fight some hillbillies up in West Virginia."

Morris stirred in his seat uneasily. "Sir, rest assured, my men will be in the best possible training should we deploy. I'll ensure it."

"How exactly are you going to accomplish that, with you stuck in hearings all the time?"

Morris felt panic setting in. Barksdale was going to relieve him. He'd known this was coming; it was just a question of when.

"Sir, the Article 32 investigation will be over by Friday. Then we just wait for the report. I can see your point if it comes to a court-martial, but that's not very likely at this point."

Barksdale frowned. "I see. All the same, I'm not comfortable with this. I won't formally relieve you—not yet. We'll place you on a leave status until you've either been cleared or until they announce a court-martial, and your XO can assume command for the time being. But let me be clear, Captain. If it comes to a court-martial, I'll be forced to relieve you of your command."

Morris hated the tone of his voice, even as he spoke. "Sir, doesn't the principle of innocent until proven guilty apply? You were there, sir. You know what happened. Why should my career be derailed when I haven't even been convicted of anything?"

He couldn't have found anything worse to say. Barksdale looked at him, his face frozen, eyes narrow. "It's not about you, Captain Morris. It's about the good of your company. I don't give a rat's ass if it's fair to you, but if your company suffers and people die because you are too busy defending yourself in court, we've got a problem."

Barksdale paused, visibly trying to control his anger, then he spoke again. "You know, that's what I don't like about you, Morris. It's all about you and your career. Not once have I heard you express concern about that boy who was killed, or even your men who were killed. Not once have I heard you ask how Private Turville is doing. But, of course, your defense rests on his guilt, isn't that right? I'd rather see you answer, 'No excuse,' and take the consequence than see what I'm seeing now. It's despicable that you would base your defense on screwing one of your subordinates." Morris almost physically shrank into his chair as Barksdale pointed his finger at him. "Captain, you may walk away from this. You may be cleared by the Article 32 investigation, and resume command of your company. But I tell you this: in my eyes, you are already done. As an officer and as a man."

"I don't know what I'm expected to say at this point, sir," Mike said. "It looks as if you've made up your mind."

"That's right."

"Sir, if I'm unofficially losing command of my company, I'd like to request a couple of weeks' leave to go to Kentucky and see my daughter over Christmas."

"Denied. You can sit around here and find out whether or not you're going to be court-martialed."

"Sir, I haven't seen my daughter since before we deployed to West Virginia."

"You should have thought about that before you became in infantry officer. Dismissed."

Morris stumbled out of the office, fists clenched, his mind clouded. Barksdale's comment was a bitter reminder of similar words he'd said to Alicia in the spring. The colonel was right about Turville, too: Morris had never been comfortable with that line of defense in the first place—never mind that it was the truth.

He went to the back door of the battalion in hopes of avoiding reporters, but it was too late. As he stepped out of the back door, a reporter and a photographer appeared in his path.

"Captain Morris, I'm Ron Reid from Newsweek. We're putting together a story about you and Captain Karen Greenfield in West Virginia. Would you care to comment?"

"No, I wouldn't. Please get out of my way."

"Is it true, sir, that your wife and daughter left to go back to your father-in-law?"

"That's none of your business."

"Well, Representative Skaggs is a very important congressman. Is he supporting you in your defense? It's curious he hasn't spoken up about it."

Mike lost his temper. "It's not at all curious, all right? And my relationship with my wife and her father is none of your goddamn business, and none of your magazine's goddamn business, and none of the public's goddamn business! Got it?"

"But sir, we've been told by sources your wife left because of your involvement with Captain Greenfield while you were in Charleston. We've got several statements placing the two of you together in West Virginia. And you dated in college for what, three years? We've got photographs. And then, to have both incidents occur the way they did—don't you think it's an incredible coincidence?"

"What the hell is wrong with you? Is it your job to ruin people's lives?"

"Well, sir, I didn't shoot a kid."

"Neither did I. Get the hell out of my way."

Morris shoved the reporter out of his way and continued walking.

"Morris! We're running the story whether or not you talk. Don't you think it's better you get your side on the table?"

"It'd be better if you were in hell."

Morris walked away.

⌘

The morning after her brother's funeral, Valerie caught her breath as she came out of the lee of the South Capitol Metro station and the icy wind slapped her. She pulled her overcoat tight around her, wishing to God she could wear a good pair of jeans to the office instead of this damn skirt. It didn't matter if she was a senior aide to a senior congressman—she still had to wear goddamn outfits that left too little to the imagination. The same old litany ran through her mind as she walked toward the office. Because only pretty girls got jobs on the Hill.

Won't matter much longer, she supposed. She wouldn't be working here more than another month or two. With Al Clark's surprise defeat, she didn't have a clue what to do next.

At the staff entrance to the Rayburn Building, she dropped her purse on the X-ray machine and walked through the metal detectors. Long experience had taught her not to bother coming to work with anything in her pockets; all of it went in the purse, so she didn't have to mess with emptying them every time she entered the building.

The office was like a graveyard. Too many changes had come, too quickly, and the staff was in shock. Virtually no one was in the office when she arrived.

Ambrose, in a well-tailored brown suit, was already sitting with Clark in the boss's office.

"Come on in," Clark said. He waved his arm in a vague gesture.

She walked in, the clicking of her heels abruptly muted on the carpet as she walked into the office. Clark leaned back on his couch, his jacket off, a cup of coffee in his hand. Valerie sat down and dropped her purse next to the chair, then smoothed out her skirt. A moment later she looked up at her boss.

"How are you doing, Al? I couldn't believe it."

Clark shrugged. "I'll be fine, as soon as Ambrose stops giving me those 'I told you so' looks. Right now we need to find jobs for all of you."

She glanced between the two, a question in her eyes.

Ambrose spoke. "Governor Slagter suckered Al into making that statement on election day."

"Now, he did not, Ambrose. I wasn't going to go out there and say something I didn't believe in. I just never anticipated the reaction would be so strong. It's actually quite interesting—it's the widest margin we've had in an election in our district in almost fifty years."

"Now there is a dubious distinction," Ambrose said.

"No, It just means I didn't understand the depth of anger back home. Do you know, two weeks ago I would have said there was no chance in the world that referendum would pass, that the citizens of our state would go it alone—possibly in the face of a war—rather than work it out."

Valerie shrugged. "Come on, boss. Who is there to work with any more? All it takes to land yourself in jail these days is to discuss this stuff in a chatroom somewhere."

"You're right. I just didn't see it."

"So what do you think you're going to do?" Valerie asked.

"Pick up the pieces," he said. "There's a hundred law firms in Washington I could go to work for, or maybe I can wangle an ambassadorship out of the next President. I think my chances with this one are shot."

She shook her head, her eyes watering. "Al, I thought you were going to be President some day."

He grimaced. "I did too, Val. I did too." then his eyes narrowed as he looked at her. "Val, how are you holding up? You've had an impossible time."

She shrugged, her body stiff.

"I'll be okay," she said, and her voice broke.

Ambrose spoke. "You don't have to keep the whole world running, Valerie. It's okay to grieve for your brother."

"It's not just that, Ambrose. It's my father. Oh, my God, you should have seen him. He's like a walking skeleton—he's lost his wife and his son and his job in the last three years. It's like the whole world is crumbling around him. Al, I'm afraid of what he might do. Do you know, if West Virginia does secede I think he's going to get himself killed. And Kenny—he was such a beautiful little boy. He would have lived if they hadn't cut the funding. And I didn't have time to do anything about it."

"Valerie," Clark said. "You don't know that. He might have gone even if the funding hadn't been cut."

"I don't think so. Three of the children who were in the program died within three days after the treatment was stopped. There's got to be a reckoning for that, but no one is investigating, no one is saying anything."

"Dear God," Clark whispered.

"Al, I just don't know what to do. My Dad is all I've got left, and I think I've already lost him."

༶

The stack of reports, presentations, paperwork and more paperwork was smaller than it had been on Murphy's arrival at the brigade headquarters, but not by a significant amount. He'd had a lot of paperwork as a battalion commander, but it appeared the volume of paper directly increased with rank.

This much was true: he had a hell of a job ahead of him. Regardless of the outcome of the debate in the State House, his job was to make this brigade ready for combat. Right now, they weren't even close. Personnel was the biggest problem—since the referendum passed, nearly five percent of his officers had resigned. More were sure to come, especially when serious war preparations began. Worse, nearly fifteen percent of the enlisted personnel had not shown up when the governor called them. They were voting with their feet, probably leaving West Virginia rather than be caught in the middle of the conflict.

He had tank battalions that could not man all their tanks, infantry companies without a full complement of riflemen, and at the command and staff level the holes were worse. One armor battalion in the southern part of the state had seen the resignation of the entire battalion staff, leaving the senior company commander, a captain, in command of the entire battalion.

Ammunition was also a problem. They had plenty of small arms ammo, but the initial estimate of tank cannon rounds was only enough for two days of sustained combat, and there was no way to get any more. The Air National Guard was in worse shape: the A-10 anti-tank aircraft company in Lewiston didn't have a single combat round on hand. Unless they could put their hands on some ammunition, the planes would be no use for anything but observation, and that was pretty limited.

As he ran through his thoughts, Murphy made a list of problems that needed to be addressed, starting with the ongoing siege outside this very building. That would have to be dealt with immediately—he would need to talk to General Peak about options. Next on the list came personnel, then ammunition and fuel, then training. He'd pull the brigade staff together first thing in the morning to look at resolving all of those areas.

His phone rang. Without looking up from the papers, he lifted the receiver to his ear.

"Colonel Murphy."

"Colonel, this is Major Johnson, on General Peak's staff in Charleston."

"What can I do for you, Major?"

"Sir, I've been asked to get in touch with you by Chief of Staff Colonel Briggs. General Peak suffered a severe stroke this morning, and—sir, the prognosis is not good. The governor has ordered you and the other Brigade commanders to report to him immediately."

Murphy closed his eyes. Things just seemed to keep getting worse.

Chapter Thirty
November 10

Two hours later Murphy's helicopter landed on the snow-dusted helicopter pad next to the Governor's Mansion in Charleston. The flight was cold and disorienting: they'd been tossed about as they hit gusts of wind between the mountains, and a sheet of white snow thrown up by the rotors blanked out visibility as they landed. Hard.

Fifty feet away from the chopper, a young lieutenant wearing fatigues and a pistol stood and saluted Murphy as he approached.

"Welcome, sir. If you'll come this way, I'll take you straight to the governor."

Interesting, Murphy thought. It was a National Guard officer who escorted him to the governor, and not a civilian aide of some kind.

The lieutenant led him directly to governor's office.

"Ken," Slagter's voice boomed as Murphy entered the office. "Welcome, welcome. I hope you're holding up okay after the loss of your son. I was very sorry to hear about that."

"Thank you, sir."

"Come in, come in, we've some things to discuss. You know Mark Brown, the attorney general?"

"Yes, sir, we've met," Murphy said. "It's a pleasure to see you, sir."

"And you, Colonel."

"I'm sure you know these gentlemen." Slagter indicated four officers who stood around the conference table.

Colonel Myers, the First Brigade Commander, was based out of Logan County. Blonde, athletic, he was the youngest officer in the room at thirty-five, and the most aggressive.

Colonel Hatfield, commander of the 501st Artillery Brigade, white-haired, had until recently been battalion commander for the Division Combat Service Support team. A former Logan County sheriff and Democratic party chairman, his brigade command had less to do with experience than political connections.

The other two men were colonels Wilson Briggs, the Division Chief of Staff, and Roland May, commander of the 450th Air Cavalry Brigade, based out of Charleston.

Murphy nodded to the other officers. "Hello, sirs," he said. Only recently promoted to full Colonel, he was the most junior officer in the room.

The governor and the attorney general sat down at the antique mahogany conference table, and the officers followed.

"Mark," Slagter said, and gestured to the attorney general.

Brown placed his hands flat on the table and spoke. "Gentlemen, I will get straight to the point. General Peak's stroke was quite serious. While he will live, he is paralyzed, and we don't know if he will recover. As you know, this is a most serious time for West Virginia. We cannot leave open the question of command of the National Guard."

Murphy glanced at the other officers. None of them spoke up, so he asked the question. "Governor, what about General Wilson, the assistant division commander?"

Brown answered instead of the governor. "I have his resignation on my desk, effective today. It seems he is unwilling to stay in command of the West Virginia guard when we may soon be called to defend our state."

"Which leaves you gentleman," said Slagter. "Colonel Hatfield, you are the most senior officer present, according to your service records. But I am very concerned, sir, about your lack of any combat experience whatsoever."

Hatfield said, "Governor, I assure you, I am quite fit for command."

"Your assurances are noted, Colonel. However, they aren't enough. I'll need an officer with combat experience. The first question I have is the one I should have asked of General Wilson. Are any of you willing to stay in command in the event the legislature passes a declaration of independence? Will you stay and fight for your state, if you must?"

The officers looked at each other. Murphy's first thought was they looked paralyzed. Whatever they said would be wrong at this point. If they answered in the affirmative, it amounted to treason against the federal government. The same federal government that killed his friends, cut off his son's medical care and shot civilians in the street.

That settled it. Murphy spoke up. "I'll stay and fight. The federal government has abandoned everything that made us American."

Colonel Briggs spoke, his tone ice. "Murphy, that's treason you are talking."

"Colonel, I swore an oath to protect the Constitution of the United States—and the federal government is trampling all over that Constitution."

Briggs frowned. "I don't know where in that oath it authorizes armed insurrection. Governor, I'll have nothing to do with any discussion of treason or secession, and I'll inform you now that I will report what is said in this meeting to the Army."

Slagter looked Briggs in the eye. "I'll accept your immediate resignation, Colonel. You may go."

Colonel May pursed his lips and shook his head. "Me too, sir. I understand where you're coming from, Murphy, but you miss the point. A lot of people will die if we end up fighting a war here. I'm taking my family and leaving the state. This is a huge mistake." He stood up and walked out.

Myers and Murphy looked at each other. With Hatfield ruled out by the governor, one of the two of them would be in command.

"Colonel Murphy," Slagter said. "Refresh my memory. You were an enlisted man in the Gulf War, correct? Infantry?"

"I was a cavalry scout, sir."

"Then an armor officer. You served in Yugoslavia and in the Iraq War."

"Yes, sir."

"And you, Colonel Myers. You were also in Iraq."

"Yes, sir, Colonel Murphy and I served together."

Slagter grunted. "And what would you do, sir, if you were in my shoes?"

"I don't know if I can answer that question, sir."

"Give it a stab."

"Sir, I would place Colonel Murphy in command."

"Why is that, Colonel? What not you?" Murphy blurted out the question before the governor could speak.

Myers grimaced. "Politics and morale. We can't win a war here. Governor, after the past year, Colonel Murphy is an instantly recognizable figure throughout America. He's looked at almost as a popular hero. It will be an early morale blow to our opponents, and a boost to our side, if we have someone of his… stature… in command."

"Do you agree with his assessment, Colonel Hatfield?"

"It appears I'm out of the running, sir. Yes, I suppose I do."

Slagter's gaze turned to Murphy, who sat there, intensely uncomfortable.

"Well, Colonel? Are you in agreement with Colonel Myers?"

Murphy attacked one half of Myers's statement, ignoring the most critical part of the question.

"Yes, sir, he is correct. We cannot win a war against the United States. It will be necessary for you to find a political solution."

"I'm asking about command. You can't dodge the question forever, Colonel."

"Sir, I'm the most junior colonel you have."

Brown spoke up. "You have more combat experience, however."

"Sir, if you choose to do this, I will accept. But I caution you, we can defend this state three days, maybe a week, against a ground assault, depending on the weather. No longer, and not without sustaining massive civilian casualties. You must—absolutely must—find a political solution, sir. There is no military solution to our problem."

Slagter cocked his head. "What if we make it clear to the President that it will cost him dearly—it will cost the Army dearly—to invade us? Look, there's no question in my mind the bill will make it through the House and Senate. Anyone who wishes to stay in office will have to vote for it. It's almost certain they would override any veto. It's just a matter of time—possibly a few weeks—before we'll have a declaration of independence on our hands. Look at what happened to Congressman Clark. If I get in the way of this, they'll run right over me. Someone needs to defend our borders."

"I'll do it, sir. I'll try to buy you time. You have to keep them from coming if you can."

Slagter turned to Brown. "Mark, please pass to the legislature my recommendation that Colonel Murphy be promoted to Brigadier General. I can at least give him a brevet rank, can't I?"

"You can, sir."

"All right, good enough. Congratulations, General."

"Thank you, sir."

"How soon can you get a defense plan to me?"

He would need to consult with the division and brigade staff and get an initial plan written. That would depend on current force strength. He had a lot of work to do.

"End of next week, sir. I'll need to bring some people here—all the brigade and battalion commanders, plus the staff for each of the brigades. We'll need to do some large scale planning exercises, and quickly. Colonel Myers, I'll be heavily relying on your expertise in this."

Myers nodded.

Slagter nodded, too. "Do what you need to do, General. The one other thing: I want the feds out of Morgantown. I won't have them surrounding one of our military installations. Use force if you must, but try to find a way to get them out without any shooting. Now that you are in command, you get the hard tasks. Oh, that reminds me! Mark, do you have them?"

He turned to Brown, who pulled out a plastic sheet with stars pinned to it. Myers and the governor pinned the stars on Murphy's epaulets.

"Congratulations, sir." Myers smiled.

"This may not turn out to be such a prize."

"Probably not. Yours may be the first public hanging, General, but I won't be far behind."

"Well, let's get to it. We've got a lot of work to do."

༄

The phone rang again, and Valerie answered it, irritated. She had asked the current receptionist, a new intern from Brown, to hold any calls. So far, the phone had been ringing off the hook most of the morning. The Attorney general had issued indictments against twenty members of the religious cult at Baughman Settlement, for the bombings in Arlington and Charleston, as well as the murder of Dale Whitt. The press was going crazy.

"This is Valerie Murphy," she snarled.

"Valerie, can you come in here if you're not too grumpy?"

Her face flushed; it was Clark. "Sorry, boss. I'll be right in."

She walked toward Clark's office and tripped over a cardboard packing box someone had left between the desks.

"Oh for Christ's sake, can't you put your box inside your cube? Someone could get hurt."

Immediately she felt ashamed of herself for the outburst. It wasn't anyone else's fault she was so upset.

Clark sat at his desk, his coat off, tie loose and collar open. Despite the frigid temperature outside, Clark had his windows open to let out the heat.

As she walked in, Valerie said, "Boss, have the engineers been up here yet? I can call them."

"Don't worry about it." He waved his hand vaguely toward the entrance. "I asked the new intern, she called them."

Valerie looked over her shoulder, and then quietly spoke. "She probably sent them to the wrong office. I'm really not impressed with this one."

"You're just getting older, Valerie," he said. "Less tolerant."

The door opened and Ambrose strolled in.

"Hey, Valerie." Ambrose sat down in the empty chair next to her and absently twirled the tip of his mustache. "What's up, boss?"

Clark leaned back in his chair and looked at the two of them. "I just got a call from Frank Slagter. He wants me to resign early and come back to Charleston."

Valerie and Ambrose met each other's eyes. If Slagter was involved, nothing good would come of it. His administration had been marked with a series of scandals and corruption investigations, and a marked lack of serious leadership. He couldn't be trusted.

Ambrose cautiously said, "What for?"

"It seems Kurt Hamilton has stepped down as secretary of state. Slagter wants me to take the job. Specifically, he wants me to negotiate our way out of a war, when the legislature passes the independence bill."

"Oh, you get the booby prize," Valerie said.

"No, Valerie, your father got the booby prize: he has accepted command of West Virginia's National Guard."

Her eyes widened. "Oh, dear God, you're not serious."

"He did, Valerie. But we won't let it come to a war, if we can avoid it. Frank seems to believe I'm the best person to negotiate with the federal government on this. But I'll need some help."

"Okay. What do you want us to do?"

"Come with me. I'll need an assistant or chief of staff or something. Do what you're doing now."

"Okay. You got it."

Clark's gaze shifted to Ambrose. "What about you?"

Ambrose continued twisting his mustache thoughtfully, then spoke.

"Boss, I'm with you all the way—but not back there. When I left West Virginia I promised myself I'd never go back, and I've kind of kept that promise. I don't live there anymore, anyway. I'll find a job around here—there's plenty of jobs for lawyers in Washington."

Clark cocked his head. "Why not?"

Ambrose cocked his head. "Look at me. I'm a gay black man. Marked on all counts. Being Black was bad enough—cops always harassing me, couldn't get a job, only option I had was to get a scholarship and get out. And I couldn't fall back on the black community; back home, being gay is worse than being white. No offense, but I'll stay here, thank you. West Virginia was bad enough, but an independent West Virginia, devoid of federal anti-discrimination protection—oh, no. I don't think so. The DHS may have some bad apples, but they don't have anything on the Klan. And now it turns out it was more crazies from West Virginia that blew up the federal building? No, I think I'll stay here."

Valerie nodded, and unbidden, felt tears begin to stream down her face.

"Hey, Val," Ambrose said. "It's not so bad. DC is a great place to live."

"I'm sorry. I just can't seem to stop crying lately."

Ambrose nodded. "It does seem like the end of an era, doesn't it? We made a good team."

"That we did," Clark said.

∽

The phone rang. Four rings. Five. Mike pictured Alicia standing there, staring at the caller ID on the phone, waiting for him to hang up. He sat in his one chair, an open beer on the floor beside him. A book lay open on the floor beside the beer. Otherwise, the room was still empty.

Six rings. Seven. Eight.

"Hello?"

"Alicia?"

"Hello, Mike."

For an excruciating moment, they were silent.

"Why are you calling, Mike?"

"Today is Savannah's birthday, Alicia. I am calling to wish her a happy birthday."

"She's fine, Mike. We gave her your present, if that's what you're worried about."

"May I speak to her, please?"

Mike heard her inhale quickly. "No, Mike. I don't think that's a good idea. It will just upset her again."

"Alicia… I am her father. You can't do this to her."

"I will do what I think is best for her. If you talk to her it will just get her upset again. She doesn't need that right now."

Mike could feel the blood rushing to his head. His heart was pounding.

"Alicia…"

"Mike, let me ask you something. You haven't once asked when I was coming home. Why not? Don't you care? Is it because of her? That bitch you dated in college?"

"What? What are you talking about? She's got nothing to do with it."

"Oh, give me a break, Mike. Everybody on earth knows you carried on with her when you were in Charleston. I just wish you had had the balls to tell me, instead of me finding out from a magazine. You disgust me, Mike."

"I don't have a clue what you are talking about, Alicia, and you weren't here when I got home from Charleston anyway. Just in case you forgot, *you* left *me*. Our house was empty when I came home."

Her response was a whisper. "Our house has been empty for years."

In the background, Mike heard a voice that made his heartbeat race again. "Mommy, mommy. I heard you yelling. Is that Daddy on the phone?"

"No, honey, you go on to bed," Alicia responded.

Mike shouted without thinking, "Savannah, it's me, Daddy!"

"Mommy! I want to talk to Daddy."

"No. I said no, now go to bed!"

Savannah shrieked, and Mike cringed.

"Alicia, let her talk on the phone."

"Do you hear what you started, you bastard?" Alicia shouted into the phone. Mike heard a crash, then the phone disconnected. She must have slammed the phone down.

Mike stared at the phone in his hand, breathing heavily, his face red.

⁂

In Morgantown, Karen Greenfield sat at her desk and looked at the cover of the magazine. The cover featured a ten-year-old photograph of her and Mike Morris in formal clothing, holding each other in an embrace. Superimposed at the bottom corners were more recent and less flattering photographs of both of them.

"Revolution?" read the cover in large bold letters. Below, the subtitle: "How two military officers ignited the West Virginian independence movement. What really happened that week in Charleston?"

She had come back to the office after dinner and found the magazine on her chair. One of the helicopter pilots must have dropped it there—they were the only people who'd been able to leave the building.

Dear God, she thought. Where the hell did they get that photograph? She hadn't seen it since she and Mike broke up. It had been her favorite: Mike in his ROTC uniform, her in a black dress, her hair tied up, her head thrown back laughing. It was taken at a formal Christmas party at BowlingGreen their sophomore year, the night Mike proposed.

The inside article was worse. First a chronicle of events in Charleston: the shootout with the DHS, complete with diagrams and screen captures from the home video.

The article read, "Karen Greenfield is described by her fellow officers as the 'ice queen,' refusing to participate in social activities within the unit. Her former co-workers at Saturn Microsystems describe her as 'cool and efficient,' and many express shock and admiration at her actions in Charleston."

Ice queen, hell, she thought. *Just because I turned those assholes down for dates.*

It got worse. A photograph of Mike and Alicia at their wedding, raising a toast. She smiled in the photograph. He did not.

He had married in a tuxedo, not in uniform. It seemed odd: the wedding took place after he'd been commissioned as a Second Lieutenant, and the Mike Morris she remembered would have insisted on wearing his uniform. On second thought, looking at the photograph of the dour father-in-law, Congressman Skaggs, maybe this made more sense.

If only, she thought. *If only.*

The worst was to come, however, for the article speculated—quite accurately—on when and where Mike and Karen met again in Charleston. Some weasel in the battalion staff had given the reporters the dates and times they'd met.

"Some members of the administration are asking whether or not the relationship between these officers had a significant impact on events in West Virginia. Confidential sources have informed Newsweek that Alicia Skaggs Morris left with their daughter Savannah immediately after Morris's return to Fort Meade. Congressman Skagg's office has refused to comment on the question, but Skaggs has called for a full investigation into Morris's activities in West Virginia."

Son of a bitch wasn't standing behind his son-in-law. *What an ass,* Karen thought. She remembered the early days when she'd fallen in love with Mike Morris. It was all wrapped in her mind with the joy of that first freedom in her life—finally away from the nightmare of foster homes and devastated coal towns, finally on her own, and passionately in love, not just with Mike, but with life.

A sidebar included a profile of Sasha Zana, a Kurdish-American who'd been arrested immediately after the bombing in Charleston. The 19-year-old college student had purple spiked hair and a diamond stud on her nose. She was suing the federal government after being held for two months without charge.

Not taking her eyes off the article, she picked up the phone and dialed information. "Fort Meade, Maryland," she said. "Captain Michael Morris."

She wrote down the number, then dialed.

Two rings, and he answered, his voice sounding anxious. "Captain Morris speaking."

"Hi, Mike."

A pause. "Karen?"

"Yes. Have you seen the article?"

"I just got home from the PX. It was all over the place—the clerk smirked at me."

She snorted. "It's like being a target, isn't it."

"Yeah, well, I'll just have to keep moving."

She smiled, then gently said, "I… I'm sorry to hear about Alicia. You must really miss them."

"Well, I miss Savannah, terribly. Today's her birthday, you know. Alicia wouldn't let me talk to her."

"What the hell did you tell her?"

"Nothing. They were already gone when I got home."

Karen felt relief flood through her. They hadn't left because of her after all. "I see."

"Yeah."

They were silent, and she could hear him breathing.

Mike broke the silence. "How are you holding up? I see you on the news every day, or at least the outside of the building you're in."

"I don't know. I've never imagined what it would be like to have the attorney general insist on the death penalty for me. I always wanted to serve my country, you know?"

"Yes, I do."

"Hmm. This is horrible."

"What are you going to do? I mean, it sounds like this thing will come to blows."

"I'm a tank commander, Mike. I'll do what I have to."

"Are you serious?"

"I couldn't be more serious. The federal government doesn't stand for anything anymore. Certainly not for freedom. You remember when we were growing up, and Saddam Hussein in Iraq was the big bogeyman? Or Russia for our parents? We live in Iraq, Mike. We live in Russia. Pretty soon you'll have to get a passport to drive to the local Wal-Mart."

Mike exhaled. "I refuse to believe that. I'd give my life for my country."

"Let's not talk about it, then. Because for all we know, one of us may have to do that soon. I don't think I could bear it," she said, her voice breaking slightly.

It was true—in a matter of days or weeks, she would be out in the field, possibly in combat against the United States.

"Karen... I meant what I said in Charleston."

Tears ran down her face. She took a deep breath, wiped her eyes, and then responded.

"Well, I didn't. I don't want you to go away. If we live through this, Mike... I want you to come find me. Do you hear? I must be a complete idiot, because I still love you, you bastard."

Before he could reply, she gently set the phone on the cradle, then laid her head in her hands and wept.

Chapter Thirty-One
November 14

Valerie walked beside Congressman Clark past the security gates and into the main terminal, then winced as a mob of reporters rushed at them, bright lights on, microphones waving in the air like giant reeds. Other passengers leaving the terminal shied away, as if afraid of being caught in the limelight and associated with a subversive event. One man literally jumped when he noticed a camera pointed near him.

Valerie moved close to Clark as the reporters crowded in around them, microphones shoved in their faces. One of the journalists pushed so close she could smell his sour aftershave. She wanted to shove him away.

"Congressman, is it true you are going to accept the position of secretary of state?"

"Congressman, are you still against West Virginia independence?"

"Congressman, what are your plans?"

Clark held his hands up, palm out, and said, "One question at a time, please."

"Congressman, Sarah Davis with Channel Four. Is it true you are accepting the position as secretary of state?"

He shook his head sharply in the negative. "Governor Slagter and I are talking, nothing specific has been decided. Think of it as a job interview. You know I've been fired, so I'll be looking soon."

The reporters chuckled. Valerie thought the joke in bad taste and nearly elbowed Clark in the side.

"Congressman, Randall Pitts from the Logan Examiner. During the election you came out with a strong statement against independence for West Virginia. Now the referendum has passed, are you opposed to the declaration currently being debated in the State House?"

Clark took a deep breath and spoke. "I believe this move will lead us to war against the United States. I'm committed to do what I can do prevent any violence. However, it is clear—very clear—how the people of West Virginia feel. I believe a declaration if independence is now inevitable. For that reason, and to prevent more bloodshed, I'll do everything in my power to help negotiate a peaceful settlement."

"Do you think it will come to war, sir?"

"I'll do my best to see it doesn't."

"Congressman, what about the indictments in the terrorist attacks? Do you have any comment?"

Clark nodded. "This is a perfect example of the system working. The way our country is supposed to work is through the law. In the case of Baughman Settlement, those folks have been arrested and they'll get a trial. Let's hope we can go through the law and diplomacy to settle these others questions. We don't need any more violence. No more questions, I have work to do."

Unfortunately, there was one more question. For the first time, a reporter leveled a question at Valerie instead of Clark.

"Ms. Murphy, how does it feel to know your father has accepted command of the defense of West Virginia in the event of a war?"

Anger flooded her. "How do you think it feels? It's frightening."

The two of them walked away, the group of reporters on their trail. A moment later they were whisked away in a government staff car to meet the governor.

"Are you okay?" Clark asked her once they were in the quiet of the warm car.

"I'll be all right. It's the first time they've ever noticed me before, much less called me by name and asked me personal questions. Assholes."

Clark chuckled. "You'll get used to it."

"I better not."

༄

Murphy called his officers together in the gymnasium of a school that had been shut down by the Kanahwa County Public School District five years before. The building was now largely used as a warehouse, and had been loaned to the state government for purposes of this meeting—and possibly for use as a semi-permanent headquarters. They were within five blocks of the capitol building, which made this a good location for a military headquarters. It also seemed unlikely the federal government would suspect a former school of housing military headquarters, another good reason to use this location.

Now the gym was filled with the officers and staff of Murphy's lopsided division. Two infantry brigades, heavy on armor. One aviation brigade, with a battalion of Apache helicopters and another of A-10 Warthogs. One Special Operations group, which luckily had some recent combat experience in South America. Not a large force, and certainly not large enough to effectively defend the state. They had virtually no ammunition. The officer corps was rapidly thinning out with resignations. They had very little fuel. If it did come to war, it would be a short one.

Someone shouted "Attention!" as Murphy marched into the room, and the hundred or so officers jumped to their feet.

"As you were," he called out, and they relaxed. He took the steps two at a time, his combat boots echoing on the empty stage, and then stood in front of the group.

He surveyed the room, and wondered what Kenny would have made of all this. The thought settled like a lead ball in his gut. Kenny hated the weekends his father went away for training, and would have hated this even more.

Kenny was alone at the end. Pushed off on his grandmother during the last two weeks of his life. Was any of this worth the pain of losing his son? Not in a million years. But if his boy had sacrificed those last few days with his father, willing or not, for this cause, Murphy would do the rest. He *would* do the rest.

"Gentlemen. Ladies. I'll open with the most important question of the day, and one that will determine whether or not you should stay here."

"You are all aware of what the legislature is debating right now. You are all aware it will almost certainly pass and be signed by the governor. Your presence here right now could be construed by some as illegal—indeed, as treason against the United States. For that reason, I'm putting it to you: you may leave, right now, and walk away. A personnel officer is out in the hall who will quickly and easily process your resignation from the West Virginia National Guard and prevent your possible trial, incarceration or execution. Does everyone understand the seriousness of this? If you choose to stay, one of several things may happen. You may die on a battlefield not far from here. You may lose any veterans benefits for your family. You may go to prison, or worse. You may even be executed as a traitor. Even if the bill doesn't pass, and we are never called upon to act to defend this state, if you stay here it will make you an active member of a conspiracy against the United States government."

"Think about it. You have five minutes to make your decision, and then we will move on."

He looked at his watch, and then walked off the stage and out the door. A moment later he heard a familiar voice behind him.

"Well, I'll be damned if that man doesn't have stars on his collar."

Murphy turned around, a smile on his face. "Vince, how are you?"

Major Vince Elkins smiled, his face crinkled into deep lines. "It's been a pretty tough time for all of us, Ken. How are you hanging in? I was so sorry to hear about Kenny."

Murphy shrugged. "I'm trying not to... I'm trying not to dwell on it very much. Not now, when so much is happening."

Elkins shook his head. "Ken, you've got a right to grieve for your son. He was a dear little boy. What an incredible loss."

"A right, maybe, but I can't right now. I've got a war to plan for. I'll have plenty of time for grief later."

"If you need someone to talk to—or to have a beer with—you let me know."

Murphy nodded. "I will. How are things back home?"

"Worse than ever. Bunch of businesses have shut down, but then, that's happening everywhere, isn't it? People are scared and out of work. Ken, we held a recruiting day in Harpers Ferry about a week ago and I had a hundred men standing in line. I've never seen anything like it."

"I hope it will be enough."

"Me too. Most folks don't realize it—in fact I'm sure the damn politicians don't realize it—but when the Army comes, they won't be pussyfooting around. I've been on the dishing out end of the U.S. Army three times now, and I don't ever want to find out what it's like on the other side. But now… Looks like we just might."

Murphy looked at his friend. "You don't have to do this, Vince. You're a doctor. You could walk away right now, just like I said in that room."

Elkins frowned, and then grunted contemptuously. "Just goes to show you they don't hand out brains with your general's stars. Is that how little you think of me? I can't walk away. Dave Firkus was my patient since he was a baby. No way am I walking away from this. Could you? After what you lost?"

Murphy placed hand on his friend's shoulder, took a deep breath. "Thank you, Vince. For understanding."

"Well, General, I'm going to head back in there and see how many of our officers turned into weasels overnight."

They stepped back to the door and Murphy caught his breath.

The room was still full. It looked as if not a single officer had left, or very few. *Don't they know they could be killed?* He raised his hand to his eyes to wipe away unbidden tears.

"All right, then. Somebody close the doors."

Murphy waited while two captains ran to the doors and closed them. The sound echoed through the room.

He looked out at the room. "Men, ladies… I never would have guessed it. I'm proud of each and every one of you."

He took a deep breath, and looked back at the room full of officers, knowing many of them might not live to see another year.

"All right. Here's the deal. We have to assume the worst right now. Some time in the next few weeks, the State House will likely issue a declaration of independence. What does that mean to us? We need to scramble—today—to be ready. My expectation is within seventy-two hours of that declaration, an army will roll into West Virginia. Make no mistake, folks: we can't win that war."

The officers stirred at this statement.

"Don't believe me? How many of you have some combat experience?" Murphy asked.

Less than a quarter of the officers raised their hands, most of them members of the Special Operations Group.

"How many of you have large scale mechanized combat experience? Tank battles?"

This time virtually no one raised a hand.

He grimaced. "It's about what I expected. We have to plan on them hitting us with virtually everything the Army has on the ground and in North America: the Third Infantry, Seventh Cavalry, Hundred-and-first Airborne, Eighty-second Airborne, Tenth Mountain Division. All of them are within a couple of days striking distance—they'd merely need to fuel up their tanks and hit the road. On top of that, if the President follows recent doctrine, they'll bomb the crap out of us first. Take out all the electric grids, communications, bridges, dams, roads. Only then will ground forces come in—when we've pretty much lost our ability to fight. Does everyone get this?"

He paused and looked at the faces. Many of them young and scared. Good.

"Now, what does this mean? Two things: first, I've made it absolutely clear to the governor that there is no military solution to this problem. The governor must find a political solution. Our job, in the meantime, is to be a deterrent. We may not be able to stop the United States Army from pounding the crap out of us, but we can make it very, very painful to do so. And that, folks, is our only hope. We have to sustain our defense long enough that the politicians can bring about a settlement. We'll not just be fighting for our lives—we'll be fighting for our freedom."

"Make no mistake. You *will* be forced back and overrun. You *will* be outnumbered and outgunned. You'll watch your men bleed and die. But they can't outsmart you. They can't out-dedicate you. You men and women will be the hope for freedom for our children. So your mission is to defend, protect, and to preserve the lives of your men. Your mission is also to preserve and protect the civilian population. Your mission is to buy us time. Especially, buy the politicians time—time to secure a peace, time to secure our future."

༒

Morris sat down in the impromptu courtroom, hopefully for the last time. Ben Wharton took his seat next to him and set his soaked cap on the table between them. The others were soon seated, with the exception of Colonel Sheeman.

"Well, I think this will be it," Wharton whispered. "You're sure you want to make a statement?"

Morris nodded. "I am."

"You're not going to do anything stupid, are you?"

"Trust me, Ben."

"Of course I don't trust you, Mike. That's why I'm asking."

The door burst open and Colonel Frank Sheeman strode into the room. Like everyone else in the room he wore his camouflage uniform, soaked from the heavy rain.

He shook the water off his cap, set his briefcase on the table, and opened it with a loud click. After removing his notebooks he sat down and surveyed the room.

"Good, everyone is here. Let's get this show on the road. First thing: as of today, I've talked to all the witnesses I had intended to call. Each of you has a binder, which contains all the documentary evidence I will review as part of my decision. Also, a reminder that my recommendation is not final, and may well be overturned by the court-martial convening authority. Does everyone understand?"

Sheeman watched for nods around the room. Everyone responded in the affirmative.

"Good, good. Earlier in the investigation, I advised each of you of your right to make a statement or to remain silent. Do I need to explain these rights to you again? Private Turville? Captain Morris? Good. Do you wish to make a statement? Private Turville?"

Captain Harris, Turville's lawyer, spoke. "Sir, Private Turville prefers to remain silent at this time."

"Thank you. Captain Morris."

In an undertone, Wharton said, "Are you sure? This could make it worse for you."

"I'm sure," Morris responded.

"Colonel, my client would like to make a statement for the record."

"Please proceed, Captain. Come around to the witness chair."

Morris stood, uncomfortable, and relocated to the seat. The change disoriented him; he sat now facing Colonel Sheeman, with the prosecutors on his left.

Sheeman spoke, almost gently. "For the record, Captain, please state your full name, grade and organization."

"Sir, I am Michael Allen Morris, Captain, and I am company commander of Alpha Company, First Battalion, Fifteenth Infantry."

"You may proceed with your statement, Captain."

"Sir, I'll be brief. Over the last several days I've given this issue a tremendous amount of thought. This was a horrible tragedy. Here we are, the very forces who are sworn to protect and defend our people, and in this case, we took the life of a young man who was filming in his own hometown. I think we've established a few facts here, sir. We've established my company was given the order to enter an American city, to escort the local police force on a law enforcement mission. Second, I think we've established the fact I—and my non-commissioned officers—gave explicit orders to my men not to lock and load their weapons. Finally, I think we've established Private Turville disobeyed that order."

Morris glanced over at Turville, who visibly shook, his jaw set. Morris looked back at Colonel Sheeman.

"I've got to say one thing about that. My instructors once taught me that it is unethical and bad leadership to give an order that is impossible to be followed. And I believe, in this case, this order was impossible to be followed. Private Turville was placed in a situation where his life might well be in jeopardy. At the time he fired his weapon, he believed he and the members of his squad were being attacked by an armed individual. It was a mistake, but not his. Mine."

To his right, Wharton sank his head into his hands. Morris heard rustling in the back of the room as the reporters stirred at his words.

"The fact is Private Turville raised the same question I did. The order for American forces to conduct a law-enforcement activity within the boundaries of the United States was clearly an illegal order. The law forbids the U.S. Army from participating in such activities, for the very reason that we face a potential civil war right now. Yet I accepted that order and went forward, even though I explicitly informed my commander of my opinion that the order was illegal."

He paused and stretched his neck. He was effectively tanking his career at this point, but he wasn't going to force a nineteen-year-old kid down with him.

"As a commissioned officer of the United States, I know an illegal order, and I know what my duty is when I receive an illegal order. I did not do that duty. Private Turville, on the other hand, was in an infinitely more difficult position. He is not a commissioned officer, and has neither the training nor the experience to recognize the difference. Yet he too was given an illegal order, and an impossibly stupid one. If anyone should be punished for that, it should be me.

"That is all I have to say, sir."

Sheeman sat back, his eyebrows raised, his mustache practically twitching. Turville and his lawyer were in a huddle. Morris diverted his eyes from them. He didn't feel the sense of relief he'd expected. If he read Sheeman correctly, he would approve of Morris' statement, professional suicide though it was. It was the right thing to do. All the same, a nagging voice doubted his motives. His move had been self-serving. Barksdale was right. He didn't care about Turville and what happened to him.

"Thank you, Captain. You may return to your seat."

Stiffly, Morris did so. Wharton put his hand on his shoulder and whispered, "You said you wouldn't do anything stupid. 'Trust me,' you said. Damn it, I don't know whether to hug you or hit you over the head!"

Sheeman cleared his throat.

"Gentlemen, this concludes this investigation. I was almost prepared to render a recommendation today, but I see I need to go back and review the testimony in greater detail. You can expect a recommendation in one week. You may go."

Sheeman slammed his briefcase shut, put his still dripping cap on his head, and walked out.

The reporters mobbed around Morris, shouting questions. Wharton waved them off and pulled Mike toward to the door. They could talk to the press another day.

Back at his house, in the midst of a pile of bills, he found a letter from Karen.

Dear Mike,

You would think, given that I've been locked up in a virtual prison the last weeks, that I would have had a tremendous amount of time to write, and to think. In fact, there has been little such luck. I've spent most of my time writing operations orders, maneuver plans, on and on and on.

Enough of that subject—we will need to agree to keep that one off limits for the time being.

Either way, I hope it won't be much longer. It's been nearly two months since that awful week in Charleston, and there is little resolution in any area. I saw on the news your Article 32 investigation is continuing. I wish you the best of luck, that you can retain your command and your career and come out of this in one piece. For my part, I'm just hoping for some aspect of freedom. For the last few days, the Homeland Security people have been blasting this God-awful fifty-year-old acid rock out of speakers big enough to shake the building. Every once in a while they shoot a tear gas grenade into the compound, but they've not been foolish enough to actually attack.

Mike, I am terribly afraid. Things are far worse than I ever imagined they could get, but it just keeps getting worse.

This is an awful thing to hope for, but in my heart I am hoping you and Alicia have not reconciled. I want to see you again, and at least give it a chance. But only if you are free.

One day we will all be free.

I love you,

Karen.

Chapter Thirty-Two
November 21

The feds started playing AC/DC at about a quarter to four in the morning. Lieutenant Austin Robear didn't mind so much; he liked AC/DC, though they were old-fashioned. For the last two days the music played by the DHS had been on a serious oldies acid rock trip. Only problem was they were playing it at around 110 decibels, loud enough to cause the guard shack to shake, even under the weight of the sandbags. Austin would be very happy to pull the plug on that racket.

It served them right they didn't hear the approach until it was too late. No one in the federal camp even looked alarmed until the ground began to shake.

Austin stood ready in the guard shack when he felt it. In full combat gear, he watched through the window with his night vision goggles, and reported back to Lieutenant Colonel Jian Chang, the new brigade commander.

Someone in the camp finally noticed the vibrations in the ground. One of the feds ran out of his tent and looked out, with what looked to be night vision equipment similar to Robear's. Then he sprinted to the FBI command center, another tent across the street. Austin smiled. After days of harassment, it was nice to see them in a flurry.

He keyed his radio. "Base, this is Red Six. Starting to get some activity." He swallowed as he scanned the scene with his night vision goggles. The feds were starting to panic.

He tensed further as he watched them. Back home in Blair, his twenty-one year old wife Melissa was probably still asleep with their son. He wanted to get home to see them. Time to be extra careful.

The rock music suddenly cut off, and Robear heard ringing in his ears, then the distinctive whine of turbine engines and the loud crack of tank tracks slapping into the pavement.

There they were: four tanks racing up the street toward them.

He keyed the radio again. "Red elements, this is Red Six. Prepare to launch."

The tanks were setting off a panic in the camp. The feds were racing out of their tents in various states of undress, throwing on their combat gear. A hundred yards away, in the enclosure designated for the press, bright lights swung this way and that, seeking the source of the noise.

Sixty seconds later half a dozen helicopters flew over the brigade headquarters, low to the ground, their rotors throwing up dust and small rocks. They settled to the left of the brigade headquarters, miniguns pointed directly at the federal camp and away from Robear.

That was Robear's signal.

"This is Red Six, go, go go."

The gates opened and two platoons of infantry sprinted out and dived to the ground in prone firing positions, their rifles aimed at the feds.

Robear walked calmly outside the gate and raised a megaphone to his mouth, afraid his voice was going to crack from anxiety. He needn't have feared: his command was clear and crisp.

"Lay down your weapons and step out into the street. You will not be harmed if you follow instructions. Lay down your weapons where you are and come out into the street with your hands up."

He had to struggle to be heard over the tank engines and the helicopters, but they heard him. For good measure, he repeated the instructions as loud as he could.

No one moved. The thirty or so federal agents—most of them just aroused from sleep—stood, disoriented. The press, however, was quite awake, and probably terrified. Secure in their positions, they filmed everything, their bright lights glaring in Austin's eyes.

Austin heard a voice on his radio—the brigade commander calling the tank platoon. "Blue Six, fire a warning shot into the hill behind the feds."

The feds jumped when one of the tanks traversed its turret to the right and fired a stream of bullets, which arced into the hill. The reporters dived to the ground.

"I say again, lay down your weapons and move into the street. You are surrounded."

The hopelessly outgunned agents moved into the intersection. Robear's men frisked them, and then tied their arms with plastic loops. The National Guardsmen ignored the press as they went about their business. The reporters fanned out, filming as the Guardsmen loaded the agents onto helicopters. All of the weapons were cleared and stacked next to the gate.

Lietenant Colonel Chang appeared at Robear's side. "Good job, Lieutenant."

"Thank you, sir. Nice to see we did this without anyone getting hurt."

"I agree, son. Any mission without anyone hurt is a success. Go ahead and get those men loaded on the choppers, and we'll get them out of here."

By the time the sun rose, the federal agents were onboard the helicopters. Robear watched, hands on his hips, as the helicopters rose again. The plan was to dump the agents in rural Pennsylvania. No need to make things easy for them.

Within an hour, the news was broadcast across America: West Virginia had forcefully evicted federal forces from within its border.

☙

Lieutenant Brady Antal and Major Vince Elkins stood on the edge of the parade ground—now deeply rutted with tank tracks—and watched the helicopter approach. A hundred yards away, Sergeant Catlett stood over ten new recruits as they did pushups in the muddy field. His shouts punctuated the otherwise quiet morning, until the sound of the helicopter overshadowed him.

Elkins stood calmly, his expression fixed. Antal felt apprehensive; for nearly two months he'd been acting company commander. Now, when things were just about to get hot, it didn't seem fair to him that he was pulled out and moved back to battalion headquarters. Regardless of the circumstance, he was sorry to lose his first command.

Elkins spoke. "Lieutenant, you look like someone just stole your favorite car. You've done a good job with the company while Greenfield was away. Any interest in having one of your own?" Antal looked at Elkins with disbelief. "Of course, sir!"

The major frowned. "Don't look so happy. This is going to be a dangerous and dirty job, and we're all likely to be dead in a few weeks. Do you get that?"

"I understand, sir."

"All right, then. Both Alpha and Delta's company commanders have resigned. Delta has a strong XO who can step in, but Alpha doesn't. It's yours if you want it. You've proven yourself."

"Thank you, sir. I won't let you down."

"Don't worry about letting me down. Worry about keeping your men alive."

"Yes, sir."

The helicopter, a fifty-year-old Huey, touched the ground. Karen Greenfield jumped out the door and ran across the field before it even touched the grass.

She stopped in front of Elkins and saluted.

"Captain Greenfield reporting as ordered, sir," She couldn't suppress the smile on her face.

Elkins returned the salute. "It's nice to see you back, Karen. Tell me what happened; all I've seen is what was in the news."

Karen chuckled. "That's more than I've seen, sir. No one told me about the operation. I was sitting having a cup of coffee, trying to wake up when I heard tank tracks outside, then the helicopters. Did you see CNN? They had a much closer view than I did."

"Well, it looks like you are going to have a much closer view of all of this than most would care to have. Let's go talk."

"Yes, sir."

The three officers walked into the armory. Someone shouted, "Attention."

The company burst into applause. Karen stared, eyes wide. A banner stretched across the room, with the words, "Welcome Home, Captain," written on them.

The first sergeant, Ken Shumaker, approached with a broad smile on his face. "Welcome back, ma'am. I don't approve of this sort of thing, but they insisted."

"Well thank, you, First Sergeant."

Antal stood to the side as she spoke. "Thank you, to all of you. We had a hell of a difficult situation to deal with in Charleston, and you all handled it professionally. We have even more difficult times ahead, and I believe you will all do your duty."

Antal realized her eyes were watering. He tried to imagine how he would feel in her position: isolated, under federal indictment, relieved of her command, under siege at Brigade Headquarters for almost two months. He couldn't. No wonder she had tears in her eyes: this was a real homecoming.

Elkins spoke when she finished. "Let's go, Captain. Lieutenant Britton and Antal, you come, too."

The officers followed Elkins into the company commander's office, now Karen's again.

In the office, Elkins set his briefcase down, opened it, and placed a stack of paper onto the desk. "This is the battalion operations order. You need to review it immediately and begin preparing your own."

"Yes, sir. I'm already familiar with the brigade plan in detail, so I've got a pretty good picture already."

Elkins glanced at her, one eyebrow raised. "Where did you get the brigade plan?"

"I wrote a good bit of it, sir."

He smiled and shook his head slowly. "I should have realized."

Major Elkins unfolded a map on the desk. "Here's is your company's sector. Your primary responsibility will be Harpers Ferry itself, and the U.S. 340 approach into West Virginia. As brief as it was, your company is the only one with any experience under fire, so you get the main approach, with Charlie Company on your right flank, covering Route 9. Alpha and Delta will take the outside flanks and serve as a reserve, here and here, blocking I-81."

She nodded.

"You probably know we're it. Brigade and division think this whole section of the state is a lost cause. We'll get cut off by I-81 and split from the rest of the state. I had to fight to get this position—they didn't want to put up a defense here at all. Now, we've got an attached infantry company, and each of your companies will be augmented by one platoon of infantry. We have a small amount of attached artillery and engineers, but not enough. We have three Special Forces A-teams up here training up irregular forces. I hope to God those folks don't get dragged into this—mostly old men and kids with shotguns, but there are plenty of volunteers."

"How is our personnel status?"

Lieutenant Antal anwered this question, pride on his face. They'd had fewer resignations than any other single company in the state. "Just about the best in the state, ma'am. You've only lost about twenty percent to resignations. We've been cross-training all the experienced loaders and drivers to take over as gunners and tank commanders. We've managed to backfill all of the vacant positions with new recruits."

Alarmed, she said, "New recruits? Did they go through any basic training?"

"We're doing it right here," he replied. "Sergeant Catlett is running the training."

Elkins replied, "It's not ideal, Karen, but there is little choice."

"All right." She nodded, face impassive. She was right on target: the new recruits had only been training three weeks, and had just barely begun to understand military organization. They were out of shape and weeks away from being in the kind of physical condition they needed to be in, and none of them were ready to crew a tank. But they could only do what they could do, and this was it. If nothing else, they were dedicated.

Elkins spoke. "I would get out there and survey your defensive positions immediately. I'd like to see your provisional plan in forty-eight hours."

"Yes, sir."

Antal placed a sheet in front of her. "You'll need to sign here, ma'am."

The sheet read: *The undersigned assumes command of Bravo Company, 2nd Battalion, 432nd Armor.*

She signed it.

Antal stood at attention and saluted. "Thank you, ma'am, for the opportunity to have my first command."

She returned the salute. "Thank you, Lieutenant. I can see you've done a great job in my absence."

"Come on, Lieutenant. Let's go introduce you to your new company." Elkins headed out the door.

Antal followed. "Yes, sir."

⁂

Murphy paid the bill to the cashier as Valerie talked, and they walked out the door into the bitter cold.

"I just can't believe it," Valerie said. "We can't even get any appointments! No one in Washington wants to talk—all I hear is they'll check and get back with us later, and of course they never do."

Murphy frowned as he watched his daughter. Her brow was furrowed, and some of the care lines on her face looked permanent. Where did the time go? In the blink of an eye she'd gone from being a gangly, shy teen to an adult, a strong, competent woman.

If only Martha were still alive. She would have been so proud of their daughter. They walked along the promenade on the Kanahwa River through the center of town. She shivered and hunched her shoulders in her coat as an icy breeze blew at them from the river.

"Why don't they talk to us, Dad? It's like they want it to come to war."

Murphy shook his head. "I don't know, hon. I'm beginning to think some people do. There's always someone who thinks war is worth it. People who don't understand how much death and pain will come."

"What are we going to do?"

"We do the best we can. You and Al Clark keep doing what you can to negotiate. Eventually someone will come out to talk to you. And I'll have to keep doing what I'm doing, preparing a defense."

"How bad can it get?"

"Oh, pretty bad. We're not prepared for this—we don't have the fuel, or the ammunition, or the personnel to defend this state more than a couple of days. And if it does come to war, the death toll, especially for civilians, is going to be brutal."

"But... They talk so much about how the military works so hard to avoid civilian casualties."

"It's nothing but a polite fiction, Valerie. You can't have a war without civilian casualties. The whole essence of the thing is chaos."

She stopped and turned towards the river, her hands crossed over her chest. She looked up at the stars.

"Dad, did you ever cheat on Mom?"

Ken was startled by the question. He glanced over at her, silent, then answered. "Once. A very long time ago."

They stood in silence, then Ken went on. "Valerie, your Mom and I... God, we were sixteen when we started dating, got married when we were nineteen, and you were born only a year later. Neither of us knew what we wanted in life, where we were going. I don't think it ever occurred to us we might ever want someone else."

"Then you didn't love each other?"

"Yes, we did. That's not at all I'm saying. Martha... She was life to me, and part of me has been dead since we lost her. We—we were partners in life. Your mother meant more to me than anything else in the world, except you and... you and Kenny. I mean, the job, the house—all that could have been gone, we could have lived in a shack, and I still would have felt like my life was good as long as I had her."

Valerie frowned. "Then what happened?"

"Oh, life happened. I guess you were about nine or ten then, I was in Kentucky for training, a couple of years before I went to Iraq the second time. One of the other students... We spent a couple of weekends together. Not much more than that." He smiled. "You would recognize her name if I told you who she was. She was one of the first female armor officers, and outranks me by a long shot these days.

"It's funny. I never intended or even thought about leaving Martha. I think we might have been a little bit in love for a time, there at Fort Knox, but that doesn't mean much compared to what your mother and I had."

"I think she would have understood."

"Martha? Yes, she did. She knew about it years ago. Things were rocky for a while, but we got past it."

Valerie smiled. "I should have known you told her the truth. Do you know, if anyone else on Earth had told me that story about you, I would have called them a liar. 'Not my Dad,' I would have said. He's… He's like a hero, the perfect man."

"I'm hardly that."

"No, but you are honest, and you've always tried to do the right thing, even when it hurt you personally. I've always admired you, Dad. I mean, even now, all this—I understand what you're doing, and why you have to do it. I guess that's what I wanted to say to you all along. I understand, and I'm proud of what you are trying to do. I just wish Mom and Kenny could be here to see you—"

She stifled a sob as Murphy's eyes watered.

"I do, too, Valerie. God, I do, too."

"Dad… All I ask is please don't get yourself killed. That's all. You're all I have left. Okay?"

"I'll do my best, Valerie. I can promise that."

"I guess it has to be enough."

He held out his hands and pulled his daughter to him, his face twisted in agony.

"Are you going to be okay?" she whispered.

"I will. I will. I just—I just miss my little boy." Murphy's voice broke and his eyes filled with tears. He sobbed and buried his face in her shoulder, struggling to contain his emotion.

"I miss him, too," she whispered. "And Mommy."

༄

Forty-five minutes later, Murphy drove back to his temporary headquarters in a borrowed State government staff car. He fumbled through the channels on the radio and found the all-news station, then stopped the car.

The newscaster spoke, voice at a high pitch. "That's right, folks, they've done it. The House has passed the Independence Bill thirty-three to twelve. A companion bill is on its way through the Senate and may pass any day now."

Murphy switched the radio off. They were headed off the edge of a cliff, and there wasn't a thing he could do about it. He couldn't help but wonder what Martha would have thought of all this. What would she have told him? Flee the state? Quit the guard, as his brother had advised?

He didn't think so. Martha would have wanted him to stick by his principles. But what about the cost?

As he drove back to the headquarters, snow began to fall.

Chapter Thirty-Three
December 6

Karen looked down into the tank. Inside, Sergeant First Class Tom Catlett sat with two new recruits and demonstrated how to load the main gun. With a clang, he opened the ammo door, pulled out an armor piercing sabot round and in a smooth motion flipped it over his arm, then slid it home into the main gun. All told, the action took about two and a half seconds. The practice round was a little shorter than a combat one: a real sabot round consisted of a ten pound slug of uranium, traveling at such a high velocity that the kinetic energy would destroy an armored target.

"You see how that goes? It's all one smooth motion. These rounds are heavy, so it's all about balance, when you flip that thing over your arm."

Catlett opened the breach and replaced the training round in the ammo rack.

The new recruits looked at each other, clouds of condensation rising from their breath.

"You try, Donaldson." Catlett climbed out the hatch to give the trainee room to move across the turret.

"Ma'am," he murmured to Karen, then looked down inside. The young man sat in the loaders seat. He looked up at Catlett, face pensive.

"Gunner! *Sabot!* Tank!" shouted Catlett.

The recruit hit the knee switch and the door rolled open. He fumbled with the catch, and then slid the round out. As he started to flip it over, it slammed into the hatch above him. He cried out in pain; he'd jammed his finger. He dropped the round on the floor. *Oh, God, these kids were never going to be ready in time.*

"Donaldson, goddammit! You and your entire crew are dead. Those rounds have a combustible casing. You put that down on the floor next to hot brass and it will explode inside the turret. Holy Christ, don't do that."

"But Sarge, I hurt my finger."

"Right, you hurt your little finger, and then you killed your crew. Think I care about your finger? Do it again."

Greenfield nodded to Catlett. "Doing a great job, Sergeant. Let me get out of your way."

"Thanks, Captain."

She slid off the cold turret, and then dropped down to the pavement. As she hit the ground again, she heard Catlett shout again, this time calling for a high explosive round: "Gunner! *Heat!* Tank!"

They were pushing as hard as they could to prepare a defense, get the supplies laid in, and train the new recruits.

Not just the troops. She had just spent three grueling days in a computerized battle simulation with the other officers in the battalion. With virtually no sleep, and with her company getting picked off by attack helicopters, she had attempted a counterattack and failed, killing her entire company in the process.

The only thing that drove her now was exhaustion.

She sighed and walked toward the maintenance platoon, where two of the tanks were being repaired. Time to get back to work.

~

Morris looked out his windowshades at the frozen lawn. No one was out there. Good.

He had called the Provost Marshal's office twice before the reporters were thrown out of the base housing area—which was, after all, on a restricted government installation. It had reached the point where neither he nor his neighbors could get in and out of their houses without being accosted by the press. It was one thing for him, but his next-door neighbor, Captain Wilson Cline, had complained loudly after his thirteen-year-old daughter had been interrogated by the press on her way home from school. She had burst into tears and run into the house, and that was the last straw.

He reached for the door and froze when the phone rang. He hesitated. Why not let the machine get it?

What if it's Savannah?

Morris ran to the phone and picked it up.

"Hello? Captain Morris speaking."

"Morris, this is Ben Wharton. The scuttlebutt over here is Colonel Sheeman finished his recommendation, and the commanding general hasn't signed off on it yet. It may be the general doesn't care for Sheeman's conclusions, which could only be good for you."

Morris frowned. "How could it be good, sir? He doesn't have to pay attention to them anyway; Sheeman even said that. General Blake can do whatever he wants regardless of Sheeman's recommendation."

"That's true, but it is extremely rare to overturn the findings of an Article 32 investigation. It looks really bad for the Army to conduct an investigation and then ignore its own findings."

"Well, I suppose it is good news. How long will it be?"

"It shouldn't be long at all. General Blake doesn't typically sit on this sort of thing. My guess is the only reason it has taken so long so far is pressure from the White House."

"Sir, if the White House wants to see me behind bars, why doesn't General Blake just salute and take his marching orders? Why the hell all the pretense?"

Wharton did not answer immediately, and when he did his tone was angry. "Because, Captain, there are still plenty of officers in the Army with integrity. Think about it this way, Morris. If Blake goes against what the White House wants, you'll go free, right? But will Blake ever get his third star? Think he'll ever get a theater command? Not likely. He might as well turn in his retirement papers when he's finished with you. So quit feeling sorry for yourself, Morris. You are not the only person who might get whacked by this thing."

As he listened, Morris heard footsteps coming up the gravel walk. He leaned out of the kitchen, toward the window, but couldn't see who it was. Whoever it was pushed an envelope through the slot in the door and it fell to the floor. From the kitchen, Morris couldn't see who it was from, but hand delivery was pretty unusual.

"Can you hold on a moment, sir?"

"Sure."

Morris set the phone on the counter and walked to the envelope. From Base Housing? He ripped it open and scanned through it, and then started to laugh.

He walked back to the phone, still half amused by the letter.

"Hi, sir, sorry about that."

"What is it? Are you okay, Mike? You sound funny."

"Just amused, sir. It seems now my wife is divorcing me and left with my daughter, I'm no longer entitled to base housing. I've been given two weeks' notice to move out into bachelor officer's quarters."

Wharton grunted, and then said, "At least you don't have much stuff to move."

Morris looked back at the empty house. "True, true. Let me know as soon as you hear anything, please."

"I will. Get some rest, Morris."

༄

The distance between Fort Meade to Harpers Ferry was only a little over an hour's drive, well within the driving distance of the two-hour limit imposed by Morris's unit's alert posture. Not that he was likely to be alerted for anything.

Morris kept the music turned up loud and tapped his hands on the steering wheel, deliberately not thinking about where he was going. Virtually all of the radio stations played Christmas music, since it was only two days away. This would be his third year in a row away from Savannah on Christmas. Three years, half of her short life. He understood why Alicia was angry, if only because of that. Would Savannah grow up never having a Christmas to remember with her father?

Morris turned the music up louder. He'd finally stopped at a gas station and picked up a disc of Golden Oldies from the Eighties. Better than the Christmas music.

Like everyone else in the country, Morris had seen the dramatic news coverage of the National Guard swooping in on helicopters and forcing the federal agents to disarm. He was amazed it hadn't turned into a bloodbath. In the end, though, it affected him on a personal level, because a few days later he got an e-mail from Karen that indicated she was back with her tank unit and in the general area of Harpers Ferry. Harpers Ferry, which was not too far a drive from Fort Meade.

He pulled around a curve in the highway, and there it was, just across the river. Karen had been hesitant when he called. She was very busy training her unit, no time to meet.

"Just a few hours," Morris had said. "We… we may not have the opportunity again for a long time."

Traffic came to a halt, and Morris leaned over, trying to see around the line of cars ahead of him. Traffic was moving, but very slowly, across the curving bridge over the Shenandoah. Beyond the bridge was a rising slope and woods. On the far side of the bridge, a lone tank stood guard, a dozen men with HUMMWVs standing around it, watching the cars crossing the bridge. They weren't stopping any vehicles, but they were watching. To Morris, it was menacing. They were there to quickly seal the border, he supposed, in the event the West Virginia Legislature passed its lunatic independence measure.

Twenty minutes after crossing the bridge, he turned left onto a gravel driveway almost in the woods and saw her house for the first time. It was a low rambler, at least fifty years old, in varying stages of restoration. Surrounded by woods, and situated with a reasonable view of the valley below, it had a rustic feel, almost like a cabin. Morris parked the car behind a mud-spattered gas hybrid. Slowly, he stepped out into the cold and approached the house.

She opened the door before he reached it, and he caught his breath. Instead of the combat gear he'd last seen her in, she wore a simple blouse and blue jeans. Her red auburn hair hung in loose curls at her neck, and she smiled. Morris looked at her, seeing her delicate neck, the swell of her breasts under the blouse, her hips. He felt lightheaded.

She opened the screen door. "Come on in, Mike."

He stepped inside the door, brushing against her, and even the small touch was charged emotionally.

"You want a beer?" She walked to the refrigerator, giving no clue she'd been at all conscious of the light touch as he passed.

"Sure," he replied. She leaned in and pulled a bottle out, then popped the top on a bottle opener mounted to the cabinet next to the refrigerator. She sat at the scarred kitchen table and motioned for him to do likewise, passing him the beer. She had a cup of coffee, sitting on the table.

He took his jacket off and hung it on the coat rack next to the door. Her helmet and web gear hung from the rack, next to a shoulder holster with the letters U.S. stamped into it, a black pistol still in the holster. She was, after all, a tank commander.

"I've only got a few hours away. I'm sure you can imagine what it's like right now."

"Indeed."

"I've missed you. Tell me how you've been." He stared at her eyes as he spoke, felt simultaneously awkward and elated to be with her again.

"Better than the last couple of weeks," she replied. "For a while there in Morgantown it was like a prison. They cut off all the outside phone lines and started blasting terrible music loud enough to shake the walls. It was a big relief to get out of there."

He took a sip of his beer. "What are you going to do now?"

"In the long run? I don't know. All I'm worried about right now is leading my company. We've got… We've got a hell of a job ahead of us. What about you?"

He shrugged. "I don't know. I'm still in limbo. The Article 32 investigation is over, but the investigating officer still hasn't handed up a recommendation. My lawyer says he thinks the investigating officer wants to drop the whole matter, but the thing is being driven by politics. Apparently someone in the White House wants to see me go up the river."

"Why?"

"They want someone to blame this mess in West Virginia on."

"Well, that's idiotic," she said, her voice contemptuous. "This thing was moving along well before you came into the picture."

"Karen, why in God's name are you doing this?"

She smiled. "I swore to protect and defend the Constitution of the United States. I love my country, and I can't stand to see politicians and the DHS ripping the heart out of it to enrich themselves. It's personal, too, Mike. Seven months ago I saw federal agents gun down a friend of mine for no good reason."

"I know that was horrible, Karen, but it was only one incident. I can see raising hell, suing them or something, but this? I don't get it."

"No, it wasn't one incident. It's been happening over and over. Think about it, Mike. The government arrests and holds people without access to attorneys on an indefinite basis. Why? They are *suspected* of involvement with terrorism. All DHS has to do is level an accusation, secretly at that, and they can pick you up from your house at night and lock you away and not tell anyone. We're being watched in churches, and in political rallies, in town meetings, on the Internet, phone lines are tapped, and it just gets worse and worse. We have to do something about it."

He shook his head. "Wow. I don't know what to say."

She closed her eyes and leaned her head back, looking at the ceiling. He watched her—the slender neck and chin—and wished he could touch her.

"Don't say anything. You don't have to understand. I'm not trying to persuade you to join us; I know it's not something you would do. So what's the point?" As she said it, tears formed in her eyes. "It was a mistake, what I wrote. Asking you here."

Morris moved without thinking, leaning close to her chair, touching her hands. "Karen, it was not a mistake. I made the mistake—the biggest mistake of my life—when I lost you. Let's not compound that mistake now."

She smiled; all the while tears streamed down her face. "It's impossible, Mike. I'm going to end up in prison or dead. For God's sake, the attorney general of the United States has publicly announced he's seeking my execution. We only get that far if we live through the next few weeks, and that's pretty chancy."

"Nothing's impossible."

"What will you do if you meet me on a battlefield?" she asked. "I won't hesitate to do my duty. My men depend on me, and I won't let them down."

A chill ran through him. "Do you seriously believe it will come to that?"

"Of course it will. At this point there's no other alternative, unless the President decides to just let it go, which is never going to happen. There's going to be a war, and unlike all these Third World little interventions all over the world, this one will be against a well-armed and well-trained opponent who knows your tactics and equipment."

"I don't care. I threw away seven years of what could have been our life together. Karen, if I die tomorrow, or get court-martialed and thrown into prison, I want my last memory to be of you."

Morris watched her slightly parted lips, her accelerated breathing, and he knew she felt something. *Something.*

"Why did it have to come to this? There's no future for us."

"Let there be a present for us, then," he whispered, running his fingers through her curls. His hand touched her shoulder, her neck, the side of her cheek, and her breath quickened.

He reached out with his other hand, framed the other side of her face. They stood, their lips just brushed, and he nearly sobbed.

"I never stopped loving you, you bastard," she whispered. "Nothing was the same after, nothing."

He stood and pulled her shaking body to stand with him. "I've hated myself for seven years."

He looked in her wide brown eyes and wondered what she thought, what she felt, as she looked back. Slowly, slowly, he ran his fingers through her hair, the red locks parting easily.

Their bodies brushed just barely along their entire lengths, and Morris nearly gasped from the shock. He kissed her, on the lips, on the chin, on the neck.

As she leaned her head back, his lips brushed her neck and he whispered, "I'd die before losing you again."

"Shut up."

They didn't talk any more.

☙

"The White House, please," Valerie said to the cab driver as she got in. She slid over to the seat behind the driver, and Clark got in beside her.

Each of them had a small overnight bag, no real luggage. This wasn't expected to be a long trip. After days of calling every contact they had in Washington, they'd finally managed to arrange a meeting—not with the President, but with his National Security Advisor. It was something.

They were lucky they'd taken an early flight. They were pulled off the plane and thoroughly searched on their arrival at National Airport. Clark had restrained any anger; it was clear the airport personnel had no choice in the matter. They rode silently in the cab. They had already talked about their strategy at length, and Valerie was still angry about the search.

Twenty minutes later they showed their identification at the gate of the White House.

It was immediately obvious something was painfully wrong. After the first secret service agent examined their identification, he said, "Please wait here," and went to a telephone. Five minute later two more agents appeared, in plainclothes.

"Come this way, please," one said, his tone brooking no argument.

The agent led them to a small room, not in the White House, but in the small guard building near it.

"This is just a formality, ma'am," said one of the agents, "but we have to ensure you have no weapons on you before you enter the building. Please hold your arms out to your side."

The other agent said something similar to Clark on the other side of the room. Valerie raised her arms at her side. She'd been in the West Wing half a dozen times, and nearly always followed the same routines. This was new.

The agent ran a wand over her, which let out a piercing tone as it passed over her shoes and her chest.

"I'll have to ask you to get undressed, ma'am," the agent said. Across the room, she could see Clark's face flushed with anger as he took his coat and shoes off.

"Why are you doing this?" she said. "It's not as if we haven't been here before, more than once."

"New procedure, ma'am. We have no way of guaranteeing your behavior, so we have to be extra careful. Those are my orders. It's nothing personal."

His eyes were cold.

"Well, go find a female agent, then. I'm not getting undressed in front of you."

"Ma'am, I'm afraid no one else is available right now. You are welcome to wait, but I don't expect we'll have a female agent around for several hours. You'll likely miss your appointment."

She stared at him. He was lying, the son of a bitch. They were at an impasse. She had to get into the building in order to meet with the national security advisor. To do that, she had to submit to this humiliating examination. She sighed, then started to take her clothes off. She could see Clark do the same thing, his face twitching in rage.

Apparently even that wasn't enough, as the agents poured out the contents of her purse and Clark's briefcase and went through them, one by one. For this, they worked as a team, with one agent identifying the item in his hand and the other writing it down in a notebook. Of course there was nothing to find.

Valerie got dressed again as they went through her purse, item by item, cataloguing her comb and compact, her lipstick and her wallet.

"Looks like about two hundred dollars in cash," the agent said as he opened the wallet.

"Cell phone, with a headset."

"Handheld computer."

It took forty-five minutes for them to complete their inventory. Clark looked at his watch repeatedly. Finally, they were led into the West Wing. Both agents flanked them as they met with a twenty-something-year-old intern.

"Hi, I'm Matt Harris. Let me escort you to the national security advisor's office. He has two more appointments lined up this morning, so I don't know how much time you will have. You're quite late."

Valerie wanted to smack the smug brat.

He led them down the hall, to a room Valerie recognized as being directly next to the Oval Office. He gave a quick knock on the door and opened it just enough to lean his head in and say something. A second later he stepped back and the door opened wide as the familiar wizened features of Carl Metzenberger came to the door. Valerie had never met him person, but she'd seen him on television enough to recognize him easily. A gaunt man with thin wisps of white hair, he looked far older than his actual fifty years. Metzenberger was an academic, and had been the chair of the Middle Eastern studies department at Princeton when the President appointed him to his current position.

"Congressman Clark? Ms. Murphy? Please come in. I'm Carl Metzenberger, National Security Advisor to the President."

The followed him into the office, significantly smaller than the President's next door. The windows were the same bluish bulletproof glass, however, and looked out toward streets that had been closed to the public for some years now.

"We're short on time right now—I'm meeting with the Ambassador of India in twenty minutes—but we have time for a quick chat. Coffee?"

"No, thank you," they said simultaneously.

Clark said, his tone sharp, "We've been here nearly an hour; we were strip-searched by the Secret Service before coming into the building."

Metzenberger chuckled a little. "Well, you know the Secret Service. They're there to protect the President, and they do take their jobs seriously. So tell me, since time is short, what exactly is the purpose of this visit. Please have a seat."

As he spoke, he pulled off his coat. Underneath, he wore a starched white shirt and blue suspenders. He sat down behind his desk and listened as Clark and Valerie sat across from him.

"We're here to try to head off an impending war," Clark said. "I'm sure you know as well as I do that West Virginia is on the verge of declaring its independence. This situation is a powder keg. We believe, however, if the federal government were to take some specific steps, we might be able to head off the vote in the Senate and prevent them from passing the bill."

Metzenberger leaned forward with his elbows on his desk, his fingers tented and covering the lower half of his face.

"What sort of steps?" he asked.

"To start with, I would close the offices of the Department of Homeland Security in the state. Announce reform of the Department. Drop the prosecution of Karen Greenfield. I would ask the President to appoint a special counsel to investigate the death of Antoine Jackson, a Harpers Ferry police officer who was killed in a bungled DHS raid, and find out who gave what orders when the Army shot a civilian in Charleston last month."

Metzenberger leaned back.

"You are asking a tremendous amount for people who are threatening treason."

Valerie met Clark's eyes. Not a good opening.

"Sir," she said, "the issue isn't treason at this point. This is a very popular issue in West Virginia. The people there feel as if they have lost all of their civil rights. They clearly identify the culprit: the Department of Homeland Security. It's not just in West Virginia; the entire country is suffering. The agency is out of control, sir. What Representative Clark is telling you is that with only a few minor steps, you might be able to prevent a war. That's not asking too much."

Metzenberger shook his head, the smile leaving his face. "Look, you and I both know there will be no war. The West Virginia National Guard has no combat power. They have no fuel. They have no ammunition. If we roll the Army in there it will be over in a day or two. How dare you sit here and threaten armed conflict if we don't give in to your demands? I ought to have both of you arrested for treason right now."

"We're not threatening anything, Mr. Metzenberger. This is what the situation is, whether you or like it or not. It's well known that I opposed the referendum in West Virginia. But it passed, and overwhelmingly. If you take seriously any of the tenets of our nation, that has to shake you to the bone."

Metzenberger shrugged. "People do stupid things," he said. "Why should West Virginia be any different than the rest of the world?"

"Sir," Clark said. "You must consider the possible consequences here."

"I'll tell you what," Metzenberger said. "I'll talk to the President about this if you promise to deliver up for me the ringleaders of this so-called rebellion so we can put them on trial. I want your governor, and that renegade National Guard Commander Murphy—you're not related to him, are you?"

"He's my father," she answered.

"Oh, wonderful. You have those two and that trigger-happy Captain Greenfield turned over to federal authorities, and we'll consider conducting an internal investigation of the DHS."

"Let me guess," Clark replied. "Then the report of the investigation will be labeled as classified, and it will be locked up and never acted upon. See, we investigated. There's no problem. Is that it?"

"Mr. Clark, surely you are not suggesting the DHS can't investigate itself with integrity."

"Of course it can't," Clark cried. "No government agency can."

Metzenberger shook his head. "Then there is nothing more to say. I'd escort you out, but I have another appointment."

He stood. The appointment was over. The two secret service agents underlined his effective order to get out.

Valerie almost cried out in frustration. "Sir," she tried one last time. "You have to at least consider some of this. People are going to die."

He looked her in the eyes. "No," he said. "I don't. Have a nice afternoon."

He turned and walked toward the Oval Office. Clark and Valerie were led from the building, defeated.

"I don't understand," she said as they walked away from the White House. "Why won't they talk to us?"

Clark didn't answer for a moment, then said, "They're being tough, I guess. Can't give in to terrorists or something. Easier than trying to actually solve the problem. Goddamn stubborn bastards."

"Do you really think that's it?"

He glanced over at her. "Yes, unfortunately I do. The President is posturing for the cameras and showing how determined a leader he is."

"I'm worried about my Dad, Al."

"I'm worried about all of us, Valerie."

Chapter Thirty-Four
December 24

The old M1A1 Abrams tank, painted in a black-and-green camouflage pattern, sat in a dug-in position surrounded by trees and covered by extensive camouflage netting, which had been further covered with snow the night before. Karen didn't know if it would be enough to fool a satellite, but there was little they could do at this point. From the position, she had an unobstructed view of the highway and the bridge across the Shenandoah, the wooded hills of the Harpers Ferry National Historic Park rising beyond. Any attack into her sector would come from one of two places: here, on U.S. 340, or the Charlestown Pike Bridge on Route 9 from Loudon County, Virginia. Crews were prepared to blow both bridges at the opening of hostilities, but her main concern was here: Route 340 was a large divided highway, the river crossing shallow enough for tanks and armored vehicles to make it across the rapids, which Sergeant Catlett told her were called the "staircase."

Her crew was inside the tank, staying warm. She sat nearby at a picnic table, with the platoon leaders and platoon sergeants of her company, going over the defense plans again. She held a plastic travel cup filled with steaming instant coffee. She hated the bitter-tasting stuff in the combat rations, but it tasted better than nothing at all, at least when mixed with chocolate.

"All right. I talked to Major Elkins. We're authorized to let the company go at 50 percent strength for today and tomorrow. I'd like each of you to let half your platoon go for the remainder of today and overnight. They need to be back in position by 0500, because that's when the rest will go."

All three platoon leaders grinned. Morale was a huge problem, and sending folks home for Christmas would help a lot. It was tough to be away from home for Christmas when you could literally see home at the bottom of the hill. She just hoped they would all come back; there were no guarantees at this point.

"Guidelines are, we keep fully operable crews so that if we are attacked we can mass at least fifty percent of our combat power. And make sure the men know not to discuss our defense plans. First Sergeant, can you make arrangements for the supply truck to take the men to their homes and pick them up?"

Schumaker responded. "Yes, ma'am."

"All right, that's all I've got. Any questions?"

They had none. She stood up and stretched, then fished in the pocket of her field jacket. "Lieutenant Britton, you want to flip a coin for which crew will go first, yours or mine?"

"Yes, ma'am."

"Here we go," she said, squinting at a dollar. She flipped it.

"Tails," he said.

The coin landed, backside up.

"Your choice. You want your crew to take Christmas day? I'll send mine today."

"That sounds very nice, ma'am." He had a big grin on his face. Britton had recently married, and had a little girl at home, six months old. Tough to be away from home on your kid's first Christmas.

She turned back toward her tank, only to see Sergeant Bowen, her gunner, climbing out. His expression was grim.

"Captain, we've been listening to the news in here. The Senate just voted for the independence bill. It passed."

Lieutenant Britton frowned. "Should we cancel sending folks home, ma'am?"

"No," she murmured, her voice low. "Let them go, it'll take a few days before the governor signs it and it's official. Let the guys see their families while they have the chance."

She climbed onto the turret of her tank, sat down between the main gun and the grenade launchers on the right side, and looked down at the valley. Spread out below, Harpers Ferry looked peaceful, covered in snow. There, far down below, was the bridge the enemy would cross, possibly in just a few days.

She crossed her arms over her chest and leaned forward, huddling against the cold. She felt a biting pain in her cheeks, and realized tears were freezing on her face. She brushed them away. Time to get inside the tank and warm up.

༄

As Karen's men prepared for their brief Christmas visits home, planning proceeded in Murphy's still busy headquarters in Charleston. Murphy was standing at the urinal when his phone rang, its irritating tone echoing off the bare walls of the bathroom.

"Dammit." He quickly zipped up as the phone rang again.

He finally flipped open the phone and answered, his voice echoing off the walls. "Hello?" "Ken? It's Tom."

A smile broke out on Murphy's face, and his voice echoed in the bathroom. "Tom, it's good to hear from you. How are you?"

As he spoke he walked out of the bathroom and toward the front of the building. He'd get some air while he was on the phone.

"I'd congratulate you on your promotion, General, but under the circumstances I don't know if I should."

Murphy sighed as he reached the door and pushed it open. Tommy's tone was cold, tightly controlled anger. An icy cold wind hit him, bracing him. The light outside was grey, as was the sky, a cold, grim day. Icy wind blew up from the Kanahwa River, stinging his hands and cheeks.

"Tom, I don't know that it's anything to be proud of. I ended up in the slot for a lot of reasons, but mostly out of a process of elimination."

"Ken, I don't understand. Why? Why is all this necessary? Did you hear the President's speech this morning?"

"I did."

"You heard what he said about the West Virginia National Guard? That as of next Monday you are stripped of your commission in the Armed Forces if you are still serving in West Virginia? They are going to charge you with treason if you don't walk away."

Murphy closed his eyes. "Tom, I don't expect you to understand. We tried to talk about it when I was in Atlanta, and you didn't see it then, either. It's not about me. It's about the future of our country. I don't want to fight a war, but I won't stand by while the President and his cronies trample everything we've spent our lives fighting for."

As he spoke, Murphy stared at the ground and wondered if that was what it was really about. Was he just kidding himself?

He heard Tom exhale at the other end. "Look, Ken, I'm sorry. I didn't call you to get in an argument—I just wanted to see how you're making out, you know… since Kenny passed away."

Murphy gave a helpless shrug, almost as if his brother could see him. "Tommy, I don't know. I… just keep going. Ever since Martha died, that's all I can do. Just keep going, one step forward. You know, I think I finally said goodbye to her, too, there at Kenny's funeral. I just feel… empty, now. It's funny—those last few weeks, he was doing so much better. I guess I thought we were going to have more time."

"Why don't you come home, Ken?" Tommy said, his voice almost pleading. "Just resign—half the officers there have already quit. The politicians are crazy if they think you can win this thing. You can come home, maybe bring Valerie with you, and have your family here. Mom and Dad are worried sick."

"I can't. I can't walk away from my responsibilities here, Tom."

"You know the President has called up 50,000 reservists, Ken. And my brigade has been alerted; we're loading our choppers with ammo. It's going to be a war."

"I love you, little brother, but I can't be turned aside from my course."

"What will you do, Ken? When my brigade rains death and destruction on you and your people. What are we going to do?"

"We just keep going, Tom. Maybe you should come here. I could use a good brigade commander."

"I would never betray my country, Ken."

"Neither would I, Tommy. The country we grew up with is gone. You're just like the guys in the *Wermacht* eighty years ago, defending the fatherland when the real enemy was behind them, giving the orders."

"Ken, I've admired you my whole life. But this… I just can't accept it. It's not just your life you are throwing away. A hell of a lot of completely innocent people will die because of your ideological spin on things. You and your militia pals out there are starting a civil war."

"That's where you're wrong, Tom. There's been a long running democratic process that made this happen. It's not me and my cronies. It's the will of the people. And they are right, Tom. They are *right*."

"I can't stand by while you betray everything our family stood for."

"I didn't ask you to."

"I love you, Ken. But I don't know if we can be brothers anymore."

Murphy's face contorted, and tears formed in his eyes. "You said that when you were eight years old and I punched you."

Tom sighed. "Yeah, but I meant it back then. Maybe we'll see each other when it's over."

"Yeah. Maybe."

"Goodbye, Ken."

"Goodbye, Tom."

Murphy closed the phone with his numb fingers and pushed it back onto his belt. He was freezing, but not ready to go back inside. For now, he'd stay out in the cold.

༄

Mike Morris looked down at his hands—and his own wedding ring—then back up at the altar. The ring. He sighed. It was way too late to be thinking of how much he'd screwed up his own marriage. He took the ring off and slipped it into his pocket.

This was one more thing to worry about. Sergeants Kevin Miller and Kathleen O'Donnell had shown up at his door this morning, hand in hand, and announced their intention to marry before deploying. Everyone knew they'd been living together for some time, but this was a shock. Married couples didn't deploy to war zones in the same infantry unit. Ever. But there was no time to replace a key platoon sergeant. That meant Kevin Miller's two sons from his first marriage would be left behind with one set of grandparents. Not an ideal situation.

After a lot of rearranging, the base chapel had been cleared, and two precious hours carved out of the deployment schedule for the entire company to witness the nuptials.

Not that Morris had much to do with it; he was still in limbo. He wasn't relieved of command, but his XO was acting as company commander. All the same, he'd packed his gear and prepared for deployment like the rest. Maybe he'd spend the time sitting in the back of a truck at battalion headquarters. Who knew?

Alicia still hadn't let him talk to Savannah. The hell of it was, he could understand her anger. He'd put her through hell, dragging her all over the country, deployment after deployment, literally years away from home. But he'd never forgive her for cutting him off from Savannah. Never.

"I do," said Sergeant Kevin Miller, standing at the altar in his elegant dress blue uniform. The scar on his forehead, normally not prominent, stood out in high relief. Kathleen O'Donnell, by contrast, looked completely relaxed. Unusually out of uniform, she wore a plain white wedding dress and a beaming smile. The chaplain turned to her and spoke.

Morris's attention was interrupted by Lieutenant Colonel Barksdale, who stood at the end of the aisle.

"Captain Morris, I need to speak to you. It's urgent."

Right in the middle of the wedding? What could be that important?

"Yes, sir," Morris whispered. He slid out of the pew.

Behind him, he heard the chaplain say the last words. "You may kiss the bride."

Morris glanced up at the smiling couple and his mind turned to Karen. Not likely they'd ever have a scene like this. A roar rose around him as his entire company stood up, clapping and cheering. The families of the couple were a little more reserved, with the knowledge that they were deploying into a probably combat zone almost immediately.

Morris followed Barksdale to the entrance area. A cold draft blew in the gap between the heavy oak doors.

Barksdale spoke quietly. "You're ready for the deployment?"

"Yes, sir."

"All right, you are back in command. Court-martials be damned, I need an experienced officer in that slot."

"Yes, sir."

"Look, Morris. The President has ordered an immediate offensive. The moment the governor of West Virginia signs that bill is our jumping point. They don't care whether all the assets are in place or not; I guess they figure the National Guard won't put up much of a fight."

"You sound like you don't agree, sir."

"I don't. That's pretty much what they said before Bull Run, too. We'll still be fighting Americans."

Barksdale turned away, and Morris said, "Sir, I have to say thank you. I appreciate your confidence."

Barksdale stopped and frowned. "I didn't do it for you, Morris. Whatever my personal feelings for you, you are a capable commander and you think clearly under stress. That may be critical for the survival of your men. For all I care, the minute we get back, they can cart you off and court-martial you."

Morris did not reply, and Barksdale relented. "Maybe this is a chance to show your true colors. I could be wrong, Captain. I hope so. I heard what you said at your hearing. For what it's worth, you did the right thing."

Barksdale walked away, and Morris turned his attention back to the cheering crowd. The newly married couple made their way down the aisle as raucous troops on either side clapped and shouted. Something else to take care of; he couldn't have a married couple deploying to a war-zone together.

No time; they were jumping off tonight. As soon as the wedding was over, his company had been ordered to gather, in combat gear, at the battalion headquarters, ready to deploy. The wedding was only allowed to proceed when the base chaplain interceded with the Division Commander. After the wedding, Mike would go straight to the company and change there.

Morris slipped outside behind Miller and O'Donnell. Miller had two sons from his first marriage, already outside with the grandparents. Morris watched as they hugged the two crying boys, who knew their parents were going away again and not on a honeymoon as planned. The remainder of the company followed, their cheering becoming mute as they saw the crying boys.

An older man with white hair approached. He wore a pin Morris recognized: a miniature Southwest Asia Service ribbon from the first Gulf War in 1991.

"Are you Captain Morris?"

"Yes, sir."

"I'm Frank O'Donnell. Kathleen is my daughter."

"Yes, sir. You should be very proud of her, sir."

O'Donnell nodded. "I am. We're taking the kids home with us. I just came to ask you... Take care of them, please. Those boys need their parents. Take care of my little girl."

"I'll do my best, sir. I promise."

"Well, that's all I can ask."

The boys—both still crying—were put into the back of a car by their parents, and a hush fell over the infantrymen who had been cheering before. O'Donnell's father walked away from Morris, hugged his daughter, and shook hands with Sergeant Miller.

In the sudden quiet, Morris heard the wind whip through the power lines above their heads. He looked at his company, mostly men, and a few women gathered around, most of them embracing their wives and children. All of them saying goodbye to someone, something.

Morris had already said his goodbyes, in Harpers Ferry yesterday.

God damn politicians and their wars. That's the way it always was—some politician somewhere wanted something, and it was the infantry and their families who suffered and died to make it happen.

"All right," the first sergeant grumbled. "Vacation is over, folks. I want everyone back at the company in one hour, locked and loaded."

The gathering on the front steps of the chapel broke up and the men and women of the company hurried home with their families, to change out of their dress uniforms and back into combat gear.

They were going to war.

Chapter Thirty-Five
January 1

"Hello, America, and happy New Year. This is Bill Warner with Washington Talk. Today we have with us West Virginia Secretary of State Albert Clark, and Vice President Robert Hamilton of California. We'll discuss the news on everyone's mind: West Virginia's Declaration of Independence, signed by Governor Frank Slagter this morning. We'll ask these gentlemen their views on these important events, and give you, the listener, the chance to call in your questions."

"Commercial," someone shouted. "180 seconds."

Vice President Hamilton, a tall and gaunt man, turned to their host, ignoring Clark.

"How's the family, Bill? Still getting along okay?"

"Oh, they're fine, sir. Dee just started college this year, believe it or not."

"Really. Well, that's wonderful. You know mine flew the coop some years ago. It's a difficult time. How is your wife taking it? Does she work?"

"Yes, sir, she's a neurology professor over at Georgetown Medical School."

"Thirty seconds."

Clark frowned. Hamilton still looked everywhere possible other than him. This could be interesting. The Vice President was nervous about something, but what?

"Ten seconds."

The studio went silent as the lights came up, and Warner spoke on queue.

"Hello, America. This is Bill Warner with Washington Talk. With me are two men on opposite sides of one of the key issues facing America today. On my right, Vice President Robert Hamilton will speak for the White House's position. On my left, Secretary of State Albert Clark of West Virginia. Mr. Clark is a former U.S. Congressman and is leading negotiations on behalf of West Virginia. The first key question: this morning, Governor Frank Slagter signed a bill, passed by the West Virginia legislature, declaring its independence from the United States. For the first time since 1861 a state is attempting to secede from the United States. Reactions? Mr. Vice President?"

"Well, Bill, I'll be brief. The action is illegal, and dangerous. It will put the lives of thousands of people at risk, all to placate the ambitions of a few men like Governor Slagter and Mr. Clark here. It is treason, and the United States will treat it as such."

"Mr. Clark."

"Mr. Vice President, one thing is clear: the people of the State of West Virginia voted overwhelmingly for this measure in a statewide ballot. The people heavily campaigned their representatives to vote for it in the legislature. I was personally opposed to the measure, spoke out against it and voted against it, but there is a time to line up behind the will of the people, and this is that time. You can't characterize this as being the ambitions of one or two men: this is in clear reaction to the repeated use of excessive force and violations of civil liberties in our state. Key point here, Bill: we're at the brink of a civil war. We need to step back the rhetoric, and especially step back the mobilization of military forces, before it goes too far. It's not too late to stop this thing from becoming an open conflict, but only the President has the power to stop that."

"Thank you, Mr. Clark. Next question: West Virginia activated its National Guard some weeks ago, and about a week ago the President ordered the mobilization of some hundred thousand troops in the United States. The impression of most of America is that we are hurtling towards a war. The question is: how do we prevent it? Mr. Vice President."

"Bill, the only way to prevent it is for the West Virginians to back off this dangerous path. One-hundred and fifty years ago President Abraham Lincoln established one undying principal that this country has stood by: the Union is indivisible, and the parts may not come and go as they will. No one wants this to come to a war, least of all the President. But the President must do his part to preserve our unique union."

"Mr. Clark."

Clark looked straight at the camera as he spoke. "Now, Bill, in most situations, you want to sit down and talk first, before you start shooting at people. Let me be clear. The United States government has refused to talk, has refused to negotiate, has refused to sit down and even meet with us. The President could stop this right now if he would merely appoint a negotiating team to sit down, meet with our people and work out our differences. Instead, the President has sent a very clear message that there will be no negotiations, and if we don't do what they tell us they'll send five divisions of tanks in to force us. We must establish a basis for negotiation."

"We'll be right back after this commercial break. This is Bill Warner with Washington Talk."

"Sixty seconds."

Across the studio, Valerie Murphy listened with one ear as she worked on her pocket computer, still trying to arrange meetings at any level with the U.S. government. As she worked, she glanced up and froze. Three men in matching black suits approached her. All three had earpieces with wires trailing into their coats, and dark sunglasses hid their eyes.

"Valerie Murphy?"

"Yes."

"I'm agent Lukeman of the Department of Homeland Security. You are under arrest. Please set the computer down on the table and stand up."

She set the computer down, slowly, and then stood as instructed.

"What is this about? Why am I being arrested? Do you have a warrant?"

One of the men approached her and said, "Please raise your arms in the air, right now."

She did, and the man thoroughly patted her down for weapons. A moment later, he twisted her arms behind her and handcuffed her wrists, too tightly. She cried out in pain.

"Relax your arms a little, it won't hurt so much," he said.

She did, and it did help a little.

The other agent quickly catalogued her purse, and placed her pocket computer in a small protective case.

"Let's go."

The agents forced her to walk out of the studio and on to a waiting elevator. She stumbled getting into the elevator and the agents simply lifted her up between them and carried her the next several steps.

"It would be best if you cooperated," the agent on her left said in a menacing tone.

"I tripped, you ass."

The agent on her right snickered.

As they exited the building, she was overwhelmed by the sudden shouting and noise. Fifty, possibly a hundred reporters crowded around the exit, filming, shouting questions.

She shut them out of her mind as the agents barged their way through the crowd, shoving reporters out of the way.

Someone shoved a camera in her face and the flash went off, leaving bright spots in her eyes. A woman screamed, "Valerie, are you being arrested for treason?" Valerie flushed.

The agents pushed her into the back seat of an unmarked car. With her hands cuffed behind her, she had to lean forward, unable to sit back all the way. Her skirt rode up to her thighs as she sat, and she couldn't fix it. Tears of frustration flooded her eyes.

The cameras continued to flash as the reporters shouted questions at her. An agent slammed the door of the car, then got into the driver's seat, but they continued to sit, even as the reporters on the street filmed her and shouted questions.

"What, did you guys call the press in advance? You don't have any grounds for charges, so you'll just publicly brand us, is that it?"

"Shut up." The order was delivered in a deadly tone.

A few minutes later the reporters moved, en masse, back to the door. Seconds later Clark appeared, flanked by two agents who pushed the reporters back. He held his head high, but he, too, was handcuffed.

They shoved him into the car in front of her, none too gently. Seconds later both cars sped away.

꒰

Captain Greenfield keyed the switch on the side of her helmet. "Block the road. No one comes through unless they have a West Virginia driver's license or can substantiate residence or family here. Pull the tank right into the middle of the road."

She watched as the tank below drove forward, into the traffic lanes of U.S. 340. Traffic immediately came to a halt as the turret swung toward the other side of the river. One car, a small BMW, backed up until it hit the guardrail with a screech she could hear all the way up here, half a mile away on the heights. A Ford pickup truck with a tripod-mounted machine gun pulled into position next to the tank.

Two infantrymen, rifles slung over their shoulders, walked toward the incoming cars and began talking to the drivers. A third stood guard at the machine gun. Good. Everything looked calm.

With her right hand she reached back down into the turret and switched the radio to the battalion network.

"Cornstalk Six, this is Bravo Six, over."

"This is Cornstalk Six, over." Major Vince Elkins.

"Cornstalk Six, Objective Green is secure, over."

"Roger, Bravo Six. I understand Objective Green is secure. Cornstalk Six out."

"How you doing, guys?" she asked the other crewmembers over the intercom.

The others answered quietly, the mood somber. All across the state right now, local forces moved to block bridges and tunnels, roads leading in or out of the state. Before the day was over, many of those bridges would be blown, reducing the lines of attack ground forces could take into the state. They had gone from taking abstract political steps to taking very concrete, military steps.

Karen wondered how many of them would survive the coming week.

꒰

"Come in, General, come in."

As usual, Frank Slagter's tone was jovial, friendly, despite the deadly seriousness of this visit.

"Thank you, Governor."

Slagter led Murphy into the office, and as before, they sat at the table overlooking the decimated site of the federal building.

"What can I do for you, General? My secretary said you needed to see me right away."

"I'm here about two things, sir. The first one is a question. How are things on the diplomatic front?"

Slagter frowned. "Not so good, General. Secretary Clark—and your daughter—were in Washington this morning, and no one has heard from them since. The news is reporting they've been arrested."

"Arrested? For what?"

"I couldn't guess," Slagter said.

Dear God. He never would have imagined Valerie would be in danger. Of course, she'd be safer in the DC lockup than here in Charleston.

"You said you came for two things, General."

"Yes, sir. I've ordered an evacuation of all the government agencies and buildings, and apparently no one has complied. I came to speak to you about it, because you are in a position to enforce it."

"Whatever for, General?"

"Governor, it is very likely most of the government buildings won't be standing in forty-eight hours—including this one."

"General, surely it's not likely to go so far."

"But it will, sir. Unless you come up with a diplomatic solution. If this thing comes to open armed conflict, one of the first things they will do is bomb every government facility, every power plant, every bridge in the state."

Slagter shook his head. "General, I just can't believe the President would authorize such things."

"Sir, why did you appoint me?"

"Why, because you had more combat experience than the other officers."

"That's right. I'm your military advisor. And I am telling you, they will follow standard operating procedures and bomb the crap out of this place as soon as they realize we're putting up serious resistance."

"All right, General. I'll order the evacuation. I do hope you are wrong."

"So do I, sir. I've told you before—when this comes to war, we cannot win. Depending on the weather and a lot of other things I can probably hold the state two or three days, but no longer. You've got to find a political solution, sir."

Slagter nodded, and Murphy had the feeling there was no political solution in sight.

The sun was almost setting as the column came to a halt on U.S. 340, halfway between Frederick, Maryland and Harpers Ferry, West Virginia. Morris, a little unsteady on his feet after the long drive in the HUMMWV, stepped out and was immediately hit by a blast of cold air.

He marched up the column, where he met the other company commanders and Lieutenanant Colonel Barksdale. The officers stood huddled in their field jackets as icy wind blew at them.

"It's cold as a witch's teat out here," Barksdale said without preamble. "Have the men put out the tents and heaters; I want everyone well rested when we jump off. Your supply sergeants can work with Headquarters Company to break the tents down in the morning after the combat elements jump off. Meet me in the command track in fifteen minutes, and we'll brief the attack."

Morris returned to his company and gave the necessary orders. The men weren't happy about putting up tents in the freezing cold and dark, but they'd be even less happy about sleeping out in it.

He quickly returned to the command tracks. Three armored vehicles, Vietnam-era M-113's, had been lined up side by side, with tent extensions stretched out to form a relatively sizeable briefing area. The whole setup could be rolled out in ten minutes, and put back in motion again in five. It was already warming up inside when Morris entered the tent.

Captain Delveccio, the Delta Company commander, was already there when Morris entered. He was chewing gum, a smug look on his face.

"Hey, Morris, isn't your girlfriend in 2-432 Armor?"

"My what?" His heart suddenly pounded.

"You know, the redhead in Newsweek? West Virginia National Guard lady? I wish I had a copy of the article. I swear she was in 2-432 armor."

"She is; she's a company commander."

Delveccio pointed at the mapboard. "Take a look, Morris. Fucking-A."

Colonel Barksdale spoke in a commanding tone. "Captain Delveccio."

Delveccio straightened. "Yes, sir."

"Do me a favor and shut up, Captain."

"Yes, sir."

Barksdale approached Morris, who stood over the map table. There it was, as he had fully expected. The map showed three companies of tanks and infantry in positions near Harpers Ferry and Charles Town, from 2-432 Armor. The map didn't indicate which company held each location, but Morris knew she was there. She was there, all right.

Barksdale spoke, his tone low. "Is this going to be a problem, Morris?"

"No, sir. I've got a job to do. So does she."

"Pretty sad world, isn't it?"

"It can be, sir."

By this time all of the officers were present. Barksdale said, "All right, everyone gather around the map board. I'll make this short; y'all are already familiar with the operations order, just a couple of minor changes. We're approaching from the east and south, right here. My understanding is that all of the bridges have been dropped except for this one at U.S. 340. The scouts will approach the bridge first with a sapper team and attempt to disable any explosives. In the event the bridge is taken out, engineers will place pontoon bridges just to the west right here, at the top of the rapids. This is the shallowest point, so even if we drop a tank or Bradley into the water, it should be able to get out: it's only about 18 inches deep there. Everybody got it?"

The officers nodded.

"Now, the bad news. We're expecting a really bad storm, with as much as twelve inches of snow. The Maryland Department of Transportation has extra plows and salt trucks deployed to ensure this highway stays open, but you can bet that there won't be any civilian plows out in Harpers Ferry tomorrow morning. Make sure your men are prepared for an ugly fight in the snow."

Delveccio, the pugnacious captain from Delta Company, squinted and said, "What about air support? Will we have any if the weather is that bad?"

"Probably not. However, the area will be thoroughly prepped with artillery. The first fire mission is scheduled for oh-three-hundred, just as we cross the line of departure."

Morris nodded. It would still be dark when they crossed the river.

"Any more questions?"

"Sir, if we don't have air support, why are we going now? Why not wait until it clears?"

Barksdale looked at them all, his eyes jumping from one officer to the next. "Because that is what the Commander-in-Chief wants, understand? Those are our orders, gentlemen. We're going into combat against the most formidable opponent this unit has faced in many years. This is no third world army you are fighting; these folks trained in the same places you did, served in the same places you did, and at least some of them are combat veterans. I expect all of you to take good care of your men, and be careful. Be very careful. Dismissed."

Slowly, the officers trailed out and back to their companies. One way or another, it would begin tomorrow.

Chapter Thirty-Six
January 2

Karen leaned against the side of the turret, her helmet providing some measure of cushion against the hard steel. The hatches were closed, but still her breath appeared before her in crystals. It couldn't be any more than forty degrees inside the tank. Which meant it was a hell of a lot colder outside.

She looked at her watch: 0245. They should get the word to move any time. Her company had occupied the same position for a week, making a nice fat target for satellite photos and reconnaissance planes. The plan was to move to their alternate positions as soon as it looked like the enemy was on the way.

A loud squeal in her ear signaled an incoming radio transmission.

"Bravo Six, this is Cornstalk Six, over."

She switched her transmitter to the battalion net and keyed her helmet forward to the radio position.

"This is Bravo Six, over."

"Intel reports movement of enemy forces west on U.S. 340. You will occupy your alternate positions immediately and prepare for enemy assault, over."

"Roger, Cornstalk Six."

"Cornstalk Six out."

Well, she thought. *This is it. No turning back from here.* Keying to the company net, she spoke.

"All six elements, this is Bravo Six, over."

Her platoon leaders quickly reported in. She relayed the order to move. No need to give detailed instructions; they'd rehearsed this maneuver four times in the last week, each time in full darkness. The ten tanks and five infantry fighting vehicles, plus the various support elements including maintenance, medics and fire support, all started their engines at once.

Immediately afterward she said, "Hey, Crump. Can you turn on the heater? It's freaking cold in here."

She opened her hatch and a pile of snow fell in around her; then she stood up, her head and upper body outside in the cold. Even with the night vision goggles, visibility was poor.

One by one, the tanks and Bradleys backed out of their positions and drove up the fire road to the new spots they would be occupying, a quarter mile away and closer to the river. She counted them as they passed: two platoons of four tanks, one platoon of infantry, her XO Lieutenant Britton, then the fire support track and the medics.

As she watched, Major Elkins called over the battalion net again.

"All six elements, this is Cornstalk Six. Intel report: the artillery units to the south are at a high level of activity, over. Prepare for incoming any minute. Cornstalk Six out."

God damn it. Most of her company was still in transit, some still at the original position. She could hear the tracks clatter against the pavement, and knew the attackers across the river must be able to hear it as well.

Where was battalion getting the information anyway? The latest intel placed the enemy artillery down in Loudon County, across the river. They must have a spy, maybe a local resident calling in reports. She tapped her fingers on the edge of the hatch, waiting as the last vehicles crossed the line of departure.

"Okay, Crump," she called to her driver over the intercom. "Let's move out. Back up slowly please. Now pivot right. Good. Do you see the track ahead of you? Good, follow him."

A piercing shriek tore the sky overhead and she screamed. "Incoming!"

She dropped down into her hatch and pulled it closed.

A massive explosion two hundred yards to their rear threw rocks and snow across the landscape, followed by another. Seconds later she heard her executive officer, Lieutenant Britton, reporting to the battalion they were taking incoming artillery.

The next hit was close enough to shake the sixty-ton tank, and pepper it with shrapnel. It sounded like rocks inside a tin can.

"Six elements," she called over the company net. "Sitrep, please. Everyone intact?"

Her platoon leaders called back in. No one hit, so far. As the reports came in, she heard someone whisper. What the hell was that? The voice was hurried, almost a chant or a prayer. She looked around, frantically. Private Haggett, her new loader, sat with his back to the wall of the turret, his mouth steadily moving. Three months ago Haggett had been washing dishes at Sally's Diner. These kids were not prepared for this.

"Haggett," she said.

His eyes shifted to her. "Yes, ma'am?"

"Can you unkey your mike while you pray?"

He swallowed and nodded. "Sorry, ma'am."

Less than a mile away, Morris stared at the ridge across from him, and at the still untouched bridge into the town of Harpers Ferry. Looking at his watch, he frowned. The artillery ripped the ridge up, the big rounds crashing into the mountain with huge explosions that echoed off the ridgeline behind them. He hoped to God the civilians had been evacuated from the area. Even as he watched, a house went up in flames.

"Alpha Six, this is Arrow Six, over."

Morris keyed his microphone and responded to Barksdale.

"This is Alpha Six, over."

"On order your company will attack across the bridge toward Bolivar Heights. Once you reach the top of Bolivar heights, engage and destroy the enemy encamped there. Your sector of fire is between phase lines Brown and Hunt. Make sure your units don't fire over that line; Alpha and Delta Teams will be in echelon to your flanks. Do you copy, over?"

"Roger, Arrow Six. Do we have an estimate of force strength on the hill, over?"

"At this point our best estimate is one M1A1 tank company, reinforced with mortars and one platoon of infantry, over. We flew a drone over there a while ago, but it crashed. The weather."

What they had expected, he thought.

"Arrow Six, this is Alpha Six. Any air support?"

"We have no air support at this time, due to weather conditions. We'll continue with the artillery until two minutes before you launch your attack."

"Roger, Arrow Six."

"Arrow Six, out."

He pulled out his map and made some notations in it, then called over the company radio net. "Alpha elements, this is Alpha Six. All six elements and platoon sergeants report to my vehicle immediately. Alpha Six out."

Climbing down out of the turret, he signaled to Corporal Porter, his radioman. "Come on, Porter."

The two of them exited the back of the Bradley and stood on the ground. Within a few minutes, the command group stood around him in a loose semicircle and they reviewed the plan one last time.

"This is it, folks. Things are about to get real ugly. Everything goes by the plan for now, keep me informed as you advance."

※

Karen's gunner swept the turret back and forth across the area, scanning for targets, and she asked herself for the hundredth time if she had made a huge mistake. Maybe she should have just turned herself in. *No.* Too late for doubts. For better or worse, she had a job to do now.

She clambered back into the cupola and looked around the position again with her night vision goggles, mentally reviewing her company's positions for the hundredth time. Two tank platoons faced the main approaches across the river, both platoons dug into recently excavated berms with additional cover from nearby houses and shops rolling down the slope. Both platoons had clear fields of view of the hill, however, and secondary positions were prepared. The third platoon was dug in on Cavalier Heights, kept in reserve to support whichever area was attacked in force. They should be able to get good defilade fire on the enemy. Stretched out between the two tank platoons, occupying houses and buildings with good interlocking fields of fire was the attached infantry platoon, which had come down from Wheeling. Though an unknown, the infantry platoon leader and sergeant were both experienced and knew their stuff. She would have to hope for the best. Not far behind the reserve platoon, her small mortar section's personnel carrier sat ready to fire on anyone approaching the hill. It wouldn't do much good against tanks, but would be very effective against the Bradleys parked across the river.

More on her mind were the twelve loaders and drivers in the company who had enlisted in November and December. None of them had enough training or experience, but the slots simply had to be filled. One of the new privates was seventeen; he hadn't even graduated high school. *What the hell have we come to, when we have children fighting our wars?*

A call came in over the radio: the second platoon leader.

"Captain, this is White Six. We've got movement; they're getting ready to cross the bridge, over."

"Roger, White Six," she replied, lifting her night vision goggles to her eyes.

Britton called the report to battalion headquarters. "Cornstalk Six, this is Bravo Five. We have movement across the river at this time, break. Estimate three companies of infantry teams, mixed mounted and foot. We can see about a dozen tanks in three groups, over."

"Roger, Bravo. Keep your people prepared to execute Clean Sweep on order, or on your judgment. Cornstalk Six out."

She grunted. Clean Sweep was the evacuation plan. The idea was to hurt them, then get the hell away before they could hit back. Stop somewhere down the road and hurt them again. She frowned as she watched the infantry battalion below move to the bridge. The first two tanks were pulling out on the bridge.

"All elements, this is the Captain. We are at weapons hold status at this time. I don't want anyone firing prematurely. We're going to let most of the infantry get about halfway up the hill before we do anything. We want them out in the open. Acknowledge."

After the platoon leaders acknowledged, she called her attached infantry platoon leader. "Red Six, this is the Captain."

"Red Six, over," responded the infantry platoon leader.

"Take out the bridge, over."

"Roger."

She waited thirty seconds, and nothing happened. The tanks were halfway across, and the explosives they'd planted must have been deactivated.

"Captain, this is Red Six. It looks like our explosives have been taken out."

"All right, hit it with TOW missiles."

Seconds later there was a bright flash and explosion. A moment later one of the supports crashed, causing one side of the bridge to sag. One of the attacking tanks, an M1A2 model considerably newer than hers, went down into the river with a crash. The other tank was already across. It swung its turret wildly, scanning for targets as it backed down the bank toward the river and a hide position.

Dropping into the turret, she put her eyes to the sight. "Gunner, sabot, moving tank."

Her crew responded rapidly.

"Identified."

"Up."

"Fire."

The cannon fired, the blast pushing the cannon a foot back into the turret. The shell casing flew out of the back and clattered to the floor, flooding the turret with the smell of ammonia. The sabot round, shining bright green in her sights, flew to the tank. She waited a second. It was still moving.

Her voice loud now, she called out, "Target, reengage."

She saw a muzzle flash as the enemy tank fired.

"Identified."

Haggett struggled with the heavy 120mm round. She reached across the turret and helped him shove it in the tube. A moment later, his face flushed, he yelled, "Up," and armed the cannon.

"Fire."

The cannon bucked again, and she looked through the site and felt a rush of elation as the turret exploded, showering fire and shrapnel across the river. A moment later the elation was gone, washed away, as it hit her that she had just killed eight Americans in those two tanks.

Seconds later the center section of the bridge collapsed into the river below.

The radio monitoring the battalion net spoke, her executive officer calling to the higher-up, "Cornstalk Six, Bravo Five, over. The bridge is down. Two tanks engaged and destroyed, over."

She looked through the sights at the thermal images of the approaching infantry. They were almost in the kill zone. Behind them, engineer vehicles were moving pontoon bridges into place across the river. She gave the order to fire.

Murphy's hands trembled as he took a sip from his coffee. Major Roth, his operations officer, sat across the map table from him as they listened to the reports come in from three battlefields.

In the north, at Harpers Ferry, infantry units from Fort Meade were attacking their positions at U.S. 340 and Route 9. Additional fights were occurring on the borders with Kentucky and Pennsylvania.

Murphy flipped open his phone and dialed.

A voice answered at the other end, "This is the governor's office."

"Please put the governor on the line. This is General Murphy."

Murphy waited, impatiently. He looked at his watch. Almost 0300.

"This is Slagter."

"Governor, this is General Murphy. We're under attack at this time on three fronts. The fighting has just started, so I don't have any status for you yet."

"Thanks, General. I'll be right down there."

෴

Shifting position inside the Bradley fighting vehicle, Morris switched the radio back to the company net.

"Alpha elements, this is Alpha Six. On my mark, I want every vehicle to fire a TOW missile at that hill, followed by chainguns. Those tanks must be suppressed while we get across the river. Short count to follow. Five. Four. Three. Two. One. Fire. Move out, move out! Get across the river. Alpha Six out."

Ttwenty wire-guided missiles raced toward the summit of the hill as the Bradleys lurched forward. Morris watched them go, knowing one of them might well be aimed at Karen. Was she up there? What the hell were they doing? It didn't matter if she was on the hill or not. If not, she was somewhere else nearby, defending against one of the other attacks. Like it or not, they were both in this battle.

"Sergeant Harris, what you got?" Morris asked, watching the faint contrail of the missile. A second later he was rewarded by half a dozen explosions on the hill as the missiles found their marks.

"Sir, I can't tell if we hit anything. The tanks backed down off the berm as soon as we fired."

"What exploded?"

"I don't know, sir."

෴

"Red, White, Blue, this is Bravo Six, give me a report, over," Karen shouted into the microphone as her tank moved into its secondary position. Her voice shook, but not as much as it had seconds ago when the missile slammed into the front of their turret, throwing the tank back about three feet.

"Bravo Six, White Six, no damage, repeat, we are REDCON one!"

"Captain, this is Red Six. One-three is gone, break. Total loss, everyone's dead."

She closed her eyes. Four people dead, at least.

"Blue Six?" she called. "Blue Six, this is the Captain, acknowledge, over."

"Captain, this is Blue Four. My Six element is dead."

"Roger, Blue Four. Take command of the platoon."

"We got more incoming."

～

SFC Kathleen O'Donnell cheered as she saw the tank explode at the top of the hill. The air was peppered with the sound of heavy small arms fire, tank cannons firing, and rockets flying over their heads. She could smell smoke, black and heavy as it drifted across the battlefield.

"Come on." She shouted at the column as they ran past a burning vehicle. "We're halfway there."

"Blue Six, Blue Four," she called to Lieutenant Wingham, her platoon leader. "Checkpoint alpha, over."

She checked her watch as she waited for a response. 0300. Christ, had it only been ten minutes since they'd crossed the river?

A moment later she frowned. "Blue Six? Blue Four."

She waited again. "Blue Six?"

Specialist Conner grimaced beside her as he squatted with the heavy radio on his back in addition to his rucksack. "Sarge?"

"Hold on, Conner," she said, and held her hand toward him, palm up.

The headset came to life in her ear. "Sergeant O'Donnell? This is Sergeant White. The LT is dead. We're pinned down by a sniper, over. Son of a bitch took out Ellers, too, and we got a couple more wounded, over."

"Roger, White. Can you make out the location of the sniper, over."

"He's in that office building up the hill, on Washington Street. It's the only big building around, we're out in the open."

His voice was high-pitched, almost in a panic. She deliberately slowed down, spoke in a calm tone.

"White, give me a description of the building, over."

"It's a five story, up the hill. It's higher than anything else around here, over."

"I see it. Wait one."

"Switch me to the company net," she yelled at Connors as she fumbled with a map.

"Roger, here you go." He handed her a microphone.

"Captain Morris, this is Sergeant O'Donnell, over."

"Go ahead, Sergeant."

"Alpha Six, my six element is dead, repeat my six element is dead. His section is pinned down by a sniper. The sniper's in a five-story office building, at the intersection of Washington and Union Street. Can we get some fire to take the building out, over?"

"Roger, Blue Six, we'll get it. You hold on there."

As she dropped the handset, bullets slammed into a car parked to their right and they all dropped to the ground. The windshield shattered, spraying them with fragments.

"Damn it!" she shouted. "Rudolph, Sheehan, get your machine gun team on that building right now. We've got to give Alpha section some cover. Connors, back to the platoon net, now."

Half a second later she realized Connor was lying on his back in a pool of blood. "Medic!" she screamed, lurching to him. A piece of flying glass had cut his throat wide open and blood poured out into the street, staining the snow black in the garish streetlight. Without hesitation, she covered his throat with her gloved hands, the blood pouring out between her fingers, steam rising into the freezing night.

"Sarge," someone screamed. "McKinley's dead!"

She closed her eyes. McKinley was their only medic. Connor didn't have any pulse, and there wasn't a thing she could do about it.

She stared around her wildly, losing control. *Goddamn sniper.* Jesus Christ, five people down in two minutes.

"Sarge, the machine guns are set!"

"Let 'em go! Kill that motherfucker!"

She lifted her hands from Connor's neck and rolled him on his stomach, wrestling the radio free. Switching to the platoon net, she shouted, "White, I got a machine gun covering you. Move out. Get past that building. Get some grenades in there while you pass—see if you can set the damn thing on fire!"

"On the way!"

❧

"All elements, this is Bravo Six," Karen called into her radio. "Execute Clean Sweep, I repeat, execute Clean Sweep. Marching order, Blue, Red, White. Move out now."

She spoke to her own tank crew over the intercom. "Back up and pull into our hide position. Good."

She reached to her side and switched the radio to the battalion net as the tank rolled back away from the position they had occupied for the last hour.

"Cornstalk Six, this is Bravo Six, over."

"This is Cornstalk Six," Elkins said over the radio. "Go ahead, over."

"This is Bravo Six. We are evacuating at this time, over. We're hurting, over, we lost four tanks and six infantry, over. I'm going to need reinforcements, over."

"Roger, Bravo Six. You've done an outstanding job."

Karen took once last glance at Harpers Ferry as they sped away. The snow had increased in intensity, almost a blizzard now. Half a dozen buildings were in flames. Behind her, the U.S. Army would was occupying the positions they'd just vacated.

They'd be after them soon enough.

Chapter Thirty-Seven
January 2

Twelve hours had passed since the defenders pulled out; the snow coming down hard enough that visibility was reduced to less than six feet. Morris didn't care how loud the President and senior officers crowed. You couldn't fight a war in this stuff.

All the same, after several hours of waiting and regrouping the company, they were ready to move out in pursuit of the retreating West Virginia forces. He'd had a chance to review their positions. It was a good, well-planned defense, made all the more impressive by the overwhelming force arrayed against them. What looked to be an under-strength tank company had defended against an entire battalion here, and won the upper hand. Not because of any failure on his men's part, but because the politicians ordered them to jump off despite the weather and the lack of air support. He had a dozen dead in his unit because of their arrogance.

He'd checked the bumper number of the damaged and destroyed M1 tanks. She wasn't there. But it was her battalion they'd fought here, her company, even. She'd been part of it. Now twelve of his men were dead. He tried to picture her in his mind—the woman he'd wanted all these years, the woman he'd held in arms, what, a week ago? All he could see was Lieutenant Wingham, his brains and blood scattered across the snow by the shot of a sniper. He had work to do now.

"Six elements, this is Captain Morris," he called over the radio. "Prepare to move on my order."

The engines in the remaining Bradley fighting vehicles and one tank started.

"Move out, marching order Blue, White, Red."

They fell in behind the column formed by Charlie Company. Morris's Alpha Company had been the hardest hit in the battle at Harpers Ferry, losing a dozen men. Barksdale had placed them in the center of the column as the weakest point.

As they advanced, plows moved ahead of them, clearing the snow.

The tank was still, engine off, and Karen could hear her ears ringing as she looked at the dark landscape through the commander's extension. Below, the thermal sights of the tank clattered, and in the far distance she could hear artillery. Someone else in the middle of a fight, somewhere else.

"Captain, this is Red Four. I've got hot spots coming over the ridgeline. Looks like our folks coming down the highway."

The call came over the landline, a wire strung from tank to tank, to enable the company to maintain complete radio silence. She leaned forward and traversed the turret to the right. There they were: scouts, in Bradleys and HUMMWVs. They would let the scouts pass, wait until the main body arrived before engaging.

Bravo Company, down to not much more than sixty percent strength after the morning battle, occupied positions to the right of Delta, all of them behind the ridgeline and out of sight of the road. The weather had taken care of air observation; no one could fly in this storm. Even if they could, there was little to see; the men had buried the tanks under a foot of snow. More snowfall had broken the uneven lines, making them nearly invisible. The gunners carefully cleared away spaces in front of the primary sights; otherwise, the snow served their purpose nicely, camouflaging the thermal signature of the tanks.

Ahead of the advancing enemy column, Lieutenant Antal's Alpha Company arrayed its tanks at a right angle to her and Delta; also out of sight of the road. Antal's company had fought along Old-Highway 340 from Virginia in the morning, losing roughly half his tanks. The battalion had linked up here, where it would back away from the enemy in this dangerous cat-and-mouse game.

She opened her hatch and stood, scanning the area with night vision goggles, then toggled her radio. "Everybody track a target, but hold your fire. We'll get the word from higher when we're ready to go. Let the scouts go by."

༄

The dismal day was turning into even darker twilight. Mike continued to scan with his binoculars when he saw a glare. It looked like a reflection. Hard to see anything in all this snow, but he scanned again and saw a regular shape: a black rectangle on its side, barely visible on the ridgeline. It was the primary sight of a tank. Panic hit him, and he reached for the radio.

As Morris moved, a green star cluster exploded in the sky above him. He gripped the side of the hatch and ducked down instinctively.

At the signal, the cannons of twenty-four tanks fired at once. Morris winced at the sudden muzzle flashes and concussions, and several tanks exploded into flame as they were each hit by two or more rounds. The explosions lit the highway and surrounding area in a bright red light

"Blow smoke! All elements, dismount, dismount!"

The attack shattered the column. Ten tanks were burning, their ammo cooking off and throwing shrapnel and dark black smoke into the air. It looked like Charlie Company had been wiped out.

Each of Morris's Bradleys launched their smoke grenades, blanketing the entire highway in thick white smoke that shielded their movements.

"Go, go, go!" Morris's men sprinted down the ramps of their vehicles, each platoon rushing to occupy a defensive position.

He jumped out of his vehicle and hit the ground with his small command group. The Bradleys pulled off into the depression in the center of the road, trying to find some cover.

The tanks behind him in the column returned fire, the cannons throwing up great clouds of smoke and flame.

He looked up as he heard a sudden ripping sound, as if someone were tearing a thick blanket.

"Incoming!" He tried to shrink further down into the slush.

The first dozen artillery shells were shot out of the air by a truck mounted laser at the back of the column, bright explosions over their heads illuminating the area. Then laser was taken out by a tank round, and the artillery came in undeterred.

The first shell landed amidst the Bradleys with a giant explosion.

He screamed into the radio, "Everybody off the road. Maintain your sectors, but expand the perimeter—I don't want anyone in the open! Report."

His platoon leaders reported in, and he crawled through the slush to the edge of the highway. The snow and ice soaked through his uniform. He glanced back: not everyone in the command group was off the road yet.

"Come on, get off the road, you're sitting ducks there!"

He heard a high-pitched crack, and another tank exploded, and another. One tank in the column, surrounded by smoke, swung its turret as it looked for a target. Four rounds hit it at once with a tremendous explosion, throwing the turret into the air.

Crawling forward, he rolled into the slush-and-mud-filled ditch. He fumbled with his binoculars and scanned the ridgeline, then keyed his radio and called his platoon leaders.

"Give me a report, six elements. First platoon."

He heard a squeal and then Kathleen O'Donnell's voice. "We're mostly intact, sir, I've got one guy with pretty bad burns, but he'll live."

"What's your position?"

"Left side of the road, sir. I'm mixed up with some guys from Charlie Company; they can't find any of their officers."

"Roger. Keep your folks low and in the ditch. They'll be coming after dismounts next. Second platoon, report."

He heard no answer except the cracking of tank cannons.

"Second platoon."

Still no answer. "Damn it. O'Donnell? Do you have contact with second platoon?"

"No sir. I don't think they all made it out of the Bradleys, sir."

Oh, no. "Third platoon, report."

"Sir, this is Sergeant Miller. We're intact, sir, no casualties at this time, I've got a good base of fire along the edge of the woods south of the road, sir."

"Are you in contact with second platoon?"

"No, sir."

"All right. You've got the best position right now. I want you to send a squad up the ridge right now with all the anti-tank weapons you have. See if you can take out some of those tanks."

"Sir I have to advise against that, at least until we get better control of the situation. They might get cut off."

Through the smoke, Morris could see muzzle flashes from tank cannons up the hill. They were cutting his company to pieces.

"Sergeant, we won't get better control unless we can do something about those tanks! Get them on the way."

"Wilco, sir."

Morris looked at his command group. "Watson, you got battalion on the line yet?"

"Right here, sir."

Morris reached out and took the microphone, winced as another vehicle exploded.

"Colonel Barksdale, this is Captain Morris."

"Go ahead, Morris, report."

"Sir, the tanks are all gone, sir. I've got one platoon on the edge of the woods; they are sending a squad up the ridge with anti-tank guns. I've got one more platoon in the ditch at the side of the road; we're preparing to advance. My second platoon is gone, sir, out of touch. I don't know if they made it out of the Bradleys alive. Sir, we're facing considerably more than one tank company here."

"All right, son, keep it calm. Charlie Company has been torn up completely—I can't reach any of their officers. If you find any of their men, pull them in under your command. Alpha and Delta companies were cut off in the attack, we'll try to swing them around in a flanking attack. Keep your squad on the ridge in touch; I don't want any friendly fire."

"Yes, sir."

"Keep me informed, Morris. Barksdale out."

Morris handed the microphone back and heard a chilling sound. Machineguns—lots of them. The enemy had finished with the tanks and Bradleys, and was shifting focus to the dismounted infantry. The rat-a-tat-tat sound of machine guns was heard all up and down the line, and tracers slammed into the pavement behind him. The sound was oddly muffled as the bullets struck mounds of snow and ice.

He keyed the radio again. "O'Donnell."

"Here, sir."

"I want you to see if you can extend your right flank and envelop most of whatever is left of Charlie Company. We need to get some control over there; no one can reach their officers. As soon as you have done so, we need to get some anti-tank mines out there, otherwise they're liable to come rolling in on top of us. And get your men into the trees, if they're not already. They're dead if they stay in the open. Got that?"

"Roger, sir."

༄

At the top of the ridgeline, Karen watched through the thermal sights of her tank as the dismounts scattered below. At this distance it was impossible to maintain accurate machinegun fire; they were well outside the effective range of the M240 machineguns. However, even random fire from two companies of tanks—each tank armed with multiple machineguns—must be murderous down there.

Below her, in the gunner's seat, Sergeant Bowen leaned away from the sights and rested his head against the side of the turret. "This is awful, Captain. Oh, my God, those people are Americans. We might even know some of them. Oh, Christ."

"I know, Sergeant, I know. This will be over soon, I hope."

By this time the battle had quieted significantly. In the valley, fires raged as fourteen tanks and a dozen Bradley fighting vehicles burned. None of the armored vehicles in the column had survived, and the infantry was scattered in pockets and ditches. Slightly to the rear of her position, her fire support team dropped mortars at the direction of her platoon leaders, but it was impossible to gauge the impact.

A call came over the radio.

"Captain Greenfield, this is Red Six. Spot report, over."

"Go ahead, Red Six."

"Ma'am, it looks like they are trying to flank us—we've got a column of tanks coming up the fire trail, looks like a reinforced company. They've got a bunch of dismounts with them as well."

"Okay, good work, Red Six, wait one."

She switched the dial of her radio to the battalion net.

"Cornstalk Six, Cornstalk Six, this is Bravo Six."

Major Elkins answered. "Go ahead, Bravo Six."

"Spot report. I have a column of tanks and infantry, estimated to be greater than company strength, moving up the eastern fire road at this time. I have a defense prepared, but we won't hold them long."

"Roger, Bravo Six. Keep me updated. I'll send a platoon from Delta Company to your position as a reserve if you need it. Cornstalk Six out."

She switched back to the company network. "Red Six, Red Six. Shift your platoon's sector of fire to their alternate positions and prepare to defend. I have an additional platoon on the way as backup for you."

"Roger, ma'am."

A moment later she heard the first anti-tank mine explode to her right, followed by the crack of tank cannons and machine guns. That was followed by a radio call to the fire support vehicle, calling in mortars on the counterattacking forces.

Her hands twitched as she peered out the vision block, trying to see what was going on over there. Nothing she could do without getting in the way at this point.

∽

Sergeant Kevin Miller peered up the hill, desperately trying to see in the dark just where his men were. He had two squads covering the edge of the woods, most of them sitting in a cold, wet ditch. The ones who weren't in the ditch were digging in.

His third squad was up the hill, steadily reporting back their positions as they moved.

A voice over the radio came at a very faint whisper—it was the squad up in the woods. "Sergeant Miller, can you hear me?"

"Go ahead."

"We've infiltrated their position. I don't know if there are any infantry up here, just tanks so far. I've split my men up, we're going to try to disable as many of the tanks as we can."

"Good, please keep me—"

Miller never finished the sentence. A random bullet from one of the tanks hit him in the face and knocked him backwards. Blood splashed out the back of his helmet and stained the snow.

"Oh, shit, Sarge!" Corporal Larry Woods, the platoon medic, ran over. "Oh, shit!" he screamed when he saw the damage. "Sergeant Miller's fucking dead! Oh shit!"

Woods, panicked now, stood up, his head swinging around as he searched for a place to run.

One of the team leaders shouted, "Get down, Woods!"

It was too late. Woods was hit by a shell fragment and fell to the ground, blood pouring out of a gash in his side. He looked down at his side, and screamed as steam and blood poured out of his body.

∽

Two hundred yards away, Kathleen O'Donnell was focused on her own platoon's problems. She had managed to get one squad to the edge of the woods before the tanks had turned their attention on the infantry, but the other two squads were still in the ditch beside the highway. She lay on her back in the ditch, her rifle across her chest, calling instructions back and forth to Staff Sergeant Roy, the third squad leader, when the call came over the company net.

"Captain Morris, Captain Morris, this is Sergeant Wilson. My six element is dead, repeat, Sergeant Miller is dead, over."

"Roger," Morris answered. "Take command of the platoon, please. Remember you've got a squad up this hill, maintain contact with them."

O'Donnell closed her eyes. *No.* They hadn't even been married two days yet.

PFC Deena Hall, their platoon's medic, called to her, "Sarge, you all right? Sarge?"

"Yeah, yeah. Just keep your head down, all right? It's a mess out here."

O'Donnell took a deep breath. Right now, here and now, she just didn't have time to mourn. Not if she got her people killed because she was too busy thinking about herself. All the same, as she rolled over and peered over the edge of the ditch, tears streamed down her face.

"Sergeant Roy!"

"Yo!"

"Here's what we're going to do. We take 'em by surprise. We all storm over the edge at once, and run like hell for the trees. No stragglers—no goddamn stragglers, because if they stay behind they'll be dead. Understand?"

"You got it!"

"All right. Everyone listen up. When I say go, jump to your feet and run for the treeline. The second you get there, dive, get under whatever cover you can find. Don't panic and don't stay behind. On three."

She paused, caught her breath.

"One. Two. Three!"

On three, she jumped to her feet and drove them like pistons, running for the edge.

The machine guns rattled and red tracers pounded into the snow around them. Someone screamed as they ran for the woodline.

One step. Two Three. She'd made twenty yards, when she heard a cry behind her.

A glance back, and O'Donnell slid to a stop. PFC Hall had fallen, her aid bag with its precious bandages strewn across the wet slush. O'Donnell ran back and pulled her to her feet.

"Run, goddamn it, run!"

Hall took off running. O'Donnell followed, her feet slipping in the wet slush. An arc of machine gun fire tracers pounded into the ground to her right, then moved in her direction. She shrieked.

A bullet knocked her off her feet, shredding her knee and throwing her to the ground. She stared in horror as blood poured out of her. She was still twenty yards from the treeline.

"Go, go, go," she shouted until she saw Hall disappear into the trees.

O'Donnell glanced down at her knee. She couldn't feel anything, but didn't really need to see it in order to understand how serious it was. Blood soaked into the snow, turning it black, spreading. Too much blood, it had to be an artery. Oh God, no.

She reached to her left shoulder, where her individual bandage hung, as it did on all the troops. Her hands shaking, she ripped open the plastic and began to wrap it around her knee. It wasn't enough. She needed a tourniquet.

"Sarge!" she heard someone call. O'Donnell looked up.

Turville was crouched beside a tree, rifle at his side.

"Can you move? You've got to get out of there, Sarge! I'm coming!"

"No. Stay there, I'll be fine." She struggled to stand, and then fell back over.

She looked up, saw the indecision on his face, then shouted, "No!" as he slung the rifle over his shoulder.

Turville ran out of the treeline. His mouth was open and he shouted as he ran, sliding the last ten feet through the snow.

"Come on, Sarge, we got to go."

O'Donnell struggled up, and a flash of tracers came their way again.

"No, damn it! Go back!"

A bullet struck Turville in the neck, and he fell to the ground. Blood showered out of the hole in the front of his throat as he screamed.

Another bullet hit O'Donnell, this one dead in the center of her flack vest. It knocked her over onto Turville. She tried to pull him up, but her knee gave out and she fell down. Blood poured out of her and all over the no longer white snow, and she realized it was too late.

She closed her eyes. Kevin was dead, a hundred meters away. What would their boys do? The dark sky poured snow like the troubles raining on Job, and she prayed at a whisper, tears and blood running freely from her body.

"Please take care of them, Lord. Please see my sons grow up to be strong and good men, and happy." She sobbed. "Let them be happy—"

A bullet ended her prayer.

⁂

Karen looked at the carnage on the highway below and wondered if God would ever forgive her.

"This can't last much longer." Sergeant Bowen's voice was framed by the loud clattering of the old thermal sights of the tank.

"I know. As soon as their artillery catches up, they'll kick the crap out of us. Good thing we had all this snow, it's got to be slowing them down. I don't understand why they're attacking without any air support, it doesn't make any sense."

"How much longer before we evacuate?"

"Not long. The whole point of this strategy is to keep them blundering into ambushes as we back up. We're stalling for time, I think, so the politicians can sort this thing out."

"We won't be able to stall for much longer," he said. "Not the way we're losing folks, running out of ammo."

"*I know that*, Sergeant. As soon as we get the word, we'll clear out of here."

He didn't reply, and she mentally kicked herself for snapping at him. It wasn't his fault.

She reached up, pulled the releases on her hatch and popped it to the full open position, then stood up and stretched. Outside, she could hear the engines of tanks, tracks creaking on the ground, and the occasional burst of machinegun fire. In the distance, to the north, there were large flashes. Another battle, by the looks of it, probably somewhere up near Shepardstown. Another bright flash in the far north, and it suddenly sank in: she could see. Visibility had vastly improved. Not good. She looked up at the sky. Still heavy clouds, but no more snow, and in a spot or two, she could see stars. With the weather clearing up, it wouldn't be long before air support appeared.

Even as the realization sank in, she heard a squelch over the radio, then Major Elkins.

"All elements, this is Cornstalk Six. Prepare to move out, please report status."

Karen called to her platoon leaders, even though she knew their status already. A few moments later, she called back to Elkins.

"Cornstalk Six, this is Bravo Six. We are ready to roll, except for one disabled vehicle. Some dismounts hit one of my second platoon tanks with a grenade earlier and blew off a sprocket. They're not going anywhere, over."

"All right, Bravo Six. Have the crew join your trains and blow that tank in place."

"Roger, Cornstalk Six."

Karen relayed the necessary instructions.

☙

At the bottom of the ridgeline, covered in frozen mud, his fingers too stiff to move, Morris heard the tanks leaving. The tracks rumbled and creaked on the ground with an ominous noise.

"Everybody stay in position until they are gone," he called over the radio. "They may have left behind snipers. Platoon leaders, get me a count of your dead and wounded so I can call in a medivac."

For fifteen excruciating minutes Morris waited, until the last of the sounds were gone. In the east, the sky was just beginning to lighten. He tried to stand, and found he couldn't move. Slowly, he came to his knees, leaving his rifle in the snow; he couldn't grip it anyway. Teeth chattering, he bent over, pulled his rifle over his shoulder and finally stood.

He could hear helicopters approach. He slowly walked back to the highway, where the fifteen Bradley fighting vehicles of his company, plus two tanks, still burned. Black smoke poured from the vehicles, and they still radiated a tremendous amount of heat, though the ammunition had long since cooked off. Near the second platoon vehicles, he could see several bodies on the ground, all of them burned beyond recognition.

Dear God. Why are we doing this? What the hell purpose did it serve to invade immediately instead of trying to negotiate? Was this all for the pride of a few men? What the hell would he tell the children and families of the dead? What would he tell the Miller kids?

The sky was light enough now to see his platoons at the treeline, gathering their dead and wounded. They were exhausted, frozen, some injured, and all of those left had watched their friends and teammates cut to pieces overnight.

He looked up as the helicopters approached. It wasn't the medivac: eight Apache helicopters, armed with anti-tank missiles, raced overhead, no more than forty feet off the ground, throwing up snow in their rotor wash as they passed overhead.

Too bad they weren't here twelve hours ago.

It was time for this to end.

༃

As they came to a stop, Karen and her loader, Haggett, jumped out of their hatches. Sergeant Bowen had traversed the turret so the main gun pointed to the side. She climbed off the turret onto the back deck of the tank and began to work loose the cover to the right side fuel tank. Haggett did the same on the left.

A moment later two trucks pulled up beside them—on the left, a fuel truck, on the right, ammunition.

Haggett and Crump, the driver, began fueling the tank. Karen jumped back to the turret and helped Bowen with the tank rounds. The driver of the ammunition truck handed the rounds off to her, and then she passed them down to Bowen, who loaded them into the turret.

Twelve rounds, then thirteen, and the driver said, "That's it, ma'am. How about small arms?"

Bowen looked up through the hatch. "We're not done yet, still down by five rounds."

Karen looked at the driver, who shrugged. "Orders, ma'am—I was told no more than thirteen rounds per tank; we're running low on ammo."

Karen put her hands on her hips and said, "Who gave you that order?"

"Colonel Elkins, ma'am."

"All right, whatever. I'll talk to the Colonel. I'll need two cans of fifty-caliber. Sergeant Bowen, how are we doing on 7.62 rounds?"

"Need about two thousand."

"Ten cases," she said to the driver.

"This war better end quick," Bowen said. "If we don't have any ammo, we're going to be hurting."

Karen looked off, down the valley, and squinted, suddenly alarmed. What the hell was that? She could see movement, and then a flash. Probably a rocket launching. *Helicopters.*

"Bandits! We got choppers coming!"

She leaned down beside her hatch and reached in, grabbed the microphone, and screamed, "Bandits! Bandits! Pop smoke!"

The truck drivers, panicked, jumped back into their vehicles, but they were too late. The first round slammed directly into the front slope of Karen's tank, throwing the entire turret, and everyone on it, into the air.

Karen saw a flash of white below, and then nothing more.

Chapter Thirty-Eight
January 3

Just before sunrise, Governor Slagter marched into Murphy's headquarters with two aides in tow. Murphy's body shook from fatigue and too much coffee. He looked at the governor, his glance dismissive, and he made no move to walk away from what he was doing. Slagter's clothes were rumpled, as if he'd slept in them, and dark circles framed his eyes. His face seemed to struggle between irritation and anxiety, and he opened his mouth to speak, and then closed it. Finally he spoke, his voice devoid of the confidence it had borne in their earlier meetings.

"General Murphy, where do we stand?"

Murphy gestured to the table. "Why don't you come over to the map, sir, and I'll show you."

The governor approached, his eyes scanning the map without understanding. Murphy pointed as he spoke.

"In the north sir, we've been knocked out at I-79: first brigade is out of the action, most of the men dead or surrendered. Here along the 340 extension, we stopped the attack in place overnight, but I had a report an hour ago that the battalion there was under air attack. I've heard nothing since; we have to presume they were defeated. In the south, it's no better. We were wiped out at I-66. I expect the war will be over sometime this morning."

An explosion, somewhere outside, rattled the windows, and the lights went out. After a few seconds, the lights came on.

"We've got generators in the building, sir. But not long ago they started hitting key points through the state with cruise missiles: bridges, power substations, telephone exchanges."

They were interrupted as Major Roth, the operations officer, called to Murphy. "Looks like they just took down the Bureau of Mines building, sir."

Slagter looked at him, his face slack, defeated. When he spoke, his voice was almost at a whisper. "Murphy, how could it be over so quickly?"

Murphy stared back. "Governor, I told you over and over we can't win this on a military basis."

The governor's response was almost a whisper. "I counted on you to win this."

"Sir, it's not too late for you to do something. We can probably hold on for a few hours yet—at least until they get troops into Charleston. Can't you get a political settlement? Of some kind?"

Slagter shook his head. "The President won't even return my calls."

"Try again, sir."

The building shook again.

"I'll do what I can, Murphy. I would never have guessed it could end this quickly."

Murphy grimaced. "Sir, you should be grateful they didn't bomb us from a distance for a month or two to soften us up. That would have caused massive civilian casualties. Someone up high made a decision to put their soldiers at risk in a ground assault to avoid civilian deaths."

Slagter turned away, hands clasped behind his back. His shoulders rose as he took a deep breath.

"What do you recommend?"

Murphy watched the governor, almost feeling pity.

"Sir, try again. Then—if we can't get the President to agree to anything—we surrender. We have no other choice at this point. The weather is clearing, so for sure, sometime today, we'll have air assault or airborne forces dropping into Charleston. You don't want a battle in the streets. The civilian casualties would be enormous."

"Surrender! General, how can you seriously advocate surrender? You and I would both be tried for treason and likely be executed!"

Murphy shrugged. "Better that than killing innocent people."

"I don't believe that will happen."

"Governor, you appointed me as your military commander. *Will you listen to my judgment of things military, just once?* I am telling you if we resist, if we fight the invading troops here in the city, we'll not only kill a lot of our own troops, and theirs, unnecessarily, but we will likely be responsible for the deaths of thousands of civilians. That is not an option. I won't order my men to do it."

"Then I'll fire you and put someone else in charge."

"Who? Colonel Hatfield? He's been captured. Colonel Myers? Missing or dead. Maybe Major Roth over here will accept command. It's irrelevant at this point. I'll say the same thing to you I've said all along, governor. There is no military solution. You must find a solution, a political one, and quickly. The war will be over in a matter of hours."

Slagter, his cheeks twitching, stared at Murphy as if he'd been slapped. Without another word he turned and walked out.

The pain was excruciating, her side burning, as if she had been flayed alive. The searing pain went down to her hips to her right knee, almost driving away conscious thought.

Karen opened her eyes. An unfamiliar medic crouched at her side, a young woman in her twenties, her face blurred by the tears that flooded Karen's eyes. The sun was high above the medic's shoulder; it must be near noon. The snow melted around her.

She tried to sit up, and nearly screamed from the pain.

"Don't move, Captain. You're pretty torn up; helicopters are on the way."

Karen's voice was gravel. "What's happening? Where are my men?"

"Calm down, Captain. I think some of your men are dead, but there's some survivors. You'll be taken to the hospital. I don't know after that."

Unbidden tears poured from her eyes. "What unit are you with?"

The medic looked at her, incredible sadness in her eyes. "First of the Fifteenth Infantry, Ma'am. I guess. Not too many of us left now."

Panic set in, and Karen lifted her upper body, despite the pain. Her voice was hoarse.

"Captain Morris? Are you in his company? Is he alive? Is he here?"

The medic jerked back, surprised an enemy prisoner knew her commanding officer.

"Yes, I'll see if he'll talk to you."

She backed away, and Karen collapsed backward, lightheaded and shaking. She must have lost a lot of blood. She couldn't tell, couldn't lift herself enough to see her own body. Above, the sky was clear and blue, crisp like winter. Her eyes closed.

Boots approached in the crusted snow, and a shadow fell over her. Afraid of what she would see, she opened her eyes. Morris knelt at her side, his face black with mud and dirt, a bandage wrapped around his left arm.

"Is it over?"

At her question, his eyes dropped to the ground.

"It is for us. They'll be taking you to the hospital, then wherever prisoners are going. I'm—I don't know where I'm going. My company is gone."

She felt her whole body shake.

"I'm sorry. I wish…" She couldn't articulate what her heart cried out to her.

His eyes blurred, and he averted them, looking away to the woods.

"So do I," he whispered, and she knew his love had become nothing more than dust.

He leaned close and kissed her lightly on the lips. Then he stood, and without another word, walked away from her.

Two hours after sunrise, the reports Murphy expected came into headquarters. Hundreds of helicopters had crossed the Kentucky border near Mingo County.

"Order all units to stand down," he told Major Roth. "Issue new orders to all commands. We are going into a ceasefire, effective immediately. The rules of engagement will be simple: avoid contact. Surrender if fired upon."

Roth, his face drawn, nodded.

"Yes, sir." He hurried away to relay the orders.

Murphy stood at the windows, looked out at the snow-covered city, his back to the officers in the room. This time last year, he had been playing in the snow with Kenny. They had gone to WalMart and bought a plastic sled, and spent the day sledding down the slope near the house until they were both soaking wet, red in the face, laughing. His little boy would never have understood this. Murphy wasn't sure he understood it. Why had it come to this? Why had he let it continue? Someone else could have taken the command. Now it all rested on his shoulders—all that pain and death was his responsibility, his cross, and he knew there was no escaping, no walking away from the lives he'd wasted.

Out near the airport, he saw hundreds of canopies in the sky: airborne troops parachuting in. Must be the 82nd; they would take the airport, and the 101st would probably secure the city. On another day, it would have been pretty; from here, the parachute canopies looked tiny.

The building shook as a flight of Blackhawk helicopters flew over. Looked like they were landing in front of the State Capitol. Many more would arrive before it was over.

He waited. It wouldn't be much longer.

༄

When it came, it was almost an anti-climax. A quiet knock on the door, and Major Roth ducked his head in.

"Sir," Roth said to Murphy. "The enemy commander is here."

"Thank you, Major." Murphy turned away from the window, looked at the young officer. "Go get him, bring him in."

Roth saluted and left the room. Murphy turned around, looked back out the window. It was all over. In an incredibly brief time, not even forty-eight hours, all of West Virginia's military forces had simply been wiped out. Their dreams for independence, their dreams for a country with the freedom of his childhood, were swept away. Footsteps, and behind him the door opened. He turned, and almost broke down then.

Tom Murphy stood in the door in his combat gear, a pistol in a shoulder holster. Several other officers crowded in behind him, but they kept their distance from Tom. He saluted Murphy formally.

Ken returned the salute. Tom's eyes filled with tears.

"General," Tom said, struggling to keep his face and voice under control. "My understanding is you are prepared to surrender your forces."

"That is correct."

"Then I formally accept your surrender and relieve you of your command, sir."

Tom turned to the other officers who had crowded into the room. "Out. Everyone leave."

All of the officers backed out of the room, except for Roth, who stayed, his eyebrows raised in question.

Murphy nodded to Major Roth. "You too, Major."

Roth backed out and closed the door behind him.

Tom spoke first. "You look terrible. Are you all right?"

"I don't know. It's been quite some time since I've slept; I could use a rest."

"General Hayes will be here soon to arrest you. I'll probably be up the creek for coming ahead of him; he'll want the glory of accepting your surrender."

"Thank you, Tom."

"Was it worth it? All this? The dead troops? The war?"

"I don't know. It all depends on whether or not our country wakes up. If it can somehow turn us away from being a police state, then yes, it was worth it. Some things are worth fighting for."

Tom's face twisted. "Ken, this may be the last chance I ever have to talk to you in private. They're going to hang this whole war on your shoulders."

Murphy shrugged. "Come on, little brother. I love my country. It's worth it. Maybe it's not about whether or not you win, but whether you try. Besides… There was nothing left to lose."

Tom's face contorted. "There's always something to lose."

They embraced.

"Take care of yourself, Tommy." Murphy's voice broke. "And please watch out for my little girl."

Tom nodded. "I will."

Eyes red, Tom Murphy backed away from his brother and wiped his face with the back of his sleeve. He squared his shoulders, tried to regain his composure. He was a Colonel in the United States Army, and needed to look the part as they left.

"Let's go."

Ken Murphy followed his brother to the door and out of his headquarters. He took one short glance back at the classroom, which had been his headquarters for these brief days, and then turned away. It was time to meet his fate, whatever that would be. He would meet it head on.

Epilogue

By noon on January 4 the war in West Virginia ended with the surrender of General Kenneth Murphy. U.S. Army troops occupied Charleston, and by the end of the week established control over the entire state.

By the time occupation troops arrived at the Governor's Mansion, it was too late. Frank Slagter had shot himself in the head, a failed suicide. Rushed to the nearest hospital, he never recovered from the gunshot wound, and spent the short remainder of his life in a coma.

Two weeks later, sixteen members of a religious community in Baughman Settlement, West Virginia, were convicted of the bombings in Arlington, Virginia and Charleston, West Virginia. The jury acquitted them of the charge of the murder of Dale Whitt, due to lack of evidence.

༄

The black sedan pulled in front of the Miller home in Gaithersburg, Maryland late in the day on January 5. The door opened, and two officers stepped out, the first a youthful captain from the Chaplain's Corps, the second a grizzled infantry sergeant major.

They walked up the immaculate gravel walkway. The sergeant major felt a pit in his stomach: he had known Kevin Miller, and dreaded giving this news to his family. All the same, he squared his shoulders and rang the bell. They waited, and then heard the sound of running feet. The door opened, and a little boy looked out. He looked up at them, then ducked back inside and yelled "Grandma, the Army's here!"

The sergeant major clenched his fists.

The door opened wide, and a woman stood there. She was a beautiful dark skinned woman, and when she saw them standing there she cried out and her hands flew to her mouth. Her face twisted.

At the sound of her gasp, a grey haired man ran to the front door. His eyes widened when he saw them, and he pulled the woman to him.

"Mr. and Mrs. Miller?" the Chaplain asked.

She wailed, already knowing what she was going to hear.

"We regret to inform you that your son, Sergeant First Class Kevin Miller, was killed in action yesterday. I'm afraid we don't have any details as to the circumstances, other than it was in a firefight in the vicinity of Harpers Ferry, West Virginia."

"No," the woman keened.

Two more adults came to the door, a Caucasian man and woman in their sixties. The man had short-cropped, grizzled hair and a neatly trimmed mustache. They spoke in low tones with Miller's parents, and the sergeant major realized they must be the parents of Sergeant First Class O'Donnell. He knew Miller and O'Donnell had just married. Someone needed to see about getting O'Donnell some leave.

"I'm very sorry to have to bring you this news," the chaplain went on.

Anxiety struck the sergeant major when he saw another sedan, identical to his own, coming down the street. What were the chances? It pulled up behind theirs, and a notification team got out.

"Oh God, no," O'Donnell's father cried. "Not my little girl."

At the top of the stairs, two boys without parents looked down and watched their lives fall to pieces.

꒰꒱

The first thing Jim Turville became aware of was the feeling of something rigid in his throat and the awareness he was unable to move at all. With that little bit of information, he passed back into unconsciousness for another twenty-four hours.

The next time he woke up, he opened his eyes. He was in a hospital; that much was obvious. His head was immobilized and he hurt like hell, but he was in a hospital, which meant he was alive.

He was alive.

꒰꒱

When Karen Greenfield awoke, she was disoriented. Her surroundings were dark, with tiny colored lights all around. She couldn't move her body or her head, had difficulty breathing. She felt pain everywhere, a dull, throbbing pain not localized to any single part of her body.

"It's all right," said a voice. "It's all right. You'll be fine, you're in the hospital."

She moved her eyes around, tried to focus and couldn't through the tears. She was alive. Dear God, she was alive.

She felt a hand slip over hers, then a brush, a light touch against her ear.

"I promised I'd find you when it was over. I'm keeping that promise."

Above her, she saw Morris's face. She sobbed. Tears rolled out of her eyes and down the side of her face.

He wiped them away.

꒰꒱

Larry Harris stood in front of the desk of his new boss, Morris Klegg. They were in a temporary office—the old one had been completely destroyed in the fighting.

Klegg looked at him, frowning. "I don't understand," he said. "You've had one hell of a career."

Harris shrugged. "I'm done, okay? I want out."

"At least explain it to me. Sit down, for Christ's sake. Is this about Hagarty? You know there's nothing more you could have done."

Harris collapsed into the chair, like nothing more than a balloon that had been pricked.

"It's not about Hagarty. It's the whole thing… I don't think I'm willing to do this any more. We've been wrong too many times. It's one thing to feel like we're protecting folks. It's another when we have screwup after screwup that ends up with the very people we're trying to defend hating us."

"It's not our fault," replied Klegg.

"No? What about the Saturn plant last spring? And you know as well as I do that Hagarty's death would never have happened had we not jumped the gun and made all kinds of wrong assumptions. The war, for God's sake—had it not been for our screwups—it wouldn't have happened."

Klegg closed his eyes and looked down at his desk. His face worked for a moment, as if he were angry. After ten long seconds, he looked up. "Look, Harris, we need you. Why don't you take a leave of absence for a little while, get some rest. You'll be good as new."

Harris shook his head, then reached into his jacket. Slowly, he pulled out his pistol and laid it on the desk, followed by his federal credentials.

"I'm sorry, sir. That's almost exactly what Hagarty said to me two hours before he died. I'm done."

Harris stood and walked out of the office.

✧

At the end of March, three court-martials convened and occupied the news for the next several weeks.

The first, of Captain Michael Allen Morris, resulted in an acquittal. The court-martial board ruled that he was not responsible for the death of a civilian minor in Charleston, West Virginia, in October the previous year. All charges were dropped, and Morris was then reassigned to the Fourth Brigade, 3rd Infantry Division, already deployed in the Middle East. Two days after the end of the court-martial, he flew out to his new unit.

Captain Karen Greenfield's trial ended three days later. She sat stoic, in uniform throughout the trial, but obviously still in considerable pain from the injuries which had kept her in the hospital for three months.

On March 18, the jury returned a verdict of guilty, and sentenced her to seven years imprisonment at the U.S. Army Disciplinary Barracks at Fort Leavenworth, Kansas. She was stripped of her commission as an officer and reduced to the rank of private, to be followed by dishonorable discharge.

On March 21, in a trial that was surprisingly quick, General Ken Murphy was convicted of treason.

༄

"Bless me father, for I have sinned. It has been twenty-seven years since my last confession."

Murphy's eyes were closed as he kneeled on the unyielding concrete floor. It was very cold.

"My sins are these. I have killed, at least four times in combat, possibly more. As a general I was responsible for many hundreds of deaths of innocent people. I have committed adultery. I have lied. I have had false pride, which led me to lead others into danger. I did not educate my children about the Church, and did not teach them of God."

He opened his eyes and looked into the priest's eyes. The priest was around his age, balding, in his black suit and Roman collar, with a purple stole draped over his shoulders.

"Father, my son died without baptism, and did not receive the last rites. I lost my faith. I lost my wife. Then I lost my soul. I don't even know if it makes sense to come to confession now, but…"

The priest spoke. "Are you truly penitent for your sins?"

"One more," Murphy whispered. "I have wished for death, father. I have prayed and prayed I would die and could rejoin my wife and son. I can't be penitent for that, father; I can't. It's all I have left."

The priest sighed. "God will understand, my son."

"Will I see them again, father? Do you really believe it? Do you believe I will see them again in Heaven, Father?"

Tears rolled from Murphy's eyes as he spoke.

The priest put his hand on Murphy's shoulder and leaned his forehead against him.

"I do, my son. Pray for strength during your ordeal. Pray your sacrifices will not go unanswered. He will know, my son, and forgive all."

"What is my penitence?"

The priest grunted. "You've already done it."

"Thank you."

They stood, and the priest knocked on the steel door. It opened, and he stepped out. Tom Murphy, now wearing the single star of a Brigadier General, walked in.

"Ken."

They embraced.

"I'm going to miss you, bro. I wish—I wish there was something I could do."

Murphy closed his eyes. "There is, Tom. Find Valerie. Find out what they've done with her, and get her free."

Tom nodded his head and stepped back. "I will, Ken. I'll find out what they did with her, and get her free, if it's the last thing I do. I'll look after her, and make sure she's safe. I promise."

"Please don't stay, Tom. Don't watch."

"I'm the only family you've got. I'm not leaving your side."

"Don't do this to yourself. Go. You belong among the living, and I don't. Please, Tom. Go."

They embraced again.

"I'd give anything to go back in time and fix it, Ken," Tom whispered. "Anything."

"Just don't let it be in vain. All those people dead—make it matter. Do what you can."

"I love you."

"You too."

Tom straightened and knocked on the door.

The heavy door opened, and two guards entered.

"Are you done, sir?" one asked Tom. "They're ready for him."

"Yeah," whispered Tom.

The guards let Murphy out of the cell, and down the hall. Tom followed close behind.

The bed was an uncomfortable looking steel device. The guards led him to it. They were clearly tense, possibly expecting a fight. Murphy wasn't prepared to give them one. He lay down on the bed. He glanced over at his brother and said goodbye. Tom shook as he stood there, just a few feet away.

Murphy closed his eyes, shut out the steel and concrete surroundings, and for a moment, he could see a beautiful woman standing, hand in hand with a little boy, tears in their eyes, waving for him to come.

"Martha."

THE END

Feedback

Thanks again for reading Republic. If you'd like to contact me with feedback, or want to find out when the next book will be released, please feel free to get in touch by visiting my website www.sheehanmiles.com or send me an email: Charles@sheehanmiles.net

I'd also like to encourage readers to post a review on Amazon.com—whether or not you liked the book. Word of mouth is what makes the publishing world go round, and for independently published authors all the more so.

Charles Sheehan-Miles

Printed in the United Kingdom
by Lightning Source UK Ltd.
122878UK00001BB/14/A